T0146492

"You ever ride a bike before?"

Her pretty pink lips turned down. "You know, oddly enough, I have not."

The way she talked, every once in a while, bespoke an Ivy League education and hard-won experience. Just who was Cee Cee? "What's your last name, darlin'?"

"Jones." She shivered in the night air and zipped up a designer leather jacket.

Daire would bet his last coin that his cousin, clothes aficionado Simone Brightston, would approve of the coat. "You're a mystery, Cee Cee Jones."

She stepped into him, bringing the scent of wild hyacinth. "I'm just a good girl out for one wild time before getting back to real life. You going to give me that, Enforcer?"

Wicked Edge

Realm Enforcers, Book 2

REBECCA ZANETTI

LYRICAL PRESS
Kensington Publishing Corp.
www.kensingtonbooks.com

LYRICAL PRESS BOOKS are published by

Kensington Publishing Corp.
119 West 40th Street
New York, NY 10018

All Kensington titles, imprints, and distributed lines are available at special quantity discounts for bulk purchases for sales promotions, premiums, fund-raising, educational, or institutional use.

Special book excerpts or customized printings can also be created to fit specific needs. For details, write or phone the office of the Kensington sales manager: Kensington Publishing Corp., 119 West 40th Street, New York, NY 10018, attn: Sales Department; phone 1-800-221-2647.

LYRIC PRESS and the Lyrical logo are Reg. U.S. Pat. & TM Off.

First electronic edition: November 2015

ISBN-13: 978-1-60183-513-0
ISBN-10: 1-60183-513-2

First print edition: November 2015

ISBN-13: 978-1-60183-514-7
ISBN-10: 1-60183-514-0

This one's for Big Tone,
because for our first date,
he took me on a motorcycle ride
to visit my Nana.
I love you.

ACKNOWLEDGMENTS

I have many people to thank for help in getting this second *Wicked* book to readers, and I sincerely apologize to anyone I've forgotten;

Thank you to the readers who've followed the Dark Protectors into the Wicked Realm, and thanks for understanding that I make up places and people in my books (the island isn't real in this one, gang);

Thank you to Big Tone for giving me tons to write about and for being supportive from the very first time I sat down to write. Thanks also to Gabe and Karlina for being such awesome kids and for making life so much fun;

Thank you to my talented agents, Caitlin Blasdell and Liza Dawson, who have been with me from the first book and who have supported, guided, and protected me in this wild industry;

Thank you to my amazing editor, Alicia Condon, who is unflappable, willing to take a risk, and is always a wonderful sounding board;

Thank you to the Kensington gang: Steven Zacharius, Adam Zacharius, Alexandra Nicolajsen, Vida Engstrand, Michelle Forde, Jane Nutter, Justine Willis, Lauren Jernigan, Fiona Jayde, and Arthur Maisel;

And thanks also to my constant support system: Gail and Jim English, Debbie and Travis Smith, Stephanie and Don West, Brandie and Mike Chapman, Jessica and Jonah Namson, and Kathy and Herb Zanetti.

Chapter 1

Daire Dunne swung his leg over his Harley, disembarking and biting back a growl. Music and boisterous voices spilled out the open doorway to the club's main bar area, and the stench of beer permeated the center concrete courtyard.

Another bloody party at Titans of Fire Motorcycle Club.

He'd spent most of the evening at the Grizzly MC headquarters, quietly drinking aged whiskey and playing poker with several friends, who were supposed to be his enemies. He'd had enough of the potent brew to be feeling nicely mellow, but with his metabolism, the feeling wouldn't last long. Especially since he'd had to return to Fire, pretending to be a full member.

Enough of this undercover shit.

He rolled his neck and erased his normal pissed-off expression, stalking inside the room heated with too many bodies and alcohol fumes. Maybe he could get a couple of Fire members to finally loosen up and give him the Intel he needed. Spilled booze squished beneath his size fourteen boots, and he felt the scowl forming on his face again.

He scoured the disorganized array of bar tables, stools, and drunks, his gaze hitching on a woman across the room, moving on, and then zooming back in.

Fucking stunning. Long, nearly white-blond hair, deep blue eyes, bone structure masterfully crafted by the gods on a seriously good day. She sat on a stool across a round wooden table, a low-cut black T-shirt revealing high breasts—pushed up and surprisingly full from what could only be described as a petite bone structure.

Her gaze met his and traveled from his head to his boots . . . and then back again. Her pink lips twitched and spread into a smile.

It was the smile that did it. Sweet and filled with challenge, which was a combination he'd never been able to ignore.

He didn't need to deal with a human female right now, especially one who appeared to be in her mid-twenties, while he'd lived for more than three centuries. Even so, his boots kicked into motion and he moved through the crush of bodies toward her.

A couple of club members greeted him, and more than one scantily clad female tried to halt his progress, but he arrived at her table soon enough.

Young and typically angry, a new club prospect sat across from her, generously pouring tequila into lined-up shot glasses and spilling onto the knife-scratched table. The kid's name was Grad, because supposedly he'd graduated from college the year before. He stiffened when Daire walked up.

"Move," Daire said, his gaze on the woman.

The kid faltered and then moved on with a sigh of disappointment. Yeah, it sucked to be just a prospect and not a full club member.

Daire straddled the now unoccupied fifties-style stool. "Daire Dunne," he said.

The woman lifted an eyebrow in a curiously confident way. "Cee Cee," she said, her voice a husky whisper.

That tone licked down his skin and planted hard in his balls. Jesus. He leaned back and studied her. Enhanced. Definite tingles cascaded from her, not too strong, but with enough force to show she was probably an enhanced human female. Either an empath or a psychic, probably.

Which explained the instant attraction.

He nudged a tequila shot glass toward her and picked one up, waiting until she'd clanked hers with his. Her fingers were small and graceful with natural nails and no frills.

They tipped back the drink, and she kept his gaze, swallowing the brew without a hitch in her breath.

Most enhanced humans either didn't realize they had special abilities, or ignored them, so he focused elsewhere. "How old are ya, Cee Cee?" he asked, pushing a second glass her way.

Amusement curved her lower lip. "Old enough. You?"

"Too old," he answered honestly. He'd been undercover at the club for nearly two months, and so far, he hadn't learned shit about the elusive drug he was tracking, a drug that harmed humans as well as his people. While he usually avoided the parties, he still kept an eye on participants. "I haven't seen you here before."

She nodded. "It's my first time. I came with a friend." She craned her neck, all grace, to look around the loud party. "I don't see her, though."

"A lot of the, ah, women who attend the parties end up in the back rooms," he said quietly. The correct term was bitch, honeybun, or even skank, but his mama had taught him better.

She smiled. "That's quite an accent you have there."

"I'm from Dublin," he said, quite enjoying her smile. "Our club merged with Titans of Fire, and I'm here for a bit." As soon as he got all the information he could from the club leader, he was getting back home.

A fight broke out on the other side of the room, drunken members arguing about bike pipes, and Daire shifted his weight to put himself between the woman and danger.

She smiled, no concern entering her stunning eyes, even as the guys threw a series of punches until one careened over the stained bar to disappear on the other side. "Your patch says you're an enforcer."

"Aye."

"Of what?" She leaned toward him, revealing more creamy cleavage.

His groin hardened instantly. Something about her, something graceful and out of place in the smoke-filled bar, kept his interest from where it should be—on his investigation for the witch nation. "Internal laws for Titans of Fire MC and whatever else needs to be enforced."

She breathed out. "You believe that *ends* justify means?"

"Yes." Unfortunately, in his line of work, he had to draw a line before any gray area. His words probably alarmed her, but he had to know more about her before she took off, as any smart woman would do. Intelligence shimmered in her eyes, so no doubt the lady had a brain. "What were you doing with the prospect?"

Her gaze dropped to the several full tequila shot glasses. "Drinking and arguing the merits of the United Nations."

Daire lifted an eyebrow. "Your opinion?"

She twirled a full shot glass with delicate fingers. "Great in theory but with no bite. A governing authority needs teeth."

Her emphasis on *bite* rioted more fire throughout him. "You like bite?"

Her eyelids lowered just enough to be unbelievably sexy. "Right place and right time, absolutely." Without moving, she glanced around at the gyrating bodies on the dance floor, despite the lack of decent music. "Not here, however."

Yeah. A woman like her didn't belong in a place like this. "Wanna get out of here?"

She sat back, studying him.

He didn't smile or try to cajole, almost fascinated by the play of expressions across her finely crafted features. When she opened her mouth to speak, he fully expected a refusal.

"You sure you're safe with me?" she asked, that throaty voice scratching under his skin.

He grinned. Not in flirtation, and not in reassurance, but in pure amusement. He was a three-centuries-old witch, an enforcer for his people, and one of the most dangerous beings on the planet. "I'll take my chances."

"Remember those words," she whispered, sliding from the stool.

He pushed back and stood, struck by her size. Even wearing spectacular black boots with three-inch spike heels, she barely reached his chest. It was a colossal mistake to spend the night with a human woman, and he was surely ignoring his duties, but for once, he didn't give a damn.

His two younger brothers, both enforcers, were out of the country on jobs, while the two prospects, who weren't quite prospects, were out clubbing in Seattle, looking for the elusive drug they were all trying to stop. None of them required babysitting for the evening. In fact, nobody needed his assistance right now, and with a woman like Cee Cee sending out unmistakable signals, he was taking a fucking night for himself. Yet he paused. "This is one night."

She threw back all of that glorious hair and laughed, deep and throaty. "I'm not looking for a ring, Enforcer. This is an adventure for one night, and then it's back to reality."

He had the oddest urge to discover her reality, but he shook it off. "Fair enough." Sliding a hand around her bicep, he propelled her through the crowd to the door, ignoring the hangdog expression on Grad's face. The kid hadn't had a chance and apparently was too dumb to know it.

They reached outside, a cool Seattle night, and he escorted her to the Harley. "You have a car here?"

"No. I came with my friend." She eyed the supercharged bike with bright eyes. "She's beautiful."

His chest lifted. Yeah, she was. "Thanks. You ever ride a bike before?"

Her pretty lips turned down. "You know, oddly enough, I have not."

The way she talked, every once in a while, bespoke an Ivy League education and hard-won experience. Just who was Cee Cee? "What's your last name, darlin'?"

"Jones." She shivered in the night air and zipped up a designer leather jacket.

Daire would bet his last coin that his cousin, clothes aficionado Simone Brightston, would approve of the coat. "You're a mystery, Cee Cee Jones."

She stepped into him, bringing the scent of wild hyacinth. "I'm just a good girl out for one wild time before getting back to real life. You going to give me that, Enforcer?"

Aye. Aye, he was. He threw a leg over the bike and held back an arm to assist her to sit behind him. She straddled the bike like she'd been born for it, and he shoved down a groan at the mental image of her straddling him. Then she slid her hands around his waist, tucking them inside his jacket.

Swallowing deep, his body rioting like a teenager's on a first date, he handed back the helmet. "Tiny blondes with big brains protect their heads," he rumbled, his voice sounding like he'd swallowed shards of glass.

She shifted against him and slid on the helmet. "I'm ready." Her voice emerged muffled.

Shit. He was more than ready. "Hold on, baby." He paused before igniting the engine. "Your place or mine?" Damn, had he really just used that stupid line?

She laughed and leaned up and into him, the helmet smacking his cheek. "Your place."

Fair enough. He had a flat across town in a high-rise building where they wouldn't be disturbed. Igniting the engine, he pulled out of the lot and opened the throttle down the quiet road.

Cee Cee held on tighter, her laugh an energetic hum of pleasure.

He smiled and slowly took a turn. She plastered her body against his, relaxing into him, allowing him to control the bike without any resistance. The woman was a natural.

What else was she a natural at?

He made record time through the quiet Seattle streets, finally driving down and into a private parking garage.

She jumped off the bike before he could assist her, yanking the helmet free. Her hair spread out and tumbled down her shoulders, and delight pinkened her high cheeks. "That was lovely."

Lovely. Not fucking great, awesome, or cool. But lovely. The little blonde had class and quite a few layers, now didn't she? Daire swung his leg over the bike and towered over her again. Small. God, she was small. He hadn't been with a human in decades. Was she too delicate?

As if reading him, she slipped her hand in his. "Stop being silly. Show me your flat in this beautiful building."

He kept his hold gentle but couldn't wait any longer. Leaning down and tugging her up on her toes, he took her mouth. Slow and sweet, he explored, shocked by the electricity ricocheting through him.

Fire. All fire and sparks.

She moaned and slid her hands over his shoulders, pressing against him, tilting her head back to take more of him. Giving as good as she got, she kissed him back, a soft, needy sigh emerging with her breath.

He leaned back, nostrils flaring, taking her in.

Surprise, almost shock, and sheer delight covered her face. Her lips pursed in a round O, and a feminine wonderment tilted her eyes.

Wonder.

Yeah, he felt it, too. So damn sweet, and he wanted more. He tightened his hold on her hand and all but dragged her toward the elevator. Slow. He had to slow down and make sure not to break her. Human. Definitely enhanced human who was already messing with his equilibrium.

And he fucking loved it.

How long had it been since a woman, any woman, had caught his attention for more than a few minutes?

Yet the surprise on her face, the innocence of the expression, still caught him off guard. "You okay?" he asked once the elevator door closed.

A delicate coral, stunning in its femininity, spread from her chest over the smooth bones in her face. She chuckled, all hoarse woman, and patted his arm. "I'm better than okay. It has just been a while, Enforcer."

"Why tonight?" he asked, not really caring about the answer.

She faltered. "Why, ah, not tonight?"

Why not, indeed? If she didn't want to tell him her story, she didn't have to, considering this was a one-night thing to scratch an itch. "Fair enough," he said, drawing her into his body. She fit. As small as she was, as fragile, she settled into his side like she belonged just there.

Unease swept through him.

As if sensing his mood, she flattened her palm over his abs and gave a slight purr. "I'm betting we're looking at a six-pack here. Maybe a twelve-pack." Drawing in air, steeling her shoulders as if for courage, she moved her hand down and over the obvious bulge in his jeans.

He stilled. A second later, his cock jumped with the force of forging steel. His balls drew up tight, and heat flushed down his torso.

If his family could see him now. The grouchy, always in control, demanding oldest brother now panting in an elevator from the touch of one tiny human.

He moved then, enjoying her sharp intake of breath, lifting her against the wall and forcing her legs around his hips. Her thighs tightened at his waist with impressive strength, and he pushed against her, seeking any sort of relief. Her core, hot as hell, caressed him through his jeans.

The elevator door opened, and he clamped his hands on her ass to keep her in place down the hallway and while he kicked open the door to his penthouse. Not wanting to wait another second, he took her lips, kissing her hard and taking her deep. A growl rose within him, a testament to his species, and he didn't care.

He kissed her long and hard until neither one of them could breathe, and then, only then, did he lift his head.

A flush covered her face, and desire danced across her skin, the intensity of it palpable. Slowly, her chest moving as she panted, her legs released him, and she slid down his body. "You're something, Daire Dunn," she murmured, her hands going to her jacket.

He breathed in her scent, feeling it seep under his skin. "Take off your clothes." They might as well get the parameters of the night straight now.

She smiled, a siren's dare, and reached for her lapels. "I do like how you kiss."

"Do as I say, and you'll get kissed again."

She gave a half nod. Regret twisted her lip.

He stiffened instinctively.

The tiniest flash of silver. She dodged forward, much faster than he would've thought, and stuck a needle in his arm, plunging instantly.

He roared and flew back, striking out. His knuckles impacted her chin, and she crashed toward the wall. Sizzling sparks shot through his veins. Gray covered his vision, and as hard as he tried to remain standing, gravity won. The last, bizarre thought he had before his face hit the cold marble floor was a hope that he hadn't hurt her.

The world fuzzed. He lay on the ground, fighting to move, urging his brain to kick back alive. Sounds morphed in and out as he lay not feeling anything. Sounds, muffled and unclear, echoed back from other rooms.

Finally, spiked heels crossed his vision.

Cee Cee leaned down and brushed his forehead with soft lips. "I'm sorry."

The touch awoke something in him, and his hand unfisted. He growled low, and she jumped back.

"You'll be okay by tomorrow," she whispered, turning on one of those deadly heels and leaving the apartment.

"This . . . isn't . . . over," he ground out. Then blackness covered his vision, and he passed out.

Chapter 2

The Seattle wind fought against Cee Cee as she rode along the nearly empty streets, passing silent storefront windows, each a reproachful mirror. Her reflection glimmered back at her, block by block, showing an unthinkable image of a wild and free woman. Something she'd never been.

Stealing the enforcer's bike was probably a bad idea, but the Harley was a lot faster than the rental car she'd had stashed around the corner. Though she hadn't lied to Daire about her lack of experience riding motorcycles, she might have left a few things out, such as her ability to figure out quickly how to drive the massive beast.

Daire Dunne. Sure, through the years, she'd heard stories about the deadly witch enforcer. But nobody had warned her about his kiss. Dark and dangerous, and for the smallest of moments, she'd forgotten her purpose.

A man like Daire could make her forget everything.

The green of his eyes hinted at the roaming hills of Ireland, a place she'd never visited. Roped muscles had made up his wide shoulders and masculine torso and had tempted her to play. With his jet black hair and fiercely cut features, a wildness had careened off him, one he apparently tamed daily by keeping a strictly organized environment. What would it take to make him lose such rigid control?

Everything in her, all feminine and real, had wanted to jump into his fire.

Yet she'd drugged him instead. She shivered. There'd be hell to pay, and hopefully she'd be the only one to pay it. But repercussions were for another day.

She'd kissed him. He'd kissed her. The thought was almost unthinkable. She'd once had a mate, and in the immortal world, mating was forever, even past death. If a mated being touched another, or was touched by anybody other than the mate, a terrible, life-threatening allergy normally occurred. Until a virus had been unleashed that ultimately broke the mating bond.

The cure, a mutation of the virus, had worked on her. Unbelievable. She'd lost her mate eons ago and had resigned herself to being alone for eternity. Yet now, after allowing the vampire queen to infect her with the mutation, Cee Cee could touch and be touched. Damn, she wished she could've stayed and touched every inch of Daire Dunne before turning him into her enemy.

If he was as meticulous in fighting his enemy as he was with organizing his apartment and business files, she was in deep trouble. What kind of wild male witch kept such a rigid control on his environment, anyway?

Right now, she was driving a Harley for the first time in her life. Rushing through the city to Seattle's underbelly was an undeniable pleasure. Nice apartments sped by, and soon enough small houses with peeling paint and brown yards lined the street. Finally, when she arrived at the seedy motel on the outskirts of the rough end of town, she cut the engine and disembarked with genuine regret.

Puddles littered the broken concrete where three older vehicles had parked. A porch light flickered in the middle of the building; otherwise, the motel was dark. Not even an old television droned into the silence. Any strangers paying to stay in the dump had given up life for the night to sleep, while her men had better be awake.

A vampire, a young one, ran out of room thirteen. "Mission successful?"

"Yes." She tossed him the keys. "Return the bike to a secured parking area and call Dunne with the location. Far away from here." She paused and slid the backpack of perfectly organized papers off her shoulders. "Were the surveillance videos confiscated?"

The kid nodded, not meeting her eyes. She had a team of four soldiers, Jon, Jay, Sal, and Simon, and none of them ever met her gaze. Darn vampires.

Jon cleared his throat. "We got all videos from Dunne's building and the surrounding areas, so you won't be identified. Also, we confiscated two new videos of Apollo victims, ah, ma'am."

She stiffened. Her chin went up. "Did you just call me *ma'am?*"

He blushed so hard and fast, her own cheeks hurt. "Sorry, ah, Cee Cee." Without meeting her eyes, he jumped on the bike and ignited the engine, swiveling the machine around and taking off.

"You're supposed to be a badass," she yelled after him, happy she'd only given him her nickname. Imagine if he knew her entire name.

The door to thirteen opened, and Jay glanced out. "You're screaming."

She pinned the young vamp with a hard stare.

He swallowed, his Adam's apple bobbing. "Well, you are."

For Pete's sake. She sighed and stepped over cracked concrete, careful not to scratch her boots. "You're supposed to be a vigilante band of vampires too tough to align yourselves with the Realm," she muttered, sweeping by the kid, who had to be around nineteen years old. "Which was a mistake."

"I know."

After the war, which had basically just ended a year ago, most vampires in the world had made peace with the Realm, which was a coalition of vamps, shifters, and witches headed by the Kayrs family. Her current followers had thought themselves too tough to align themselves with the Realm until a rogue band of shifters almost ate them for dinner. Of course, it was her good fortune to need a band of Merry Men right at that time.

Her nose twitched as she entered the stagnant hotel room. A dingy flowered bedspread sprawled over what appeared to be a lumpy mattress, and the orange shag carpet had turned to a dirty rust. Thank God she didn't have a blacklight with her, because she truly didn't want to see beneath the surface to the germs and bodily contaminants.

Two other vampires, both young and blond, fiddled with connecting a brand-new laptop to an ancient television set. "Let's see the recording of the victims," she ordered.

Jay shut the door behind her, smelling like French fries and pizza. "Our deal stands?"

She barely kept from rolling her eyes. "Yes. You helped me with the mission, and now I'll make sure the king lets you into the Realm." By all that was holy. If the kids just showed up at King Dage Kayrs's house, he'd feed them dinner and provide lodging for them, making sure they were trained. Hell, knowing Dage, he'd adopt the young warriors into his own vampire family. They didn't need her introduction.

Good thing they didn't know that. They'd been invaluable in scoping out Titans of Fire, the Dunnes, and the Apollo drug. After she sent them to Dage, she should probably let him know some of the outliers didn't realize he welcomed all vampires into the fold.

Something to worry about another day, and only if she survived double-crossing Daire Dunne, which seemed to be a bit impossible after meeting the guy. It was too bad the only kiss she'd had in eons had come from a witch who no doubt was about to put a bounty on her head and then collect it himself.

It wasn't like she could blame him, because man, had she worked him. Who would've thought, her biggest curse and greatest regret would be an advantage in subterfuge? She might be damaged, and she might be weak, but this time, she was going to win. Finally.

It was odd how life worked out.

Hers was no doubt reaching its expiration date, but she had one job to do before she could rest, and Daire Dunne or no, she was going to do it.

The old television sprang to life, and a grainy video took shape of a couple of twenty-year-old girls dressed in shimmering tops and high heels hanging out in the private lounge area of Tod's Bar in lower Seattle. They smiled and flirted with men in suits, and the shortest girl finally drew slim vials of bright orange liquid from her knock-off purse. Apollo. The newest drug on the market.

They drank the entire vials.

Jay glanced over his shoulder. "This gets bad, Cee Cee. Sure you want to watch?"

If the kid had any idea what she'd seen through the years, he'd feel like an idiot asking the question. Yet she appreciated his concern, even as her stomach rolled. "Yes," she murmured, her gaze remaining on the screen.

The girls continued to party, one even making out with a much older man in a corner booth. An hour passed and the room began to clear out. Soon, the girls began to wobble on their heels while returning to the bar.

For water, probably. At that point with Apollo, their spit would be drying up.

Sparks crackled on the shorter girl's arm. Then waves of fire, blue and orange.

Her friend gasped and stumbled back, only to shoot plasma, oddly purple, from her fingertips.

A bouncer quickly reached the girls, but it was too late. Fire cascaded around them, on them, even inside them. Soon they both dropped to the ground, scorching the carpet around them.

The bouncer, a huge bald man with multiple earrings in each ear, shouted orders and sent the few remaining patrons scrambling for the door.

He didn't reach for the phone.

The taller girl went into convulsions, and fire roared from her fingertips to scald the far wall. Then she went silent and still, her eyes open in death. Colorful striations marred the whites of her eyes.

The other girl gasped, smoke streaming from her mouth, and tried to crawl toward her friend. She almost made it before collapsing in death, a trickle of flame burning out the side of her mouth.

The television clicked off.

"So sick," Jay said. "What's in Apollo? Nobody knows, Cee Cee."

She knew. It was a mineral mined in Russia that had several names, and her people called in planekite. It stole the power of witches and ultimately killed them, and now it was part of a designer drug that gave witchly power to humans before incinerating their internal organs. "I don't know what's in it," she lied.

He flicked off the television. "The bouncer ends up carrying them outside, where there's no camera. The bodies haven't been found yet."

That figured. "Track down the bodies and make sure they get a proper burial, and make sure their families are notified, if they have families."

Jay cleared his throat. "You'll contact the king?"

"Yes." She glanced at her watch, her heart aching for those poor, stupid girls. Youth made mistakes, but they shouldn't be deadly, damn it. "Finish the job here, lie low for two weeks, and then show up at Realm headquarters. Dage will be waiting with open arms."

That would give her enough time to get her job done before anybody figured out what she was doing.

"Thank you," Jay whispered, the gratitude on his rugged face sweet and kind of sad.

"You're welcome," she said, wanting nothing more than to give the kid a hug. But now she had a plane to catch and a pissed-off male witch to escape. With a sigh, she turned and headed back into the cool Seattle night for the next part of her grand plan of revenge and death. Then, finally, she could rest.

Time started to tick by as Daire fought to regain control of his body on the smooth tile floor. His other hand unclenched. Then tingles cascaded up his legs. If he could just get—

The door opened.

Fuck.

A second clicked, and then two well-trained bodies launched into motion. One jumped over him, green gun out, scouting the empty penthouse. The other hauled him up by the armpits, all two hundred fifty pounds of him, and shoved him onto a brocade chair by the entrance.

Garrett Kayrs, nephew to the vampire king, kept Daire from falling over and peered into his eyes. "Do we need backup?"

Daire shook his head and forced out a word. "No." It was bad enough the two young soldiers had found him. But better them than his brothers. He'd never live down one of them finding him helpless on his own damn floor.

Garrett's metallic gray eyes narrowed, and his massive shoulders rolled back. For a vampire only in his early twenties, he'd settled into command mode incredibly quickly.

Logan Kyllwood jogged back into view, rubbing his crew-cut hair. "Condo is clear."

Daire swallowed, and the taste of sulfur burned down his throat. Whatever had been in the syringe had been created to take down an immortal, more specifically, a witch. "I'm fine."

Logan snorted, his lighter green eyes twinkling. Coming from a vampire and demon hybrid, it sounded more like a call for war. His square jaw was all demon, while the sharp angles of his cheekbones were all vampire, making for a predatory combination. "Dude. You are not fine."

Had the fucking demon just called him *dude*? God save him from soldiers two decades old. Yet as much as he tried, he couldn't help liking the two young males, even though they were slobs who kept violating the order of his condo. One a vampire, one a demon. Man, had humans gotten them wrong. Vamps could go into the sun, and demons had nothing to do with hell. They were just two different species on earth, like witches. But the smartass comments needed to stop.

Daire cleared his throat, finally able to move his mouth. "What was taken?" He'd heard Cee Cee rummage through his place, and his gut clenched.

Logan grimaced. "Your office looks like a pack of feline shifters went through it, and it's gonna drive you crazy, believe me. A lot of papers everywhere, and the drawer on mine holdings is almost empty. Any files pertaining to Russia, Norway, and Canada."

Daire breathed out. Oh, she had not taken those. Who the fuck was that woman? He stretched his ankles, and spikes of needles pricked through them. "Is that all?"

"No. It looks like Simone's penthouse was also ransacked." Logan shook his head. "Boy, is she gonna be pissed."

Simone? As a member of the Council of the Coven Nine, the ruling body for the witch nation, Simone surely had confidential papers at her penthouse, which was adjacent to Daire's. He tried to grasp on to reality. "Go get the video surveillance for the building. Now."

Logan nodded and sped out the door.

Garrett released Daire and sat back. "What happened?"

"Nothing. Coven business." As an enforcer for the witch world, he could claim privacy from the vampire. "How was hunting?"

Garrett studied him, almost too much knowledge on his young face. More and more, every day, he was starting to look like his father, badass Talen Kayrs. Talen was one of the most dangerous vampire soldiers Daire had ever met, and that was saying something.

Garrett and Logan were undercover as prospective members of the Titans of Fire Motorcycle Club and had been scouting Seattle bars all night for a lead on the drug they were all investigating. The idea of the two soldiers, who had seen real war and death, fighting to be included in a human motorcycle club was silly at best. But they had been doing a good job getting information about the drug, and

Daire had actually enjoyed having the kids around, even if they did mess up his normally ordered life.

Garrett shook his head. "No new Intel tonight from the bars we frequented. The dealers are getting sneakier."

Daire tried to clear the numbness in his head. "Are the cameras at Fire operational?"

"No. We disabled them weeks ago, not wanting Logan or me caught on surveillance."

Aye. At the time, Daire had agreed with the decision. "Those papers hold the locations of every planekite mine on earth as well as the deeds we hold." He purposely kept all information off computers, which could be hacked, because, hey, he was a hardass enforcer who could protect paper. Well, except from one very tiny blond, enhanced human. Fuck, shit, and double-damn fuck. "I can't believe this." He wiped his forehead, his hand shaking.

Garrett swallowed. "Um, were there a bunch of them? The ones who took you out?"

"No. One woman with a syringe knocked me on my ass." One woman.

Garrett's eyebrows rose in his hard-cut face. "A woman?"

Daire growled. "Yes. Very pretty."

Garrett pressed his lips together, and his gray eyes lightened to a sparkling silver.

"If you laugh, I'm going to throw you out the window," Daire snapped. A ten-story fall would teach the young vampire a lesson.

Garrett's mouth twitched, and he cleared his throat.

Logan shoved his way back inside the door. "The surveillance system was knocked out all night. No videos."

"Smart woman," Garrett coughed.

Logan glanced down at his buddy, who was still crouched beside Daire. "Woman?"

Garrett stood and took a step away from Daire. "Yes. A woman with a mighty syringe."

Logan stood straighter, a frown drawing down his dark eyebrows. "Shifter or witch?"

"No." Daire planted a hand on the wall and shoved himself to his feet. He would've recognized a witch, and he hadn't gotten any hint of shifter from her. Vampires were male only, and demons gave out stronger vibes than any other species. Plus, ninety percent of the demon nation was male, and a female would never be out on her own like that. "Enhanced human."

Logan's mouth dropped open.

"Shut up," Daire growled. "She was beautiful, and it has been a while." Could he sound any more like a dumbass? "If you two tell anybody, and I mean *anybody*, I'll cut off your heads myself."

The kids shuffled their feet. Garrett was no doubt under orders to report anything and everything to his uncle Dage, the king of vampires. Logan was probably similarly under orders to report all progress to his brother, Zane Kyllwood, the leader of the demon nation.

Daire sighed. "The woman and the mine holdings don't concern the vampire or demon nations, so I'm asking you, at least for now, keep this between us." Considering they'd done nothing but create chaos in his perfectly ordered life while also eating him out of house and home, they could grant him a solid.

The soldiers nodded.

Good. Now he owed them, but he'd worry about that later. Right now, he had to figure out the Apollo drug and Cee Cee's connection to it and the mines. Besides killing humans, the drug had been injected into darts and fired at witches, thus killing them. They'd learned that Seattle was just a test-drive for the drug, and soon it would be unleashed on his homeland. That simply couldn't happen. "So no progress on Apollo tonight?"

"No." Logan leaned back against the closed door. "It was a shitty night."

A shitty night? Yeah, that about summed it up. But it was nothing compared to the night little Cee Cee was going to have when Daire caught up to her.

Chapter 3

Wind pierced Cee Cee's thick clothing, digging with sharp blades right to her skin. She shivered, her gaze on the frozen landscape of Fryser Island in the Arctic Sea. The sun shone weakly down, glittering along the ice, failing to provide an ounce of warmth. The chill banished any hint of fog, leaving the arctic tundra in crisp focus.

She had taken three different private planes to arrive in the Arctic, and her eyes stung with the need to sleep. First she had a job to do, and at least the cold was keeping her awake.

"Begging your pardon, ma'am, but this is a very bad idea," said her pilot, a local from the mainland and a barrel of a man with the thickest beard she'd ever seen. "Ms. Jones. Please come back to the plane with me, and I'll return you to the mainland." Concern, and an unwelcome note of duty, echoed in his tone.

She smiled. "I asked you to call me Cee Cee." They'd spent hours together in the small plane to reach the island few people knew even existed in the Norwegian Sea. "Mr. Agard, I assure you, I have a guide meeting me any minute."

They stood on an ice-covered wooden dock, facing away from the quiet sea and toward a series of abandoned buildings staring back at them. Barren and rugged, the fierce desolation of the area appealed to her on a primal level. Even the massive mountains piled so high and sharp held a beauty that stole her breath.

He cleared his throat. "We have another abandoned city called Pyramiden on Spitsbergen Island. It's cold and desolate like this, but sometimes tourists go there, and graduate students study the environment. There are hotels not too far away, and more importantly, there are people. Please let me take you there."

Pyramiden hadn't been mined in years and was of little interest to her. This place? Yeah. It looked abandoned, but mines often went far into the mountains, and there were a hell of a lot of mountains behind the tiny entrance. More danger chased her than the man could imagine, but his instincts, like those of most humans, were spot-on. "I like abandoned," she murmured.

He shook his head. "There's nothin' here but old buildings, cold, polar bears, rabbits, and arctic foxes." Almost on cue, a white shaggy beast with horns loped across the landscape. "And Svalbard reindeer."

"I'll be fine," she said, her eyes tearing from the chill, even from behind protective contacts. Since the mine in her sight was obviously dead, she only needed to check on two other mines, because she'd already discovered the secrets of the third, and they would end tomorrow. The wind slapped her face, and she made a mental note to slather on face cream at first chance.

"You don't understand. The polar bears are vicious and many just had cubs. If they scent you, they'll attack." He cast wide eyes around the desolate area and shivered.

A grating noise pinged against the mountains, rising in pitch, coming closer. Soon a figure in a thick white coat zoomed around a far building on a powerful black snowmobile. The man wore a knit cap, light-refracting glasses, and snow pants. His gloved hands rested easily on the handlebars, and even at the impressive speed, his body remained relaxed.

"Idiot isn't wearing a helmet," the pilot muttered.

The idiot was a witch and didn't need a helmet. The man slowed to a stop and cut the engine, remaining in place, gaze shielded behind the glasses.

"Good. He's bigger than you, so the polar bears will eat him first. You could run for safety while he gets eaten," the pilot said. "One last chance, Ms. Jones. Come with me and leave this lonely place." He quickly crossed himself.

She turned and gave him a gentle nudge toward his seaplane. "I'm stronger than I look. Thank you for your help, and please don't give me a second thought."

His brown eyes warmed, even as he backed away. "I hate to tell you this, little lady, but you'd be a hard one to forget." His frown reached his eyes as he glanced toward the rider, who still hadn't moved. "You know anything about this guy?"

"I do. We're old friends," she lied. Truth be told, she'd heard about him from a friend of an acquaintance of a friend. A mercenary for hire—one with excellent connections.

"Okay." The pilot finally gave up and ambled back toward his plane. "Good luck."

Yeah. She needed luck. She kept in place, waiting until the pilot had steered the plane out to the calm sea and taken off. Keeping her expression relaxed, she slowly strode toward the silent rider, stopping a couple of feet away. The plane flew over her head. "Vegar Bergan?" she asked.

He nodded and tipped down the glasses to reveal cold blue eyes. "Ms. . . . Jones?"

"I am today," she returned easily. They were business acquaintances, and he didn't get to know her real name. "I take it you received the first half of the payment?" She'd wired the five million dollars the previous night.

"Yes." He glanced from her hair to her fur-lined boots. "You're not a witch."

"No." She steeled her shoulders and pointed to the entrance to the mountain, shielded by a frozen orange metal building. "I'd like to start with this mine."

His gaze didn't waver. "That one's empty, one we can't reach, and two are very heavily guarded and difficult to get to, even with a snowmobile. I told you that before you came all the way out to the middle of nowhere."

She tilted her head. "Yet you took my money anyway, so I want to see the mines."

His chin lifted. "You're not a shifter, either."

"No."

"Something, though. Something light." He frowned. "Fairy?"

Had the low-browed witch just called her a *fairy*? Fire lit inside her, a testament to her heritage. Fairies stayed in their communes and didn't venture out. Well, most of them. She'd only met a few in her life, and she was nowhere near that calm or gentle. "I'm not a fairy," she muttered.

He leaned back, eyebrows drawing down. "You're human? An enhanced female?" Without losing a beat, he threw back his head and laughed, long and hard. The sound slapped against the deserted buildings and pinged back. "You're kidding me. Human."

She gritted her teeth together and barely forced out words. "My heritage is irrelevant, and I hired you to do a job. So do it."

He sobered and slowly drew out a snub-nosed pistol. "I thought this would be much more difficult, but I figured you for a witch. Considering you're looking for planekite."

She settled her boots in the snow and drew in a deep breath. The guy was a foot taller than she and about a hundred pounds heavier. At least. She'd have to be fast and brutal if they fought. "If I don't see the mines and reach safety, then you don't get the other five million."

He smiled then, revealing oversized teeth and sharp canines. "You're apparently worth twenty million."

Heat flushed down her torso to slam into her stomach. "You know who I am."

"No clue, lady." His gaze raked from her freezing head down to her chilling toes. "Care to tell me?"

Somehow she didn't think that would help her cause. The wind picked up again, lifting her hair and biting her ears. She glanced around at the barren area, not sensing anybody else near. "Who hired you?"

He shrugged. "Don't know and don't care. Received directions via the Internet, and payment via the Caymans."

That was all right. She knew who'd hired him but truly hadn't expected retaliation quite yet. "What's your plan?"

He kicked back on the seat. "We're going to take a nice ride around the coastline, go north, and meet transport on the other side of the island. I'll radio from there." He gestured her forward with a gun.

She stepped toward him, forcing her muscles to go lax. "If somebody wants me that badly, you won't shoot me."

He lifted both eyebrows. "I was specifically told I could shoot you in the leg if necessary." His grin widened. "We both know that ain't gonna be necessary, don't we?"

She nodded. "We both do know that fact." Leaping up, she kicked out with both feet, nailing both the gun and his chin. His head snapped back, and he flew off the snowmobile. The force knocked her onto her back, and she flipped up, hampered by the heavy coat and boots. Her sunglasses went flying.

He shot to his feet, blood dripping down his chin. "Bitch."

"Well now, that's just not nice." Her breath panted out, and adrenaline burst through her veins. Bunching her knees, she leaped across the vehicle and slammed into him, one fist plowing into his trachea. He bellowed, twisted, and threw her hard.

She landed on unforgiving ice and rolled, snow gathering in her hair. Pain rippled up her elbow and to her shoulder, but she shoved the sensation away, rose to her feet, and ran full bore for him.

He braced his feet, ready to catch her, when she suddenly jumped up and clamped her knees on either side of his face. With a sharp twist, she cracked his jaw and slid around his back to tuck her arm beneath his chin and pull up.

His scream echoed against the buildings, zinged around, and seemed to come from every direction. He reached up and grabbed her hair, yanking hard.

Agony lanced along her scalp, and she loosened her hold, suddenly flying over his head and smashing into the snowmobile. Her vision fuzzed and her ears rang. She fell down, her butt on the ground. It had been too long since she'd been in a real fight. Bile rose in her throat, followed by panic.

He cupped his jaw, fire shooting from his eyes. Real fire, red and angry, danced down his neck.

Shit.

She tried to scramble up, but plasma balls formed on his hands. Damn it.

He spit out blood. "You're no human." The plasma morphed and danced, waiting to burn. "Let's see what you can take."

She swallowed and tasted blood. "I'll triple your price."

"No way. I want you to burn."

A shadow fell across the sun for the briefest of moments. She squinted and looked over his shoulder, gasping. What the hell? A figure in all black, straight and true, hang glided from the east in perfect formation. Her mouth gaped. The guy had to have jumped from the high peaks of the jagged mountain. Crazy.

Vegar half turned to see the figure.

Cee Cee launched herself off the snowmobile, hitting the witch mid-center and throwing him on his back. He clamped her arm, burning through the material. Pain cut into her, and she cried out, shoving against his chest to stand. Crying, swearing, she stomped onto his hands, throwing snow.

He clasped her ankle and shoved her back toward the snowmobile. She no sooner hit than she jumped up and aimed for him, punching and kicking strategic points. The traitor defended himself, hitting back, but not getting enough time to form more fire. If he created more, he might incapacitate her. His fist connected with her jaw, and she dropped, her head spinning in sharp pain.

Then he grabbed her hair and pulled her back up.

She helped him, punching both fists into his groin. The sound he made defied description. Using her hair, he swung her around and flung her again.

She landed on her front, the air knocked out of her lungs. Her gloved hands scrambled to stop her as she turned around and around on the ice, spinning away from the threat. She had to shut him down before he created more fire.

A plasma ball landed next to her, and she yelped, rolling out of the way and crouching up on her knees.

He stood, blood flowing down his face and turning his teeth red. "You're gonna pay." As if remembering just then, he half turned, but it was too late. The man on the hang glider kicked two large boots into Vegar's face, throwing back his head. The snap of bones breaking ripped through the chilled air. Vegar crashed onto the ice, arms outstretched, out cold. Probably with a broken neck.

Cee Cee pushed herself up, her legs wobbling. She squinted as the sun reflected across the ice. Spotting her sunglasses, she reached down and planted them back on her face, protecting her eyes.

The hang glider dropped and sent the glider across the frozen tundra to slide into the orange building. He was big and broad and easily controlled his body in a graceful jog to stop within a yard of her. A black headgear mask covered his face, and a knit hat covered his hair. A dark Klim Latitude jacket covered his wide torso, and Klim pants led down to thick boots. Even mirrored eyeglasses hid his eyes.

But she knew. Damn it, she knew.

He ripped off the face mask. "Cee Cee."

Ah, crap. "Daire. How in the world did you find me?" Spirals unfolded in her abdomen, sparks of unwelcome pleasure. Her body was happy to see him. Her brain was not. "Seriously. How?"

He tucked the mask into his back pocket and shoved his glasses atop his head.

Furious. Green eyes, ringed with darker green, shot sparks at her. His body was relaxed, and yet, a tension now lifted the breeze, sparking along her skin. "You might have taken my surveillance cameras, but cameras are all over town, baby."

Baby. When was the last time anybody had called her baby? Had anybody ever called her baby? She didn't think so. "I see. You caught up surprisingly quickly." Trying to be casual, she moved slightly toward the snowmobile.

He smiled, and she halted in place. The smile wasn't kind or remotely amused. It was a warning.

She was smart enough to heed it.

"Considering the files you stole, I tracked you here."

"I have to admit, you made it so easy to find the exact right maps with your freaky organizational skills. Do you have OCD?" she blurted.

He drew back, irritation all but wafting from him. "No. I just like things orderly."

Must be nice. Her world was usually full of chaos these days. "I could've gone to the mines in Russia instead of here," she murmured, and she still fully intended to do so. Where was the key to the snowmobile? She had to move to see the ignition.

Daire lifted a dark eyebrow in a dangerously rugged face. "The key isn't in the ignition. I assume he has it." Daire jerked his head toward the unconscious witch, whose neck should be repairing itself. "Who is he, anyway?"

She sighed. "Vegar Bergan."

Daire coughed. "The mercenary?" He kicked the downed man, who didn't even moan. "You trusted Bergan?"

Heat climbed into her freezing face. "I paid him well."

"Not well enough," Daire drawled.

"Obviously." Her chin lifted.

"Everyone knows Vegar is available to the highest bidder. If you have an enemy, then you're vulnerable when working with a guy like this."

Yeah, she'd learned that the hard way, but enough chitchat. It was time for some action, even if it hurt. She'd lost any patience for waiting around. "If you and I are going to fight, I'd like to start now. It's getting cold."

He rubbed his chin with what looked like thick glove insoles. Witches probably didn't need full gloves. "Well, I have to admit, I caught some of your earlier fight. You can hit, darlin'."

She breathed out evenly. That didn't sound like a compliment, but even more, it didn't *feel* like one. She was damaged and had needed to learn to fight physically, but she didn't need to share that fact with him. "I took karate."

"Nice try, but you're not human. It took me a while, and I don't really understand what's going on, but now at least I know what you are." He took two steps toward her, casting an intimidating shadow across the icy beach. "Take off the sunglasses, Cee Cee."

She swallowed. There was no reason to keep them on—one hit from him and they'd fly off. She slid them up her forehead to hold back her hair. "Why?"

He glanced down, no expression providing insight to his thoughts. "And the contacts."

She blinked. The thought occurred to her to deny she was wearing contacts, but instead, she lifted her chin. "No."

"Take them out, or I will."

She glanced down at his huge hands. No, she didn't want one of those fingers in her eyes. Apparently the gig was up, anyway. "Fine." Yanking off her glove, she reached up and removed the colored contacts to fling them onto the snow. The cold instantly enfolded her hand and dug into her eyes. Then she faced him squarely, her eyes no longer blue. "Happy now?"

He slowly, very slowly, shook his head. Anger vibrated on the arctic breeze. "Fuck no, I'm not happy. Demon."

Chapter 4

Daire stared at the stunning woman facing him so bravely. White-blond hair, sparkling black eyes, tiny stature, and hoarse voice. A purebred female demon. They were so rare as to be almost extinct, and not for a second had he considered she was part of the demon species. She looked much more angel than anything else. Of course, angels didn't exist, and demons were just another race with no ties to heaven or hell. Just earth.

Most demons gave off intrusive vibrations of energy, and it usually took years, centuries really, for one to be able to temper the waves. But this one? This one didn't give off any hint of demonness. "Why couldn't I tell what you are?" he asked, ignoring the freezing wind cutting into his eyes.

Her gaze faltered and then strengthened. "Maybe you're not all that talented."

At the moment, he didn't appreciate flippancy. Standing this close to her, even knowing what she was, his body rioted. Not even the sub-zero temperature could cool his raging cock. "How old are you?"

She huffed. "What a rude question."

"Answer it, or I'll show you rude."

She rolled those stunning eyes. "Fine. I'm a hundred and twenty-five." Then she frowned, looking no more than twenty-five years old. For her species, she was young. "How old are you?"

"Over three centuries." He narrowed his gaze, fighting every animalistic urge he owned not to tackle her to the ground and take what she'd offered the other night. "You're not old enough to be able to mask your energy. Not *nearly* old enough to do it so well." He'd met demons over a thousand years old who couldn't mask to that degree. "Explain."

She lifted one small shoulder, and the wind kicked in, lifting her light hair. "We all have unique gifts, Enforcer. That's mine."

He frowned as the cold slapped his bare face. Nothing about the woman was adding up, and even so, his fingers itched to run through her hair.

She shivered.

He swore. "Put your glove back on."

She slowly slipped her delicate hand back into the glove. The wind stirred up snow, and it swirled around, turning her into a magical princess. "I'm going to ask you again, how did you know to follow me to Norway and not Russia?" The woman spoke with intelligence and a hint of demand.

The combination only turned him on, which made absolutely no sense. He liked quiet, sweet, structured women. "The mines in Russia are public knowledge; the mines here are not." He'd figured she'd check out the secret mines first, and the bet had paid off. "What do you want with the Fryser Island mines, Cee Cee? If that's your real name."

"It is." She slid the glasses down her forehead to protect her eyes. The wind rolled dark clouds in from the sea, and the temperature instantly dropped further. "At least, that's what my mother called me."

"The mines?"

She shrugged, the movement oddly sensual. "I'm hunting a demon with strong connections to your people and your mines. You own two of the four here, and he owns the other two. Apparently this mine of yours is truly not producing."

"I don't deal with demons," he said, trying to keep derision from his tone. Truth be told, until he'd gotten to know Logan recently, he'd never liked a demon. "Who are you, ah, hunting?" It was hard to imagine the petite blonde hunting anybody, but looks were obviously misleading.

She just stared at him, no expression on her smooth face.

"Who are you?" he asked softly.

She blinked, as if not expecting the question. "Nobody you need to worry about, Enforcer." She slid one very small boot toward the sprawling snowmobile.

"You became my business the moment you drugged me and stole

my files as well as the private files of a member of the Coven Nine."
The second she'd smiled at him, he'd been in a constant state of
arousal. "What did you drug me with?"

She craned her neck toward the empty ignition slot and then
sighed. "It was a horse sedative with a few tweaks. Quantum physics
at its finest."

He widened his stance and fought a shiver as the blackened clouds
started to cover the meager sun. "You hired a witch to alter the sedative and take me down."

"Not all witches belong to the Coven Nine," she murmured.

No shit. One of them was sprawled, unconscious, on the ice in
front of him. "I'm well aware."

She smiled. "You're fine, with no permanent damage, so how
about we call it even?"

Even? His chin lowered as his temper tried to spike. "You're
joking."

"No." She mirrored his stance and planted her hands on her hips.
"I don't want to fight you." Turning slightly, she glanced toward the
empty orange building, revealing a wicked bruise along her jawline.

"Holy fuck." He moved before thinking, prowling toward her
through the swirling snow, cupping her jaw. The bruise was too fresh
for him to have done it the other night, thank God.

She tried to step back, and the snowmobile stopped her. "I'm
fine."

Rage, the real kind, roared through him. He released her and took
a quick step away before fire flared through his right glove, burning
it away. Taking several deep breaths, he quelled his temper and the
flame.

Her mouth formed a perfect O.

Keeping her gaze, he drew a knife from his boot.

She paled. "Wh—"

"He dies," Daire said, turning toward the prone witch.

"No." Cee Cee rushed toward him, grabbing his arm. "It was a
fair fight, and then you knocked him out. Why would you kill him?"

Daire stilled. The entire world halted, and he touched her with his
now bare hand, running a finger along the darkening bruise. "For
this." Gladly. Her skin was softer than silk and twice as fragile.

Snow licked against her surprisingly dark eyelashes and melted on her nose.

Her finely arched eyebrows drew down, and she leaned back against the snowmobile, breaking his hold. "Um, we're enemies. You get that, right?"

"Aye." It didn't matter. Nothing mattered at the moment but avenging that purple mark on her face. "But I wouldn't do that to you. Ever."

She tilted her head to the side, confusion all but rolling from her. "So you're basically harmless to me."

He chuckled, even pissed off. "Oh, I didn't say that." She'd tell him everything he wanted to know, but he'd never punch a woman. He turned back toward the immediate problem.

"Daire, please do not kill him," she whispered.

He sighed. "Why the hell not?"

"There's been enough death, don't you think?" She pushed the glasses up her head again, her eyes onyx jewels. "No more."

The war had ended a little more than a year before, and too many immortals had died. Yet when he again glanced at the bruise on her face, he wanted to draw blood. He needed to harm the witch on the ground. But it didn't have to be today, and it didn't have to happen in front of Cee Cee. His chest hitched. "Well now, what kind of deal shall we strike?" he asked.

She swallowed. "I'll return your deeds and surveys to you, as well as the documents taken from Simone Brightston."

He smiled. "I assume they're in the backpack you're still wearing, and I believe I can get them if I so choose." He faced her fully, more than a little curious how far she'd go. What would the little temptress offer?

Her nostrils flared, and a little color returned to her angled cheeks. "Fine. How about I don't melt your brain out of your skull?"

He slid the knife back into his boot. "Speaking of which, why didn't you unleash a demon mind attack on Vegar here?"

She rolled her eyes. "Please. It takes energy to shoot pain and terrible images into somebody else's head, especially a witch's. You must know that."

Aye, he did understand her people's gifts and the toll it took on them. "You were about to get your ass burned."

She scoffed. "Hardly. I was just getting started."

Maybe. Maybe not. He cocked his head to the side. "Heal your face, Cee Cee." Her people had just as much healing power as witches, and she should've already sent healing cells to her jaw. The bruise was making it difficult for him to focus, and it needed to disappear.

She pursed her lips. "I will when I'm ready."

What the hell? "Do it now, or I cut off his head."

She glanced around at the now churning sea, the darkening sky, the silent buildings, and mumbled something.

He leaned in. "Didn't hear you."

She exhaled, sparks shooting from her eyes. "I'm too cold."

The admission slammed him in the chest. Sometimes he forgot not everybody burned with fire inside. Damn it. He instantly shrugged out of the Klim jacket.

"No." She moved back and tumbled, falling on the snowmobile.

"Yes." He hauled her up by the arm and shoved the coat around her. "Put your arms in, or I'll do it for you."

Her lower lip trembled. "I'm not weak."

He tilted his head. "Never said you were."

She cleared her throat, vulnerability darkening her eyes. "Right."

What kind of land mine had he just stepped in? He couldn't handle an emotional female at the moment. "Being cold isn't the same as being weak. Now put on the fucking coat."

She pushed her arms in, and he zipped her up, noting how the coat dropped nearly to her knees. She ducked her face inside the collar. "Petrichor," she murmured.

"Huh?" he asked.

"The smell after the rain is petrichor," she said. "Even in the bar at Titans of Fire, that's how you smelled." Her throaty voice seemed to kiss his skin, and he'd give every possession he owned to have her whispering something, anything, against his cock.

He shifted his weight.

Waves crashed into the shore, water spreading over ice. He grasped her arm. "What was your plan here?"

She glanced down at the prone witch. "He was supposed to pick me up, get us to shelter, and then show me the three remaining mines on the island. The orange one right there is obviously defunct." A fox yipped in the distance, and she slid her hands into the pockets. Then she frowned. "By the way, a hang glider?"

He eyed the oncoming storm. "I own this abandoned mine as well as the functioning coal mine up beyond the bluff. My employees hang glide for fun, and when I saw you through binoculars, it was definitely the fastest way of getting down here."

She eyed the far peaks. "How did you get *up* there?"

"Plane, helicopter, and parachute," he said easily. From the island, snowmobiling was the only way to get to the coal mine, and that was fine with him. "About twenty years ago, I had a hangar built on the western end of the island. We need to get there and to the helicopter to get off this damn island." A gust of wind blew in, and she stumbled toward him. Lightning zigged across the sky. He crossed to the downed witch and searched his pockets, getting the snowmobile key. Fire crackled along his arms. "I'll wake this guy up and ask who offered him money to betray you."

She coughed. "No need. I already know."

Daire glanced over his shoulder. "Who?"

Her lips pressed tightly together. Her very blue lips.

He sighed and moved toward the vehicle. "We need shelter until the storm passes." At which point, she'd finally tell him everything. "Give me the name, Cee Cee. I'm not going to ask *why* right now, but I want the name." Getting information from the woman was as difficult as getting money from his cousin, Simone. Women.

She glanced down at the barely breathing witch on the ground. Her shoulders moved forward just an inch. "Ivan Bychkov."

Daire jerked his head. Bychkov, the damn demon, owned half of the mines in Russia, including a couple that had formerly mined planekite. So he also owned the other two mines on Fryser. Interesting. Daire had traced the ownership through several dummy corporations that hadn't led back to Bychkov. "The plot thickens," Daire muttered. For now, he had to get the woman out of the storm. He sat on the snowmobile, his butt instantly freezing, and held out a hand. "We've been here before." It wasn't a motorcycle, but close enough.

She faltered and then accepted his hand. The wind whipped her hair around, and her beautiful eyes teared.

He stopped her before she could straddle the machine. One more question needed to be answered before he could move on and make a plan. "Was any of it real?" he asked.

"Any of what?"

The looks, the kiss, the fucking need. "Us."

She blinked snow from her eyes, her gaze down. "No."

He studied her, noting the vibrations in the air. "You're a terrible liar."

She gasped, her gaze meeting his. "I most certainly am not."

Was she protesting his claim that she was a liar or a *terrible* liar? "Aye, you are." He leaned in, not missing her quick intake of breath. "Admit it was real, or I'll prove it." Damn, he really wanted to prove her wrong.

Even bruised, her chin was stubborn. She leaned toward him, bringing the scent of female and hyacinth. "There's nothing to prove. I worked you, Enforcer. Deal with it."

He moved then, clamping his hands on her waist, and plunking her down, facing him. The handlebars bracketed her, as did his arms.

She sucked in air and tried to lean back and away. The move scooted her core closer to his, and he shoved against her, his dick jumping at the vee in her legs. Her eyes widened. Desire all but rolled off her. Both hands pressed against his chest with impressive strength.

"Admit it, Cee Cee."

"No." She didn't hide her gaze, but her fingers curled into his chest. Anger and denial danced in her eyes, but beneath them, there was something more. Curiosity? She held her breath, not moving.

His gaze narrowed. She wanted to know as badly as he did if the other night had been about tequila and drugs or something else. Yet instead of saying so, she denied any feelings and waited for him to pounce. His biceps vibrated with the need to do exactly that and go deep. So he slid his hands down to her hips and tilted her, rubbing his shaft between her legs.

She gasped, and her lips half lowered. Desire competed with the storm now beating around them.

He leaned in so close his breath brushed her lips. "I don't play games, sweetheart, and you've done nothing else since the first time I met you."

Her tongue flicked out to wet her lips.

He fought a groan and pressed harder against her core. Even

through his snow pants and hers, he could swear he felt her heat. The woman called to him on a level he couldn't explain, but he'd give anything to feel her wrapped around him, crying out his name.

"I'm not playing games," she ground out, her voice so sexily hoarse he almost came in his pants right there.

"You are." He closed the inch between them and settled his lips a breath away from hers. There was an innocence to her game playing, a real curiosity, that gave him pause. She was a demon, no doubt closely protected by family her entire life, considering female demons were incredibly rare. Had she been with a man? The other night, the woman had known how to kiss. Really known how to kiss. Was the curiosity real? "Enough game playing."

Her eyelids fluttered shut. "Fine." Quick as any witch, she shot her hands into his hair and yanked his mouth against hers. Soft as petals, she kissed him, flicking her tongue along his lower lip.

Desire, hot and desperate, roared through his blood. Flexing his hands, he tipped her back, taking her lips and stealing the kiss. His tongue swept inside her mouth, tasting woman and fine wine. The combination lit him on fire, and he had to force flames away from his skin. Something he hadn't had to do since he'd been a randy teenager centuries ago.

He pressed against her, allowing the beast inside him off the leash. Then she groaned. The sound reverberated up her throat, eased into his mouth, and set his nerve endings alive. Kissing her harder, he pressed his chest against hers, allowing the handlebars to carry their weight. With only his mouth working hers, he tilted her head to the side so he could go deeper. His hands went to her jacket, just as her cold nose brushed against his cheek.

Freezing nose.

He broke the kiss and leaned back, his entire body throbbing with the fierce need to strip her bare and bury himself inside her tight body. "You're cold," he rumbled, his voice rougher than any demon's would ever be.

Her eyelids fluttered open, and her pupils widened. Surprise and need glittered in the depths of her eyes. "Not cold. Very hot."

He grinned. Even now, his body on fire, her likability soothed him. Oh, he didn't trust her and had no doubt they were on opposite sides of whatever was going on. Yet she had a sweetness to her he wanted to explore, consequences be damned. "Shelter, baby. We need shelter."

The atmosphere ticked. A change around them, a tension in the storm, had his shoulders stiffening. He leaned back, taking Cee Cee with him, and surveyed the area.

She stilled, her head turning toward the orange building. "Something is there."

Aye. The storm had strengthened, swirling snow around, making visibility nil. But he could *feel* something. Or someone. Darkness through the white. Eyes. Animal eyes.

Slowly, on the prowl, a series of polar bears stalked around both sides of the orange building. The beasts were well known in Norway, their kills a normal occurrence when anybody was stupid enough to set foot on Norwegian islands.

Cee Cee swallowed. "Shifter or animal?"

He ducked his head. Many shifters lived on the island, and most of his employees in the coal mine were actual bear shifters. But these? All animal, which was unfortunate. He moved his hands incredibly slowly around the woman's stiff body. The switch inside him flipped, turning him from lover to killer in an instant. Protecting the woman in front of him became his entire focus. "I'm going to ignite the engine, and I need you to flip around me and hold on at the same second."

"Okay," she whispered, her thighs tightening around his waist.

"Now," he muttered, twisting the key. The engine roared to life, and Cee Cee moved, gracefully swirling around him and planting her butt in place.

The lead bear charged, teeth sharp and bared.

Chapter 5

Oh God. There were at least eight large beasts running at them.

"Hold on, Cee Cee," Daire said, twisting the throttle. The powerful vehicle jumped forward, and snow sprayed.

She clamped her hands together, her body flush with his, her legs vibrating. Piercing cold air rushed against her face, and she leaned her cheek into his back. "What about Vegar?" she yelled.

Daire swerved to avoid the head bear.

Two more leaped toward them, hitting their bodies square on and knocking them off the rapidly moving snowmobile. Daire turned in midair and tucked her close, wrapping his body around her as they landed hard on the ice and skidded several yards. Before she could catch her breath, he was up and in front of her, facing down a line of snarling beasts.

She scrambled to stand, her boots sliding on the slippery surface. Panic cut off her air, and the wind shoved at her from behind. The snowmobile continued on without them for a distance, slowed, and slid to a stop, its engine still running.

The nearest bear lifted its head and growled. Insanity glowed in its eyes, or maybe that was hunger. Definitely pure animal with no shifter inside. Judging by size, three of the animals were male, five female. All were a mangy white with thick coats and deadly claws, ranging from nine feet to seven feet tall, and about a thousand pounds. How in the hell could she and Daire take all eight of them?

A female to the leader's left turned and ran over to Vegar on the ground. Cee Cee cried out and tried to move toward the downed witch, but Daire shoved her back behind him.

"Too late. Concentrate on the immediate threat," he ordered, his stance set, his large body between her and the snarling beasts.

A sickening crunch echoed as one of the beasts sank its teeth into Vegar's neck. Within seconds, the animal had beheaded the witch. Two more bears leaped over and started to feed.

Oh God, Oh God, Oh God. Cee Cee swallowed down bile.

Daire angled slightly toward the sea, facing the remaining five beasts. "I'm going to charge them, straight in the middle, and you run for the snowmobile," he said under his breath.

"No." She couldn't leave him to five of the snarling monsters. "You're tough, Enforcer, but one of those animals just ripped off a witch's head with minimal effort." She'd never fought a real bear before. "Go for the throat and incapacitate quickly," she whispered.

He nodded. "Get to the damn snowmobile. The throttle is the right handlebar—just twist forward the second you jump on. I can't charge them and cover you."

She quickly calculated scenarios in her head. He was right. The five remaining bears began to spread out and circle them. "Okay."

"When you get on, go north, past the buildings, and keep going until you reach the base of that peak over there. I have allies, polar bear shifters, and they'll help you. Tell them you're mine." Daire shook out his hands and angled to keep himself in alignment with the leader as it moved. "Now. Go." With a breathtaking roar, he jumped forward, arms outstretched, taking down three of the massive bears.

Cee Cee ducked to the side and ran full bore toward the snowmobile. Panting and the clacking of nails on ice sounded behind her. Claws raked down her arm, shredding the coat and digging into her skin.

Pain flared—hot and brutal.

Her heart rate increased, and her lungs panted out. She half turned and kicked out, nailing the animal in the snout. It went down, and Cee Cee turned to run again. Blood poured from her torn artery, but she didn't have the time or resources to heal herself right now.

She reached the snowmobile, leaped onto the seat, her hand already twisting the handlebar. The machine lurched forward, and she jerked to the right, swinging the back skis around. No way was she leaving Daire to the animals. The machine wobbled, and she tightened her hold, opening the throttle wide. Ducking her head, she drove over the ice, straight at the melee.

Blood already flowed across the white tundra. Daire stood in the middle of the four remaining predators, kicking and striking, forming fire balls and throwing. The beasts used sharp claws and deadly teeth, alternating between striking and avoiding the burning plasma.

Cee Cee ran right into the biggest animal, hitting it in the back and sending it flying toward the sea. She whipped the vehicle around and reached out a hand for Daire. Blood covered him forehead to ankles, and most of his clothing was shredded. "Get on," she yelled.

He shook blood from his eyes and threw a succession of deep green fireballs at the bears, swinging his arm and creating a graceful arc of flame. With his free hand, he grabbed hers and jumped behind her, still forming and throwing deadly fire through the swirling storm. The horrifying smells of burned fur and blood swirled with the barrage of snow. "Go," he bellowed.

She leaned down and opened the throttle again, kicking out with one leg to nail a bear in the neck. It fell back, teeth mashing together.

Daire wrapped his body over her, his thighs outside her hips, bracketing her. With an unholy howl, the lead bear came at them from the left, while another male came from the right. "Strike to the right," Daire ordered.

Her lungs compressed. She held on to the handlebars and cocked her leg to kick. Daire threw fire from both hands, nailing each bear before turning to deal with the lead Alpha bear.

The other male yelped as fire impacted his chest but didn't halt his trajectory. He hit the front side of the snowmobile, thick paw sweeping out. His claws raked into her forehead and ripped down, opening up the side of her face to the bone. Raw agony set her on fire. She screamed and jerked her head away, trying to protect her eye.

The lead bear roared in fury and pain, but she didn't turn to see. Daire leaned over her, a ball of fire in his palm, and smashed the flames into the other male bear's face. It shrieked and fell back.

Daire grabbed her hands over the bars and pushed farther, driving fast into the storm and dodging around the orange building. Dizziness rippled through her, and she tried to focus, but too much pain pierced her nerves. The freezing cold clashed against the raw bones in her face, and nausea lurched across her stomach.

He steered the vehicle through a deserted town dotted with abandoned buildings, including a schoolhouse and small store. Daire continued on, fighting the storm, and finally reached a crumbling brick building with a haphazardly hanging sign that read: ISLAND SKOLE. *Island School.* He drove around back and cut the engine, grabbing her up in one smooth motion and running through a partially open back door.

The smell of must and snow filled her nose. He moved gracefully, but every slight jostle sent excruciating pain through her head. Her arm had gone numb, which was not a good sign.

He carried her through the small building containing overturned desks and tables into what appeared to have been a kitchen, where he gently sent her down on an red metal table. Old pots littered the ice-covered floor, while a wide frozen oven took up one whole wall opposite a crumbling brick fireplace. "How bad?" he asked, walking around and stopping short upon seeing her face. "Holy fucking shit."

She wobbled, her vision graying.

With a gentleness surprising in such a large man, he unzipped the coat and removed it. Even so, when he reached her injured arm, she bit back a scream.

"God." He peered down. "Your artery is clawed, baby. Can you heal it? You're bleeding like a geyser."

Her teeth chattered, and she tried to concentrate and send healing cells to the wound, but she'd lost too much blood. She was too damn cold. "No."

"Okay. Hold on. I've got you." He jerked around and grabbed an overturned wooden chair, one of four. Quickly kicking them into small pieces, he shoved them into the brick fireplace. Fire danced down his arms, and he shot it toward the wood, which sputtered and died out. He looked around frantically and then yanked off his shirt, tore it into shreds, and placed the pieces under the wood.

"No, Daire," she said weakly. He'd need his shirt.

"Shh." He formed plasma balls again and set the material on fire. Claw marks marred his incredible back and arms, even his head. Through the temporary carnage, she spotted an intricate tattoo that began at his left shoulder blade and wound up his back and down his arm. A myriad of complex Celtic lines with a barely discernible C9E combined in the middle. His designation as an enforcer for the

Coven Nine, the ruling body of witches. A sexy warning on his
warrior's body.

As she watched, the wounds began to close. Incredible. Witches
could heal faster than any other species, probably because of the
whole fire thing and their ability to alter matter through the use of
quantum physics. She giggled.

He turned. "You're going into shock."

God, she hoped so. The pain was too much, and if she threw up,
her head might really fall off.

The wood caught fire, and warmth began to permeate the small
room. "Won't the animals see the smoke?" she asked drowsily, swaying on the table.

"They're animals, sweetheart. Not shifters." He moved toward her
and peered down at her arm. "Your head is bad, but nowhere as bad
as your arm. You're still bleeding too much." Regret colored his tone,
but she was so close to falling into the darkness, she didn't wonder
why. He smoothed the hair from her face. "You're too weak to heal
yourself, so I'll have to. This might scar you. I'm sorry."

She blinked.

He held her good arm, and a very pretty green fire danced on his
free hand. Then he pressed it to her injuries along her bicep.

Agony! She screamed, her entire nervous system misfiring. All
instinct, she kicked out, shoving against him and trying to get away
from the flame. He held tight, giving no quarter. The scent of burned
flesh banished the clean scent of wood on fire. Tears poured down
her face, burning in her injuries.

He finally let go, and she leaned back, all fuzziness gone. Several
gulping breaths brought her back to control.

"You okay?" he asked, smoothing bloody hair off her face.

She swallowed and tried to stem the tears. "Yes." Her voice shook.
"Thank you."

He grimaced, and his warrior's hand shook. "I know that hurt, and
I'm not done." He turned her arm over to reveal three thick, bloody
lines down her forearm. "If we don't stem the blood, you won't be
able to heal your face."

If they didn't stem the blood, she'd go into a coma and might
not recover. "I know." She tried to straighten her back, her gaze seeking his.

Sorrow and regret mingled with fury in his amazing green eyes. This was costing him more than her, if she had to guess. So she swallowed and tried to smile with the half of her face that still worked. "I'm fine, Enforcer. Let's see your fire."

Daire kept his hold gentle on her wrist and hid the turmoil slashing through his gut. There was a chance the burns he was inflicting on her would scar if she didn't get the strength to heal them and soon. "I'm sorry," he said.

"It's all right." She tried to smile again, her beautiful face something out of a horror flick. The right side of her face was in ribbons, down to her cheekbone, and to her skull. The roots of her teeth even showed. Waves of pain, excruciating in their intensity, rolled off her, and yet the woman was trying to smile for him. So he could do what had to be done. Her dark eyes held trust and reassurance. "Let's get it over with, Daire," she said, the words slurred through one side of her mouth.

He drew in air, altered the oxygen molecules around his hand, and formed a green plasma ball. Toning down the intensity took enough concentration that sweat slickened his forehead, but he hadn't healed completely yet, and his power had ebbed. Finally, he reached the right mixture and wiped his palm across her forearm.

She jerked, and he clamped a hand on her good shoulder to hold her in place. But he didn't need to. She stayed still, any color still remaining in her skin wiping away to leave pure white. Her gaze held his, even as her eyes filled with tears.

But she didn't make a sound this time.

It was almost worse. To witness the struggle in her, to see the strength, humbled him. It was one of the bravest things he'd ever seen, and he wondered what kind of monsters she'd faced to learn to keep silent in pain. Smoke rose from her arm, and he lifted his palm. He'd cauterized the wounds, leaving raised burns, red and swollen.

A shudder racked her entire body. She swayed again, and he held her in place. "If we could get you warm, maybe you could heal your head without my having to cauterize it," he murmured, taking the damaged coat and tossing it on the cold ground. She needed sustenance, and so did he. His remaining injuries weren't life threatening, but he required fuel to create more healing cells.

She blinked, shock coming back into her eyes as she coughed. Yeah. He couldn't leave her on the table. So he lifted her, as gently as possible, and placed her on the coat near the fire.

"I'll be back in just a minute."

She leaned against the wall. "You're not wearing a shirt. Take the coat." Half lifting her butt, she reached for the material, her gaze unfocused.

"No." He loped toward the door. "I can create fire, and you need to stay warm. I'll be right back." Without waiting for an argument, he shoved his way outside and pushed the door closed to keep out the storm, even while reaching for the knife in his boot. The arctic air bit into his skin, and he dug deep to ignore it, unable to create much fire after the fight and loss of blood.

He kept to the sides of buildings, hoping the freezing wind and storm would mask his scent. Yet his mind remained on the woman he'd left behind. Smart and strong, the woman could fight. Who was she? It was time to get some answers, as soon as she was healed. Her interest in his mines made him uneasy. Why would the demons want planekite, which only harmed witches? And humans. Plus, if she was correct, and Bychkov wanted her betrayed and alone in the wilderness, she had a hell of an enemy. The woman was a mystery, and Daire was finished being in the dark.

More than that, he wanted her. All of her. Not just her body. Her spirit, even though she was lying to him, intrigued the hell out of him. When she'd had the opportunity to ride to safety during the fight, she'd turned and challenged danger to help him. Then she'd smiled at him, to reassure him, when he'd burned her flesh together.

Aye. It was the smile that did it.

Chapter 6

A small cove protected the luxury yacht from capsizing in the boisterous storm but failed to keep the sea from battering the hull. Ivan Bychkov sat at his desk in the office portion of the boat, a glass of aged Scotch sliding around on the top. His stomach lurched with the Norwegian sea.

Demons didn't get seasick, damn it.

He took the glass and tipped back the warm brew, heating the nausea away.

The table was a burnished teak, as were the walls and floor. The boat pitched, and he sucked down some air. Maps covered one wall, antique and valuable, while windows showed the churning sea outside. Even the smell of Scotch failed to banish the salty scent of the sea. Man, he wanted to go home to warmth and solid ground.

Where the hell was Vegar with the woman?

He shoved the stack of papers to the side, having already signed contracts for the recent acquisitions. As the leader of an elite and powerful group of Russian demons, he had to continue buying and selling to keep the money flowing well. Good thing he had a knack for the stock market and an IQ beyond high, even for a demon. Plus, he truly enjoyed the strategy of figuring out what would happen next. His money was on biofuels and vaccines right now.

A discrete knock announced his first in command, Vadim Deeks, who stepped inside and closed the door. "The storm is too intense to leave the cove and explore along the coastline."

"Satellite?" Ivan asked.

"No. The cloud cover is too thick." The six-and-a-half-foot blond took a wide stance as the boat tipped. Dressed in all black with knives and various guns tucked into his uniform, the soldier narrowed his dark eyes. "If you wish, I could walk the shoreline around to the southern side and look for Vegar."

"No." Ivan gestured to the chair on the other side of the desk and poured another glass of Scotch, appreciating the loyalty if not the wisdom in such an offer. "The storm will ground everyone, and I assume Vegar took her to shelter to wait it out." They were both strong and well trained——surviving one arctic storm would be simple. Plus, Ivan had paid the witch twenty million dollars and promised to match it the second he delivered the woman. "Let's wait for the storm to abate, and then you and I can go looking." He had two other soldiers and a captain on the yacht, but he didn't require their help at this point.

Vadim nodded and prowled across the rocking boat to settle his bulk into the seat. "I've investigated the money trail further, and so far, I don't believe her people have any idea she's looking for you here. In fact, my source in her organization thinks she's on a luxury cruise right now in the Bahamas. She gave her name as Cee Cee Jones when she hired Vegar to show her your mines." Vadim swirled the glass around in his massive hand, gaze intense on the spinning liquid.

Ivan smiled. "Her mother called her Cee Cee when she was a young child."

"'Tis a sweet name for a demon." Vadim took a healthy drink of the brew, humming in appreciation.

"Female demons are notoriously sweet as well as deadly." Ivan refilled both glasses. "That one more than most. On both counts."

Vadim stretched his long legs out and crossed his boots, appearing relaxed yet always on the ready to protect and defend. "And intelligent, considering she's eluded you for three decades." Pure fact and no derision echoed in his hoarse tone.

"Three decades? That woman has eluded me for over a century." Ivan inhaled the scent of the expensive liquor, his blood thrumming at being this close to her. Finally.

"Yet you're willing to take her back. To make her a partner in your life."

Of course he was. "She's stunning, brilliant, and dangerous. Most important, she's a purebred demon." Ivan drew out his wallet to remove a photograph. It had been taken at the turn of the current century, in black and white, and had faded almost to white. Yet her outline, the beautiful blond hair and sparkling black eyes, remained in place. But maybe the paper had faded to the point that only he could see her. He frowned and returned the picture to its rightful place before sliding a manila folder across the desk.

Vadim opened the top to reveal a recent picture of her in Seattle. She wore modern jeans that cupped her ass and too-dark glasses that masked her glorious eyes. "She is beautiful—and so rare. A real purebred female demon."

True. Although she had defects, she was still a purebred and beyond incredible. A mixture of kindness, femininity, and deadliness that formed the sexiest woman he'd ever met, and he'd lived nearly two hundred years. Nobody, not one woman, regardless of species, had ever come close to her.

Vadim lifted his head. "You're a lucky man."

Lucky? Hell, no. He'd been chasing her for so long, he had begun to despair that he'd ever catch her. Yet when the war had ended more than a year ago, he figured it was time for her to make a move. So when he'd been approached with an intriguing offer for his planekite resources by an outside partnership, he'd figured the timing was fortuitous as well as perhaps fated. He'd begun mining again, in Norway as well as Russia, to see if he could draw her out. Surely she felt safe enough, settled enough, to pick up the game again. And here she was on his island, just a few miles away, no doubt ready to meet him head-on. "Now here she's come, trying to find me."

"Why not just call you up?" Vadim asked. "Why the game of hunting you down through the mines?"

Ivan lifted a shoulder. "I guess it's because she's ready to kill me now."

The smell of cooked meat and freezing snow permeated the small school kitchen, banishing the scents of blood and burned flesh. Daire had caught, skinned, and cooked a rabbit over the fire, and now only a small plate of meat remained in the room.

"Finish eating that bite, Cee Cee," he rumbled, sitting next to her, the play of firelight dancing over the hard angles of his face and down his ripped torso.

She took another bite, trying not to grimace, and working hard to keep the food on the good side of her mouth before swallowing.

"Don't like rabbit?" he asked.

"Don't eat meat usually," she murmured, eating more to regain strength. Wild rabbit was much greasier than she would've thought.

He chuckled, his broad chest moving nicely. "A vegetarian demon."

She leaned her head back against the wall. "I hope it was really a rabbit and not some shifter."

He snorted. "No such thing as a bunny shifter."

She sighed. Shifters were either feline, wolf, or multis. "A multi-shifter could become a rabbit, I think."

He shook his head. "When was the last time anybody saw a multi-shifter?"

She shrugged. "Bears. All sorts of bears."

"Yep. Prevailing theory is that all multi-shifters evolved into some sort of bear."

Maybe. She didn't really care. "How bad is my face?"

"It's killing me," he deadpanned.

Humor bubbled through her, but she kept a smile at bay to avoid more pain. "Hilarious."

"I'm the funny one," he said, finishing his meal and wiping his hands down his destroyed pants before turning toward her. "Time to heal your face."

She nodded and closed her eyes, trying to send healing cells to her temple. A nice tingle began under her skin for the briefest of moments and then petered out. "Darn it."

"Okay." Daire pivoted and drew her onto his lap, one arm cradling her shoulders and the other planted flat on her solar plexus.

She gasped and tottered on his lap, warming instantly.

He leaned against the wall and stretched out his legs, holding her securely. Warmth cascaded from his palm, and her stomach heated. "Draw strength from your center mass, right where my hand is heating you."

He was giving her his strength. More than just her abdomen warmed. Her nipples hardened beneath the heavy clothing. She coughed. "No, I—"

"Now, Cee Cee. Worry about the rest later. Right now, let's close the open wound on your face before you form scar tissue or lose any more blood." His voice remained low and steady, but the clear tenor of command came through bright and clear. His hold was gentle but firm, and she knew she wasn't going anywhere.

Tears gathered in her eyes from his kindness, and one rolled down her cheek, burning her raw skin. "Daire—"

"No tears," he said, a snap in his tone. "Shut your eyes, focus on my hand, and heal your damn face."

She sniffed and shut her eyes. Drawing in air, she filled her lungs, focusing on the heat he was generating within her. She imagined the warmth flowing through her skin, up her arms, over her neck, to her aching skull. Tingles zapped, and she caught her breath at the power. It was always inside her, but Daire had harnessed and focused it for her.

Healing hurt like hell.

She kept her breathing even, gasping only with the sharpest of pains, allowing tears to fall. Every time she jerked, Daire's arms tightened, and his body stiffened, as if he shared the pain. She kept all sound at bay, refusing to cry out and cause him any more distress.

The process took nearly an hour, and by the time her face felt healed, they were both sweating. She blinked and then slowly turned her head back and forth. A residual pain thrummed through her head, but it was more of an afterthought.

As the pain finally ebbed, her body focused elsewhere. On the hard thighs beneath her butt, and the thick chest holding her close. Hair covered his chest and led in a nice trail down to his pants. A manly chest. He stirred beneath her, and she realized some of the hardness wasn't his thighs. Heat flared into her face, zinged down her torso, and bloomed in her feminine parts.

He looked down. "All healed." Satisfaction glittered in his eyes along with something else. Hunger.

She nodded, her body crashing, even with desire fluttering through her. Her eyelids grew heavy. "Why are you being so nice to me?" she whispered.

He tucked her face into his neck and caressed a broad hand down her hair. "I'm not nice."

The sheer comfort of the moment almost made her purr. "Yes. I drugged you and stole from you." While the idea had seemed fine before she had gotten to know him, now it seemed shameful, although she'd had no choice. She'd done enough research to know his weaknesses, and she couldn't afford to let him know the full truth. "You're a good guy, Daire Dunne."

He chuckled, and his heated breath stirred her hair. "Don't think for a second that I'm a good guy. I'm just a guy who gets things done, and sometimes it's bloody, and sometimes it's necessary. Healing your face was necessary."

She struggled to remain awake. "Thank you."

He held her tight, keeping her warm and protected, even as he rested back his head. "You're welcome. Now get some sleep, finish healing, and tomorrow you're gonna tell me everything."

She wanted to protest, because she truly couldn't tell him everything. He was an enforcer, and if he had any clue who she was, he'd ship her home. Or at least he'd try to, and she really didn't want to fight with him now. For years she'd done what she had to do, and now it was *her* time. Her time to set right the wrongs of years ago, and nobody, not family, allies, or even deadly witch enforcers, was going to stop her. "I wish things were different," she whispered.

"They will be tomorrow." His words had the sound of a vow.

She snuggled closer, enjoying the feeling of male all around her. It had been so long. "Is there anything you *have* to do? A calling or a duty? Something nobody else can do?" she mumbled.

"I'm an enforcer for the Council of the Coven Nine," he said simply. "It's not a job."

It was a calling. "You're a protector, Dunne."

"Aye."

"I don't need a protector." She couldn't afford one right now.

"Well now, Cee Cee. Considering you have drugged me, stolen from me, and basically lied to me, if you did need a protector, it'd be *from* me."

Enough truth existed in the statement that it gave her pause. "It's hard to be scared of a half-naked man holding you tight," she murmured.

His hold tightened imperceptibly. "Keep pushing, and you'll be naked, too. Then we'll see how brave you are."

Her eyelids opened and then closed again. "I don't think so."

"Think whatever you want, baby, but at some point in the very near future, you're going to be spread out in front of me, all of that glorious skin revealed, and I'm gonna take my time."

A shiver trembled through her that had nothing to do with the cold. The very idea of spending a night with Daire Dunne, enjoying his obvious attention to detail, heated her in places she hadn't used in far too long. Yet his arrogance grated. "Here I thought we were becoming friends."

His bark of laughter moved his chest. "No. We may be enemies, and we may try to be allies, but I don't fuck my friends until they whimper my name."

Whimper? Seriously. Whimper. She tried to catch hold of anger or even indignation, but her energy had been depleted. Her mind fuzzed, but she needed a decent comeback. Something that would put him in his place. Unfortunately, her brain refused to kick into gear. "I don't fuck."

"Good thing I do."

She fell asleep as his amusement wandered around them.

Colors, crazy and bright, filled her dreams, but she slept in contentment, protected after so long. The arms around her were temporary, but the sense of safety seduced her into a deep sleep.

A few hours later, her eyelids jerked open. Wind whistled a pissed-off sound around the building, sliding through cracks in the far wall. The fire had died down to a soft crackle, and rolling thunder moved the earth. Her heart rate picked up, instinct kicking in. What had awakened her?

Daire's arms tightened, and he set her away. "There's somebody outside."

Chapter 7

Daire crouched low on the frozen kitchen floor and concentrated on the vibrations outside. The storm had died down a little bit but still competed with other energy sources. He could detect energy waves better than most witches, and he knew those signatures. Demons. At least two—maybe more. Either way, they waited outside in the swirling snow.

"Stay here and be ready to run out the front. A half mile to the north is an old gas station. I hid the snowmobile behind it," he said to Cee Cee. "They're out back." He hadn't heard any sort of vehicle, so they'd walked. He pointed to the jacket she'd sat on. "Put that back on."

Cee Cee stood, her eyes wide, her hair wild around her face. "They're here for me, not you."

Yeah. He got that.

"You don't even have a shirt, Daire." She visibly steeled her shoulders and tried to move toward the back door.

He planted a hand in the center of her chest, halting her easily. "I don't need a shirt, and you're not at full power yet. No way could you be after healing your body like that last night." Plus, he was a fucking enforcer, and nobody was going to harm her on his watch. "They might not know you're here, so just stay out of the way until I figure out who's out there."

She glanced down at the hand at her chest, and a flush worked over her cheekbones. "I told you I don't need a protector."

That was too bad. He leaned down and yanked up the jacket to shove over her shoulders. "Zip it up."

He waited until she'd complied, pure defiance on her face. She could wear any damn expression she wanted so long as she did what he said. He turned away and opened the door to find two demons to the left, and two to the right against a crumbling building of old apartments. "You all about to square-dance?" he called through the lightly falling snow.

One man stepped forward. Curly blond hair, dark eyes, firm but young jaw. Ivan Bychkov looked like a handsome teenage heart-throb and hadn't seemed to age in the years Daire had read security updates on the Consortia leader. "Bychkov," Daire said.

Ivan blinked and settled his stance. "Daire Dunne. What is a Nine enforcer doing on my island?"

Daire lifted an eyebrow and kept his stance loose. The odds sucked, especially if the soldiers were as well trained as they appeared at first glance. "I own two of the mines on this island, as you know."

"Yet I own the actual island as well as two of the working mines." Ivan smiled, youthful and charming. The soldier next to him was Vadim Deeks, one of the deadliest assassins around, and rumored to be completely loyal to Bychkov. They seemed to have a peaceful alliance with the main demon nation, which was currently being led by Zane Kyllwood, Logan's older brother. If Daire killed Bychkov, there might be a problem with Kyllwood.

Daire didn't recognize the other two soldiers. "Well, this has been nice. Go away."

Bychkov sighed. "Where is she?"

"She?" Daire asked. Instead of letting the exhausted woman sleep all over him, he should've demanded answers. Right now, he didn't know shit, and that was not a good place to be.

Vadim lifted a green gun and pointed it at Daire. A laser gun that turned into bullets as it hit flesh. Immortal flesh.

Daire responded by allowing fire to dance down his arms and morph into plasma weapons in his hands.

"Enough," Cee Cee said from behind him, crossing to his side.

Bychkov sucked in air. "I've been looking for you."

Anger, female and strong, cascaded off her slim form. "I hadn't planned to meet up so quickly."

"Yet here you are," Bychkov drawled.

She chuckled, the sound low and hoarse. "I'm here to check out Dunne's mine. Not yours."

Her voice plus the double entendre rippled through Daire to his groin. When all four men facing her discreetly adjusted their stances, his temper moved from simmer to *bring it the fuck on*. A chuckle from a woman like her was a dangerous thing.

Bychkov's gaze raked Daire's bare chest. "Still slumming it, I see."

Slumming it? Had the woman been with a witch before? Daire angled his body so he could cover her if anybody fired. "Would somebody tell me what is going on?" If he was going to fight, he wanted to know the reason, damn it.

Bychkov sighed, his gaze remaining squarely on Cee Cee. "We have an agreement, and you're going to honor it."

"Not a chance in hell," Cee Cee spat, glancing up at the thick cloud cover.

What was she looking for? "Agreement?" Daire muttered under his breath.

Bychkov crossed his arms. "We were betrothed decades ago, and you ran away." He shuffled his feet. "We could've worked things out."

She stretched her neck, her body one tense line. "I'm not property to be bargained with, Ivan. There's no betrothal." Her boot made no sound as she took a step forward. "You should've let go, and you will pay for what you've done. In ways you can't even imagine with your tiny mind. I will see you dead."

He smiled. "There are four of us against two of you."

She chuckled again. "Oh, I didn't mean today. You get to live a while . . . first." So much threat lived in the words that the hair on the back of Daire's neck stood up.

Bychkov frowned. "You've forgotten how well I know you. Everything about you."

Her chin snapped up. "I haven't forgotten."

"Then you know you can't beat me. Can't come close, in fact." He finally turned his focus to Daire. "You know she's damaged, right?"

Daire was more interested in the woman's preoccupation with the clouds. "What are you doing?" he whispered, the sound slight.

"Time. Can't see sun," she whispered back.

The sun? Why did she need time? But Daire could go along for a moment. "Damaged? If you ask me, she's pretty fucking perfect."

Cee Cee smiled at him.

Bychkov growled, demon low. "Then she hasn't told you, Enforcer." A tickle, one of pain and death, vibrated through the air toward Daire's frontal lobe.

Daire smiled and threw up a mental shield. His expertise for the last three centuries had been in learning to shield against demon mind attacks, because the Coven Nine had always expected war with the demon nation. "That all you got?"

Bychkov's eyes turned beady. "No. But it's more than she's got."

Daire kept any reaction from showing. Was Cee Cee incapable of demon mind attacks? Was that even possible? "Regardless, you asked for the lady's hand, she apparently said no, and it's over. Tuck your tail between your legs and go home."

Bychkov shook his head, his face contorting. Emotion, deep and dark, charged the atmosphere. "We have a contract, struck by families, and she's mine. The Coven Nine will not interfere in such matters, and you know it. *You* go home, Dunne."

True. The Coven Nine wouldn't even think of interfering in another nation's matters, including betrothals and all that crap. "I guess I'll just have to interfere on my own, then." He kept the mental shield in place, although even he wasn't delusional enough to think he could protect his brain from the attacks of all four soldiers. They weren't going anywhere, and the matter was about to escalate, so it was time for action. He molded the fire still burning across his hands into smaller projectiles.

"Wait a second," Cee Cee said. "Give me just a few more minutes, I think."

"For what?" Daire asked.

She lifted her head. "I like the enforcer. I owe him and have brought enough trouble to his doorstep. You have one chance here, Ivan. Forget the contract and walk away. I'll do the same."

Bychkov studied her, the heavy wind blowing his hair around his classic face. "No."

She exhaled, her breath misting in the cold air. "I'm glad you said that. To be honest, I'm not sure I could've walked away."

He took an involuntary step toward her and then stopped. "I didn't think so. You've wondered about us."

"No." She shook her head.

"Yes, you have. I was your first kiss." Triumph lifted his pale lips.

She wrinkled her nose. "That was decades upon decades ago, and I have to tell you, there was way too much teeth."

Daire bit back a grin at the sarcasm, even as his muscles tensed for the fight. The crumbling building shielded the soldiers from the gentling storm, and they'd make a move soon.

The ground pitched. Air paused, and the atmosphere held its breath. A rumble echoed, the entire tundra rocked, and an explosion rippled through the storm. The icy ground cracked. Fire billowed into the air, even through the storm, shooting sparks and debris into the air a couple of miles away.

One of the soldiers slipped and fell on his face.

"What did you do?" Bychkov yelled, spittle flying from his mouth.

Daire bunched and threw both fire balls, impacting the crumbling building at its stress points. Sheet metal flew out, sharp and jagged. The building toppled. The soldiers ran in different directions, sliding on the unsteady ground, trying to avoid the piercing metal.

"Run." Daire grabbed Cee Cee's arm and yanked her into the schoolhouse, releasing her to run through the building and out the front. "Follow me." He zigged across the street and behind another row of buildings, leading her through an escape route he'd planned the other night while hunting, just in case. The pressure of the chase descended upon his neck, and he angled quietly, moving between buildings and sometimes through them, until they reached the old gas station at the end of the small town.

Cee Cee kept on his heels, as quiet as any predator, staying close.

He eyed the icy tundra. "We need to go east, keep to the shoreline, and reach the helicopter hangar," he said, breathing out heavily.

"They're not behind us any longer," she panted out.

"Aye. We lost them at the third apartment building." Unfortunately, that meant the soldiers had headed back for transportation, which was probably a boat moored where Cee Cee had docked.

The ground continued to rock its displeasure.

"Do you think they know about the helicopter?" she asked, hands on knees, catching her breath.

"I don't know." Probably.

She sucked in air, her cheeks rosy. "The sea has to be roiling. Following us would be foolhardy."

He shook his head. "The storm isn't as bad as it was, and if they hug the shoreline, they'll be fine." No way was Bychkov letting her go, if Daire had to guess. "Want to tell me what just exploded?" As if he didn't know. He pinned her with a hard gaze.

She glanced toward the flame-filled smoke billowing into the sky. "One of Ivan's two mines, of course."

Of course. Daire bit back anger and tried to stick to the matter at hand. "Why?"

"I'm taking him down." Passion and a dangerous light glittered in her eyes. "You should thank me. The asshole was mining plane-kite, and I had that fact confirmed before giving the order to blow the entire place up."

"What about the miners?" he asked, disbelief rippling through him.

She rolled her eyes. "Gas leak. The place was cleared of personnel before being blown up and closed forever."

He shook his head. "I swear to God, you're one fucking unpleasant surprise after the next." Grabbing her hand, he yanked her into the garage and picked her up to plunk her on the snowmobile seat before sliding in front of her. "Who planted the explosives?"

"Men I hired." She reached around him and laced her fingers against his abs. His very bare abs. "I came to check out your mine before deciding whether or not to blow it up, too."

He paused in turning the key. "You thought I was in business with Bychkov?"

Her palms chilled his skin. "He's in a partnership with a witch, and you own many mines, so I had to be sure. Don't worry." She patted his abdomen, and his cock stirred. "They won't plant any explosives in your mine here or your mines in Russia unless I give the order."

"That's just great," he snapped, twisting the key. "Who's the witch that is in business with Bychkov?"

"Obviously I don't know."

He shook his head. "Lady, I trust you as far as I can throw you."

She patted his gut. "You're all muscle, Dunne. You could throw me quite a distance."

He growled, his temper really, really, really wanting out.

She nodded, her forehead between his shoulder blades. "My plan was to check out your mines here on Fryser, leave orders, and head on to Russia."

"Oh, baby, you ain't going to Russia," he muttered in Gaelic.

She sniffed. "I don't speak Gaelic."

"I figured." He shook off the very strong desire to flip around and shake some sense into her until she told him everything. "What about Bychkov's other mine here? It has to be the Sjenerøse mine, right?" The only way to reach it was by parachuting in and snow-mobiling down and out.

She sighed. "I haven't figured out how to get there yet."

He didn't like the *yet* in that statement. Right now, he had to get them off the island. "Hold on, and if you see them on land or sea, let me know." There was only one path to the helicopter and no way to hide from the sea. He twisted the throttle, and the machine jumped forward and into the storm.

Chapter 8

Her heart raced, and her head spun, even as she held tight to the enforcer as they sped the snowmobile across the shaky frozen ground. Mountains rose high and sharp in the background, while the red and orange of fire crackled inland through the air. Smoke billowed up into the darkening sky, spitting embers.

"Anything near the shore, Cee Cee?" he bellowed back, anger still in his voice.

She blinked against the swirling snow, trying to squint at the ocean. Dark and merciless, it churned as if answering the call of the storm. "Not yet," she yelled back. By all that was holy. She'd blown up the planekite mine, and if all else had remained on schedule, her people had just imploded several mines in Russia owned by Bychkov. Her plan was coming together nicely.

Except for Daire Dunne. Although the enforcer had shown much more restraint than she would've ever thought, his patience seemed to be coming to an end. Unfortunately, since Vegar had betrayed her, she needed Daire to help her off the island. Her men would've planted the explosives and immediately retreated, which left her either with Bychkov or Dunne.

Dunne was the safer choice at this point.

Probably.

Ice flicked up from the skis, and she ducked her head.

As a fighter, he was legendary, and now she'd seen him in action. While he'd been incredibly gentle with her so far, there was no question a deadly predator, a fierce fighter, lived easily within Dunne's handsome skin. He hadn't treated her as an enemy, that much she knew. And the reason, as difficult as it was to admit, was because he didn't see her as one. He didn't see her as a threat.

Was she?

She'd held her own physically with Vegar, and she was more than holding her own intellectually with Bychkov. But with Daire? He'd found her in the middle of nowhere, and now he'd taken command of the mission. She hated feeling weak, and pride insisted she hide her frailties from him. He treated her like a woman, whole and strong, even if he was pissed.

His scent surrounded her, both masculine and earthy. She liked him, and damn, she wanted him. But she couldn't have one more person in her life who couldn't see past her size or looks. No matter how much he heated her blood.

Something dark cut through the haze of the sea.

She leaned her cheek against Daire's bare back, stunned by the continued warmth. Out in the sea, hugging the shoreline, something moved. She patted his stomach. "I see something."

He nodded and lowered his chin, twisting the throttle. "Hold on," he bellowed. "We're going in hot."

Her thighs clamped against this, and she held on with all her strength. Ice popped up next to her, and Daire swerved. More ice, and he swore. Somebody on the boat was shooting at them?

She glared through the mist, trying to make sense of the shapes. A man stood at the front of a long yacht, pointing a rifle. The storm and distance masked the sound, but bullets continued to ping around them.

Daire's head was thrown back, and he hissed. His body jerked against her. The smell of blood clogged her nostrils.

She held on tighter, patting up his torso. "Where are you hit?"

"Right arm," he ground out, turning sharply to the left.

She yelped and struggled to remain in place. A white hangar sat against a stark outcropping, barely visible. He skidded to a stop and was off the vehicle and kicking open a door in the span of a heart-beat. Dashes of blood followed in his wake.

How badly was he hurt?

She scrambled off the snowmobile and ran after him, sliding across bloody snow he'd tracked inside. A sleek silver helicopter took up the center of the concrete hangar. It had small wings with propellers as well as the rotor on top. Definitely a new design and nothing she'd ever seen before.

"Get inside," he yelled, his voice echoing off metal walls as he ran for a button on the far wall.

She nodded and ran to the machine, pulled the handle, and jumped inside. The interior smelled like leather and Daire. The roof began to open, and snow billowed down.

Daire reached the other side and leaped into the pilot's seat. "Buckle up." Blood coursed down his arm, dripping onto the leather.

She whipped off the coat he'd made her wear and pressed the material against his wound.

He swore and jerked away.

"You're bleeding," she said, trying to stem the flow again.

He nodded, shut his eyes, and stilled. The atmosphere changed, and tingles bit through the oxygen. The hole in his arm slowly closed.

Man, she'd never seen anybody that fast at healing themselves. "That's amazing," she murmured.

He turned and pinned her with flashing green eyes. "I told you to buckle up."

She blinked, her hands already in motion to obey. Though she didn't like the tone, meaning she *really* didn't like the tone, she'd deal with him when they were safe. The buckle clicked into place. "What is this thing, anyway? It looks like some sort of hybrid."

"I call her Stella." He handed over a helmet and shoved one over his head, waiting until she'd done the same so he could talk through a microphone. "The humans have created a few designs close to this, but they don't have the power or maneuverability we do. Not yet anyway." He flicked a bunch of buttons, and the machine began to vibrate under her legs.

His voice in her ear caressed down her body, and she shifted in the seat, her heart rate picking up. She tried to focus on the concrete wall in front of her. "When we rise up, will they be able to shoot at us?" she asked.

"Aye. Depending on the type of firepower they have on the boat, they might hit us." He clicked more levers above his head, and the copter began to shake in earnest. "I haven't flown her in too long. This might get bumpy."

She swallowed, feeling a little hemmed in by the helmet. "Stella is your design?"

"Mine and my brother Adam's. He's the genius in the family."

Ah. She'd heard of Adam Dunne, and he was known to be brilliant. Smart and ruthless, just like his brothers. Demons and witches rarely mixed, so she'd only heard rumors. The dossiers she had on the family just listed facts. "I hadn't realized you'd be so kind," she said softly.

He turned toward her, his hands still moving levers and flipping buttons. Green eyes, dark and true, lasered through his face shield. "I've used up my well of kindness with you."

"When?"

"When you kept to yourself the fact that you were having explosives planted on the island, putting us both in danger of an earthquake." He turned and pulled back on the throttle. "Hold on."

They lifted high and fast, leaving her stomach down on the ground. Wow. The Dunne boys sure had tweaked the machine.

She held her breath.

The wind batted at them, and Daire swore in her ear, his muscles bunching as he jerked the controls. Something pinged loudly against the side of the craft.

"Fuck, fuck, fuck," he muttered, turning sharply away from the shore. "They've got enough weaponry."

Cee Cee said a quick prayer, her muscles so tense, her body felt a millennia old.

More bullets hit the craft, and they rocked. She bit her lip to keep from crying out.

They flew low, moving up quickly over mountain peaks. The smoldering mine lit the ground below them, and gaping holes revealed burning levels all the way into the mountain. Man, she'd really demolished the mine.

A shrieking alarm pierced the craft. Several lights flashed on the dash in rapid succession.

"We're out of firing range," Daire said, his arms visibly shaking. "Come on, Stella. Stay true, sweetheart."

The soft crooning in his deep voice created a yearning in Cee Cee's abdomen. In his tone she heard a sweetness she neither deserved nor would ever have. "How damaged is she?"

Daire shook his head. "She's not good, and we're losing fuel."

Cee Cee craned her neck as the destroyed mine faded from sight when they flew out over open waters. The ocean threw up whitecaps and churned a deep black. She shivered.

Daire growled and wrenched on the controls. "The craft has been damaged too much. We won't make it to Greenland."

"What about Russia?" she breathed.

"Nope." The copter pitched and he struggled to regain control. "The best I can do is hit one of the islands in the Franz Josef Land."

Those were uninhabited and cold. She blew out air. "What then?"

"One thing at a time." Sweat dotted his brow. "Just hope we make it to an island."

She nodded and held still, as if that would help, her gaze wide on the furious water below. It seethed dark and deep . . . waiting. They flew, losing altitude, for what seemed like eons but probably was just a few minutes. "What about Svalbard?" she asked, remembering the other island with abandoned mines.

"Too late and in the wrong direction." The helicopter pitched, rocked, and then started to go down. She cried out, her body tensing, her nails digging into the leather.

Daire's arms shook and his muscles clenched as he fought with the steering wheel, pulling back. The sea rose up to meet them, and this time, she did scream.

They hit so hard, her head rocked back onto the seat, and she saw flames of white. Water poured over the window. She unclasped her belt, her body in serious pain. Adrenaline roared through her veins, and her heart beat frantically against her rib cage.

Daire kicked open the front window. Freezing seawater poured in. Her lungs compressed, and her skin shrieked. He leaned down and yanked a bag from under her seat and then grabbed her hand. The helicopter sank, and she held her breath as the water consumed them both with a chill too piercing to overcome. Salt and sea pounded against her. How would they survive? Her legs kicking, she pushed off from the drowning craft with all her strength, trying to look up to air.

All she could see was dark and icy water.

Daire kept a firm hold around Cee Cee's wrist and another around his bag, kicking his feet and propelling them toward the surface. She kicked next to him, her white-blond hair billowing out all around and small bubbles emerging from her mouth. The sea fought them, black and alive, trying to shove them back down.

Finally, they burst through the surface, and he sucked in air, his lungs burning.

Cee Cee coughed next to him, jerking her arm free to tread water. A wave crashed over her head, and she emerged sputtering.

He looked around, trying to see past the battering waves. "I think this way." He was disoriented, but he'd seen the outline of an island as they were going down.

She nodded and started to swim through waves behind him.

He kept a brisk pace, trying to fight the sea's chill. Energy poured out of him. He paused and waited until Cee Cee stopped. Her skin had frozen, and her lips had turned blue. A human would be dead. Icicles formed on her eyelashes. "We're almost there," he said.

She nodded.

He turned, keeping her partially in sight, and continued swimming. An outcropping finally came into view, and relief flushed through him. Minutes later, they crawled across sharp rocks to a barren land. Chunks of ice so dense as to glow a light blue dotted the landscape, leading to a full glacier between two mountains. Outcroppings of rock protected the small cove somewhat.

Cee Cee sat on the ground, her arms around her knees, her body shaking violently, her teeth smashing together.

He yanked open the bag, hoping it was as weatherproof as advertised. He felt inside. Thank goodness. Yanking out a satellite phone, he quickly dialed his brother with frozen fingers.

"Daire?" Adam asked.

"My helicopter went down outside the Franz Josef Land islands, and I don't know which one. Lock on the phone and send rescue." He clipped out the words, wanting to get warmth into Cee Cee. She was freezing in front of his eyes, but they needed help.

"Hold on," Adam said.

Daire reached down and hauled Cee Cee up, tugging her wet clothes over her head. She struggled, shoving against him. Then he drew a heavy sweater from the bag and yanked it down over her body. The sound she made, pleasure and pain, warmed him right up.

"Daire?" Adam asked.

"Go." Daire studied the nearly frozen woman in front of him. Did he have the strength to start a fire?

"I'm still in Russia researching the planekite mining, and there's a blizzard going on. As soon as possible, I'll pick you up. Might be first light tomorrow. Be ready." Adam's voice roughened. "Are you hurt?"

"No. Just get here. Bring clothes for me and for a petite woman. And food." Daire clicked off before Adam could ask any questions and then yanked a waterproof tent from the go-bag.

Cee Cee's lips trembled in the parody of a smile. "Aren't you prepared?" Her teeth chattered as she spoke.

"Always." He unfolded the tent and quickly hammered it into place against the nearest rocks, and then he grabbed a rolled-up sleeping bag to toss inside. "I keep an escape helicopter on a remote island north of the Arctic Circle." Testing the ties of the tent, he nodded. "A go-bag for bad weather seemed like a good idea. Just in case." The current situation was by no means the worst he'd ever been in, although he'd never had a small blonde to worry about before. He held open the flap. "Take off the jeans and get in."

She glanced down at her wet jeans and boots before shivering. Surprisingly, she didn't argue but shrugged out of the wet clothing and then hightailed it inside.

The wind pierced him, and snow began to fall. He sucked in air and tried to force fire to the surface.

Nothing.

He shivered. Wet clothes weren't going to help. His hands shook as he kicked out of his jeans and placed them right inside the tent before toeing off his boots and socks. His limbs were heavy, and his head pounded. Being naked was the last of his worries. Without a word, he opened the flap and crawled inside to find Cee Cee in the bag. She'd unzipped it and tossed open the side.

"Get in," she said, her voice cracking.

He climbed in and zipped up behind him. The wind moved the top of the tent back and forth. Her scent wafted lightly around him along with the smell of salt and ocean. "I can't make fire, but if we sleep, we'll both heal." The woman felt like one long piece of ice. Trying to be gentle, he turned her back to his front and spooned around her. "Body heat will have to do."

She trembled, shivers rubbing her skin against his. Even through the wool sweater, she felt cold.

He rubbed her arms and tucked his knees up and under hers.

"Sleep will help." Not that there was a choice for him. After fighting, being injured, helping Cee Cee to heal, and then crashing a helicopter into the freezing sea, his body was done. So he tucked his nose into her wet hair, took a deep breath, and let himself fall.

Even sleeping, his subconscious kept track of the woman in his arms and the storm berating the tent, but he went under deep enough to allow his body to heal, resting for several hours.

A strong gust of wind whipped across the tent, and he came fully awake with a jerk. No light permeated the darkness, so it wasn't dawn as of yet. He'd slept for the rest of the day and then a good portion of the night. Heat surrounded him in the tight sleeping bag. As his mind settled, his body kicked alive. Smooth, soft hands were caressing very lightly across his chest and down his abs, soothing each one as if counting them.

Cee Cee faced him, one smooth thigh between his legs, her hands exploring.

Desire, desperate and hot, burned through him. "What are you doing?" His voice was beyond rough.

She lifted her head, her soft and now dry hair brushing across the bristles of his whiskers. "I didn't mean to awaken you."

That voice. That sexy, hoarse, *fuck me* voice. His cock sprang hard as steel. "Yet you did," he rumbled.

She finished counting the last rib, her small hand so close to his dick, he stopped breathing. "You're just so hard and ripped, I wanted to feel."

The sweetness in the confession competed with the feminine need in her tone.

He shut his eyes and tried to breathe evenly. Almost on its own volition, his hand caressed down her torso to pure heat. So smooth and inviting. Her moan lit him on fire. She was wet and ready . . . and in about two seconds, he was going to lose all control. So he removed his hand. "Cee Cee? Either move away from me or say yes."

Quiet ticked.

Her palm flattened across his abs, the touch firm. "It has been a while, Enforcer. But *yes.*"

At the word, he finally did exactly what he'd craved since first seeing her across the bar. Grabbing her hair, he plundered her mouth, rolling them over and shoving himself inside her with one hard thrust.

Chapter 9

Cee Cee gasped, her body arching up into the solid concrete of Daire's. Pain and an incredible pleasure rippled through her. Thank goodness she'd been ready. Her nails dug into his chest.

He reached down and tore the sweater over her head, his mouth absolutely conquering hers. Hard and deep, he kissed her like he owned her, giving no quarter. Hot and male, with a fierceness too late to tame. Finally, he lifted his head, allowing her to breathe.

She filled her lungs, overwhelmed. Yeah, she'd wondered. Wondered if she could really do this—if she could have sex now. Apparently she could. God, he felt good. Muscle, toned and deadly, filled her palms as she caressed up his chest and down the rigid contours of his arms. His cock pulsed inside her, awakening nerves she'd forgotten existed. "So much for foreplay," she murmured, her lips tingling and swelling from the hard kiss.

"The last two days have been foreplay," he ground out.

Fair enough.

He levered his body up on his elbows, pressing himself even deeper inside her. She moaned, pleasure shooting hot sparks along every nerve ending. The hand tethering her hair twisted, turning her head and elongating her neck. He lowered his head and scraped his teeth along her jugular with a bite of pain he then soothed by licking back up.

Her sex convulsed around him, and he groaned into her ear before biting her earlobe. The erotic pain blazed down her body, zinged across her breasts, and planted hard in her clit. "Daire," she murmured.

"How long has it been, sweetheart?"

"Decades." Sadness, surprising in its intensity, swamped through her. Her mate had been a good man and her best friend. Vulnerability followed.

"Hey." Daire nibbled along her jawline to press a kiss on her chin. "Stay here with me. Just here and now."

She blinked. "Here and now." At the moment, she had free rein with one of the most incredible male bodies ever created, and real life could wait until the next day. The emotion had been unexpected, but as he ran a hand down and rolled a nipple, she shoved sorrow away to just feel the moment. And damn, did he know how to make her feel good.

As he slid out and back in, creating slow friction, pleasure careened up her torso. *Delicious.* She'd known the first time he'd kissed her that he'd be beyond delicious. A hard kiss along her neck had him pausing.

She swallowed. The bite marks from her mating. Even though the bond was gone, and she was free, the barest of marks had remained. "Um."

He licked the two small indents. A new tension coiled around him. "Shifter?"

"Vampire," she responded, her mind whirling so quickly she could hear the blood roaring through the veins in her ears.

Daire jerked inside her. "Mated?"

She closed her eyes. Nothing in her wanted to discuss this right now. "Yes, he died, and I took the mutated Virus-Twenty-Seven to negate the bond. Willingly."

"So it works," he murmured.

"Yes." Her heart beat in her ears, while the tension in the small tent increased. "It's in the past, Daire."

An emotion, dark and male, rolled off him. "So you know the queen."

She and the queen were good friends. "No, but we share acquaintances, and when I sent her a message that I was interested in taking the mutated virus, she called me. We did the experiments from there."

Daire frowned. His arms rippled as he held himself in check. "Okay, but as of now, I'm done with your secrets. We do this, no more secrets."

She couldn't promise him that, not now, and as much as she wanted to, she couldn't trust him. "This is one night." Maybe more than one night, but definitely not eternity. If her plan worked, she'd have more enemies than he could imagine, and while she'd fight, the odds stank. "We're already doing this."

He pulled out and hammered back in. Hard.

Pain, edged with a wicked pleasure, clawed through her. She'd never been treated roughly in bed, and she kind of liked it.

He lowered his head until his mouth was right above hers, and his green eyes lasered through the darkness. "I don't bluff, make threats, or use unnecessary words, Cee Cee. I'm inside you, and I'm all around you."

She swallowed again. "I know."

"No more secrets and no more lies. You don't want to cross me." He slid out and then pushed back in, slowly this time.

"Okay." The feeling was beyond incredible. A man inside her. Something she'd never thought to have happen again. It was wonderful. But she'd failed to factor in the instant emotion that engulfed her, especially since she had secrets to keep. She loosened her hold on the enforcer, and her body stilled.

"Baby? There's a whole lot coming off you right now, and if you want me to stop, now's the time to say so." His body tensed, and the cost of the words, of the promise, lived in every undulating muscle.

Tears instantly pricked her eyes. "Please—don't stop," she gasped.

He exhaled and pulled out of her, relinquishing the hold on her hair.

"No." Her sex tried to keep him in, and her hands curled over his shoulders.

He kissed her, his tongue flicking inside her mouth, his free hand pressing against her clit. "I thought to take the edge off fast and then play, but let's get you out of your head now. We can discuss reality in the light of day."

His wrist twisted, and he slipped a finger inside her.

She arched against him, pleasure overtaking any residual sorrow.

"There we go." He licked down her neck, kissed her collarbone, and suckled one nipple into his mouth.

She detonated. An orgasm rushed through her so quickly, she could only open her mouth in a silent scream. Her legs widened, and he ground his palm against her. Fast. That had happened so fast. Finally, she came down with a soft sob.

He chuckled around her, the sound reverberating through her chest. Light nips and flicks struck her nipple until he moved to the other breast, paying equal attention. She moved restlessly against him, hunger awakening again. Another finger joined the first, rubbing against a spot inside her that flashed lights behind her closed lids.

She shook her head. "Too much."

"Not enough." He alternated kisses between her breasts, each one shooting a craving much lower. The sleeping bag caught him, and he swore, turning to jerk down the zipper and shove material out of his way. Cold washed over her, replaced by the heat of his body.

Then his mouth found her core.

She cried out, her nails cutting into his shoulders. "No, I——"

He sucked her throbbing clit into his heated mouth, and she stopped speaking. Stopped moving. She held her breath, unsure, her body rioting.

"Did you just say no?" he asked, sending vibrations through her most intimate parts.

"No, I, we, I mean," she gasped, trying to find words. It was too much. Too intimate. "You."

He chuckled, nearly sending her into another orgasm. "Yeah. *Me*." He released her, rubbing the spot inside her, and then turned to nip her inner thigh with sharp teeth.

She gasped, her legs trembling.

His canines sank in deeper, piercing her skin. She cried out and tried to yank her flesh from his mouth.

He let her go. "It won't scar, but you'll wear my mark for the week." Masculine satisfaction, lazy and dark, echoed in his tone.

She opened her mouth to protest, but one long, slow swipe of his tongue across her clit forced a whimper from her instead. He did it again, faster this time.

"Let's get one more from you before we get serious," he whispered, his heated breath all but killing her. Then he went to work, alternating between soft kisses and harder licks, keeping her on the edge, but not letting her fall over.

Sweat rolled off her forehead, and she moved against him, seeking relief, losing any sense of shyness. All that mattered in the world was reaching that peak he held so tantalizingly away from her. His fingers worked magic inside her, twisting and rubbing, but not quite giving her enough to ease the tension.

He increased the pressure, and a moan caught in her throat. "Now, baby." He sucked.

She pushed against his mouth, waves crashing through her. The orgasm shook her, head to toe, emanating from his talented tongue. He prolonged the ecstasy until her body fell in limp abandonment onto the warm sleeping bag. She murmured a sound without any real meaning.

He drifted up her body, his skin hot, until his mouth took hers. The drugging kiss slid through her, soothing her ragged breathing. Then he clamped a hand across her butt, half lifted her, and powered inside her. Even with her body satiated, her core wet, the strength in his stroke took her by surprise and forced the air from her lungs.

Her eyelids flew open, and she pressed both hands against his fiery hot chest.

"Now we get serious." He held her tight, moving out, and hammered back into her.

She'd thought she was done. Not even close. Hunger, edged with a pained demand, hit her so hot and so fast she could only hold on tight. He pounded into her, showing no mercy, a dangerous predator fully unleashed. She kicked her other leg free and wrapped them around his waist, tilting her pelvis for more. God, so much *more.*

He fucked her, hard and fast, his harsh breath panting in her ear. Each thrust jarred her clit, shooting lava across every nerve. The slap of flesh against flesh filled the tent, along with the overwhelming heat that was Daire Dunne. The thrusts increased in speed, and a galvanizing heat seared her, rippling into fire, as she exploded into a violent orgasm. It washed over her, cooling her, taking everything she had.

He stilled, ground against her, and came hard, his body shaking.

Finally, he rested against her. Her legs dropped to the ground. Still inside her, he reached around and drew the bag over them. "Now you talk."

She shut her eyes, her body too damn relaxed to drum up the energy to fight.

A ripple sounded through the night. Then a piercing light shone down, even through the tent.

"Damn it." Daire withdrew and shoved his way out of the bag, tossing the sweater at her. "Get dressed." Helicopter blades pounded through the weakening storm outside.

She shrugged into the sweater and stood. "You're naked."

"If it's my brother, he's seen me nude before. If not, we're in a shitload of trouble, and my bare skin is the least of our worries." He unzipped the tent and peered out, turning back to pin her with a dark green gaze. "It's Adam, which is good news. Don't think for a second our conversation isn't going to happen. You have a reprieve, baby. Take it and get ready to tell all."

Daire kept one eye on Cee Cee and the other on the papers spread out in front of him on the table. The plane was small, with a green sofa along the back wall, a bathroom behind that, and four chairs around a table. The carpet was an odd yellow with blue dots. "Finish that steak," he ordered, ducking his head to read another printout. He waited until she rolled her eyes. "I saw that," he said slowly. Things had changed, whether she liked it or not.

She blinked, and color slipped into her cheeks. But she took another bite of the meat from her perch on the sofa.

Adam had quickly flown them via helicopter to the mainland, shepherded them into the plane, and cooked steaks in the microwave. Now he sat across from Daire, curiosity bright in his eyes, as the pilots flew them through the Arctic storm to refuel in Greenland. Then they'd jump over Alaska, head south, and land in Seattle. Adam had followed orders perfectly by bringing both food and clothing.

The wool sweater and faded jeans had pleased Daire greatly, and the darker jeans and blue sweater fit Cee Cee well enough. The denim stretched nicely across her rounded rear, and he wanted nothing more than to strip her out of them.

Adam cleared his throat and shoved another set of papers at him. "There were seven explosions in Russian mines last night, in addition to the one on the island."

Cee Cee hummed happily from the sofa.

Daire cleared his throat. "Don't tell me. The mines belonged to Ivan Bychkov."

Adam glanced over his shoulder at the woman and then back at

Daire, who already faced her. "Either Bychkov or his people. Rumor has it that the Consortia is pissed and out for blood—Bychkov's and whoever attacked the mines."

Daire cut Cee Cee a hard look. "It would take an incredible amount of time and resources to coordinate such an attack, don't you think?"

Adam frowned, no doubt catching undercurrents. "Why yes, Daire. Yes, I do think that."

Daire turned his focus on his younger brother. "Sarcasm?"

"What is going on?" Adam growled.

"I'll let you know as soon as I know," Daire said evenly. Oh, the woman was going to tell him everything, but he preferred to hear it first before sharing with his brother. "Which will be soon." The second he got her home, to be clear.

She finished eating and stretched out on the sofa. Exhaustion created dark circles under her eyes that all but emanated from her too pale skin.

He grimaced. He'd used her hard, and that was after she'd been severely injured, healed, and dunked in freezing water. According to Bychkov, she was weak. How, Daire didn't know. In fact, he didn't know shit, now did he?

Adam cleared his throat. "Five of the mines, including the one on the island, were mining planekite."

Daire's attention focused. "So they're destroyed?"

"Yes, but we've been able to determine all five sent shipments to Seattle before being attacked." Adam sat back, nostrils flaring.

Then it was getting from Seattle to Dublin, somehow. "How big were the shipments?" Daire asked, standing up and having to duck to keep from hitting his head.

"Pretty damn big," Adam said.

Wonderful. Daire reached into a cupboard and drew out a blanket before settling it over Cee Cee. He dropped to his haunches and smoothed the hair from her face. "Go to sleep and let your body heal itself. When we get home, we're gonna talk."

Her lips trembled, and a definite apology glimmered in her beautiful eyes. "I enjoyed last night," she said softly. Then she shut her eyes, and before he could respond, she slipped into sleep.

He returned to the table.

Adam lifted a dark eyebrow. "What the heck?"

"Later." Daire reached for the nearest shipping manifest. "We have work to do." And work they did. They went through all the mine records, all the official shipping records, and everything they could glean from their allies. He catnapped every once in a while, but tension rode him hard and he couldn't completely sleep. The plane refueled in Greenland and took them on to Seattle.

Daire awoke Cee Cee twice to make her eat something, and each time, she fell back into dreamland with a grateful sigh. Her body naturally sent out tingles as her flesh healed, and true relief swept through Daire when the burns on her arm slowly faded. Thank God, he hadn't scarred her for eternity.

Even when they landed, she barely stirred when he carried her from the plane to the car on the private Jetway. They drove through town, and she slept peacefully in his arms. He enjoyed holding her, allowing himself a moment to just relax and feel.

Finally, they reached his penthouse and he carried her up to the door. She struggled, and he set her down on the marble floor. "Whatever your escape plan is, it's not happening." He pushed open the heavy door and nudged her inside, closing it firmly behind them. His place was warm and clean, and he settled into home. While Simone had decorated it with black leather and green accents, he liked the peaceful feeling of the sofa, chairs, fireplace, and massive Brenna Dunne landscape painting of Ireland.

Noise clanged from the kitchen area followed by the scent of waffles. Damn it. He'd forgotten he'd told the prospects they could hang at his place while he was out.

Garrett came into view first, chuckling. "I think the brunette was much—" He stopped short, mouth dropping open.

"I'm back," Daire said, belatedly realizing the kid was staring at Cee Cee. "This is—"

Nicholai Veis, a demon ally and right hand to demon leader Zane Kyllwood, prowled behind Garrett, his hands full of plates of scrambled eggs. He barely stopped in time to keep from running into Garrett. His dark eyes focused on Daire and then on Cee Cee, before he slowly set down the plates on the round glass breakfast table. "What in the world is going on?"

Daire frowned. "What are you doing here?"

Nick's gaze didn't leave Cee Cee. "Checking on Logan Kyllwood."

As if on cue, the young demon jogged out of the kitchen carrying jars of syrup. He smashed into Veis and slid to the side. "What the heck?" Then his gaze followed his friends', landed on Daire, and moved to Cee Cee. "Mom?"

Chapter 10

Cee Cee winced and didn't miss how quickly Daire rocked back on his heels. Forcing a smile, she crossed the room and leaned up to press a kiss to her youngest son's cheek. He stood so tall all of a sudden and so handsome. Light green eyes, pure black hair, angled features. "Hi, sweetie."

He inhaled and his nostrils flared. His sharp gaze went from her face to Daire and back. Then he moved.

Crap. He could smell Daire on her. She tried to grab his arm, but he was quick. Good thing Nick was prepared and even quicker. The older demon jumped in front of Logan and pushed him back a foot.

"Hold on," Nick said. The demon lieutenant was dressed casually in black slacks and a gray shirt, his eyes onyx and his hair a dark blond. Tall and powerful, his voice nevertheless held a note of reason, as usual. Oh, he'd kill, but he'd think it through first.

"Cee Cee," Daire said slowly, the consonants rolling off his tongue. "Your mother called you Cee Cee."

She swallowed, half-turning to face him. "Yes."

"Short for . . . Felicity. Felicity Kyllwood, to be exact," Daire said, ignoring everyone else in the room.

Her hands trembled, so she tucked them discreetly in her pockets. "Yes."

Fury. Hot and bright, the emotion blazed through the enforcer's eyes. A swell of terrifying, searing, snapping heat filled the room. Anger etched into the hard line of his rugged jaw, and his lips pressed together. She took an involuntary step back.

Nick cleared his throat. "So, Felicity. How was the luxury cruise?"

She pierced him with a hard look. "Lovely. Thank you for asking."

She tried to summon dignity, but considering she wore no makeup, her hair had dried full of salt water, her jeans were too tight and her sweater was too large, she didn't have much to work with.

"Everybody get the fuck out of my flat," Daire ordered.

A ball slammed into her gut. She really had enjoyed their night together and had hoped they could remain at least friendly. Gently, she took her son's vibrating arm. "Let's go talk."

Daire slowly, way too slowly, shook his head. "Oh no . . . *Felicity.* You're staying here. We're overdue for a little chat."

She shivered, and a warning blast of heat flicked her skin.

Logan growled, Nick half turned, and even Garrett pushed clear of the table.

Testosterone, a whole barrel of it, rolled through the room like a prelude to a hurricane.

She shook her head. Logan was seconds from charging, and while Nick would try to stop the fight, in the end, he'd fight with Logan. Garrett was Logan's best friend, and while he respected Daire, he'd have Logan's back. "Are you crazy?" she whispered.

"If I am, it's because of the last three days," Daire said evenly, anger still swelling from him. "They want to fight? We'll fight. But in the end, baby, you and I are having a long overdue discussion."

Felicity winced. Her son wouldn't like the *baby* comment.

Yep. Logan exploded.

He hit Daire full on, propelling them into the door. The steel door cracked. Daire grabbed his lapels, pivoted, and slammed Logan up hard. Surprisingly, neither Garrett nor Nick moved.

"Listen, kid, believe me, I get it." Daire slowly lowered Logan. "But here's the deal. Your mom's an adult, and this is none of your business." Daire released him and took a step back.

"I'm going to kill you." Logan's voice shook with rage, and he bunched his fists.

Felicity hustled forward. "Logan Henry Kyllwood." She put every ounce of motherly snap she owned into the words.

He slowly turned his gaze from Daire to her. "What?"

She put her hands to her hips. "I realize this is confusing, but you will not provoke a fight. Got it?"

His ears turned red. Then his head went back. "Wait a minute."

She bit her lip.

He cocked his head to the side, glanced at Daire, and then looked back at her. "There is no way I should smell him on you. You used the mutated virus?"

How did she admit to her son that she'd voluntarily undergone an experimental procedure to negate the mating bond she'd had with his father? "Logan, I—"

"Mom!" he exploded. "What the fuck?"

Daire put him back into the door with one hand. "Knock it off."

Logan swiped Daire's arm away. "You touch me again, and I'll fucking rip off your head, witch."

Oddly enough, Logan's anger seemed to sweep some of Daire's away. "That's fair," Daire said. He rubbed the back of his head. "Listen up. Your mom was in a fight with a witch, attacked by a polar bear, in a helicopter wreck, and nearly drowned."

Logan's mouth dropped open, and his eyes widened. "Mom?" he gasped.

She tried to keep from glaring at Daire. Her son didn't need to know any of those facts. "I'm fine."

"Who's the witch she fought with?" Logan asked, his chin lowering.

Approval lit Daire's eyes, and his lips twitched. "A mercenary by the name of Vegar. He's polar bear food at this point."

Logan shook his head. "Mom, I—"

"My point is"—Daire continued—"your mother needs a hot shower and some clean clothes. Then we have a matter to discuss, and after I'm finished, I'm sure she'd love to explain to you where she has been the last few days."

Felicity's chin lifted. "While I do not owe anybody an explanation, Logan, I would like time to shower and get refreshed before we sit down and chat." She gave him her hardest look, swung it to Garrett, and then landed on Nicholai. "I trust that you three will keep my current location a secret?"

"Mom—" Logan started.

"I mean it," she said, her voice hoarse.

Logan swallowed, shuffled his feet, and nodded.

Garrett cleared his throat. "Yes, ma'am."

Nicholai smiled as he shook his head. "Sorry, Felicity."

Yes, she'd figured Nick would report back to Zane, her eldest son and the ruler of the demon nation. So she turned and smiled at Daire. "I suggest you speak with your friend, or your flat will be overrun with demons. If Zane shows up, you know Dage won't be able to stay away, he's such a busybody of a vampire king."

Daire's eyes flickered, but to his credit, his expression revealed nothing. "Nick? If you call Zane, I'm going to sic Simone on you."

Nick's eyes gleamed. "Please, do. I've been waiting for your cousin's temper to explode so I can take care of unfinished business with her."

Felicity sighed and glanced around, seeing an open doorway. "I assume the master and bath are through there?"

"Aye," Daire said.

"Good. If there's any way to get fresh clothing here by the time I'm finished with a very long shower, I'd appreciate it." She moved to go.

Logan stopped her with one gentle hand on her arm. "Mom? Come with us. You don't have to stay here."

She swallowed and forced a smile for her youngest. No way did she want them all to fight, and after everything, she did owe Daire an explanation. Heck. Not only had she drugged him, she'd almost gotten him killed. More than once. "I know, but I do have matters to discuss with Daire. I'll call you when I'm finished."

Logan shook his head. "No."

She stilled. "Excuse me?"

He kept her gaze, but his ears turned red again. "I'm not leaving you with him."

"Why not?" she asked, her temper prickling up her back.

"Because you're, I mean, you're——"

Hurt smashed into her stomach. Of course her own kid knew how weak she was. How she'd failed him and his brothers. Even so, the agony of that fact spurred her anger. "I'm what?" she yelled up into his face.

He sucked in air. "You're my mom!" he yelled back.

Oh. Her body relaxed. "Huh. You're right. This has to be weird." The poor kid. She gentled her voice. "Logan, I'm barely over a century old. That's hardly an adult in human terms. I was young when I had you boys, incredibly young for a demon."

"I know." The blush moved to his face. "But . . ."

Nick strode toward the door. "The boys and I will go out to dinner, and you two can catch up later." He opened the door and paused. "Felicity, I am going to have to report to Zane. There were a series of mines blown up in Russia earlier, and while I haven't connected the dots as of yet, something tells me you weren't attacked by polar bears on a tropical cruise."

She glared at Daire. Man, he had a big mouth. "Enjoy your dinner," she said sweetly.

Nick herded the boys out, giving Logan a rather hard-looking shove to get him to leave. The door snicked shut.

Felicity breathed out.

Daire leaned back against the wall. "Felicity or Cee Cee?"

She shrugged. "Both. It's like calling a Katherine Kathy or Juniper Junie. Cee Cee is a nickname, and I answer to both."

"So at least you only *kind of* lied about your name."

Ah, the anger had only been banked temporarily. "Yes," she said. She tried to brush by him, not surprised when he wrapped a hand around her bicep and halted her in place. "You said I could borrow your shower."

"Yes." He leaned down, his breath heated at her ear. "Just so we're clear. I don't give two flying fucks who your kids are, who your friends are, or who your allies are." His hold tightened just enough to be threatening without causing any pain. "You lie to me again, and the last few days will seem like a dream vacation compared to what I'll do."

Reality hit her in the face. He really didn't care. Daire Dunne didn't see her as a damaged demon, a widow, or even the mother of the most powerful demon on the planet. He didn't see any of that. The enforcer saw her as all woman.

She turned and smiled at him, so much warmth rippling through her she nearly swayed.

He released her and stepped back, his brows furrowing together. "Don't even *try* to charm me."

She couldn't help it. Her smile widened, and delight bubbled up.

He growled and gave her a not-so-gentle nudge toward the bedroom. She couldn't quite make out the words he muttered as she moved away, but it sounded something like *it's always the fucking smile.*

Daire finished yanking fresh jeans up after a superbly hot shower, his mind reeling. He'd prepared some scrambled eggs for Cee Cee, *Felicity*, for her to eat after she'd showered. His kitchen of dark granite countertops and stainless steel appliances was no longer in order, considering the kids had cooked an earlier breakfast. But he'd put it back together later. Right now, he had enough to deal with.

In his line of work, getting involved with a woman was complicated. Becoming friends with a female demon was intricate. But bedding the mother of the leader of the demon nation was fucking crazy. Yet Daire didn't see her as a mother or even as a demon. She was sweet, she was hot, and the sounds she made when he thrust inside her would haunt his dreams until he died.

But he liked an orderly life, and he liked peaceful women. Felicity, on her own, was a barrel of crazy schemes and too much energy. Plus, she came with three grown sons and tight ties to the demon nation, which might create even more problems for him as an enforcer.

She was smart enough to drug him, and she was brave enough to face down powerful enemies half the world away from safety.

Just thinking about her made his pants too tight.

He crossed into the living room where she sat on the leather sofa, firelight caressing her skin. Her hair, long, shimmering, and blond, had dried down her back. No curls, no wave. Just delicate femininity. Dark yoga pants covered her toned legs, and a red T-shirt, a good one, her top. Freshly scrubbed with no makeup, the woman looked about twenty years old. Her feet were bare.

"I forgot to borrow socks from Simone," he rumbled, leaning against the door frame.

Felicity jumped, her dark eyes flashing to him. "The fire is warm and so are my feet."

She had cute feet. Small, pale, fragile. Yet she'd kicked that polar bear with enough force to break its nose.

"I usually know exactly what I'm doing and what I need to do next," he said, his arms crossed over his bare chest.

She smiled. "That must be nice."

"I don't know what to do with you."

A very pretty pink fluttered beneath her skin. Well, at least they were on the same wavelength. Yet she arched one fine brow. "I'm not yours to do anything with."

From any other woman, the statement would've been a challenge. Yet with her regal tone of voice, her bearing, the woman actually believed every word.

He smiled. "Why are you damaged?"

Her head jerked.

Hadn't been expecting that one, now had she?

Her chin lifted. "I'm not damaged."

All right. Enough. "Nobody has ever called me patient, lady, and I have to say, I've showed more patience with you than anybody else in my entire life." He hadn't even dealt with the fact that she'd drugged him and ransacked his office yet.

"So?" She met his gaze full on.

Heat flushed through him. "So? I'm done. Either you start talking, or I strip you naked, fuck you senseless, and then you start talking." In fact, that was a damn good idea. He pushed off from the wall.

She choked and held up a hand. "Wait a minute."

"Talk."

Her hands fluttered in her lap, and she cut a discreet glance at the clock on the mantel. What in holy hell was she up to now? She cleared her throat. "Fine. Not many people know this, but I, ah, I am unable to perpetrate a demon mind attack."

Perpetrate? Jesus. He'd rather have her screaming at him than using that monotone of a voice. "So?"

She blinked. "I'm damaged. Handicapped. Half a demon."

That was fucking crazy. "Says who?"

She shook her head, surprise glittering in her eyes. "Everyone."

"Can you teleport?"

Her shoulders slumped. "No."

He could just rip the head off everyone who'd ever made her feel like less. And by the hurt in her eyes, they'd done a number on her. In fact, until Zane Kyllwood had killed his uncle and taken over the demon nation, the world hadn't known Zane was half demon or that Felicity existed. "Your family hid you?" he asked.

She shrugged. "My parents were protective, but they died, and then Suri took over."

Suri was her older brother, the former demon leader, and a real bastard. "Willa was your sister?"

"Yes."

Willa was a demonness who was a torturing bitch. Both Suri and Willa were dead now.

"All right." Daire's brain sorted facts. "So Suri betrothed you to Bychkov in order to secure a treaty between his nation and Bychkov's people."

"Yes, but I'd met Dane Kyllwood, and we ran away together. Had the boys and lived a nice life in Africa until he died." Sadness twisted her lip.

Daire leaned back, narrowing her gaze. "How exactly did you meet Kyllwood?"

She shrugged, her gaze sliding away. "You know. At a bar downtown."

"Felicity."

The pink turned to red, and not with embarrassment but shame. "Dane lived with a small coalition of vampires, and the demons had attacked them for land, so he infiltrated Suri's headquarters to assassinate him. Instead, Dane found me, and I was injured, so he, ah, got me to safety."

Everything inside Daire stilled. "How were you injured?"

She lifted a shoulder and sighed. "Suri and I didn't get along well."

"He beat you?" Daire growled.

Her gaze met his. "I hit him, too."

Jesus. "So you got away, gave birth to three sons at a very young age, and then Dane died, leaving you alone in the world."

"Yes."

The only question remaining, he figured he could answer himself. Every move she'd made in the last week had been focused specifically on one target. Yet he wanted confirmation. "Bychkov killed your mate."

Her eyes flashed and she stood. "Yes. It's Bychkov's time to suffer before I kill him."

Chapter 11

Felicity settled her stance. The enforcer stood, legs braced, torso bare. Man, he was ripped. Dark hair curled at his nape, and he'd shaved in the shower, revealing the razor sharp cut of his jaw. A slight shadow already darkened his skin, all masculine.

Her vampire mate had been a kind man, much older than she, and he'd been incredibly over-protective from day one. She'd been injured and then pregnant so young, that she'd understood. But she'd never really had the chance to become the strong woman inside her until recently.

Daire treated her like a woman and not like a fragile flower. She liked that.

His green eyes pinned her in place. "Lemme get this straight." Every once in a while, his Irish brogue broke through.

She ignored the quivers in her abdomen from the deep accent. "All right."

"Your plan is to financially cripple Bychkov by destroying all of his mines, and you needed my records to find the hidden ones, because you figured I'd be investigating anything having to do with the mining of planekite."

"Yes."

Daire didn't react. "Why take Simone's records?"

Felicity glanced down. "She's on the Council, which is investigating the planekite mines, so I just emptied her file cabinet." Her heart rate picked up. "You seem angrier about her files than yours."

"Aye. My job is to protect her."

"That's not all," Felicity said.

"No. Simone is my cousin, and I've taken care of her since she was a little girl." Loyalty and fondness strengthened his voice.

That's exactly what Felicity had feared. "I understand."

"So, you've blown up his mines. Now what?"

She breathed out. "I have several corporations making moves on his business holdings, and I have groups devaluing any physical property he has around the world." She'd also implemented a strategic securities attack to destroy his stock market portfolio, as well as the portfolios of his entire consortia group.

"Is that all?" Daire drawled.

No. But telling Daire about the upcoming three bank heists for all of Ivan's cash seemed like oversharing. "Yes."

"Then what, Cee Cee?" Daire unfolded his body.

Her breath hitched. "Then I finish him."

Daire gave a short nod, the sides of his eyes crinkling in realization. No amusement. "Fight to the death, huh?" he murmured.

She cleared her throat and glanced at the clock again. Plenty of time. "That's my plan."

Daire followed her gaze, landed on the clock, and returned. "Have a hot date?"

"No, but very soon, I must be going."

He chuckled then. The sound pulsated against her skin, licked down, and settled between her legs. "Do you really think you're going anywhere?"

Her nipples peaked, even as her temper stretched cautiously awake. "Excuse me?"

He blinked, slowly. Like a predator, almost intrigued, yet with lazy indulgence. "You know, you're at a disadvantage here."

Her head snapped up. "Oh, am I?"

"Aye. I've seen the real you since day one. The fighter, the strategist, the woman." He cocked his head to the side in a curiously dangerous movement. "You haven't seen me."

What the heck? "I don't understand."

"I agree."

God save her from enforcers talking in riddles. "I'm pretty much a straight shooter and don't really catch subtext, Dunne."

"Ah." He reached her in two long strides, lifting her by the elbows, turning, and dropping to the sofa with her legs bracketing his.

She slapped her hands against his very strong chest. Outrage filled her along with a heat she couldn't banish. "What in the hell are you doing?"

"Whatever the hell I want to." His hands clamped her hips and held tight. "Which is something that surprises you."

"I'm not accustomed to being manhandled," she breathed, trying to ignore the iron-hard thighs between hers.

His cheek creased. "I'd think not." Slowly, deliberately, he ran one hand up her side, over her shoulder, and threaded his fingers through her hair. "But here's the thing, sweetheart. I don't give a shit who your family is, and they sure as hell don't scare me. I don't care who your parents were, your brother was, or your kids are. In fact, I not only don't see you as a mom, I don't see you as a demon."

She swallowed, her heart hammering against her ribs. In her entire life, she hadn't met anybody like Daire Dunne. For so long, she'd been afraid of her siblings, thinking demons were the most dangerous beings on earth. For the first time, she wondered. Was anybody more dangerous than a Coven enforcer? "You don't scare me," she barely ground out.

One dark eyebrow lifted. "Then you're not as smart as I assumed. You're young, and you've been fairly sheltered from the world, Felicity. Watch yourself." A twisting of his wrist in her hair accompanied the warning. "Any man who'd attempted to drug me would be dead. Any woman I didn't know would be brought before the Coven Nine and probably seriously burned. And a woman I've fucked three ways to Sunday? Well, now. She'd be wincing every time she tried to sit down for the near future."

The hand tethering her head kept her from moving, so she glared. "Careful, witch."

"As I was saying, we haven't properly dealt with the fact that you drugged me and made me chase you across the world and nearly drown."

She swallowed, her body tensing. "You're not serious."

Both eyebrows went up.

She held perfectly still. Her lungs compressed. Though she was trained, and she had power, she'd seen him fight. The man was made for it. "Listen, Enforcer. When I drugged you, I didn't even know you." They sure hadn't been intimate before she'd tricked him. Then she caught herself. What in the heck was she doing, reasoning with him?

"Good point." He leaned in, his eyes an inch away. "I've been inside you now, and you've moaned my name, so that changes things."

"No." Regret mingled with the desire blazing through her. "I'm sorry." Because she did see him. No way, *no way*, would he allow a woman he cared about to fight to the possible death, which was something she *had* to do. It had to be her. Forget equality, forget feminism, he was an enforcer and a protector. He wouldn't stand by as somebody he cared about walked into danger, and if they continued to be together, he'd care. Whether he knew it or not, he acted from the heart and not the head. "What we had was one night in a blizzard. That's all."

"Prove it."

"Wh-what?" she breathed.

He closed the small distance between their faces, his breath stirring her lips. "Prove you don't want me. You don't want more."

Her panties dampened. She was at a distinct disadvantage when it came to experience, and she knew it. Her mate had been her first and only, and he'd been more a gentle roll and sweet trust. Although Daire had definitely tried to be gentle, there was nothing sweet about him. He was all fire and storm, and a part of her, a female part she'd denied for so long, wanted to feel the bluster and ride the burn.

His nostrils flared, no doubt scenting her arousal. "Go ahead. Say it."

Denying the obvious was silly. "You know I want you, but I have a job to do, and if we continue, you'll just get in the way."

"I'm in the way now, baby." His lips took hers.

Sparks exploded in her blood, and her mind blanked. He worked her mouth, bending her back, forcing her sex against his hard cock. Demanding, even through the jeans, it jumped against her.

She couldn't move. He held her right where he wanted her, their mouths fused, her legs spread, her butt on his hard thighs, her breasts flattened by his chest.

Yes, Yes, Yes. She kissed him back, her hands frantic on his flesh, her body alive.

Warning clanged in the back of her head, and she knew she was making a colossal mistake, but she didn't care. Right now, in Daire's arms, she just wanted more. Wanted to feel like a woman, alive and whole. He gave her that. Even so aroused she could barely think, she knew, deep down, that Daire gave her that sense of completeness.

He released her mouth so she could breathe and peppered hard kisses across her jaw and down her throat, tilting her down between his knees and toward the thick rug. She arched against him, the decadence of the position thrilling.

With the grace of any panther, while holding her aloft, he dropped to his knees and stretched them both out. The second his groin settled against hers, they both groaned.

He ripped her shirt over her head in one smooth motion, and then his mouth found her breasts. Nipping and suckling, licking and kissing, he hummed enjoyment as he made her writhe with need. Electricity charged from her nipples to her clit, whipping up a maelstrom of hunger she never could've imagined. "So much," she gasped.

"Just wait." Without missing a beat, he shoved off her yoga pants. Then, levering himself up on one elbow, he held his hand, palm down, over her breasts. Fire crackled.

She jumped.

He chuckled, the sound dark and aroused. "Don't move."

She sucked in air, her eyes widening.

Fire cascaded across his palm, dancing and threatening, primal in its beauty. He waited a beat, then another one, and finally lowered his hand.

The heat caressed across her, biting softly. The air whooshed out of her lungs, and she laughed.

He smiled. "You like fire."

She *loved* fire. At the thought, she sobered.

"Nope. Stay with me." He rolled off her, throwing his jeans aside with the movement, and then sat with his back to the couch. Grabbing her, he pulled her toward him.

Big. Huge. Way big. She couldn't look away from his fully erect penis. "Um—"

Both of his hands at her hips lifted her, and her knees dropped to the sides of his thighs. "Take your time," he ordered, sounding like he'd swallowed gravel. Sweat dotted his upper lip, and the muscles in his arms flexed as if he held himself back.

She pressed her hands against his rippling abdominal muscles and slowly lowered herself down. Several times she had to stop and breathe out, relax her body, in order to take all of him. Finally, her rear rested against his thighs. He filled her, and mini-explosions rocked rhythmically through her sex. "You're big," she said, and sighed.

He laughed and smoothed hair away from her face. "I like the sweet, honest side of you, Felicity."

She tried not to wince. In less than an hour, he wasn't going to like her at all.

His lips firmed. "Whatever you're planning, don't do it."

It was too late. She caressed down his abs to his thighs and then tilted her butt and lifted up.

His sharp intake of breath spurred her on. So she did it again. Tension crackled around them. Every time she moved, he scraped against nerves inside her, sparking shards of raw pleasure to her clit. Although she wanted to go fast, wanted to reach that climax, torturing him held its own appeal. Having command over such a powerful being, such a deadly one, was better than any aphrodisiac.

Just how crazy could she drive him? It was their last time together, that was for sure. She cupped his hard jaw, enjoying the faint scratch of whiskers against her skin. His eyes glowed a fathomless green in the firelight, which slid over the hard planes of his face. With his black hair and full lips, there was no question as to his Irish heritage. So handsome. He kept her gaze, emotion bright in his, a warning glint not far off. "Felicity," he said, rolling the sound of her name with his brogue.

A small voice in the back of her head told her to tell him how much the last few nights had meant to her. How much he already meant to her, and thank him for what he'd done. He'd reminded her of who she could be. But first, she had a job to do. So she kept silent and tried to memorize his face.

He was visibly struggling to control himself, and power flushed through her. She wiggled her butt and clenched her internal muscles.

Strong hands clamped on her hips. He lifted her and set her back down, starting a wild rhythm that ricocheted pleasure so far inside her, the sensation had to spiral out. She cried out, holding his arms, trusting him to get her there.

He stopped, fully embedded in her, his cock pulsing in time with her ragged breaths. She tried to move, gasping when he held her firm. "What?" she panted.

"Stay still." One hand kept her in place while the other lifted, green sparks careening between his fingers.

She sucked in a breath. "Daire——"

He reached down and ran his palm and the fire over her nipples.

The sharp bite overloaded her senses. So damn good. Beyond good. Her internal muscles quivered. "Oh."

"My name fits me," he said, pinching a nipple.

She glanced down, her mind blank, her body clamoring. Fire crackled between his fingers, licking her flesh. So much power. "Name?"

"Daire," he whispered, his hand caressing down her abdomen.

"No." Her gaze flew up to his. "I, ah." The look on his face, she'd never forget. Male. Intent. Possessive.

The fire crackled, and she jumped.

He chuckled, low and male. "I wouldna' move, were I you."

She stopped breathing, her body clamoring. The flame torched over her stomach, and she tried to back away, but he held her fast. His heated fingers separated her labia.

Her eyes widened, and she met his gaze, almost straining toward the flame.

Fire flicked her clit.

She exploded, throwing back her head, hissing his name. He shoved up inside her, moving her, pounding so hard she could do nothing but hold on and feel. The orgasm, if that's what it was, consumed her, burning through her, taking every ounce of energy she possessed. The waves crashed endlessly, prolonged by the heat and his furious thrusting.

Finally, her body went lax, and she sighed in relief.

He manacled one of her shoulders, one of her hips, and held her in place for one final thrust. His body, all sleek power, shuddered as he came.

When he released her, she fell against him, kissing his salty jugular. He dropped his head to the vulnerable area where her neck met her shoulder and planted one soft kiss.

She sighed, her attention caught by the clock ticking on the mantel. "Oh God." Her head lifted. "Daire, I——"

The door blew open and glass shattered. Flash grenades popped all around them. Men in black filled the room.

Daire jumped up, shoving her behind him onto the sofa. He grunted as five tranquilizer darts were instantly shot into his chest. His hand shook as he reached back for her.

She scrambled away and yanked on the yoga clothes, stumbling a little from the grenades. Even though she'd known they were coming, she hadn't had a chance to fully duck her head first.

He growled and reached for her, and two soldiers immediately turned and fired shots into his neck. He dropped back onto the couch, fury glinting in his eyes.

Oh man, this was so bad. Sure, she'd made certain the tranq was temporary and wouldn't harm him in any way. Her hands trembled when she reached him. "I'm so sorry. I'm so, so sorry, Daire."

Rage, the real kind, contorted his face right before he passed out. She grabbed an afghan off the end of the sofa and tossed it over him. There was going to be hell to pay. She just knew it.

Chapter 12

Daire rolled over and hit the floor with a hard clunk. Sparks lit across his rug. Smoke filled the penthouse and his phone buzzed from the table. An alarm should've gone out immediately upon breach, but Adam and Simone were out to dinner and Kellach was in Ireland.

Backup would take precious minutes.

He sucked in air, focusing on the tranq in his blood. 'Twas the same as the drug Felicity had first used to incapacitate him.

Big mistake.

His body would've created antibodies from the first dose, and he could actually feel the energy rippling through him as his blood negated the interloper. Closing his eyes, he focused more power into his cells, taking the energy of fire and burning away the drug.

Minutes later, he reached for his jeans and yanked them on.

Boot steps clamored up the stairs.

Adam and Simone rushed inside, green guns in hand. "Status!" Adam barked.

Daire shot a slightly numb hand through his hair. "We're clear."

Simone slowly tucked the gun into her waistband.

Daire growled. "A member of the Council of the Coven Nine does not double as an enforcer, even in case of emergency."

Her dark eyes sparkled, and she tossed back curly brunette hair. "I'm here as your cousin, not as a pseudo-enforcer." As a purebred witch, her voice was husky, low, and amused. For her dinner out, she'd donned dark jeans, designer boots, and a leather jacket that probably had cost more than his flat. She was a brilliant smartass, quite happy being a bitch, and made no apologies. Ever.

Daire adored her. "Put yourself in danger again, cousin, and as an enforcer, I'll lock you down." His main job as an enforcer was to protect the members of the Nine, and if anything happened to the spirited witch, the world would lose too much beauty.

She rolled her eyes. "Please tell me another little blond human didn't just take you out."

He paused.

Adam glanced around at the smashed window and broken glass strewn across the floor, his frown dark. "Again? Who is this Cee Cee?"

The feeling finally returned to Daire's legs. "She's actually Felicity Kyllwood."

Simone gasped, her eyes widening.

Adam stiffened, his mouth pressing together.

"Exactly." Daire grabbed his phone. "They couldn't have gone far. Simone, get to your flat and hack into every camera within a mile. Relay the information to us through the earbuds." He jogged to his room to yank on a dark T-shirt and motorcycle boots.

Adam followed him. "The smart move is to notify Zane Kyllwood and let the demon nation handle the woman."

"*I'm* handling the woman," Daire bit out, reaching for his key from the dresser as he passed by.

"Shit." Adam, always the strategist, shook his head and followed. He stepped over rubble and broken glass, his phone in his hand, already punching in orders. "I had no sense she was a demon. None at all."

Daire prowled out of the penthouse and reached the stairs, running down. "She doesn't have the ability to attack minds, and she can't teleport. So she doesn't really give off demon vibes."

Adam coughed from behind him. "She can't mind attack?"

"No."

"Interesting."

"Not really." Daire didn't give a shit if she could attack minds, but it made her vulnerable if she was going after an enemy. At least he wouldn't have to waste energy shielding against an attack when he caught up to her.

Adam leaped onto his Harley next to Daire. "She seems so innocent."

"Ha." The woman had drugged him . . . twice. Yet there was a sense of wonder to her, and even though she'd been sheltered, she'd dealt with pain and loss. Not that her history mattered. As an enforcer, he had the present to deal with, and that pertained to planekite and mines. As a man, he had his woman to deal with—whether she liked it or not.

Adam ignited his bike.

Daire glanced down at his aching hand and slowly turned it over, already knowing what he'd see.

Adam caught the gaze, saw Daire's palm, and quickly turned the key. The pipes silenced. "You're kidding."

"No." An intricate Celtic knot, the emblem of his people, stood in raised relief on his palm. The marking that a witch transferred to a mate. "It just appeared."

Adam shook his head. "Wow. She's a demon, bro."

"Aye."

Adam scratched his chin. "Demons brand their mates with the letters of their surnames. If you brand her, will she brand you?"

Daire lifted a shoulder. He'd never met a witch mated to a demon. "If it's a brand, I'd have to allow it to remain on my skin, I think. Besides, you and I both have had the marking appear before on our flesh."

"True. Remember that crazy wolf shifter I almost mated? The marking appeared, and I willed it away. Thank God. So don't worry, you can will that marking away and don't have to mate the demonness who keeps making you look like an ass."

Daire cut him a sharp look.

Adam gave a body shudder and reached for his phone to quickly dial. "Simone? What did you find out?" He listened and then nodded. "Keep looking." The phone disappeared in his pocket. "Felicity and her gang went north, and Simone is sending tracking information to our cell phones."

Daire twisted the key and his bike roared to life. A marking might appear just because a *possible* mate had gotten close; it didn't mean he and Felicity were fated. He didn't believe in fate, and if he did, fate would have a nice, docile, sweet woman ready for him. One who didn't get in the way of his job and was a soft place to land when needed.

Fate definitely wouldn't stick him with a wounded demon who'd rather drug him than work with him. No way. He jerked his head toward the exit and swung his bike around, heading out at full speed.

Felicity Kyllwood, demon or not, wasn't getting out of his reach this time. He reached into his pocket and grabbed an earbud to shove in his ear. Heading north, he swerved around cars, past restaurants, and around drunken pedestrians. Simone gave directions in his ear, her keyboard clacking across the line.

"They're on bikes and just turned east onto Bentley Road," she said.

Daire cut Adam a look. "Bears' territory?" he mouthed.

Adam exhaled heavily and twisted his throttle.

Oh, the bear shifters had better not be in on this. The bears lived in plain sight as the Grizzly Motorcycle Club and usually kept to themselves. Anger tightened Daire's hold on the handles, and he pushed his bike harder. A rumble from up ahead disturbed the airwaves. He focused, realigning oxygen molecules, applying quantum physics in a way humans would never understand. Five riders, about a mile ahead.

His blood thrummed with the thrill of the chase. He'd forgotten. Actually forgotten the excitement of a challenge. It had been so long since he'd had one.

Felicity was one hell of a challenge.

He leaned over the bike and let the wind roll across his shoulders. Lights. Up ahead, he saw lights. So he kicked it into gear, fire all but burning through his skin.

Her scent. That hyacinth sweet scent wafted back, and his nostrils flared. *Mine.*

Forgetting his job, forgetting formality, even forgetting diplomacy, he chased her. She sat behind a large shifter, her arms around his back, her glorious hair streaming in the wind.

The sight of her with her arms around another male had fury careening through him until green sparks shot from his fingers.

She turned her head and caught sight of him. Her eyes widened and her lips pursed. Then, slowly, her mouth curved in a smile, and challenge filled her eyes.

Oh, baby. It was on . . . and it was the smile that drew him toward her. Aye. That damn smile.

Felicity held on tighter to Lucas Clarke, bear shifter, her heart leaping to life. Daire Dunne, on a Harley, chasing her down looked like every nice girl's dream of a bad boy fantasy.

Yet the enforcer was all man, and he was *pissed*.

Green fire crackled across his hands, and even the air around him seemed charged.

Wind whipped across her face, yet she couldn't look away. Determination stamped hard on his rugged face, anger tightening his lips into a line. Moonlight slanted down, glinting in his furious green eyes. Yet something else lived there.

The thrill.

The thrill of a chase, the excitement of a challenge.

Her breath panted out. When was the last time she'd felt so alive? Never.

Dark anticipation crossed Daire's face as he drew near.

She shivered and pressed closer to Lucas, who was one of the top lieutenants in the shifter organization and currently under contract to work for her. "Go faster," she yelled.

The shifter handed back a green gun. "Shoot."

The weapon chilled her hand. Drugging the enforcer was one thing, actually shooting him another. Yet she swung around, tightening her thighs on the seat, to point the barrel at him in warning.

His foot lashed out, and he kicked the weapon from her hand. Holy hell. How had he moved so quickly?

The bear shifter swerved to the left, and Daire followed. Adam Dunne pulled up on the right, bracketing them. A second later, a shifter drove up beside Adam and punched him in the jaw.

The bike beneath Felicity swerved, and she cried out, holding tighter to the leather. Daire reached for her, his hand enclosing her nape. She yelped and kicked out, throwing up an arm to sever his hold just as the shifter driving her kicked Daire's bike.

Daire swerved away, both hands slamming on his handlebars to control his bike.

Felicity bunched against the shifter. "Go, go, go," she yelled. Daire had tried to grab her, and his hold hadn't been gentle. Not even close. For the first time, she doubted her safety, no matter her allies. "Hurry up, Lucas."

The shifter ducked his head and opened the throttle. Felicity jerked back and then dug her fingers into his leather cut, holding on, trying to see as the wind made her eyes tear. Pine trees spun by them, their scent competing with the misty air.

Daire reached them again, and this time, he struck out and nailed

Lucas in the face. The shifter's head jerked to the side, and he let off the throttle. Then Daire reached out and grabbed Felicity's hair, twisting his wrist until he reached her nape. She punched him, yanking her head, pain scoring her scalp. Fury roared through her and she kicked out, nailing him in the thigh.

His hold tightened.

Lucas regained control and sped up, his muscles bunching.

"Wait," Felicity cried out as her head was yanked back. Daire wasn't letting go.

Lucas opened the throttle, while Daire slowed down. Time ended. Felicity flew off the bike, and only Daire's impossibly quick reflexes kept her from spinning right into the night. He shifted his shoulders, tugged, released her hair, and she landed on the seat behind him. She hit hard enough her thighs bounced, bruises instantly forming.

Pure instinct had her hands clutching his T-shirt.

Son of a bitch. "You could've decapitated me," she yelled into his ear.

His chuckle only fanned her fury hotter, and she punched him in the kidney. He didn't even flinch. She swallowed, coughed back fear, and tried to concentrate. She didn't have any leverage or power seated behind him on the bike, and if she forced them to crash, she'd get hurt, too. The ability to attack minds had never been more necessary, but she didn't have any way to do it. Her inadequacies settled like hard lumps of coal in her stomach.

Lucas swerved his bike in front of them, turning to face them and driving straight at them.

Daire's entire body tensed. Anticipation popped in the air around them.

Felicity shook her head. What were they going to do?

Lucas held out a hand, and Felicity instinctively put hers out. If she could grab him, she could jump to his bike. Daire neatly countered by hitting the brakes. The bike skidded and tipped up on the front wheel. She screamed, landing on his back and then slapping back down. Lucas barreled past them.

Daire chuckled and twisted the throttle again.

Felicity smashed into his back and held on, her mind reeling. The man was crazy and having too much fun. Over to the side, Adam and two bear shifters fought full on while steering their bikes. They were all insane.

She stopped struggling and just held on. At some point, the enforcer would have to stop the bike, and then she'd fight. Right now, she needed to get her breathing under control so she could think.

Buildings appeared on the sides of the road, and suddenly, Daire swerved and stopped the bike before hitting a massive garage.

Felicity swallowed and looked around. Daire and Adam sat on their rumbling bikes, a garage behind them, a wall of shifters on bikes in front of them. Oh, this was so not good.

Massive lights clicked on, illuminating the concrete courtyard. Garages took up three sides, while the shifters blocked the only road.

Daire's body stiffened, and his legs bunched.

A smaller door to the main garage opened, and a man prowled out. He looked like a bear. Broad and graceful at well over six feet tall, he had shaggy brown hair and honey-chocolate eyes. A primal sense of danger cascaded off him, and he moved with the ease of a wild predator. Sleep cleared from his eyes as he took in the scene, obviously having yanked on a pair of jeans so old the white creases had creases. His lightly haired chest was bare but roped with fierce muscles. "What the holy fuck?" he rumbled.

Even over the bike engines, his words were clear.

Daire glanced at him. Apparently making a decision, he cut his engine. Adam did the same.

The guy jerked his head, and the wall of shifters on bikes followed suit.

Quiet roared in on the echoes of the pipes. An owl hooted in protest through the trees.

"I thought we were allies, Bear," Daire snapped.

Felicity peered at the leader of the bear shifters, who at the moment, no longer appeared sleepy. Instead, a slightly pissed-off curiosity glimmered in his honeyed eyes.

"We are," he said, his gaze moving to Lucas, who sat alert on his bike. "Luke?"

Lucas jerked his head toward Felicity. "Side job."

Bear glanced at Felicity, Daire, Lucas, and back to her. "Somebody talk," he ordered.

Felicity started to swing her leg from the bike. Smooth as silk, Daire half turned, grabbed her waist, pivoted, and plunked her down in front of him, her back to his front. One arm banded around her rib cage with enough pressure to compress her lungs.

Bear cocked his head to the side. "The human is yours?"

Felicity winced. "Demon," she rumbled.

Now Bear's eyebrows lifted. "Interesting."

She shrugged, hampered by the strength of Daire's hold. His body, warm and solid, shielded her from the wind. Almost against her will, her body relaxed right into his strength. "Human or not, I'm not a puppy, thus I am not his. Kindly order him to release me."

Daire stiffened.

Bear threw back his head and laughed, the low rumble echoing around the garage doors. "The Coven Nine enforcers don't take orders from me, sweetheart, and you're far too beautiful to be a puppy. I meant no offense." Quicker than a thought, he sobered, his gaze hardening as he glanced at the shifters. "In contrast, they do answer to me. So I'm wondering why I have a pissed-off ally here surrounded by my own men."

Felicity shivered. Okay. Bears could be scary. "I, ah, hired them to do a job."

"Which was?" Bear asked silkily.

"To bomb my apartment and shoot me full of tranquilizers," Daire barked. "You'll receive the full bill for damages within a week."

Bear kept his gaze on his men. "Lucas?"

Lucas shrugged. "We often take side jobs."

"Not against allies," Bear shot back. He scratched his head. "Lucas, I'll deal with you later. Daire, Adam, ah, demon lady? Why don't you all come inside?" Without waiting for a response from anybody, he turned and loped back toward the still open doorway.

"Felicity." She raised her voice. "Instead of demon lady, call me Felicity." Maybe Bear would be an ally after all. She could currently use one.

He stopped moving, and his bare shoulders went back. Almost in slow motion, he turned around. "Felicity?"

She swallowed. "Yes."

His gaze darkened and focused over her shoulder at the tense enforcer. "As in, Felicity Kyllwood?"

Mutely, she nodded her head.

"Well, fuck me." Bear turned back around and strode for the door.

Chapter 13

Daire leaned back in the cushioned chair in Bear's rec room, eyeing the bar set against the corner. In contrast to the play room at Fire, this one was clean, shiny, and comfortable. Bear might be a deadly shifter, but the guy liked his comforts. Several plush lounge chairs faced a huge screened television. Pool tables, dart boards, and various video games took up the other room, while the scent of orange cleanser filled the air. He sipped his whiskey. "The damage to my penthouse is going to cost you a mint," he said, savoring the liquid.

Bear grunted from a nearby chair.

Felicity sat to Daire's left, flanked by Adam. She swirled the brew and downed a good portion of the drink. Color sprang into her cheeks. "I paid Lucas enough to fix your place, Daire. Now, if you don't mind, I do have work to do."

Amusement, the kind that would get him shot, pinged up through Daire. "Actually, Cee Cee, I do mind."

Bear shifted his weight, stretching out his bare feet. "Why do I feel like I'm going to be the one screwed here?"

Daire lifted a shoulder.

Bear sighed. "You can't keep a member of the demon ruling family a prisoner, Daire. I sure as hell won't help you."

"I'm not asking for help," he rumbled.

"I am." Felicity turned a sparkling smile on the shifter.

He perked up.

Daire growled.

Felicity leaned forward. "I hired Lucas and your men because I needed help, as I still do."

Bear frowned. "To be honest, I don't like any woman being held captive, demon ruling family member or not. What do you want, pretty lady?"

Daire cut him a hard look. Was the shifter flirting?

Felicity's dimples winked, making her both cute and undeniably sexy. "I just need a ride to the airport. Nothing big."

Bear scratched the whiskers at his chin. "Does your, ah, family know where you are?"

Her eyebrows lifted, suddenly regal. "My *son* doesn't need to know my whereabouts, Bear."

"Well, shit," Bear said.

"That about sums it up," Adam said cheerfully.

Daire fought the urge to hurl the heavy crystal glass at his brother's head. "Where is the plane heading this time?" he asked.

She turned her focus on him, and he felt the punch from those stunning eyes right in his solar plexus. "A spa in Alaska."

Cute, and a terrible liar. "I wonder if I spanked you right now, whether anybody would try to stop me?" he mused.

Fire snapped from her eyes.

Bear cleared his throat. "This ain't no sex dungeon, kids. Keep it PG rated."

Daire rolled his eyes. "Where are you planning to go, and don't lie to me again."

She kept her lips tightly together.

He leaned forward. "What's the name of Bychkov's partner, Cee Cee?"

Her eyes widened.

Yeah. He'd figured out she had an inkling as to the identity of the traitor witch, and it was time she helped him instead of hindered his mission.

Bear's phone buzzed and he glanced at the face, frowning. Then he reached over his shoulder for a remote control with enough buttons to launch a space shuttle. "I think it's for you," he murmured, pointing the device at the massive screen and pushing a key.

Vivienne Northcutt, the leader of the Council of the Coven Nine, slowly took shape.

Daire and Adam both snapped to attention and stood. "Aunt Viv," Daire said.

Her black eyes shot all sorts of sparks. "Don't you even think of

Aunt *Viving* me, Daire Dunne." She'd pulled her dark hair atop her head and wore a sparkly dress enhanced with diamonds, obviously having been interrupted doing something fancy.

"You look lovely, Aunt," Adam said.

"You're in trouble, too." Viv leaned toward the camera, which distorted her face. "I take it you're Felicity Kyllwood?"

Cee Cee stood. "Yes."

"Ah." Viv glanced to the side. "Bear?"

"Yes, ma'am." Bear stretched to his feet, all lazy grace. "I'm innocent in all of this." Charm coated his smile.

Viv sniffed. "Right. The term has never been applied to you, young man."

"Fair enough," Bear returned. "Why is the leader of the entire witch nation using my phone number?"

Viv glanced at the enforcers. "Rumor has it my enforcers are holding Zane Kyllwood's mother hostage in your territory, so I went to the source. After leaving a very nice ball, I might add."

Daire shook his head. How the hell had she gotten such quick Intel? "This is enforcer business, and we've got it handled." He ignored Adam's snort.

Blue fire crackled in Viv's eyes. "This is Coven Nine business, and you're out of it. Ms. Kyllwood? Per your earlier request, I guarantee your transport to the airport, as soon as you give me the name of the witch mining planekite in Russia."

Daire slowly turned toward Cee Cee, whose skin darkened to a nice color of strawberry. Somehow, the woman had sent a message across the world in order to bargain with the Coven Nine. Yet again three fucking steps ahead of him. "How?" he asked.

She lifted her chin. "I may have borrowed Lucas's phone before leaving your penthouse."

Ah. So she'd been smart enough to know Daire would come after her. "You offered a deal to the Coven Nine?"

"Yes."

Bear rolled his shoulders. "All due respect, this is Coven Nine and demon nation business, and I'm out of it." He turned to head toward the doorway.

Cee Cee shook her head. "You can be out of it, but Lucas promised me five men on the next mission."

Bear turned back around, eyed Felicity, looked at Viv, and then landed on Daire. "No."

Felicity huffed. "Yes."

Bear grinned, dimples flashing. "No way in hell, Blondie. My men are out of it." He loped back toward the doorway, pausing just long enough to throw over his shoulder, "If you and the enforcer reach peace, give me a call. You haven't lived until you've ridden on the back of my bike."

Daire's muscles tightened. He was going to kill Bear . . . when he got the chance. Right now, he eyed his aunt and boss. "Kyllwood will declare war on us if we allow his mother to be harmed, and believe me, whatever crazy plan she has right now, she will come to harm."

Felicity pivoted in a stunningly graceful move and kicked him in the jaw.

His head snapped back, and stars exploded behind his eyelids. Slowly, fighting every urge he owned, he lowered his head and kept from grabbing her and tossing her over his knees.

Viv chuckled. "Nice move."

"Thank you." Felicity stepped closer to the screen. "My mission is my own, and I don't require my son's permission or assistance. If you want my information, then I give you my word I'll send it to you once I'm in the air."

Daire growled low, about to give in to temper. He wasn't known for restraint, and yet he'd showed nothing but with Felicity Kyllwood since day one. Enough was enough.

Viv's eyes glimmered. "Isn't it an odd world when the kids whose diapers you changed start to give you orders?" Her gaze slammed both Daire and Adam.

Felicity nodded. "Yes, yes it is. You and I both know it's unacceptable."

"Yet I don't need war with the demon nation," Viv said, calculation littering her tone.

"I can see how that would be troublesome," Felicity murmured. "Holding me hostage isn't the path to peace, I assure you."

Viv played with a ten karat diamond at her throat. "Turning you over to Zane would guarantee peace with him, and yet, I agree that we can't allow the younger generation to dictate our lives."

Felicity smiled, obviously thinking she'd found an ally.

Daire knew better. Viv was a master negotiator as well as manipulator. "Get to it, Aunt Viv."

"Here's the offer. Felicity, I will ensure you meet your plane at the airport. When you reach cruising altitude, you'll send me the name of the witch working with Bychkov to mine and distribute planekite." Viv leaned in.

Felicity nodded. "That's acceptable."

"And Daire accompanies you to your destination," Viv finished.

"There it is," Adam whispered.

Aye. There it was. "I'm not taking her anywhere," Daire bit out.

"Enforcer? You are hereby ordered on protection detail of our good ally, Felicity Kyllwood." Viv leaned over and signed something with a bold stroke.

Felicity clasped her hands together. "Absolutely not."

Viv sighed. "It is my understanding that the forces you thought you had just walked out the door with Bear, which means you're going it alone. Sending you off on a dangerous mission, without even informing the leader of your people, regardless of your affiliation with him, would be a colossal mistake I am not prepared to make."

Daire relaxed his stance. Felicity was tough, but Viv had about six centuries on her and understood family and duty. He wanted to believe there wasn't the slightest glimmer of matchmaking frenzy in her eyes, but he wouldn't bet his bike on it. Viv loved to get them tied up in, well, love. "Whatever you are planning in your head, Auntie, knock it off," he said.

She rolled her eyes. "Don't worry, nephew. I can already see she's too good for you . . . as well as too young. Ironic, right?"

Now that was a direct hit. Daire lowered his chin, recognizing a challenge when one rammed him full in the head. "Felicity? Coven Nine orders or no, you're not getting on a plane without me. Period."

Felicity took several moments to think, a myriad of expressions crossing her face. "In exchange for allowing the enforcer to accompany me, I'll require his assistance in several matters."

"Done," Viv said.

"Good. I will send you the name of the witch you seek upon completion of these matters," Felicity said, meeting Viv's gaze head on.

Viv lifted her chin. "That was not the deal."

"We hadn't struck a deal, Ms. Northcutt." Felicity kept her stance. "I've just offered you one. Take it."

Damn, the woman had balls.

Viv breathed in. "The traitor witch is causing havoc and mining planekite as we speak. I can't wait for the name."

Felicity smiled. "I assure you, the witch and Ivan Bychkov are distracted right now and not mining. They will, I'm sure, begin doing so again in the near future, at which time you'll have the name. If you and your enforcer cooperate."

Daire leaned back and watched the women play chess. If Felicity called him the enforcer one more time, he was going to retaliate for that kick to the face. Oh, he wouldn't hurt her, but she'd think twice before kicking him again.

"Fair enough," Viv said, and the screen went dark.

Felicity turned toward him. "How do you feel about bank robberies?"

Felicity leaned into Daire as he took a corner, acutely aware of the hard body in front of her and the rumbling machine between her thighs. How different from when she'd ridden behind the shifter. Daire had wasted no time in setting her on the back of his bike and taking off, his back a rigid line of anger.

While she couldn't blame him, not really, she had to finish what she'd started in order to protect her kids. Finally. She wouldn't fail again. Clouds began to cover the moon in true Seattle fashion, and soon the wind carried a bite. After thirty minutes of riding, she realized they weren't heading for the airport. In fact, they had turned in the opposite direction.

She dug her nails into Daire's flat abdomen and levered herself up to yell in his ear. "Wrong way."

He didn't answer.

She wiggled and tried to move the bike, but he slapped a hand over hers and held her in place. When she struggled, his grip tightened. A warning.

Damn it. Not for one second had she even considered he'd disobey a direct order from the leader of the Coven Nine. He was an enforcer, for Pete's sake. Anarchy would ensue if enforcers just willy-nilly decided not to follow orders. She fumed behind him, her hand caught, the inside of her thighs tight to the outside of his. His hard, very masculine, oh so hot thighs.

Her nipples peaked.

Of all the ridiculous reactions. So, she'd had sex—great sex—for the first time in decades. Daire was creative, full of fire, and sensual as hell. Her body didn't need to react to such a degree.

More than ever, she wished she could melt minds with her brain. No such luck.

They drove down a dirt road with overhanging trees covering them. Soon the rush of a river competed with the pipes of the bikes. How Daire could see, she had no clue, but he drove on as if knowing exactly which potholes to avoid. Finally, he stopped outside of a rustic cabin and silenced the bike.

She immediately launched into speech. "This is kidnapping and treason, Daire Dunne." Sucking in a full breath in order to let him have it, she choked when he yanked her in front of him, cradled between the handlebars and his length. "Why you——"

His mouth was on hers. Not gentle and sure not nice, he conquered her mouth like the soldier he was. No mercy, no cajoling, just pure, raw male. Demanding and strong, his tongue swept inside her mouth, stealing even her breath. One arm secured her back while the other held her chin right where he wanted her.

Her legs dangled over his knee, and if she kicked, she'd only hit air and then the bike on the down swipe. But she didn't think of kicking.

In fact, she stopped thinking the second he released her chin and palmed her breast. Need licked down to her clit. A moan rumbled up from her abdomen, through her chest, and into his mouth.

"Knock it off, you two." Adam's voice jerked her back to the present.

Daire released her mouth, his hand remaining in place.

She panted, her body rioting. A corner of her mind cataloged Adam stomping up wooden steps and shoving his way inside the cabin.

Green eyes pinned her through the darkness. Slowly, deliberately, Daire tweaked her nipple through the thin cotton.

She bit her lip, her brain fuzzing.

He leaned in, pinching with just enough bite to keep her still. "I'm done being played by you, Cee Cee. Agree right now to work with me; no more secrets and no more lies."

She could only blink.

He caressed down and palmed the flesh between her legs. Even through the jeans, his hand heated her. "I can see you need persuading."

"No." She finally regained some sanity. "I've got it."

He paused. "You sure?"

"Yes." There was no doubt he could bring her to orgasm, probably multiple times, and she didn't want to scream with Adam in hearing distance. Yet a part of her, one on fire, almost challenged Daire. How much could one little orgasm hurt? She shook her head. "I'm sure."

"Good." He released her and swung her to the ground. "Let's go inside, and I want your whole damn plan."

Chapter 14

Felicity stumbled after Daire across the wet leaves. A cranky enforcer was no fun. She bit back a smile at her sarcastic thoughts, feeling almost high from his kiss. Even now, her lips tingled and her body ached for more.

And the damn man knew it.

Of course, she hadn't missed his deliberate shifting to ease what had to be rather tight jeans. Take that, witch.

She clomped up three wooden steps, inhaling their cedar scent and walking across the long porch. The smell of cedar continued to fill her nose when she stood inside the quaint cabin. Adam crouched near a fireplace, setting paper on fire with his own energy.

Witches had it cool.

A small kitchenette took up one wall, fronted by a long oak table. A gathering area with bluish green sofas and chairs snuggled cozily around the stone fireplace.

Two doorways led to the north, probably to a bedroom and bathroom.

Papers were scattered across the table, and she inched forward, noticing the red circles around Russian mining interests. She pointed to a mountain near Nijoy. "There's another mine here. Coal, planekite, and supposedly some silver."

Daire glanced at her, grabbed a red pen from the center of the maps, and made a circle. "Owned by Bychkov?"

"No." She rubbed warmth back into her hands, not realizing how chilly it had been on the ride. Her attention had apparently been on the hard body driving the bike. "I've traced the owners through several dummy corporations, but I haven't connected the dots yet."

Daire nodded. "We'll have allies check it out tomorrow."

She shrugged. "Good luck. There's one road in, and it's secured. My plan was to take care of that mine last, and I figured on parachuting in."

Adam stood, dusting off his hands. "Have you ever parachuted?"

"No."

He grinned. "Cool."

Daire rolled his eyes. "Not cool."

Felicity pointed to three more areas across the Russian tundra. "There are mines here, all closely held corporations, but I think they're diamonds and not anything else. My people haven't had the chance to check them out personally."

Daire drew more circles with question marks. "We have more allies than you do in Russia and will take care of it."

"Actually, you don't." She'd spent years gathering allies and favors. When her brother, Suri, had died, she'd quickly confiscated all his Intel. She'd also continued with his allies, having blackmail information on many of them. Once this mission was over, she planned to burn it all. "But go ahead." She moved across the map and tapped on Fryser Island. "We need to get into Sjenerøse mine somehow."

He nodded. "I know. My people will take care of that mission as well as checking out Bychkov's other mine on Fryser."

"Good. That'll free up my people for other work."

"Speaking of which, what's your grand plan?" Daire dropped into a chair and stretched out his legs, his fingers tapping on a closed silver laptop. "You mentioned bombing mines, stealing companies, and robbing banks. What's next?"

She slid out a chair and sat. "Banks."

He eyed her, his green gaze revealing nothing. "Is this all for revenge?"

"Yes." She met his gaze evenly. "Ivan took the father of my boys away from them, and I had to return to hell in order to protect them, which I did a very poor job of doing. This is all about vengeance." Before her sons discovered the truth and put themselves in more danger than ever before. Would the enforcer understand?

"Does Zane have any clue who Ivan is?" Adam asked, leaning against the wall.

"No." She reached for the laptop.

"Zane has impressive forces as well as ironclad allies," Adam said gently, his gaze no less intense than Daire's. "Why not let him wage war?"

"There's been enough war," she spat, her body vibrating. "We finally have peace, and Zane has a one-year-old daughter to protect. All of this is because of me, and I need to take care of the threat." She'd failed her sons enough.

Adam shook his head.

Her gaze focused on Daire, and she lifted an eyebrow.

No expression crossed his chiseled face. "You need this?"

On so many damn levels, she needed this, and she had to protect her kids for once. Daire seemed so close to his cousin, Simone, and that woman was tough and independent. Maybe he could see that side of Felicity, too. Instead of going into details, instead of trying to convince him, all she did was nod. "Yes."

He studied her, a knowing intelligence in his eyes. "All right, but not by yourself." Flipping the laptop around, he pushed it toward her. "Show me your plan to rob banks."

Relief flushed through her, even as her phone buzzed. She winced and pulled it out to answer. "Hi, Logan. I'm fine, and I'm sorry we didn't get a chance to talk tonight."

"Mom? Where the hell are you?" Logan all but yelled. "I'm at Daire's, and the place is trashed."

"I'm on a plane—long gone. Please keep doing your job in Seattle, and I promise I'll be back soon to talk. Also, tell your brothers not to worry, that everything is taken care of." She winced as she lied about her location. "Love you." On those words, she disconnected.

Daire shook his head. "His next move is to call Zane, who will call Vivienne. She doesn't know your plan, so you're all right for now. But I wouldn't be surprised if we meet up with demon forces soon enough."

Felicity nodded. "I know. But even Zane doesn't understand the forces that Ivan has amassed through the years."

"But you do," Daire drawled, his posture relaxed but waves of tension cascading off him.

"I do. For years, even while dealing with Suri, I've watched Ivan and kept track of his every move. I've waited until my boys were safe and the war ended to make my move, and now is the time." She leaned forward. "Ivan is in bed with the witch trying to take down your people, and they both deserve to die."

"Aye." Daire reached over and flipped up the laptop lid. "Show me the plan for the cash."

She booted up the laptop and connected with her online server, bringing up the schematics for the three banks in the Caymans. "Only one of these is owned by shifters; the others are owned by humans. It's funny that immortal species have to use mostly human depositories to keep track of cash and gold, right?"

Daire lifted a shoulder.

Adam loped over and reached the table. "You're not going along with this scheme to rob banks, are you?"

Daire studied her, his gaze serious and then softening. "Hell ya. I've wanted to rob a bank forever."

Felicity smiled. "You're an outlaw."

Adam rolled his eyes. "This isn't the logical thing to do right now, gang."

Daire shrugged. "I don't know. If Ivan and the witch trying to kill us have money stashed away, why not take it? Cripple them internally." He leaned forward. "But as the enforcer now tasked with your protection, Ms. Kyllwood, I can't allow you to be put in that kind of danger. We'll find a safe place for you to issue orders from as we infiltrate the vaults."

Now he followed the Coven Nine orders? Felicity smiled as sweetly as she could. Panic bubbled through her veins. He had to see her. The real her. "I appreciate the concern, but if you want to participate in my plan, you'll knock it off."

Adam coughed. "You want to rob a bank."

She nodded. Frankly, it sounded like fun.

Daire sighed. "Fine, but I'm in charge, and if I tell you to get free and safe, you do it."

Adam shook his head. "You're a freakin' perfect match, you two."

Heat climbed into her face. There was a danger, not quite reckless but close enough, in Daire Dunne that called to her. Were they a good match? He was so complex, sweet and deadly, she wasn't sure. It would take years, probably centuries, to even come close to understanding him.

God, she loved a challenge.

But no more hiding and planning. Now was the time for action. Finally.

A car sputtered outside.

Daire jumped up, already at the door before Felicity could move. He threw it open.

A petite woman with long blond hair half carried a redheaded human. Blood poured out of the man's nose, and flames danced across his neck.

"He's on fire." Daire took the guy and deposited him on the sofa. "How much did he take, Tori?"

Tori? Felicity scrambled for a kitchen towel to wet in the sink and hurried to press it against the guy's neck. He moaned and blood slid from his ears to run in rivulets down his neck. Steam rose with a hiss from the liquid mixing with fire.

The woman stood back, tears in her eyes, shock whitening her pretty face. "I don't know. Bob was outside after our last set, so I brought him here."

"Why here?" Felicity asked, her stomach roiling. Poor guy.

Tori shrugged, panic fluttering her hands. "The hospital doesn't have a cure, and I know you guys are studying the drug. Please tell me there's something you can do."

Adam growled and all but pushed her into a chair. "I put a man on you. Where is he?"

Her blue eyes widened. "I didn't have time to talk to a bodyguard, Adam. Back off."

Irritation, true and sharp, sizzled through his eyes. "Oh, I don't think so."

So, Adam could get emotional. Interesting. Felicity eyed the woman with speculation. Human, definitely enhanced, emitting soft waves. An empath?

Daire lifted the guy's eyelids. Striations of red, yellow, and blue marred the whites of his eyes. Fire shot from his fingertips right at the chair.

Tori yelped, and Adam shoved her entire chair backward, covering her with his body.

Was he keeping her from seeing anything?

Daire pivoted and put Felicity behind him. He held out his hands, and fire crackled across his palms as he crouched. "This might work." Setting his hands on the now convulsing man, Daire allowed fire to spread out over his chest. "Shit. He's on fire inside."

The guy screamed, the sound full of agony.

Felicity took a step back and chills rippled down her spine. She shivered, her eyes wide. The guy convulsed, and blood arced across the room.

"This is Apollo?" she coughed out.

"Aye." Daire sat back, his shoulders slumping as he dropped to his knees. "This is Apollo."

The guy rattled something from his lungs and then went silent. Death hung in the air.

Felicity took another step back. Oh, she'd seen the drug on video and understood and what the concoction did to humans, but she'd had no clue as to the agony. Or the smell. The stench of burned flesh and organs made her cough up bile.

"Who was he?" Daire asked, half turning on his knees.

Adam lifted Tori from the floor, and the woman trembled as she neared the couch. "Bob Bailestorm. He is, I mean was, our bass guitarist." Tears ran down her cheeks. "He was twenty-two years old."

"I'm sorry." Daire stood and wiped a hand across the back of his neck. "Any idea where he got the drug?"

"No." Tori shook her head. "There were a couple of Titans of Fire members in the bar earlier, but I didn't see them do anything."

Daire glanced at Adam. "Since Kellach has been gone, we haven't been involved enough in the club. If this is a new batch of Apollo, then the distribution wasn't shut down like we originally thought."

Adam grimaced. "I'll go to the club meeting tomorrow and check in. It's possible Fire isn't involved, though. There have been different distribution avenues and an odd mix of dealers from the beginning."

Daire shook his head. "I don't understand why, though. The drug has evolved and now can be put into darts to shoot at, ah, our people at home. Why keep feeding the poison to Seattle citizens?"

Felicity lifted her head. So Tori must not know anything about witches, humans, or the true purpose for Apollo.

Adam glanced at Tori and then at the dead guy. "Seattle citizens connected to us in one way or another."

Tori swallowed, her gaze hollow. "Or to the Grizzlies. I mean, that motorcycle club has been involved since the beginning, and I've been dating one. Well, I've gone on a few dates with one."

Adam stiffened. "Excuse me?"

Felicity hid a grin. The *oh so cool* enforcer was quickly losing his cool. "Did Bob have family?"

Tori shook her head and then seemed to focus. "Oh, I'm sorry. I'm Tori, Lex's sister."

Ah ha. Lex, a Seattle cop, had recently mated with Kellach Dunne, and they were currently in Ireland meeting with the Coven Nine about Apollo. Felicity smiled. "Cee Cee Kyllwood."

The woman nodded. "Are you Daire's girlfriend?"

Felicity faltered. Could a century-old demon be a girlfriend? "Ah—"

"Yes." Daire crossed around her and slid an arm over her shoulders. "Cee Cee is in, ah, banking, and she handles my accounts."

Adam snorted.

Tori held out a hand. "Nice to meet you."

Felicity shook. The woman had no idea about the world she'd entered. Interesting. "You too."

Tori's gaze strengthened. "Wait a minute. The prospect? His name is Logan Kyllwood. Is he your brother?"

Brother? "Cousin on my mother's side," Felicity lied smoothly. She cut a hard look at Adam. If they were going to draw humans into their world, they should at least be honest and upfront about everything. Playing the woman for a fool didn't set well with her. "What Grizzly have you been dating?"

"Lucas Clarke," Tori murmured.

"Like a bad boy, do you?" Felicity asked, not missing Adam's sharp look.

Tori nodded. "Always have."

Now that was funny. Adam Dunne was probably as bad as they got, but with his current cover, he seemed rather tame compared to Lucas. Man, could appearances be deceiving.

Tori ran an obviously shaking hand through her thick curls. "I guess we need to call the police?" She turned toward Adam. "Your people are working with the local authorities, right?"

Felicity kept quiet. What exactly were their covers, anyway?

"Aye." Daire reached for a blanket to place over the corpse. "If you don't mind, I'd like to take care of the situation and not deal with the local cops, especially since your sister is in Ireland. Alexandra is the only local cop I like or trust."

Felicity moved forward. "Are you sure Bob didn't have family?" No way would she let the enforcers cover up his death if he had family out there looking for him.

Tori nodded. "I'm sure. His only living relative was his great-uncle, who died last year from a heart attack. Bob was alone."

Poor Bob. He'd looked so young and frightened in the last moments of life.

"We'll take care of him," Daire said. "Right now, Adam is going to escort you home."

Tori nodded, her lips trembling. "That's fine, but at some point, you all are going to have to level with me, Dunne."

Daire stilled. "Excuse me?"

Tori's eyes flashed all sorts of blue fire. "I'm neither naive nor stupid, but I've been waiting for my sister to get home to discover the facts. If she's not here soon, one of you is going to bring me up to speed. Like it or not." She turned on a high-heeled boot and stomped out into the night.

So much for the cute and clueless human. Felicity grinned. "I like her."

"You would," Adam retorted as he followed the human and shut the door.

Chapter 15

Daire returned to the cabin after burying Bob's body beneath an outcropping of rocks far away from the river. Burying bodies too near a moving stream only ended with their being found miles away. His gut hurt and his head ached from failure. For months he'd been chasing the distributors and manufacturer of Apollo, and he'd only shut down one main distributor, Yuri Demidov, who currently was decomposing under dirt without his head.

The river gurgled behind him, and the sweet scent of pine surround him, but his mind refused to relax. So he took time and several deep breaths to calm himself as he strode across damp earth, letting the silence finally seep in. The cabin came into view, and his heart kicked back into gear.

Setting the shovel by the front door, he stomped mud off his boots and walked inside.

The spicy scent of simmering pasta sauce stopped him cold. Felicity turned from stirring something delicious smelling in a pot, her feet bare, a faded yellow apron hugging her kick-ass body. "Hungry?"

She'd made him dinner? He staggered inside and toed off his boots. The hominess of the scene dug right into his heart and settled deep. "Aye."

"Good." She pointed to the table, which she'd set with matching plates. A bottle of Cabernet breathed next to two wineglasses. "Pour the wine, would you?"

He shook his head, his chest warming. "Sure." First he went to the sink and washed off the dirt and death. It was probably a sad state of affairs that he could bury a body without mussing his clothing, but his jeans and shirt were as clean as when he'd left. Leaning over, trying to concentrate, he poured two generous glasses. "Where did you find enough food to make dinner?"

She laughed and turned to dump pasta on their plates. "I didn't find much. No salad or bread to go with the pasta. But there were enough spices to make an interesting sauce." After setting the pot back on the stove, she drew the apron over her head and turned to take a seat. "I also found a bottle of Rémy Martin Cognac hidden under the kitchen sink behind cleansers, mousetraps, and sponges."

Daire's mouth dropped open, and laughter burst from his chest. "That's where Adam hid it? Dumbass." He'd spent a good afternoon one day trying to find Adam's stash. "And you cooked with it?"

"Just some of it." She smiled and set her napkin on her lap.

Daire grinned. "Nicely done." Aye, he understood she was a mother and probably had fed families many times, but he hadn't really seen the domestic side of her before that night. Oddly enough, this side was as appealing as her daredevil and vengeance-seeking sides. In fact, her domesticity made his belly warm, his heart heat, and his cock stretch. Her brain, her ability to strategize, was fucking brilliant, if her plan to rob a couple of the most fortified banks in the world was any indication. He could've used her abilities during the war.

Yet her motivations were personal, and emotion clouded missions and got people killed. One of the banks was owned by a coalition of shifters, so surely they'd have immortal weapons and guards.

The mission was more dangerous than just dealing with a few human security guards.

Shifters didn't mess around, and anybody trying to breach their security would be dealt with swiftly and without mercy. Which was exactly how he'd run a bank if he owned one, actually.

"Your looks are very deceiving," he murmured, taking a taste of the meal and humming in appreciation.

"I know," she mused, swirling her wine around in her glass. "People think I'm small and helpless, or cunning and ruthless. No middle ground."

Aye, beauty had a price, yet she seemed more factual than worried about it. "Who knew that you're a ruthless sweetheart with a penchant for trouble?"

She lifted her head. "Trouble?"

He cocked his head to the side in a *come on* gesture.

She dismissed him and picked up her fork. "One little helicopter accident doesn't equal trouble."

Ha.

"I hadn't seen the results of Apollo up close before." She took a bite and chewed slowly, her eyes dark. "It was horrible."

"Aye."

"Does the drug really have the same effect on witches?"

He nodded, his shoulders tensing. "Aye."

She shook her head. "That's terrible." Her hands, pale and graceful, were clasped together. "The witch working with Ivan is called Rudger."

Daire stilled. "You're giving me his name?"

"Aye," she mimicked his brogue. "I've been selfish in my pursuit of justice and hadn't thought of anybody but my own family. Rudger is just a nickname, but it's a start for you."

Damn, but her sweetness pretty much flayed him. "Thank you." He drew out his phone and sent the information to his brothers and the Coven Nine.

"You're welcome. I think his partnership with Bychkov started just as Apollo was created, so it's only been a year or so. Before that time, there was no record of Bychkov and any witch working together." She leaned forward on the table, the movement pushing her breasts together. "The witch brought capital, and several of the mines started up again."

Daire continued eating. "I appreciate the help."

"Of course." She ate several bites. "Tell me about your brothers."

Daire paused and then reached for his wineglass. Small talk? He sucked at pleasantries. "Ah, Kellach is the wild one, Adam the logical one, and I'm the cranky one. I give orders and people follow them." Or he cut off their heads. He smiled. "Everyone but you, of course."

"I don't follow orders well."

"No shit."

She cleared her throat. "Your parents?" she asked, sipping her wine.

"Retired and currently working on the food crops in Ireland. Both scientists." He poured them both more wine. "I think they're still stunned they gave birth to the three of us."

She chuckled, the sound flicking across his nerve endings. "I'm sure. What about Simone?"

Most people were curious about the stunning witch. "Her mother is Vivienne Northcutt, and nobody has ever known who her father is. So when she was little, the three of us kind of enfolded her into the family." He rubbed his chin. "Viv was often busy, and Simone was lonely, so she became ours."

"You love her," Felicity said slowly.

"Aye. She's more of a sister." He'd failed her once, long ago, and he'd never do so again. "I'd do anything for her. We all would."

Felicity sighed. "Family man."

He grinned. "Exactly."

They ate in silence for a while. Oh. Maybe he should ask questions, too. "Tell me about your boys."

Her eyes lit up. "Zane is the oldest, as you know, and is now the leader of the demon nation. As a boy, he was so serious and determined to protect us." She glanced down. "I failed him."

Daire reached out and patted her hand. "No, you didn't. You did what you had to do to protect him from Ivan."

"I know." She swallowed. "But I didn't realize how bad it would be with my brother, or how hard he'd train the boys." She sighed and visibly shuddered, as if shrugging off the past. "Sam is the middle kid, and he acts like it. Is a total peacemaker with more patience than a saint."

"Sounds like a good kid."

"He is, until he isn't." Felicity took a healthy swallow of wine. "When his temper goes, it's legendary."

Daire snorted. "Adam is like that." When Adam really blew his fuse, they all got out of the way. "And Logan, the massive beast who's been eating me out of house and home, is your baby."

She set her napkin on the plate. "Yes. He's a sweetie, right?"

Ah, no. The kid was cunning, dangerous, and deadly. But he couldn't organize worth crap. "Aye. He's a nice kid." In fact, Daire liked him, a lot. Were he and Cee Cee getting close? He liked her, and she liked him, so what the hell. Secrets and lies were behind them, and maybe, just maybe, after they shut down Apollo, he might court her. A long courtship with lots of fun for them both.

She stood and grabbed the plates.

He fumbled. "I'll, ah—"

"Go sit down." She set down the plates and turned to hand him the cognac and a crystal glass. "When I make dinner, I like to clean up to finish the entire act. Please."

If the woman wanted to be all domesticated and take care of him, he was totally on board. "I sure like this side of you."

She lifted an eyebrow. "This side?"

"Aye. As opposed to the side that drugs me and gets me shot." He turned and banked the fire before dropping into a chair and stretching out his legs.

She hummed as she cleaned up the kitchen, and a coziness filled the room. Finally, she crossed near him. "Family is family, Daire." Her words held a hint of warning and a thread of sadness.

His instincts started to hum. He tipped back the cognac and set the drink aside. "What are you up to, Cee Cee?"

She smiled, the sight slightly lopsided. "Nothing for once. Just that I'm glad we're working together. I'll send you the file I have on Rudger. I hope it helps." She sauntered over and poured him another glass of the cognac. "I should've given you the name earlier."

His ears pricked. Numbness settled in his belly and spread out to be quickly quashed. Temper swirled through him and then blew out in heat. "Son of a bitch." He jumped to his feet and grabbed her forearms. "You drugged me. Again."

She winced. "I know. I'm sorry."

His knees wobbled.

She shoved him back into his chair. "I really like you, Daire. I do."

He tilted his head to the side, noting the rapid pulse in her neck. "What the fuck?"

She sighed. "I just put a little in the drink, I promise. You won't be out for long."

He wouldn't be out at all, actually. "Where the hell was it?" he ground out, trying to focus as his vision fuzzed.

"I've had a vial in my boot. Figured I might need it."

His hold loosened on her arms.

She set his hands down and patted his knuckles. "Like I said, I'm so sorry. But there's no reason for you to accompany me on the mission since you now have Rudger's name and should probably run him down. Believe me, you don't want the conflict of interest."

What conflict of interest? Daire frowned as he sent antibodies to the poison in his gut. None of this was making sense, but he needed his faculties to cure himself before she got outside. She turned and quickly made her way to the door and opened it. Rain splashed inside.

He'd been so ensconced in the sense of comfy domestication, he hadn't even noticed it had started raining. Man, a woman cooked for him once, and he turned into a moron.

He shoved himself to his feet. "Felicity."

She slowly turned around, her eyes widening. "Wh-what?"

"You should probably know something about witches," he said, his legs strengthening.

Her chin lifted and her hand went to the doorknob. "What is that?"

"We can create antibodies for a drug if we survive the first injection," he said, gauging the distance between them and her ability to kick him in the face. "It's a gift we're hoping will be useful in dealing with Apollo."

She swallowed. "Well, crap." Quick as any cougar, she pivoted and ran into the rain.

He smiled, his muscles bunching. Oh, the race was on. He cleared the front porch without hitting one step and landed in the mud, his boots spraying. Rain mashed down, coating his face. A blur of white crossed his vision toward the river, and he turned to follow. With that blond hair, she'd be easy to spot. His blood thrummed in his veins, and his breath evened out.

The rain carried her scent toward him—woman and hyacinth. Even through the storm, he could smell her clean scent tinged with both fear and arousal. He loped into a jog, winding around trees, avoiding stumps. Every inch of the property was familiar to him, and he wasn't surprised when she found the barely there trail to the river's edge.

He reached the bank in time to see her bounding across the massive rocks he'd placed in the middle. The rain matted her hair down her back, but she fought against the wind and reached the rocky shore, as graceful as any doe. Her soaked clothing clung to her, showing every inch of her spectacular body.

The drug tried to cling to his system, and he burned it away, temper alighting anew. She had drugged him after making him such a nice dinner and getting him to relax. The idea that she still didn't trust him bunched his fingers into a fist, and he ducked his head as he ran for the rocks and made it across the rushing river in record time.

Small footprints showed her way, but he didn't need to glance down, so strong was her scent. Or maybe he just recognized her smell, because he knew exactly which way to run.

Lightning flashed across the dark sky. Unlike his brother Kellach, Daire loved the rain of Seattle and enjoyed the storms. It pounded in his blood, spurring him on.

Ahead of him, she slipped and scrambled to her feet, her arms flailing. Tree limbs fell down and she ducked to avoid them.

Enough. The storm had turned dangerous, and it was time to catch her. So he turned to the north and backtracked along the trail, ready for the moment when she barreled into his arms.

She bounced back, her eyes wide, her cheeks flushed.

He bent his head, absolute on his task this time. "Why did you drug me yet again?"

She gulped in air, her pale hand wiping rain from her face. "I don't need help with the bank robberies."

"Try again." He crossed his arms, raising his voice above the storm.

She settled her stance. The wind whipped around, shoving her hair, no match for the wildness in her eyes. "No."

He wanted that wildness, needed it set free and alive around him. Nothing in him, not one inch, wanted to tame that. He just wanted to ride it, be a part of it. "Why?" he asked.

Drops of rain danced on her full eyelashes. "I don't like you."

He grinned. Wild as hell and a shitty liar. "Aye, you do. Tell me the truth, Felicity."

Her slight turn of foot gave away her intention, so when she turned to run, he smoothly stepped in front of her. She smacked into him again, and this time, he didn't let her go.

Grabbing her biceps, he lifted her a foot off the ground and set her against a massive pine tree. The brand on his hand pulsed in angry pain. His brother had mated his cop out in the forest by the cabin, and Daire kept in mind the warning. He wouldn't mate Felicity by accident, and he'd have to be careful. But the woman had pushed him enough.

He planted his mouth over hers and swept his tongue inside, taking what he wanted. Sensations bombarded him, stronger than before. Hunger. Need. Craving. Possessiveness. Protectiveness. He consumed her, feasting at her mouth like a starving man.

She returned the kiss, nipping and licking, her tongue playing with his.

The flavor of wine and woman exploded on his taste buds and rocketed through his body. He shoved his groin between her legs, rubbing against her. She gasped and reached down to unzip his jeans, sliding her hand inside.

Her smooth skin almost sent him over the edge. He groaned into her mouth. She stroked him and he growled, reaching down to shove her pants to the ground. When freed, she immediately clasped his shoulders and wrapped her legs around his waist.

He kicked out of his jeans, needing more than anything else in the world to be inside her. He grabbed her nape and her butt, plunging inside her with one ferocious thrust. She arched against him, a hoarse cry of need echoing from her throat. Her nails bit into his skin, and the sharp pain almost snapped his control. He was right where he wanted to be in the world, and suddenly, the fog cleared from his brain. This woman was meant to be his, and it was time she leveled with him.

Drawing on control he hadn't thought he'd have, he held her tight and stopped moving. "Now you talk, Felicity."

Chapter 16

Felicity blinked, her body gyrating with a hunger so great it hurt. The tree bracketed her back, surrounding her with the scent of pine. Rain dripped down around them, plopping on the wet earth. "What?" she breathed, trying to get Daire to move inside her again.

He leaned down, and his breath heated her face. "Now you tell me why you drugged me yet again. What are you afraid of?"

She shook her head, spraying water. "I'm not afraid. I just don't want you in the way." Even as she said the words, she could hear the hollowness in them. "Trust me, Daire. You want to be out of what's going to happen." She had to protect him, somehow. "I'm sorry."

He slid out and shoved back in, sending spirals of sparks through her sex. "You're all logic and wild passion, baby. So the smart thing, the logical thing, would be for you to accept help and allies robbing those banks." Two more hard thrusts.

Her mouth opened in a silent groan.

"I've promised not to alert your kids, and yet, you still try to drug me." His hand on her butt tightened and then released her. Slowly, keeping her attention, he lifted his palm to show the Celtic knot.

She gasped. The branding mark? The witch branding mark? Her core convulsed around his shaft at the very thought of mating the sexy enforcer.

He lifted an eyebrow. "You like that idea."

Her body did, anyway. "Now isn't the time for a discussion, Daire," she panted out, trying to rub against him.

The hand at her nape clenched, and she winced. "Listen, Cee Cee. Stop moving, or I'll plant my hand on your ass to keep you still."

If he did, and if he kept thrusting, then he'd only have to bite her to mate her. She stopped moving. "Talk later," she ground out.

"Oh no, baby," he murmured, his nostrils flaring and making him look like a deadly predator on the hunt. "You're going to tell me right now why you're leaving me and going off alone to danger. It doesn't make sense."

She was leaving him because if she gave him the truth, it would force him to choose between her and his family, and he wouldn't choose her. Which she totally understood. "This is just sex."

"That's it." He lifted his hand, and green fire danced across his palm.

She sucked in her stomach, and mini-orgasms rippled through her body. "No."

"Oh yeah." He lowered his palm across her chest, and her shirt caught on fire, burning away to embers without harming her. Then he scraped the fire across her breasts, and fire bit into her with an erotic burn.

She cried out and arched against him, needing just a little more friction. Her nipples turned a bright pink and harder than diamonds, their sharp points jutting out. He tweaked one, and she bent into his fingers, the pleasurable pain fuzzing her brain. He turned to the other nipple, tweaking and pinching, finally caressing fire across it.

She tried to rub against him to find relief, but he pressed her too tightly against the tree.

His lips dropped to her ear. "Wanna tell me now?"

Everything in her wanted to give him what he wanted so she could find relief. "No," she almost sobbed.

"Fair enough."

Fire crackled near her face, and she jumped. He warmed down her side, along each rib, and then partially slid out of her.

Panic careened through her. "No."

"Aye." He reached between them.

So she did the only thing she could. She grabbed on to his hair and thrust her sex right into the fire. Sparks flew, and she detonated. The orgasm shook her with powerful jerks, shooting so much edgy heat through her she could only close her eyes and feel. Her core rippled around his cock, holding with a fierce grip.

He groaned and started to hammer into her, clasping her tight, his body rocking hers. Finally, with a moan, he stilled and dropped his head to her neck.

She slid her arms around his shoulders, holding on for dear life. Her breath panted out against his rapidly moving chest. Slowly, reality returned. Rain dripped down and across her face. She opened her eyes and blinked. The chilly wind caressed her wet shoulders, and bark from the tree scratched her butt.

Daire leaned back, his eyes the dark green of a mountain stream. Without a word, he released her to slide down him, and waited until she'd regained her footing before jerking up her yoga pants and his jeans. His gaze intent, he drew his shirt over his head and then tugged it over her.

She shivered in the wet cotton. Vulnerability and uncertainty stilled any words in her throat.

He ducked his head, and suddenly her stomach hit his shoulder. She coughed out, upside down over the enforcer. "Hey."

Turning on one thick boot, he jogged back through the forest.

She shook her head, trying not to get dizzy. "Daire? Put me down." The blood rushed to her face, and she reached out to smack his butt.

He planted one hand gently on her rear end, flattening his fingers in clear warning before turning to nip at her thigh.

She stilled, her head slightly swinging. Water splashed as he gracefully jumped from one rock to the next while crossing the rushing river. The man carried her as if she didn't weigh a damn thing. She thought of kicking him a good one in the stomach, but if he fell, so would she. Not that he'd fall. Even so, the hand heating her ass by a simple touch remained in place, and those teeth were too close to her vulnerable flesh.

They reached the cabin and crossed inside. Instant warmth soothed over her, and she fought a soft moan. He stalked into a bedroom with a red and silver rug on the floor. The quilted bedspread had matching colors in a comfy country look. The room tilted. He set her down on her feet, holding her forearms until she'd regained her balance.

Quick movements on his part had clothing tossed out of drawers. She scrambled out of the wet clothes and into a dry yoga outfit with dark pants and a light blue shirt. Yet more clothing borrowed from Simone Brightston. The warmth eased Felicity's shivers, and she rubbed her arms to banish the goose bumps.

Finally, he faced her, his body planted directly between her and the door. "Why did you drug me, Felicity?"

Ivan Bychkov paced his office, staring out at the Seattle skyline in a downtown commercial building. The floor was oak, the walls textured, and the furnishings modern. "That bitch." Fire roared through him, and for once, he wished he could throw flames like a witch. A bar was set against the far wall, and he eyed the Scotch in the crystal decanter.

Rudger chuckled, seated on a tight leather guest chair across the sprawling desk. "She is innovative."

Ivan spun around to face his partner, his shoes squeaking on the wooden floor. "Innovative? The sociopath had twelve of our mines blown up. Twelve." At least four of them would never be operational again. "When we created our partnership, I figured you'd do a better job with security."

Rudger's fingers tapped against the arm of his chair. "My brother is checking out the security right now, and since Sjenerøse mine is still operational, we're putting additional forces there. It has enough planekite to suit our immediate needs."

What had he been thinking, getting involved with witches? Ivan shook his head. "This was a mistake."

Rudger shrugged. "Not my problem."

Ivan lowered his chin and studied the witch. Black hair, blue eyes, about four centuries old, Rudger had provided needed capital in exchange for ownership in the planekite mines. "I don't think you're quite understanding the issue here," Ivan ground out, fighting the incredible urge to melt the asshole's brain in his head. "All of my mines except for Sjenerøse were attacked, including the coal and diamond mines. My people are going to be furious." Not only were the mines affected, but several of his stock portfolios were facing attack. Felicity had used the last thirty years well, preparing to take him down.

Rudger shrugged. "Again, not my problem. Besides, we have enough cash and gold stashed around the world, don't we?"

Yes, but only half of that belonged to Ivan and his people. "We had an agreement that I wouldn't ask why you're creating a drug that will harm your own people." Damn witches never made sense.

"Yes, so stick with it." Rudger stood.

Ivan smiled. "I've kept to our agreement and haven't asked."

The witch stilled, his eyes flashing a lighter blue. "Good."

"Yet my investigators have turned up a bit of information on you and why you're after the Coven Nine." The sizzle of upcoming negotiation straightened Ivan's spine, which made him tower at least five inches over the six-foot-one witch.

"Is that a fact?" Rudger drawled.

"Yes." Ivan gathered energy in case he needed to demolish the man, although that would just bring Rudger's twin brother running, and that guy was psycho. "Turns out your mother was kicked off the Council of the Coven Nine . . . decades ago. In fact, I believe her ass was kicked in battle by one of the Dunnes." Turned out Moira Dunne, cousin to the male enforcers, had taken out Grace Sadler in order to place her sister on the council. Witches always went for family.

Fire crackled down Rudger's arms. "Believe me. That fact is only one of several that went into our decision."

"Ah, but what's your end game?" Ivan braced for a ball of fire, just in case. He really did want to know.

"None of your business." Rudger shook his head. "Watch yourself, demon."

Ivan clasped his hands at his back. "I'm thinking this would be a good time to renegotiate ownership of real property as well as intangible. I mean, if you want me to stop the e-mail headed to the Coven Nine right now."

The fireplace came out of nowhere, hit his chest, and threw him into the wall. Pain radiated and burrowed deep. Sucking in air, he ducked his head and aimed devastating images and pain at Rudger's frontal cortex. The impact jerked the witch's head back. He hissed and tried to gather more fire in his palms.

Ivan narrowed his gaze and pinpointed raw agony to the center of Rudger's brain with the finesse of any surgeon with a blade. The witch cried out, slapping both hands to his temples.

Almost casually keeping up the assault, Ivan reached into his drawer for a dagger. Ancient and jeweled with diamonds from his mines, the blade had been sharpened to a deadly glint. He crossed around the desk, his body shaking from the fight, and reached his enemy.

"M-my brother will kill you," Rudger gasped out.

Ivan smiled. He was a two-century-old demon, with immeasurable power. How had the witches ever even thought they were on the same footing? Immature idiots. "Your brother is the least of my worries." He had enforcers and a pissed-off demon on his ass, not to mention his angry people. They were a greedy bunch of bastards, and the fact that he'd lost billions of their money was setting rumblings through the group. "I'll take care of him when he shows up." Or he'd have his right-hand man, Vadim, take care of Phillipe. Vadim hadn't killed anybody in at least a month, and that made him edgy.

With a graceful arc, Ivan plunged the knife into the witch's throat and then twisted.

Fire burned up his arm.

He bit back a curse and finished slicing through the last bit of cartilage. Rudger's head rolled off his body and under the desk.

The smell of blood and burned flesh filled the room. A truly grotesque scent. Ivan wiped the bloody knife on the headless corpse. "Millicent?" he called out.

His secretary, a mousy demon with dirty blond hair and oddly fat thighs, lumbered inside. "Yes, sir?"

"Clean this up."

Daire crossed his arms over his chest, facing inside the cabin's cozy bedroom and blocking the way out. He didn't give one shit whether or not he looked intimidating. He was finished handling Cee Cee with kid gloves, and he was done trying to hold on to patience. He'd never had any, and trying to find some with her had only backfired. So the woman could just get used to the real him, cranky bastard or not. "Talk."

She backed away until her thighs hit the bed.

After their jaunt in the forest, her eyes glowed with bright contentment, and a flush covered her fine cheekbones. All of her glorious hair cascaded down her back, drying slowly. Her hand trembled as she reached for the bed and sat, scooting back until her shoulders rested against the headboard. "You don't want to know. Just trust me."

He barked out a laugh. "Trust you? No dice. Try again." While he kept his voice hard, he had to appreciate her gumption. Even now, she was trying to play him, which wasn't easy and definitely took balls. "We're not moving until you talk."

She eyed his body, the door, and the rest of the room.

He grinned. "We can fight first, but I don't play fair, baby." His legs tensed with the anticipation of a good tackle.

She rolled her eyes. "I've already kicked you in the head, and apparently there's nothing in there. The kick didn't knock one semblance of sense into you."

Warmth rolled through his chest. Spunky and cute, wasn't she? "I do have a hard head." As did she. In fact, he hadn't met anybody more stubborn than the little demon. But the woman had a heart, and he could get to it. Though she tried to hide her soft side, she wasn't very good at it. "You're hurting my feelings by not trusting me."

Her eyelashes fluttered, and she studied him, her fingers picking at the bedspread. "I'm trying to protect you from having to make impossible choices, you big oaf."

"How sweet," he drawled. "How about you let the big, bad enforcer protect himself?" And her. Whether she liked it or not.

She shook her head. "Go away."

"Nope." He let loose his brogue. "Not garna happen. You have a choice here. Either start talking, or I'll see if you're ticklish."

Her eyes widened, and she wrapped her arms around her legs. "You're joking. The big, bad enforcer tickles for information?"

He slowly nodded, enjoying her discomfort. Yeah, he'd thought she was ticklish after sleeping with her in the tent. When his foot had rubbed the bottom of hers, she'd nearly jumped out of the sleeping bag. Was that only a couple of days ago? "I often tickle for data, and by the panic in your eyes, I'm thinking I'd get what I want."

She swallowed and didn't move.

"All right." He prowled toward her, keeping his movements slow. Where to start? Feet or ribs? He liked her ribs. Then he put one knee on the bed.

"Wait." She held out a hand. "Fine."

He bit back another grin. She must be incredibly ticklish, and boy, was he going to explore that later. "Well?"

She drew in a deep breath and then exhaled, dark regret filling her eyes. "Fine, but I warned you. One of the banks I'm planning to rob holds evidence against Simone Brightston, the woman you love as a sister. She's involved with Bychkov and Rudger, and she owns two of the mines currently supplying planekite to the manufacturer of Apollo."

Chapter 17

Fire crackled and spread warmth across the cabin's main room. Felicity sat at the long table and moved from the maps to the laptop, quickly accessing her online storage server. "I'm sorry, but I've looked at the documents I could find, and I've traced the original incorporation documents to the bank in the Caymans."

Daire shook his head, no warmth in his gaze. "Impossible."

She shivered, not realizing until right that second how heated he'd been with her. "It's true. Simone initially signed on to a limited liability corporation with Trevan Demidov, another witch, and when he died, his son took over. It's called Triad Financing, and it owns the land that contains the mines owned by Ivan."

Daire frowned. "Ivan doesn't own the land?"

"No. He, or rather, his people control the mineral rights and several easements to bring material in and out. He actually does not own the property." The arrangement was fairly normal, even in the Pacific Northwest with silver mines.

Daire relaxed. "Trevan was Simone's lover, and he used her to go after our family. He died decades ago, and his son died very recently."

"I figured." There hadn't been any activity in Yuri Demidov's accounts for the last week, and considering his connection to the planekite mines, she'd figured the enforcers had taken him down. "Did you kill him?"

"No. Kellach did." Daire leaned back. "So any connection Simone had with Demidov ended years ago, and she must've forgotten about the corporation."

Felicity's stomach cramped. "The corporation has gone through several restructurings, and one time, Simone was even out of the documents. But she joined back in about five years ago and has been an integral part of moving property." She swallowed. "The connection of Triad to the planekite mines was difficult to find, but I've had years to plan and study Bychkov. He's in bed with a witch, and they're going after the Coven Nine, I believe."

Daire shook his head. "Simone wouldn't ever do that."

Felicity sighed. "Are you sure?"

"Yes." His face darkened. "For years, she got involved with one bad choice after another, but that's over."

No, it wasn't. Ivan was handsome and charming, and even though Simone was a tough bitch, Felicity had studied her from afar. The woman had a gooey center and was looking for love. "You might be blind where family is concerned."

"I am not." He crossed his arms, muscles flexing. "Simone doesn't know anything about Triad, and her involvement stopped when Trevan Demidov died."

Felicity twirled the laptop so he could see the screen. "Simone made a series of bank transfers a week ago, and here's her signature."

Daire leaned over, his expression revealing nothing. Yet his jaw clenched. "That's her signature, but it was just to transfer money."

Felicity swallowed, trying not to throw up as she reclaimed the laptop and typed in keys. "And here?"

He crossed around to read over her shoulder. "Aye. That's her signature."

"This was on a shipping manifest from Russia to Seattle that should arrive any day." Keys clacked as she typed in an order, and the manifest came up in full view. "This is one of the five shipments from planekite mines, and the manifest states that it is mining materials and minerals to be studied at the University of Washington."

Daire moved away, taking his heat with him. A clank of crystal on crystal echoed behind her. "Tell me you didn't drug all of the cognac," he muttered.

She stiffened. "No. Just your glass."

"Good." Swirling a snifter, he prowled toward the fireplace. "Simone would never bring planekite into the country, and she'd never betray her family or her people. There's no reason."

An extremely strong urge to bang her head on the table made Felicity clench her teeth. "There's a movement, a strong one, to remove Simone from the Coven Nine."

The line of Daire's back tensed. "Bullshit."

"I'm sorry," Felicity whispered. "Simone has been in the States for too long and has made it apparent she doesn't want to return to Dublin. She has a history of affairs with bad men, enemies of the Coven Nine, and she no longer is representative of the mild council. You know they're trying to redo their image into wholesome and kind."

He jerked around. "Simone is both wholesome and kind."

"Simone is perceived as a wild woman with terrible taste in men. There's a demon in her past, and while I think that should be a mark in her favor, apparently it is not with your people." Felicity sat back, wanting to offer comfort but knowing better.

Daire growled. "Simone's affair with Nicholai Veis happened a century ago."

"Right. Then she took up with a few renegades, a couple of mercenaries, and finally Trevan Demidov, the guy who wanted to take down the Realm." Felicity winced. "I believe she also dated Dage Kayrs, the king of the Realm?"

Anger flushed across Daire's rugged face. "So?"

"So? Considering the Realm has now aligned itself with the main demon nation, pissing them off is a bad idea. Having any awkwardness at functions is a bad idea, and you freakin' witches love functions and balls and stuff like that."

She drummed her fingers on the tabletop. "The movement is gaining force, and even her mother won't be able to keep her from being challenged. Tell me, Daire. When was the last time Simone actively fought another witch?"

He jerked his head. "She doesn't fight. I do."

Felicity bit her lip. "Right. But if she's challenged, she either has to fight, or she has to step down. Would she win a fight?"

He didn't answer.

"I didn't think so." She didn't want to finish this conversation. "If Simone found out she was about to be ousted from the Coven Nine, her entire existence and sense of purpose, what would she do?"

Daire swigged back the remainder of the cognac. "She wouldna' do this."

Felicity shook her head. "You're being blind, and as an enforcer, you have a duty to report any threat to the Coven Nine." Which was exactly why she'd tried to drug him and go rob banks on her own.

He wiped off his bottom lip. "You're wrong, and I'm going to prove it." Grabbing his phone off the table, he quickly dialed. His nostrils flared. "Simone? Call me when you get this message." He shoved the phone in his pocket. "Looks like we're off to rob the Cayman bank first, baby, so I can get my hands on those papers that show Simone's trail."

"You think it's possible Simone is involved?"

"Hell, no. But I'll need the papers to save her ass, if somebody is setting her up. Pack a bag, and get ready to be a Bonnie to my Clyde."

Daire settled himself into the leather seat, forcing his fingers to remain uncurled on the armrest as the private airplane rose into the air. He'd hated flying even before crashing into the Arctic, and now he knew how quickly metal plummeted from the sky.

This plane was a rental and probably hadn't even been checked out properly. Even the chairs, six in all, were sprawled around the cabin in an odd configuration he couldn't quite figure out. Yet the pilots were his—a couple of witches the Coven Nine kept on retainer, and boy, could they fly. Thank the gods.

Felicity reached over and patted his hand, hers several shades lighter and far more delicate. What was he thinking, taking her away from safety in Seattle? Her kindness warmed his chest as she tried to offer comfort.

Adam loped in from the cockpit, eating a ham sandwich. He wore long dark slacks with a button-down shirt, looking more like a paid assassin than ever. His eyes were serious, and his jaw hard. "I swear, if Alexandra doesn't take care of the issue of a bear shifter dating her younger sister, I will."

Felicity sat back and released Daire. "Tori seemed to be in her mid-twenties and more than able to choose her own dates."

Adam muttered a bunch of somethings about shifters being lower than dung as he dropped into a chair.

Daire barely caught Felicity's quick grin before she smoothed her pretty lips into a straight line. The woman was just messing with Adam. Brave girl. She opened her mouth to say something that would probably put Adam over the edge, so Daire leaned over and yanked her hair.

Her expression was priceless. "Did you just pull my hair?"

Man, he loved when she got all regal and royal on him. "Aye."

She turned all sorts of crimson, clearly searching for something to say. "I thought you'd be mad at me."

"Nope. You're wrong about Simone, but your research was good." His body relaxed as the plane leveled off. "Protecting me for my own good was a bad idea, and I hope to hell you don't try that one again. In fact, I strongly recommend you don't."

Adam finished off his sandwich. "You two going to fight?"

"No." Daire released his seat belt and stretched to his full height. "I have a phone call to make, and you two need to play nice while I'm gone."

Adam's brow wrinkled, and Felicity's lips smoothed into an innocent smile.

Oh man. Daire shook his head, fought the urge to pull her hair again, and stalked toward the cockpit. A console desk was located to the left of the two witches flying the plane. He gave a head jerk to the co-pilot before sitting at the desk, turning on the monitor and dialing a call. As the call went through space, he drew headphones down over his ears and positioned the microphone closer to his mouth.

Vivienne Northcutt took shape before him. She'd pulled her dark hair back in a ponytail that could've been softened with some escaping curls. But not Aunt Viv. No curls and no softness. Dark red lipstick slashed across her mouth, and deep coal made up her dark eyes.

She was a looker, but a severe one.

"Aunt Viv," he murmured.

She leaned toward the camera, her lips pursed. "I've heard a rumor you've become intimate with the demonness."

He blinked slowly. "My personal life is irrelevant."

Viv waved perfectly manicured nails. "Don't be ridiculous. A mating between a Coven enforcer and the mother of the demon leader would be very advantageous for us. Talk about allies that remain allies." Her eyes widened. "If you procreated, that'd be even better."

"Then I'd better go fuck her silly," he ground out before he could stop himself.

Viv paused and then rolled her eyes. "For goodness' sake. Political matings have taken place for eons, and often they're the ones where people seem to be the happiest. Stop being such a wimp."

His shoulders went back. "Watch it, Auntie, or I'll come up with an imminent threat and have to shut you down somewhere safe." For an eternity.

She sighed, and quite possibly mouthed the word *pussy*, but he must have misread her. "Fine. Update me on the situation in Seattle."

He gave a quick rundown of the recent human deaths as well as the known five shipments headed for Seattle. "No more attacks on witches that we know about." The previous week, somebody had fired darts of Apollo into several witches in the area, who had died torturous deaths. "We think Titans of Fire is still distributing Apollo, and we intercepted an e-mail message about a week ago, but it was routed through several different servers all over the world, and we can't trace the source."

"Who was the message meant for?" Viv asked.

"Parker Monzelle. We took his phone when he was arrested again."

Viv sat back. "I'm surprised that human is still alive, considering."

Aye. Monzelle was actually Alexandra and Tori's father, and he'd shot Alexandra not too long ago. The police had taken him away before Kellach could rip out his heart, and Daire wouldn't be surprised if Kell still had a plan to rid his mate of Monzelle forever. "For now, Aunt Viv, Kellach is the closest to the leaders of the Titan's of Fire MC, and he's still in Dublin."

Viv nodded. "Your point is well taken. I will send Kell and Alexandra back to Seattle tomorrow."

Daire lifted an eyebrow. "Alexandra works for the Seattle Police Department, not the Coven Nine."

Viv shrugged. "She's mated to Kellach, which means she does work for us now. Or she will in a century or so, since she can't very well stay in Seattle as the fact that she's not aging becomes apparent."

She pursed her lips. "I like Alexandra, quite a bit, although she doesn't seem taken with the idea of being immortal."

Daire grinned. His brother's mate was a paradox, to be sure. When a human mated a witch, the mating increased the human's chromosomal pairs, leaving the mate immortal. Alexandra hadn't quite wrapped her mind around that reality. "Aunt Viv, is there a movement to remove your daughter from the Coven Nine?"

Viv leaned away from the camera. "The political workings of the Nine are not an enforcer's business."

"I'm asking as Simone's cousin," he said simply.

Viv inhaled. "Yes."

Holy motherfucker. "Are you kidding?" Daire leaned forward and ignored the fire dancing between his fingers. "Who's leading the charge?"

"I haven't figured it out." Her shoulders slumped, and for the first time, dark circles slashed below her eyes. "There are rumblings everywhere, and I have no doubt Simone will be challenged for the seat within the year."

Daire rubbed his chin. "It's interesting this coincides with the appearance of Apollo." He examined scenarios and banished anger. Now was the time for strategy . . . later he'd use the power derived from righteous fury. "Is Simone being targeted because she's the weakest member, or is this attack personal to her?"

Viv shook her head. "I don't know. She is the wildest member with the, ah, most interesting lifestyle. Before her adventures were viewed as a possible strength, but there are rumors going around that she's joined up with Nicholai Veis again, and you know about his troubled past."

Well, the demon had killed more than one witch sent to assassinate him, so Daire couldn't exactly blame him. "Nick has proven himself as an ally."

"Perhaps. But he's a demon, and you know they can plot for years when it comes to strategy."

Aye, he did know that, firsthand. Felicity was a master at plotting, and the trait seemed inherent in all demons. It was possible that Veis had been plotting against Coven Nine for years, but Daire's gut said otherwise. "I won't allow Simone to be harmed."

Viv winced. "I've heard that evidence against her has been collected by the Guard, but I don't know what it is or what they think they have on her. If she's challenged, there's nothing you can do. Right now, stay on mission and shut down the mining, manufacturing, and distribution of Apollo. We confiscated three weapons on the Dublin streets last week that shoot darts."

Daire's head jerked up. "In Dublin?"

"Yes." She held out a hand as he began to stand. "The Guard is working overtime, Daire. We don't need the enforcers here; we need you there doing your job."

If the Coven Nine members were in danger, his first priority was in Dublin. Of course, that would entail his forcing Simone back home, which might be part of the plan of her enemies. "You have no idea who's behind the rumors?"

"No." Viv paled. "I have a couple of investigators on the situation, but so far, all they've confirmed is that she and Veis have spent time together in Seattle."

"They've worked together—no romance and definitely no sex." He had to get Simone away from the demon before her past relationships were used against her. "I give you my word it's just been work, and she's been incredibly bitchy about it."

Viv sighed. "She wouldn't be bitchy if her emotions weren't involved, and you know it. Whatever is going on between them must be ended and right now."

"Understood." Daire flirted with the idea of asking Viv about Triad and Demidov's company, but if she knew anything about it, she would've already told him. There was no reason to worry her about a possible problem until he'd taken care of it. "Be careful, because whoever is after Simone is well funded and has this thought out."

"I know," Viv said. "There's a rumor I can't track down that somebody has damaging information about Simone beyond her wild lifestyle. Concrete evidence that she's working against the Coven Nine."

"That's impossible." Damn it. Daire needed to take care of the issue and now.

Viv nodded. "I hope so. Contact me with any new information."

"Ditto." Daire punched in a couple of keys, and his aunt disappeared. He dialed another number.

Kellach Dunne came into view, his nostrils huge across the screen. "Back away from the phone," Daire rumbled.

"Oh." Kell backed away, and his face took shape. "What's going on?"

Daire leaned in. "Somebody is going after Simone, and they're in Dublin. While you're there, I need you to investigate."

Chapter 18

The plane bumped a couple of times as it flew through some turbulence. Felicity clasped her hands together in her lap, acutely aware of Adam Dunne's probing eyes on her. When would Daire return from the cockpit? Finally, she couldn't stand it any longer. "What?" she asked.

He lifted a shoulder. "Did Daire show you the marking on his palm?"

She blinked. Her siblings had been lunatics, so they'd pretty much stayed out of one another's lives until her brother had tried to betroth her to an asshole. "Is that really your business?" she asked, curious.

He smiled. Adam Dunne had a shocking smile . . . slow and masculine. Intelligence sizzled in his eyes, and he definitely had been blessed with the Dunne good looks. "My brother is my business."

She grinned. "That's incredibly sweet."

His chin lifted and he studied her. "You mean that."

"I do." How fortunate that Daire had a brother who cared. "Don't worry. I'm sure your brother isn't going to mate a demon."

Adam chuckled. "Are you kidding? I *hope* Daire mates a demon, witch, or shifter. Somebody immortal with some power."

She shifted on the seat. "I, ah, don't have much power."

"I've seen you kick, Cee Cee. You have training and power." He rubbed his hands together. "I really like Alexandra, and I'm happy Kellach found a mate, but how terrible to worry all the time about a former human. Sure, she'll be immortal, but she won't really have power for a long time."

"True." Humans eventually gained powers from their mates, but it could take centuries. "So you're not interested in Tori?"

He paused and rubbed his smooth chin. "God, no. She's sweet and spunky, but she's human." He shook his head. "My mate, when I meet her in a few centuries, will have enough power of her own that I'll gain from her as much as she gains from me."

Felicity bit back a smile. "It sounds like you have your future all planned out."

"I do find that having a plan takes care of the vagaries of fate." He leaned back and stretched his neck. "Now, let's talk about Simone and the evidence you've found."

Daire pushed open the door. "Felicity's files are up on the computer. Why don't you study them, and then we can chat about your conclusions? I'd like fresh eyes on the documents."

Adam stood. "Sounds good." He moved by his brother. "Did Viv confirm?"

"Aye. The rumor mill is working overtime, which means that a challenge is probably coming. We don't know from which direction, but I'm thinking the documents in the Cayman bank will provide a clue or two." Daire brushed by his brother and headed straight for Cee Cee.

Her stomach clenched, and she instinctively pushed back in the chair. Adam disappeared into the other area and shut the door with a soft click.

Daire reached her, lifted her easily, and reversed their positions.

Her knees knocked the sides of the chair, her feet tucked behind her, her butt on his hard thighs as she faced him. "You sure like me on top."

The lines at the sides of his eyes crinkled. "I surely do."

She flattened her hands on his strong chest. "You have your serious face on."

"Yes. I'd like your word that anything we find in the documents will remain confidential."

Ah. He wanted to protect his cousin. Felicity rocked back. "Let's make a deal."

"I figured," he said dryly.

"You let me handle Ivan, and I'll stay as silent as you want about Simone's extracurricular activities." Truth be told, Felicity held no interest in Coven Nine politics.

Daire sighed and ran his hands down her arms. "You donna' know me very well if you think I'd let you fight a demon soldier to the death."

Which was exactly why they couldn't be together. She shook her head. "I've been training since birth, and you have to back off." There had to be a way to explain it better. "I'm not some silly cheerleader following the knife-wielding villain into the forest." That would make her too stupid to live. "I've waited and planned since my mate was murdered, and during that time, I had people investigating Ivan. I know everything about him."

Daire shook his head. "When you sought refuge with your brother, why didn't Ivan follow through on the betrothal?"

Ah ha. So the enforcer was finally listening to her. "After I mated Dane, Ivan was furious with Suri and took out several of our holdings in Canada and Greenland. Suri was a bad enemy to have, although no matter how hard he tried, he couldn't get Ivan vulnerable and take him out."

Daire smoothed hair from her face. "What about Zane? I mean, he's well trained and deadly. In fact, I've met all three of your sons, and not one of them strikes me as the kind of man who'd let their father's killer walk the earth."

She swallowed, and heat flushed into her face. "Ah, well——"

"Cee Cee?"

She sighed. "I may have told them that Suri had their father's murderer killed."

Daire's eyebrows rose. "You may have?"

"Yes." She played with his T-shirt. "If I hadn't, even as boys, they would've gone hunting the killer." They would've been killed at that point.

"I understand." Daire leaned into her, bringing the scent of man and rain. "What about now? Zane leads the entire demon nation."

"And admit I lied to them for decades?" She shook her head and hair flew. Her stomach ached with the knowledge of how badly she'd already let them down. No more. "Absolutely not. Besides, all of my sons, as young as they are, have too much blood on their hands, and that's on me. No more killing for any of them, I hope." During the war, she'd been unable to protect them from fighting and killing. Now she could.

He quite expertly turned her motivation. "So you must understand the need to protect family and those you care about."

Ah, shoot. "I don't need protection from Ivan." The asshat of a demon needed protection from her, damn it. "You need to see the real me, Daire, and not the pretty blond crippled woman."

"You're not crippled." He brushed gentle knuckles across her cheekbone.

Sure, she was. "I'm a demon who can't mind attack or teleport." No illusions plagued her. "Which is why I've prepared for this for decades." Why couldn't he see what a threat she could be? Of course, that was part of her strategy with Ivan.

Daire cupped her chin. "I see the real you, Cee Cee, and I'm allowing you to help rob the bank. But you have to acknowledge that I'm not the type of guy who'd let his woman go fight hand-to-hand with another man. You wouldn't want me to be, would you?"

His woman? "Whoa there, John Wayne." She tried to scramble off his legs, her body humming. "I'm not your possession. Hell, I'm not your anything."

He let her go. "We both know that's not true."

Tears threatened to prick her eyes, and she batted them back. "We are so over." She was fucking tired of people seeing her as weak or damaged. For the briefest of seconds, she'd really thought Daire had seen the real her. The woman who could protect her family instead of the shell she'd been for so long. "Done."

His eyes burned a devastating green through the small cabin. "If you really think that, then you've lost all touch with reality."

She dropped into Adam's deserted chair and crossed her arms. What she wouldn't give for one more vial of the tranquilizer, although the last one hadn't done her much good. No part of her wanted to fight physically with Daire, and not only because he was a more experienced fighter. She swallowed to keep the tears at bay.

His gaze didn't soften. "You don't want to cross me on this."

She lifted her chin. "I'm neither crossing you nor arguing with you." In fact, she was finished trying to convince him of anything. They'd had a good time, and now it was over. Well, it would be over after they finished robbing one of the most secure banks in the world.

Really. What could go wrong?

* * *

Daire found himself surrounded by demons in a small hotel room, and his ears began to itch. Too much tension poured off the immortals as they double checked the plan and went over the bank schematics one more time. All furniture had been piled against the wall so they could suit up, and their boots clomped on the smooth tile floor. The room lacked sufficient windows and fresh air to allow for the amount of tension.

Felicity slammed a plastic knife into one boot, leaning over to do so. Her creamy breasts almost spilled out from her top, and he fought a growl.

"Since Simone appears to own the safe-deposit box, I'll go in as her and try to reach the inner vault," she said, her throaty voice strong and assured. "While there, I'll set the charges on the other security boxes, and the second they blow, you all come in."

Daire straightened his Armani suit. They'd gone over the schematics and plan several times, and the woman certainly had accounted for everything. He was to accompany her as a bodyguard, and even he had to admit, the fake beard and the gray sprinkled in his hair appeared authentic. Brown contacts masked his green eyes, and putty changed the shape of his face, especially his nose.

Felicity wore a long, brown wig, dark glasses, and several layers of clothing to create the illusion of Simone's natural curves. The boots had four-inch heels, but even so, she didn't come close to Simone's height. But there wasn't a better way to create height, so they were going with what they had. At some point, when the video was studied, it'd become apparent that the woman who'd robbed the bank was not Simone Brightston, which eased one of his many concerns.

He rolled his shoulders back and tried to calm his racing heart. The shifters guarding the place would recognize him as a witch just from his natural vibrations, and hopefully they'd assume Felicity was, too.

Her people were all demons, so it made sense for him to go in with the Simone decoy.

Felicity turned, all business, her eyes sparkling.

The damn woman was having a ball.

Energy poured off her in straight anticipation, and she nearly hopped when she neared him. "You ready?" she asked.

He wanted to tuck her in the getaway vehicle and tie her up safely, but for the plan to work, she had to impersonate Simone. "No."

She smiled, all excitement. "Good. Let's go." Shoving the dark glasses back up her nose, she stepped out of the storage van and walked crisply down the sidewalk toward the bank.

"I think I should be inside for backup," Adam complained once again from his position in the getaway car.

Daire tapped his earbud as island heat assaulted him. "I need you outside ready to get us out of here." If they ran into trouble, Adam had the biggest brain around and would figure out an escape route. "I can't believe we're about to do this." If he had his druthers, he'd just take out half the bank with a missile and steal what he wanted. Felicity had finesse, though.

He stalked behind her, rolling his shoulders forward and trying to appear shorter than he was. He followed her, noting how her ass swung with every step. Damn it. Now wasn't the time to admire her ass.

He swung his gaze around, trying to look like a hired bodyguard and not an enforcer. All he needed was the shifter nation to know a Coven Nine enforcer had tried to rob them. Either there'd be instant war, or his people would have to give up something big to avoid bloodshed. Tourists in loud flowered shirts milled around, and several people licked rapidly melting ice cream cones. Tourist shops with sparkling jewels and oil paintings lined the way.

The heels of Felicity's boots clicked as she sauntered into the air-conditioned bank.

He breathed out as the cool air smoothed over his skin.

A wide counter to the left held five tellers, all handling customers. Three desks with bank executives lined the windows on the right, and they all had patrons before them.

The place felt like money and smelled like the ocean.

Felicity moved instantly toward a desk at the back as if she had every right to do so, her heels clomping on the silver tiles. The woman had some serious style.

A guy dressed in pure silk sat behind the desk. Tall, broad, and in fighting shape, he had eyes that sparkled with intelligence. Wolf shifter. He smiled. "Can I help you?"

"I'm Simone Brightston," Felicity said, her voice higher than normal. "I called earlier."

"Of course, Miss Brightston. Do you have identification?" the shifter asked, standing.

Felicity handed over the identification she'd stolen from Simone's apartment the first night. It had been altered a bit.

Daire stood with his arms crossed, discreetly scoping out the cameras. There were a lot of them. He could make out seven guards within yelling distance.

Finally, the guy led them through a long hallway lined with pretty oil paintings to a massive steel vault flanked by two fully armed guards. "I am Anton, and I'm here to assist you in any way you need." He turned and apologized. "I'm so sorry, but we must follow formalities first."

Felicity nodded and held out her arms to be frisked.

Possessiveness rose in Daire so quickly his chest heated.

When the guard had finished with her, he turned and patted Daire down with much less finesse.

Anton smiled and yanked out a palm reader. "Very good. Hand, please."

Daire held his breath. Felicity had somehow obtained a full hand print from Simone's apartment and then had some pretty dicey vampires create a fleshlike print to coat her fingertips. She clicked over and flattened her palm over the scanner. It quickly scanned, and a green light flickered.

Daire breathed out. God, she was amazing. If they survived the robbery, she should plan another one. By the delight all but wafting from her, she'd be just fine with that. What in the hell had he gotten involved with?

A retina scan was next, and by this time, he was confident Felicity had it all figured out. Yep. The scan went off without a hitch.

The vault opened, and Anton swung open another steel door before preceding them inside to box 1287. Felicity shoved in Simone's key, and Anton did the same before pulling out a long box to place on the center table. "Let me know if you need anything else," he said, moving toward the steel door and discreetly shutting it.

Hopefully he wouldn't close the outside door and lock them in the vault.

Felicity smiled and flipped open the box to reveal several manila files.

Daire shrugged out of his jacket and reshaped it into a pack by drawing out hidden ties. He fought the urge to read the files and instead shoved them inside the pack.

Felicity was already moving toward the other boxes. She leaned down and kicked off the wedge part of both boots. Small discs fell out.

Daire winced. "Be careful."

She laughed then—low and throaty.

His mouth gaped open. Even in disguise, her beauty shone through as she exuded such delight.

Grabbing the discs, she quickly placed them on several of the boxes. Daire overturned the table and grabbed her, covering her completely. "Sure you want to do this?" he asked.

She snuggled under him and reached for a detonator disguised as a shirt button. "Hell yeah." She took a deep breath and pressed hard.

Chapter 19

The explosions rocked the room. Shards of metal flew hard and fast, embedding themselves in the floor and twanging an odd tune. Felicity shoved against Daire, her body vibrating with the air. Wow. She'd never set off a bomb in person before.

He lifted his head and glanced around. "Holy fuck." Stretching to his feet, he pulled her with him, his hold firm.

Smoke filtered through the room, and outside, an alarm blared. Gunfire pinged as if a world away, and the grunts of men fighting hand-to-hand broke the patter of gunfire.

"Go," Daire ordered, nudging her to the south wall. "If your tech guy is good, really good, he'll be able to keep the vault open for less than a minute."

If Eli wasn't good, then they were screwed. Felicity gaped at the huge holes in the wall. Scorch marks scored down the steel to the floor, and smoke swirled through the air. "Only take from the boxes we discussed." She had no intention of harming anybody other than Ivan and his crew.

Stepping gingerly over smoking metal, she reached the first box, shrugging out of her jacket to form another bag. "Ah. Diamonds, emeralds, and rubies. Oh my." Feeling almost giddy, she tugged out the velvet-lined box and dumped the priceless gems into the bag, already reaching for a box full of cash, United States currency.

Daire looted the other side, and they hustled, meeting in the middle. One box held more files, including deeds and land trust documents.

"We have to go. Now." Daire reached for her hand.

She slung the bag over her shoulder, blinking from the burning air. The alarm was suddenly cut off.

Daire growled. "Not good." He shoved open the steel door.

The vault door was slowly closing. Shit. Daire barreled through, pulling her along. Her boot caught at the end, and he gave a hard jerk, taking her right out of the leather.

One of her men grappled with a shifter against the wall, the two throwing furious punches and kicks. She loped into a run behind Daire just as two guards, fully armed and bleeding, ran around the corner.

Daire instantly dropped into a slide, taking them both out like bowling pins. Without even a hitch, he rolled onto the first guy and punched him in the face several times, spraying blood. The guy roared and started to shift into what looked like some sort of feline. Daire shot a hard jab into his neck and then his left temple, knocking him out.

Felicity leaped forward and kicked the other guard under the chin. His head jerked back and hit the floor with a sickening *thunk*.

Yet he turned to get back to his feet.

Daire growled and leaped forward, taking the guard with him and slamming the guy's head into the wall.

Felicity took the opportunity to kick out of the remaining boot. No way could she run with only one four-inch heel slowing her down. She was already in motion when Daire jumped up and ran for the end of the hallway, his boots smashing against the silver tiles.

Her earbud crackled to life. "Authorities are dealing with the road blocks right now. You have about two minutes to get free," Adam said, tension riding his voice and hard.

She gulped, and the hazy bank reception area took on a surreal tinge. Time seemed to slow down. Patrons ran out the door, spilling over the luxurious chairs. The tellers had disappeared, as had the bank executives.

"Run," Daire bellowed. He turned just in time to get plugged three times by a guard. Without missing a step, Daire lunged for the guy and ripped the gun from his hand before slamming it down on the guard's neck. The guard, a huge guy with wolflike features, dropped to the ground like a stone, his body jerking.

Cee Cee flew into motion, kicking a female guard out of the way as she went. Her men fought hard around them, and in the distance, sirens trilled through the sunshine.

Daire motioned her forward, and she ran toward him at the front door. Blood flowed from his chest.

Sudden shooting pain ripped into her shoulder, and she tripped, falling flat on her face. Pain bloomed across her forehead. Blood spurted from her arm, and darkness covered her vision.

Rough hands grabbed her up, and her stomach hit a hard male shoulder. Her fake hair flipped down Daire's long length. Hopefully the attachments she'd used for the wig would hold while she was upside down. Her entire right side went numb, and bile rose in her stomach to be quickly swallowed. Every running step he took bounced her against his shoulder, and she had to concentrate not to vomit.

Heat blasted her as he ran outside, his boots clomping on the hot concrete.

Sirens rose in pitch, obviously coming nearer.

A car door opened and Daire jumped inside, twirling her around to land on his lap. "Go," he ordered.

Adam pulled away from the curb and into traffic, driving with speed and contained recklessness. "I can't believe you just fucking robbed a bank," he yelled.

Felicity blinked. So Adam Dunne could get emotional. Fascinating. Darkness covered her vision again, and she swayed. Daire yanked her shirtsleeve down and poked at her arm. Red hot agony sliced along her nerve endings, and she cried out, trying to jerk free.

"Hold still," he commanded, peering closer. "It's a through and through, but you need to heal yourself. Now."

Tears fill her eyes and she nodded, letting a couple loose. Then she sucked in air, trapped it in her lungs, and concentrated. Her nerves tingled and then sparked as healing cells swam toward the injury. Healing an injury internally was much like an external surgery without anesthetic. Her body shuddered with the pain, but the wounds slowly closed. By the time she was finished, she was panting and sweating against Daire.

His eyes remained closed, and slowly, the wounds on his chest closed. Man, he could heal fast.

Adam drove into a parking area. "Take the white Buick to the helicopter, and I'll ditch this car and then head to Dublin."

Daire set Felicity next to him and quickly threw all the bags into the adjoining car.

Felicity yanked out the earbud, which Daire quickly crushed with his.

"Call me when you reach safety," Daire ordered, slipping from the car and taking Felicity with him.

She allowed him to lead as she tried to regain some energy. The second she sat in the passenger seat, she reached for the bag already there and started changing her clothing. Her scalp burned when she ripped off the wig.

"Go easy," Daire said, shrugging out of his suit and tugging off the fake beard. He already wore jeans and a T-shirt underneath, so he deposited the clothing in her empty bag before igniting the engine. "We can't face any more fights. One of the bullets pinged my heart, and I need rest and protein to get back to full strength."

She swallowed. "Are you okay?"

"Yes. Just not strong enough to fight anybody right now." He continued driving.

The bullet had hit his heart? Talk about tough.

Felicity finished wiping the blood off her neck just as they reached the helicopter waiting for them. The pilot was a demon mercenary, and she'd already paid him a small fortune to be there. He'd get the other half as soon as he dropped them in Jamaica, where they were to meet a private plane and head to Miami and then Seattle.

They didn't exchange words and were soon flying low, really low, over the ocean. At least it was warm this time if they crashed.

Daire studied her, puzzled and pissed off. Anger rolled off him in slow waves, not quite ready to explode, but burning slowly and increasing in pressure.

She shifted in her seat, acutely aware of his mood. Her hands clasped together, and she tried to shrug off anxiety. Sure, they were almost caught in robbing the bank, which would've been a disaster for them both. But she'd tried to hide how much fun she'd been having, and from the look on his face, she hadn't succeeded.

They reached the private plane, bribed several officials, and were in the air before she could really settle herself.

She sat in a comfortable chair, and delight bubbled up. "We did it." Her gaze caught on the loot across the plane. "I mean, we actually did it." She threw back her head and laughed. Her other two teams had reported in, and all three bank robberies were a success. Who knew she'd be good at something like this?

Daire leaned forward and rubbed the gray from his hair. "You're certifiable, you know that?"

She laughed harder. "I do know that."

He lifted an eyebrow over a sizzling green eye. His skin was still pale from healing himself, but other than that, he looked good. Really good. "You never had a chance to have fun, did you?"

She blinked and sobered. "No."

He nodded slowly. "Your childhood was dangerous, you got free and became a mom, and then you had to go back to Suri and danger." He shook his head. "Now you're free, your kids are set, and you can do what you want."

Exactly. She smiled. Energy and adrenaline rippled through her veins, and for the first time in so long, she felt alive. "I can do what I want." Her nipples peaked, and her body thrummed. "Right now, I want . . . you."

Daire held her gaze. They had a long flight ahead of them, and while he trusted the two witches in the cockpit, he was nowhere near a hundred percent. Even so, her confident gaze licked across his skin, and his blood started to burn. "I've had a constant erection since the first night I met you, lady. But we should both get some rest, finish healing ourselves, and regain our strength."

She chuckled, and the throaty tone might as well have been wrapped around his dick.

Then the vixen dropped to her knees and gracefully made her way between his legs. "I can think of a better way to regain our energy." Her shoulders made room for her, and she hummed as she unzipped his jeans.

Heat flushed down his torso. "You're awfully brave right now, baby."

Her tongue darted out to lick her lips, and he fought a groan. "I've always been brave." Smooth as silk, her hand slipped inside his pants and ran along his cock.

Nerves sparked, and his body shuddered. She was the exact opposite of what he thought he wanted in a woman, and yet he'd never hungered more for one. Never. "You're the wildest woman I've ever met," he murmured.

Absolute delight filled her dark eyes.

He breathed out, an unwilling smile rising up inside him. "That was not a compliment." Giving in, he caressed a hand through her soft hair. Her former mate had been a smart guy to knock her up so quickly. God knew what kind of havoc she might've wreaked if she hadn't had responsibility right off the bat.

"What are you thinking?" she asked, continuing to stroke him.

"Nothing." Which suddenly became true. But a ringing clamored through his ears, and his vision was still blurry. He needed to heal and get his faculties back.

Her sweet hand on him shoved all thoughts to the abyss.

She leaned down and placed a very gentle kiss on the tip of his dick.

That was it. He grabbed her shoulders and pushed, following her down until he lay flattened on top of her. She bent her knees, making more room for him right where he wanted to be.

Her gaze dropped to his mouth. "I really like you, Daire."

Such sweetness and unusual honesty from her pierced right to his chest. "I like you, too." Slowly, just to keep things in control, he reached down and released the buttons of her shirt, revealing a pretty flowered bra with a front clasp. He loved front clasps. One quick flick, and the material sprang free, her delicious breasts pouting at him.

He peppered kisses along her neck to take one nipple in his mouth. She gasped and slid her fingers into his hair. His body rioted, and his vision wavered even more. "I'm not a hundred percent here, Felicity."

She reached down and yanked his shirt over his head. "You feel ready to me."

He grinned and paid homage to the other breast. Her nipples were pink and fully erect, and he could play with them all day. "My vision is fuzzy," he admitted.

"Then close your eyes," she whispered, sliding off her pants and helping him to kick his off.

Good plan. He closed his eyes and just let himself feel, sliding inside her with a couple of hard pushes.

Her sex convulsed around his shaft, and he groaned, moving up her so he could stretch out. "No fire this time," he whispered against the rapidly beating pulse in her neck. He didn't have the energy.

Smooth and toned, her thighs clapped against his hips. "Don't need fire. Just need you," she whispered.

That sexy voice licked right down his spine. One quickie might give them both energy, and when they were done, they could sleep. Getting shot in the chest hurt more than he'd thought. His vision went completely dark, but his body thrummed with hunger. It slaked through him, aimed solely on Felicity Kyllwood.

Her nails bit into his butt.

He licked her jugular and started to pound. She met him thrust for thrust, her fingers digging into his ass, her hot core caressing around his shaft. The sounds she made, hoarse and sexy, whispered through him, straight to his heart. He thrust harder, giving in to his need and hers.

Fine tremors shook her feminine body. Her core gripped him with enough strength to catch his breath. He tilted his pelvis, just a bit, and scraped over her clit.

She stiffened and then cried out his name. Waves ripped through her body and crashed against him. Fire lit his ass, hot and desperate, shooting electricity through his veins. Her teeth lashed on to his pec, and she bit. Deep.

He held her tighter, gripped her hip to lift her, hammering into her with everything he had. His canines lengthened. All instinct, he sliced into the vulnerable flesh at her neck and held on. Sparks burned through him, igniting every nerve, throwing his senses into overdrive. Lava scalded down his spine to land hard in his balls.

His release stole his breath, jerking rapidly through him. His teeth met in the middle, and a sense of contentment filled him. Finally, he went lax.

She panted against him, her palms drawing soothing circles on his aching butt.

Wait a minute. His canines retracted, and he instinctively licked her wound clean. His body flared awake, and he opened his eyes. He could see, but she was blurry. He'd bitten her.

Oh God.

Glancing down at his hand, he slowly slid to the side and pulled her over. His brand, bright and Celtic, was healing on her hip. "I mated you." His voice was hoarser than hers would ever be.

She blinked, and her mouth formed a perfect O.

He hadn't been strong enough to fight both biology and fate, and he had known better. He should've rested up before having sex.

"Um," she said.

He winced. "Let's just keep calm minds and talk this out."

She twisted her lip and then drew her arm up to glance at her hand. A perfect Z appeared in the center, dark and somehow feminine.

Both of his eyebrows lifted so quickly his head jerked. "What the fuck?"

She winced and then tilted to the side, peering around his body.

Almost in slow motion, he turned his head to see a perfect match on his left buttock.

She bit her lip. "I marked you, too." Then, crazy woman that she was, she threw back her head and laughed, long and hard.

Chapter 20

Ivan Bychkov threw a paperweight across the home office. The heavy disk smashed into the window showcasing a lovely view of the Seattle skyline and dropped to the antique rug in three perfect shapes. "I can't believe this."

Vadim Deeks continued reading a tablet that looked impossibly small in his massive hands. "The consortia is holding a vote tomorrow morning about your leadership. My sources confirm that you're about to be voted out." He tapped the tablet with strong fingers, causing a protesting ping from the computer with every stroke. "There's also rumor of a vote to cut off your head."

No shit. Once leaders were replaced, they weren't wanted any longer. If he set foot on his continent, he'd be dead within hours. "Any idea who's behind this?"

Vadim shrugged. "Doesn't matter. There's enough momentum that if you don't turn the tide and now, you're out." He spoke without inflection. "We need to regain the cash, jewels, and gold from the bank accounts, or we're both finished with the consortia."

"That bitch," Bychkov said, running a shaking hand through his thick hair. He had seriously underestimated Felicity. The bank strikes had been perfectly orchestrated, and combined with the mining incidents, had crippled him financially. More important, it had crippled the consortia, which meant his head was wanted on a stake. "She went right for my weaknesses." Before the last week, he hadn't realized he even had weaknesses.

Vadim nodded. "Now we go after hers."

A computer dinged on the walnut desk, and Bychkov hurried over to read the screen. His stock portfolio. "We're bleeding money," he muttered, leaning over to type in several commands. What in the world? As he watched, the stock values plummeted. His gut rolled over, and he swallowed down puke.

How the hell?

Vadim crossed the room to study the numbers. "How would an enemy make that happen?"

He fought to keep his temper at bay, but the effort cost Ivan. "You make a coordinated strike on individual businesses, infuse capital into competitors, and cause rumors that prompt people to dump stock." Apparently Felicity hadn't been hiding out cowering from him the last several decades. "When I learned that Zane had killed Suri, I figured it was time to make my move on the woman."

Turned out she'd been making her move the entire time.

Vadim's phone buzzed, and he read the text. "The Intel is coming through on Felicity Kyllwood, her allies, and her weaknesses. Also, we've upped the security at the Sjenerøse mine in Russia."

Ivan turned away from the sight of his portfolios bleeding currency. "There's no way she can get a team to the Sjenerøse mine to take it out. I just sent orders for the planekite mining to continue around the clock." If the damn Coven Nine enforcers thought they could work with Felicity and harm him, they had another think coming. He'd only worked with Rudger and his brother for money, but now it was personal. "It's time we wiped the witch nation off the map, anyway. Weak bastards."

Vadim rubbed his chin. "They've always been our most dangerous enemy, and I'm glad we're finally going to take them out."

Damn witches could shield against mind attacks with enough training. His computer dinged again, and he turned back to key in the response. Phillipe Sadler took shape. Ivan smiled. "Hello."

"Where is my brother?" Phillipe said, his eyes a bizarre blue and his hair a wild brown mane.

Ivan frowned and feigned surprise. "How should I know?"

"Last I heard, Rudger was in Seattle meeting with you."

Which hadn't gone well, now had it? Vadim had taken care of the body, so Ivan wasn't even sure where the corpse now rotted. "Your brother got some tip about the Coven Nine and headed off to Dublin. Something about Simone Brightston."

Phillipe's eyes blazed.

Yep. Ivan kept his face concerned. His sources reported Phillipe was enamored with the pretty witch. "I don't know what the tip was, and he wouldn't share."

Phillipe's face darkened. "I'll check it out, but he never pursues a lead without calling me. If you've done anything to my brother, Ivan, you're going to want to find a guillotine now."

Ivan tilted his head to the side. "I don't appreciate the threat, and I assure you, I take our allegiance seriously." He clicked off.

Vadim leaned back and crossed his arms. "Want me to take care of him?"

"No. Right now we need his distribution channels for planekite, and so far, he hasn't revealed the manufacturer of the actual drug." Nor had he revealed the ultimate puppet master. Somebody wanted the Coven Nine destroyed, and for the life of him, he couldn't narrow down the suspects beyond Phillipe's family.

Vadim shook his head. "I thought we were staying out of the Apollo trade. The infusion of capital to the mines was all we wanted."

That was before the witches had teamed up with that bitch Felicity. They'd all pay by the time he'd finished with them. "I hadn't realized the financial opportunities available when marketing a new drug to humans, and a new weapon to immortals." If he could get a cut of the profit being made, he could rebuild his portfolio and keep his position as leader. And his head. He could keep his head. "But for now, let's teach little Felicity a lesson in strategy and weaknesses."

Vadim glanced at his watch. "It's about midnight."

Anticipation lanced through Ivan, and the blood roared through his veins. While he didn't like losing his fortune, the thrill of the fight sang through his veins. Felicity was much more of a challenge than he'd hoped, and her moves against him, as devastating as they were, only made him want her more. She'd pay for making him hide and fight to keep his life, and oh, how much fun that sweet moment would be.

He chuckled. Midnight was the perfect time to go hunting in Seattle.

Felicity settled onto the sofa in the bumpy plane, her heart beating hard enough to rattle her ribs. She'd just mated the enforcer. In fact, she'd mated him before he'd mated her. Only one of them needed to transfer a brand, but they'd both done so.

Doubly mated.

Sleep threatened to drag her under, but she had to focus.

Daire stretched out next to her and curled her into his side, yanking a blanket to cover them. "Get some sleep and heal your shoulder," he whispered.

She coughed. "We should talk."

"We should heal and then talk." His tone held a touch of whip sharpness this time. "I can feel vibrations of your pain."

"Are you worried about the public relations issue with us?" she asked, her eyes closing of their own accord.

"No." He ran a gentle hand down her hair.

She cuddled closer and fought the need to purr. "Are you worried about my sons?"

"No." He continued to stroke her.

She sighed. "What are you worried about?"

"You've never had much of a choice in life, and you're just starting to learn how to live." He shifted his weight and tucked her closer. "What happened tonight happened fast and without much choice."

Did he regret it? She winced, and the sharp pang to her heart surprised her. Being mated to Daire would be exciting, and she couldn't deny she had feelings for him. There hadn't been two seconds to sit down and figure it all out, but if he didn't want to be mated, she wasn't going to keep him. "I loved my husband and mate, Daire."

He stiffened. "That's good."

"He was older, and we were good friends. It's different with you." She placed a hand over his chest. "You're young and exciting, and you see me as an equal." And not weak. Not once, even when he was being all enforcer-esque with her, had he treated her differently than he would any other woman. Of course, he was an overprotective enforcer with any woman he cared about.

He reached under her hair to knead her nape.

Pleasure relaxed her muscles.

"Go to sleep, Felicity," he whispered. Then he smiled against her forehead. "I'm not young. In fact, considering how young you are, I just robbed the cradle."

She chuckled. Everything in her wanted to ask if his feelings for her were strong enough to explore, but for the first time, she hesitated to speak her mind. What if he didn't know? What if he said no? What if, and this was the worst one, he lied to spare her feelings?

It wasn't as if she'd dated anyone . . . ever. She had no clue how to read the signs. If there were signs. Maybe there weren't any signs.

His grip tightened. "The pain rolling off you is increasing in intensity. I promise we have tons of time to talk before we reach Seattle. Right now, I need you to fall asleep and let your body finish the healing process."

Bossy. Her new mate was a bit bossy. And handsome, exhilarating, and sexy. A part of her, one she would never admit to, wondered if she would've stopped herself from marking him if she hadn't been so caught up in the moment. Daire Dunne was everything she had ever wanted in a man, and he was strong enough to handle her boys and any problems they might have with him. She could handle them as well.

Her body tingled as the mating brand took effect, and it was different from when she'd mated a vampire. The tingles held a pop of fire, and her limbs loosened naturally. Daire Dunne's energy was dark and strong, and it flowed through her as her body adapted to the mating. She wasn't a big believer in destiny, especially considering her past, but ever since Daire had first kissed her, she'd tasted him on her lips. His scent surrounded her, and when she closed her eyes, his face filled her mind.

Was it love, or was this her first real crush?

Either way, the queen had assured her that the mutated virus that had negated her earlier mating bond would fade from her system and not affect any future bond. If she wanted to stay mated to Daire, she could.

Her mind was mushy and her body exhausted, so even though she didn't care for his bossiness, he was correct that she needed to rest. Even so, it took a while for her to drop into dreamland. Life had always been difficult, and she'd learned young that if any happiness stormed her way, she should grab on to it with both hands.

Daire made her happy when he wasn't driving her crazy. If she could just get a handle on his overprotectiveness, and if she could just get him to see her as an equal, even in battle, then they stood a chance.

If he wanted a chance.

Maybe he didn't.

That thought made her heart hurt again, almost competing with the pain pounding in her shoulder. She'd never force him to stay with her, and she should probably get some sleep before trying to figure everything out.

She tried to open her eyes, but they remained shut. "When we awaken, we really need to talk," she mumbled.

His hand tightened on her nape and then quickly released. "Oh, baby, you can count on it."

Chapter 21

The plane turned and then leveled off again. Daire read through the many manila files he'd stolen from the vault, his mind spinning and his gut churning. Felicity slept on the fold-out couch running the length of one side of the airplane, and he sat at a table working across from her. He'd slept a few hours and had awakened in Miami, where they refueled.

He'd mated her.

Shit. She'd mated him.

They both could've probably healed the markings, although the mating would've stayed. But, without any discussion, apparently they'd both decided to leave the markings in place.

Now the woman, *his woman*, slept like the dead on the sofa.

She was disorderly, disobedient, and disorganized. The woman loved to rob banks and blow stuff up, for goodness' sake. But suddenly, a peaceful, calm woman sounded, well, boring. Even unappealing.

A mating needed to be planned out, though. What had he done? He had tortured Kellach with the fact that he'd mated a human without any planning or discussion, and now he'd done the same thing. Even though he'd been weak from healing himself, he hadn't fought the instinct for a second. The moment her marking scorched his flesh, any fight or discussion had been over.

He'd been drawn to her from first sight at the Fire bar. Not once had he considered the role of fate in his life. He was an enforcer, and he chose his own path. If there wasn't a path, he bulldozed one.

But looking at her now, her face so young and relaxed in sleep, he allowed himself to wonder. Did fate play a part? Was there a reason he'd been so drawn to her? He'd always seen a snapshot of his future mate in his head, and the picture sure as hell didn't include a bank-robbing insane demonness. Maybe he'd dodged a bullet by avoiding the boring life he'd assumed would be his.

Felicity Kyllwood was anything but boring.

His phone buzzed, and Adam took shape on the screen. "We had an attack against two members of the Coven Nine," his brother said without preamble.

Daire stiffened. "Who?"

"Aunt Viv and Brenna Dunne Kayrs, who was in Dublin on business," Adam said. "Viv's guard took care of the threat, but one of them got caught with a dart. He's recuperating."

Daire glanced at the clock. "How's Brenna?"

"Fine. Jase was with her and put the assassin through a wall." Adam shrugged. "Jase took several darts to the neck, and nothing happened. So now we have definite confirmation that Apollo doesn't harm vampires."

Daire exhaled a ragged breath. Vampire soldier Jase Kayrs was a good friend as well as being his cousin Brenna's mate. Thank goodness the darts hadn't hurt him. They also now had confirmation that the drug had reached Dublin as a weapon, so things were about to get dangerous for the leaders of the witch world. Well, more dangerous than usual. "I'll have the pilots chart a new course."

Adam shook his head. "I've got things covered at home. As soon as I reach Dublin, I'm sending Kellach and Alexandra back to Seattle to find the distributor and manufacturer of Apollo. We need information more than we need bodyguards right now, and you have to take down the Titans of Fire and get the facts, Daire. Enough is enough." He glanced to the side. "I'm several hours from reaching Ireland."

How odd they could talk from airplanes going in different directions. "Remember when we had to send letters to communicate?" Daire rumbled.

Adam nodded, his eyes tired. "Aye. The modern way is easier, but it has led to all sorts of new problems."

Like the creation of Apollo. Daire shuffled the papers. "So long as we have a connection right now, let's talk. I've gone through the papers we found, and Simone is all over them."

Adam frowned. "You don't think she's involved with the manufacture of Apollo, do you?"

"Of course not." While Simone came off tough and bitchy, she was the most loyal person Daire had ever met. Plus, if she wanted to take out the other members of the Coven Nine, she'd use missiles and not subterfuge. She completely lacked any sense of subtlety. "But somebody has taken great pains to set her up."

Adam sighed and rubbed a hand over his eyes. "Okay. When you get to Seattle, send me copies of all the documents. We'll have to start tracing all of the evidence."

Before it showed up publicly? "We need to warn Simone. Things are going to get dicey before we figure it out." Being removed from the Coven Nine would hurt her, so he had to make sure it didn't happen. "When I find whoever is behind this, I'm ripping off his head."

Adam nodded. "That's a plan I support."

Yeah. Daire grinned. One could always count on Adam to go for the quick kill and not screw around with it. He cleared his throat. "Ah, one more thing."

"What?" Adam said, focusing in.

"What kind of a disaster are we facing, PR-wise, if I mated Felicity Kyllwood?" he asked, keeping his voice low.

Adam's jaw went slack and his chin dropped. "Are you joking?"

"No."

"Planning ahead?"

"No."

Adam blew out air, disbelief darkening his eyes. "Have you lost your fucking mind?"

Daire glanced over at the pale features of the goddess sleeping so peacefully on the sofa. "Aye."

Adam coughed. "Well, let's see. If Zane Kyllwood found out you touched *his mother*, he'd probably put out a hit on you. When he finds out you *mated* his mommy, he's going to come for you himself and rip off your head."

"She's way too young to have a grown son, much less three of them," Daire mused. "She could have kids well into her nine hundredth year." As a demon, she was barely an adult, really. Compared to a human, she'd be around twenty-five years old.

"So what?" Adam exploded.

Daire frowned and turned down the volume on his phone speaker. "I'm just saying. Sure, she's Zane Kyllwood's mother, but she has an entire life to live still. And the woman is fuckin' crazy, Adam. No way would she just sit quietly and, I don't know, knit sweaters or anything." She was meant to live a full life, and something in him, deep down and insanely possessive, wanted to live it with her. "She's meant to blaze trails, not sit on the sidelines."

"You have it bad," Adam muttered. "Assuming Kyllwood doesn't slice off your dick and feed it to alligators, your response in the witch nation will be split. Strategists like Aunt Viv will love the idea of a permanent alliance with the demon nation, but right now, especially with Simone's alliance with the demons being used to hurt her, you could face some opposition."

So the hell what? He'd never given one whit about public opinion, and he sure as shit wasn't going to start caring about it now.

"Not for nothin', but Zane Kyllwood is barely more than thirty years old, is now happily mated, and recently had his baby girl turn one year old." Daire stretched his neck.

"So?"

"So, Zane couldn't take me in a fight, thus I'm not worried he's coming after me. Plus, I'll deal with any opposition in the witch nation."

Adam snorted. "Forget the witch nation and worry about Zane Kyllwood. He may be younger and lack your centuries of experience, but geez. You *mated* his mother."

Well now, that was a good point. Did that make him a stepdad to Logan? His head pounded.

Adam shook his head. "With the mutated virus, you know you could negate the mating bond, right?"

Fury roared through Daire's blood, and he tamped it down, swallowing several times.

"I guess not," Adam said slowly, his gaze widening. "All righty then. Congrats on your mating, bro." The screen crackled and the picture morphed. "I'm about to lose the connection. Good luck, and let me know if I can do anything." The screen went black.

Daire shook his head.

"Do you want to stay mated?" Felicity asked, scooting up to sit.

He eyed her. "How are you feeling?"

"Better. My shoulder is all healed and my arm doesn't hurt any longer." She scrubbed both hands down her delicate face. Her blond hair was mussed, and her eyes sleepy, giving her a sexy *let's go back to bed* look. Or perhaps that was just his interpretation.

He nodded. "I want to stay mated."

She blinked. "I like that we have a choice these days."

Yet how much easier would it be if they didn't? The mutated virus could negate matings, and he wasn't sure he liked the new ways. "I'm kinda' all in or all out, baby." He didn't know how else to put it to her. If they were going to make a go of it, there was no *out clause*.

Her eyes widened, sparkling like onyx jewels. "You want a decision on forever right now and this quickly?"

Aye. If he was going to give it a shot, he wanted to know she was, too. "It's how I work."

She snorted. "You're going to have to learn how I work, Enforcer."

"I do know." He needed to learn some finesse, and he might as well start now. "I don't mean to pressure you."

"I'm not feeling pressured." She stretched her neck and rolled out her healed shoulder. "I just, ah, need time to think."

He smiled. The woman who seemed perfectly comfortable jumping right into any dangerous situation needed time to think about being mated to him.

The plane started its decline, and he motioned for her to take a seat and buckle in. She did so and added an impressive eye roll. The rainy Seattle weather jostled the plane around, but finally, they touched the ground. The pilots hit the brakes, and within minutes had driven inside a private hangar.

Daire unbuckled and reached the door first, pushing the button to open it and unfold the stairs. He loped down them and held out a hand to help Felicity.

She jogged down and shivered. "Seattle is always chillier than I think it's going to be."

Daire nodded. "We'll get you a jacket." Their car must be right outside the door.

His nape tickled. A scent wafted on the breeze. He turned and set Felicity back on the stairs. "Get back into the plane. Now."

She turned, confusion crossing her face.

Men in black poured in the large open door of the terminal, guns out, wearing masks. Daire planted his body between the stairs and the soldiers. "Get back inside," he ordered under his breath, his hands up.

The soldiers secured the area, taking posts all around. The nearest one stalked up and ripped off his mask.

Ah, hell.

"Zane!" Felicity pushed past Daire and barreled into her eldest's arms. "What in the world are you doing here with guns?"

The leader of the demon nation smoothly set his mother behind him. Zane Kyllwood was six and a half feet of muscled killing machine. His eyes were green, his hair black, and his face scarred down the jaw.

"Give me one good reason not to cut off your head right now," Zane said.

Daire bit back a sharp retort.

Zane leaned in, and the men around them tensed. Make that the *demons* around them. "You take my mother to the Caymans to rob a fucking bank?"

Daire kept silent.

Felicity slid to the side and shoved her son in the ribs. "You mind your manners."

Zane blinked.

Daire fought a chuckle.

"Mom, please let me handle this," Zane said.

Felicity shook her head. "The bank robbery was my idea. Daire just came along and wouldn't leave."

Zane glanced down at her. "Don't try to cover for him."

"Nobody has to cover for me," Daire said, more than a little curious. Felicity barely reached Zane's shoulder. How in the world had the petite woman birthed three such hulking sons? "The bank robbery was my fault." He should've put the brakes on the entire affair and not allowed Felicity to join in. "But I have to admit, your mom can create a hell of a good plan."

Zane's eyes flashed black through the green. "She was injured."

Man, the kid had great Intel. He must've already gotten the videos of the robberies. "How did you know it was her?"

Zane cut him a hard look. "Once I figured out she wasn't on a cruise, thanks to Nicholai, it wasn't that hard to track her down . . . and watch her get shot."

"Aye. Her injury is on me."

Felicity scoffed. "Don't be silly. It was one little bullet."

Zane paled. "One bullet is all it might take."

Daire winced. "Again, my fault."

Felicity shook her head. "No, it wasn't. For goodness' sake. Daire was shot three times in the chest."

"Good," Zane spit.

Felicity grabbed his arm. "Now you knock it off. My getting shot was no more Daire's fault than was the polar bear mauling. And I assure you, I healed from both."

Zane stilled. His gaze slowly moved from Daire to Felicity. "Mauling?"

She nodded, her cheeks rosy. "Yes. Before the helicopter accident but after I fought with a witch on the ice."

Zane rocked back on his heels.

Daire could almost feel sorry for the guy. "As you can see, your mother is fine."

Felicity lifted a shoulder. "You should also probably know that we mated."

Tension roared through the hangar. Daire braced himself just in time to take the impact from Zane's fist. Pain ripped through his skull. He stepped back and accepted the ringing in his ears. The demon hit hard. "That was one, demon, and it's all you get."

Zane smiled then. "The fuck it is." He moved forward, and Daire settled his stance, more than prepared to go to the ground. He couldn't really beat the crap out of Felicity's kid, could he? And he sure as shit couldn't lose the fight. So he'd have to contain Zane, and that wasn't going to be fun and would probably put the demon and witch nations on another path to war.

"Stop it right now." The crack of command in Felicity's voice echoed throughout the entire building. "I mean it, Zane."

Zane lowered his chin. "Mom? I'd like to speak with you alone. Outside."

She clasped her hands together. "Excellent idea. Daire, I'll be right back."

"Absolutely not." He stepped forward. Enough people in her life had forced her into boxes, and son or not, Daire wasn't going to allow Zane to do the same thing.

Felicity smiled, winking an adorable dimple. "It'll be okay. I promise. Please give me a moment with my son." Turning, she led the way toward the opening outside.

Zane glared. "We're not done here."

Daire kept his expression blank. "It's cold outside, and she doesn't have a jacket. Find her one."

Chapter 22

Felicity's cheeks burned as she walked past all the soldiers outside. She probably shouldn't have just blurted out the information about the mating, but her mind was spinning, and she'd just gone with it. The breeze slapped her face and rain sprinkled down, but she followed the metal hangar around another corner, her stockinged feet slapping the wet concrete. Trees covered the area past the concrete, silent in the breeze.

Zane followed right behind her.

She finally stopped and turned around.

For the moment, she could only gape. How was it possible the sweet boy who'd picked her flowers had grown into such a strong man? So big and dangerous looking. But his green eyes were soft nonetheless.

She smiled, her heart full. "How are Janie and Hope?"

He blinked. "Fine. Mom—"

"Fine?" She put her hands on her hips. "How are the girls, Zane?"

He shook his head, his dark hair spraying rainwater. "You just saw them a month ago at Hope's first birthday party. They're fine."

Men. Even when you had known them their entire lives, they still didn't know how to communicate. Felicity nodded. "Thank you. What would you like to discuss?"

His eyes widened. "Seriously?"

She bit back a grin. "Let's just nip this in the bud now. You have an entire nation to worry about, and I can take care of myself."

A vein in his neck filled. "Mom. I have no idea how Daire Dunne got you to go along with this ridiculous mission, but I promise I'll take care of it. And him. You don't need to stay mated."

What a sweetheart. "I will decide whether or not I want to stay mated."

"Ah, no." Zane grasped her arm and tugged her closer to the building so the eaves shielded them from the rain. "I'll take care of it."

Wow. Sometimes her kid was a little dense. "I've got things under control."

Zane took a step back. "Control? Are you kidding? You just robbed a bank."

Warmth fused through her. "Yes, I did. Quite successfully." She leaned in, even though the rain surely masked their voices. "I had two other banks robbed at the same time. I'm telling you, Zane, if the demon nation ever needs cash, I have some ideas."

He shook his head like a dog with a face full of water. "We're good," he bit out. "No cash problems."

Truth be told, the answer was a little disappointing. "All right."

He crossed his arms. "What were you saying about a polar bear attack?"

"Oh, that." She dismissed the question with a wave of her hand. "I was checking out the mines on Fryser Island and ended up in a little scuffle."

He jerked. "In Norway?"

"Eh, close enough. I think there might still be some dissension about who owns the island." She wiped rain off her cheeks. "We done here?"

"No," he exploded, his cheeks turning a deep red. "We are not done here. What was that about a helicopter crash?"

She winced. Nobody wanted their mom to be in a helicopter wreck. "Daire and I flew from the island, but enemies shot at us and we went down."

"In Barents Sea?" Zane shouted.

"Well, close. Sjenerøse Island is actually in the Arctic Sea." She tilted her head. Her eldest son usually kept a much better rein on his temper. His face had now lost all color, and he was looking at her like she'd completely lost her mind. "I'm fine, Zane."

He took several deep breaths. "I'm going to kill Dunne."

"Why?" she asked.

Zane's chin dropped. "Why? Well, how about his extreme bad judgment in taking you to the Arctic and getting you shot at, attacked by bears, and then in a wreck? Or how about his getting you shot in a bank robbery. Or how about his getting you shot at all?" By the end of the statement, he was yelling again.

She couldn't very well tell Zane that she was on her own mission and had been lying to him most of his life about Ivan Bychkov. Zane had a baby and mate to worry about, and this was her fight. But she also couldn't let Zane blame Daire. "I'm not working for Daire."

Zane stilled. "You are working for somebody?"

Ah ha. "Yes." She grabbed on to the idea the way she would a lifeline in the middle of the Arctic, easily creating a little cover story and lie. "I've been hired to do a job, and part of that includes researching the planekite situation."

Zane frowned. "And bank robberies?"

"Yes." She smiled. "I needed to get into a couple of safe-deposit boxes for my, ah, job."

"You don't need to work."

She shook her head. "Honey, I'm only a hundred and twenty-five. That's younger than most demons are when they first get mated. I can't just sit around and goof off."

"But, Mom, you're—"

"What? What am I?" Anger and hurt careened through her. "Weak?"

"No."

She put her hands on her hips. "Crippled?"

He sighed. "Of course not."

Water soaked her socks, and she fought a shiver. "I can't attack minds or teleport. So what exactly am I, Zane?"

His gaze softened again. "A grandmother."

Well, geez. "Only because I had you incredibly young, and then you had Hope very young. I'm not ready to retire from life, Zane Kyllwood."

"I'm not asking you to retire. I am asking you not to get shot at." His shoulders seemed to vibrate as he tried to control himself. "Who are you working for, Mom?"

"Can't tell you," she retorted.

"Is it the Coven Nine?" he asked.

She smiled. "Nope."

"Then why is Daire Dunne apparently accompanying you on every insane mission?"

Footsteps sounded around the corner. "Because she's my mate," Daire said evenly, a jacket in his hands. "Now stop bugging her."

Zane tensed and his hands fisted.

"There will be no fighting," Felicity ordered. Her phone buzzed in her back pocket. Thank goodness. She needed an update on what deeds had been discovered in the other two bank robberies. "Excuse me for a minute. You two play nice." Without another word, she opened her phone and sloshed through water to a few feet away. "Hello?"

"Felicity. I can't believe how soon we're going to meet. Finally," rumbled a hoarse voice.

She squinted. Adrenaline zinged through her blood. "Ivan?"

"Ah, how nice you remember my voice." He chuckled.

She pressed the phone closer to her ear, a chill clawing through her. "How did you get this number?"

"Oh, it was in a phone I borrowed," Ivan said.

Her breath whooshed out, and her head lifted. Oh God. "Whose phone?"

"That opens up our next issue. I have something of yours."

No. She swallowed. "Is that a fact?"

"Yes. Here."

A small scuffle sounded, and then the crunch of bone being cracked. "Fucker," hissed a low voice.

Her heart stopped. "Logan?"

Ivan chuckled. "Your youngest has a head stronger than rock. I'll enjoy chiseling through it. I'll be in touch."

Tears burned her eyes. She turned, her mouth agape, her heart shattering. Daire and Zane stared at her, both frowning.

She coughed, fear piercing right through her breastbone. "They have Logan," she whispered.

Daire caught her before she fell and lifted her up. "Bychkov?" he asked.

She nodded, tears streaming down her face. "I didn't think. I just didn't even consider he'd go after Logan. Why didn't I think?"

Daire hadn't considered Logan being in danger, either. "It's okay. We'll figure this out." He turned and headed for the SUV waiting quietly for him by the doorway.

Zane grabbed his arm. "Who is Bychkov, and where is Logan?"

Felicity wiped tears off her face. "Bychkov is an enemy, and I don't know where Logan is. Yet."

Zane opened his mouth and Daire held up a hand.

"Meet at my penthouse in thirty minutes to figure out a plan. For now, reach out to every ally you have and prepare them for war. Once we find Logan, we'll need to go in and fast," Daire said. He didn't wait for a response but jogged through the rain to place Felicity in the front seat. She trembled, and her face had gone so pale that light blue veins could be seen under the skin. "We'll find him, baby. I promise."

She lifted tear-filled eyes and basically sliced his heart in two. "What was I thinking?" she asked, dazed.

He lightly shook her arm, struck by how fragile she appeared. "On the ride to the penthouse, you need to concentrate. I want you to tell me absolutely everything there is to know about Bychkov by the time we get home." He shut the door, wanting nothing more than to gather her close and soothe her fears. If he was going to find Logan, the cuddling would have to wait.

Running around the car, he barely took note of Zane moving his soldiers out. He twisted the ignition, already barking orders into his phone for reports on Bychkov and his consortia. He also put on ready all Coven Nine forces before making a call to Garrett Kayrs.

"Yo," Garrett answered.

Daire swerved to avoid an idiot in a minivan. "Garrett? We've had reports that Logan has been taken by Ivan Bychkov. Do you know anything?"

Garrett sucked in air. "No. We hit the bars last night, scouting for Apollo distributors, and Logan went home with a redhead. Sexy woman." Rustling came through the line and then running footsteps. "He's not in his room."

"Where are you?" Daire used one hand to steer around a kid on a scooter.

"Simone's penthouse. She's the only one with food in the cupboards." A door slammed shut. "Who is Bychkov, and why would he have Logan?"

Daire rolled his shoulders and tried to keep his mind calm. Terror flowed from his mate, and he had to block some of the emotion to keep his brain engaged. "We'll have a full debriefing in thirty minutes in my penthouse. For now, you try to trace where Logan went last night."

"You got it." Determination and irritation filled the vampire's young voice. No fear. That was good.

"And Garrett? Be careful."

"Copy that." The kid hung up.

Daire glanced at Felicity, who huddled with her arms around her legs. "Garrett will call all their friends and then trace Logan's movements last night. The kid is a bloodhound."

She nodded and rested her chin on her knees. "I was so stupid."

He frowned, much preferring her spunky, slightly crazy attitude. "Trust me, mate. It'll be okay." He cleared his throat and punched in another phone number, a call he had to make for both diplomacy and his peace of mind.

"Daire?" the king of the Realm asked.

"Hi, Dage. Quick update. We think Ivan Bychkov kidnapped Logan from a Seattle bar last night. Garrett is fine and is investigating, but I figured you'd want to know."

"Do you need troops?"

Daire shut his eyes. The question came from a friend and not an ally, and there had been no hesitation in the offer. "Not until we have a location." Daire purposefully refrained from explaining more, not wanting to alarm Cee Cee.

"You think he'll be moved from Seattle?"

"Aye." If Daire had to guess, Logan was already on a plane bound for a more secure location. Maybe on the East Coast? The kid had been gone at least fifteen hours, so he could be anywhere. "If your computer gurus wouldn't mind finding out everything you can about Ivan Bychkov, I'd appreciate it." If all his allies were looking into Bychkov, the better.

"Not a problem." Dage cleared his throat. "Did Zane find you?"

"Aye."

Silence ticked across the line. "Well?" Dage asked.

Damn vampire was the nosiest person on the planet. "Well, we had a nice talk, found out his brother had been kidnapped, and we're going from there." Daire sighed. "And I mated his mother."

Dage coughed. "You did *what?*"

Daire pressed harder on the gas petal. They had a limited time to trace Logan before he disappeared, and Seattle traffic was pissing him off. "You heard me. I'll be in touch." He clicked off.

Felicity reached across the seat and took his hand with her chilled fingers. "Please make me a promise."

"Anything," he said, fully meaning it.

"When Ivan calls to trade me for Logan, let me go."

Chapter 23

Felicity stepped over the threshold and followed Daire into his penthouse. Smoke still clung in the air from the flash grenades, but the broken window had been boarded up with rough plywood. She bit her lip, noting a scorched area on the leather sofa.

"Man," Zane breathed, following her inside. He'd arrived right on the heels of the SUV. "What happened here?"

"Your mother happened," Daire retorted, dumping several of the bags from the robberies onto the damaged sofa.

Zane's lips pursed and he slowly scouted the room, his brows drawn down. Then he cut his eyes to her. "What in the world have you been doing?"

She lifted an eyebrow. "Watch your tone."

"Who's Ivan Bychkov?" he returned evenly.

She sucked in air.

Daire cleared his throat. "I'll go grab Simone and some drinks. I'm all out." He nearly passed her and then paused. Slowly, he leaned down and pressed a kiss to her forehead before pinning Zane with a hard look.

Zane narrowed his gaze.

Felicity breathed deep and waited until Daire had kind of shut the damaged front door. "Ivan Bychkov is a demon, and my brother betrothed me to him years before you were born."

Zane coughed. "All of this is about a lover's spat?"

"Of course not."

"Who are you working for?" he shot back.

She faltered. Her stomach hurt. "Nobody. This mission is all mine."

"Why?"

She had to tell him the truth for Logan's sake. "I figured that Ivan would leave me alone after I mated your father."

Zane's chin lowered. "He didn't?"

"No." She took a deep breath and put her shoulders back. "Ivan killed your dad."

Zane stepped back. "Excuse me?"

"Ivan is the demon who killed your father." Her heart hurt now.

"But, but you said Uncle Suri killed the man who murdered Dad." Zane flattened his hand on the wall as if needing support.

She clasped her hands together, trying not to throw up. "I know."

"You lied?" Shock glimmered in Zane's eyes.

"Yes."

"Why?" he shouted.

Her head jerked. "Why?" she shouted back. "Are you kidding me? You were barely a teen, while Sam and Logan were even younger. If one of you, and I mean just one of you, knew your father's killer was alive, you would've been obsessed with finding him."

"Damn straight," Zane bellowed.

"You would've been killed," she said, her voice softening.

Zane swept out an arm. "So you waited until now, until we were all safe, to go after the bastard yourself?"

"Yes."

Breath burst from his lungs. "By robbing banks and blowing up mines?"

"For starters."

"Are you crazy?"

She lifted a shoulder, trying not to cry. "Maybe a little."

Zane shook his head and huffed out a sound of complete denial. "Who *are* you?"

She was still trying to figure that out. "Zane, I know I let you down, and I'm so sorry. But I'm trying to make it right. I'm trying to fix things."

"I don't understand."

She bent slightly at the waist because her chest hurt so badly. "When Dane died, I didn't know what to do. Ivan was still after me, and as you know, we demons weren't aligned with the Realm, so I didn't know Dage would help. I was so weak. I'm so sorry. You'll never know how sorry I am." Tears spilled out over her eyelids and cooled her face.

Zane frowned. "What are you talking about?"

She threw up her hands, finally speaking the whole truth. "I can't attack minds, and I can't teleport. I desperately wanted to fight Ivan, but I couldn't leave you boys alone if I lost. More than that, I couldn't protect you by myself. I'm so sorry. So sorry I had to take us back to Suri for protection. Everything that happened, all that you've been through, is my fault." The guilt almost swallowed her whole, every night.

He frowned down at her. "No, it isn't."

"Do you think I don't know?" she yelled. "About how hard he trained you? About your being forced to become a soldier, to fight and kill? I know all of it."

Zane settled his stance, back in control. "I'm a soldier, Mom. Even if we'd stayed in Africa, even if Dad had lived, I'd be right here now."

She shook her head. "I couldn't protect you." A tear fell from her face to plop on her shirt.

"You protected all of us." He reached her in one long stride and gripped her hands. "We're strong, and we're safe. Going back to Suri was the only way you could keep us safe." Releasing her, he gently wiped the tears from her face. "Stop torturing yourself. We all did our best, and I love you."

"You don't mean that."

"Yeah, I do." He smiled. "Let this go. Trust me."

She wiped her eyes, finally releasing some of the burden. "I love you, too."

He tugged her close for a hug, as always, holding her like she was made of glass. "I didn't know you felt like this, and I should have. I'm sorry."

She sniffed against his chest. "This is all my fault."

"No, it isn't." He leaned back, green eyes serious. "You need to understand that I have never thought you were weak. Abilities like teleporting are just abilities and have nothing to do with strength. You're one of the strongest women I've ever met."

Well, geez. More tears filled her eyes. "Zane."

"And I'm sure that a lot of this mess we're in right now, even though it was your grand plan, is the enforcer's fault." Zane grinned.

Humor tickled up and she chuckled. "Oh, Zane. I've been just awful to him, and he's tried so hard to keep me safe. I drugged him. Three times."

Zane shot both eyebrows up. "And he let you?"

"Well, once." She sobered. "Not once did I think Ivan would take Logan. He's a bad guy, and now he has my baby."

Zane lifted her chin. "Logan is as tough as they come. I know he's young, but he's fought in a war. He's a soldier, and I've trained him. I promise he will be okay."

She swallowed and nodded. "I know. Daire and I already talked, and he promised not to get in the way when I have to go and meet Ivan in exchange for Logan."

The door opened. "I most certainly did not," Daire said, fire crackling down his arms.

The cell deep in the mine was surrounded by black rock on every surface. A lone lightbulb had been strung across the top and hung down, swaying just a little.

Ivan sat on one of two metal chairs across from the young vampire-demon mix, curiosity burning through him. Logan Kyllwood met his gaze evenly, eyes sizzling, the bruise along his jawline already healing now that he'd fully gained consciousness.

They hadn't had a chance to talk until now. "I've wondered about you," Ivan said, the smell of rock and earth wafting around.

The kid leaned back in the chair, and a veil dropped over his eyes. Even bound tight with titanium shackles, a sense of danger cascaded from him. Not once had he complained or asked for any bit of mercy. His gaze had remained sure and determined, his body relaxed. "I don't give a shit about you," he returned.

"You might," Ivan drawled. "Considering I'm going to be your mother's mate."

Logan smiled then.

A chill clacked down Ivan's back, and he fought a shiver.

"There's no way in hell you're getting close enough to whisper to my mother, much less mate her." Absolute confidence echoed in the kid's low tone.

"Do you have her weaknesses?" Ivan asked.

Logan's chin lifted. "My mother doesn't have any weaknesses."

Fair enough. Ivan gathered strength from the atmosphere around them, centered himself, and pushed images of death and decay toward the kid's brain. He waited a beat and propelled blades of pain into Logan's frontal cortex.

A mental shield slapped so quickly into place, Ivan's head jerked back.

Satisfaction filled him. "So you can shield." Good. Any kids he had with Felicity wouldn't be weak like her.

Logan didn't answer.

"Any chance you'll attack me back?" Ivan asked. If he could just determine that the kid had basic demon-fighting abilities, he could rest easier.

"Fuck you." Logan stretched his neck, his eyes blinking.

Was the kid getting sleepy? Jesus. He wasn't scared at all.

Ivan cocked his head to the side. "I could decapitate you right here and now."

"If you were gonna take my head, you would've already done it," Logan drawled.

"Maybe I'm waiting until your mother offers herself as a sacrifice."

Logan lifted a shoulder. "Even if you do take my head, saying you could, I have two brothers who will gladly take yours, plus a best friend who's more dangerous than you'll ever be. And allies, including the Coven Nine enforcers." He kicked out his legs. "My mom will be safe from you, which is all that really matters."

"Well, aren't you cocooned in love and security?" Ivan snapped.

Logan chuckled. "Yeah, I guess so. Who knew we'd end up here?"

Ivan shook his head. He really was going to have to kill the kid, and it was almost a shame. "You ever kill anybody, kid?"

Logan sobered. "None of your business."

"I thought so." Rumor had it Logan had fought during the last war and was a hell of a soldier. "Stays with you, doesn't it?"

"Fuck you."

Ivan smiled. His phone buzzed, interrupting his fun. He sighed and glanced down to see Phillipe Sadler's contact information. Slowly, he lifted the phone to his ear. "Have you found your brother?" he asked without preamble.

"No, but I'm tracing his whereabouts, and if you hurt him, I'll end you," Phillipe said, his voice a throaty threat.

Ivan sighed loudly. "I don't kill my business partners, and if your brother met with trouble, it's more likely that the enforcers tracked him down."

"You know, I think you're full of shit, Bychkov." A rustling echoed over the line.

"I don't know where Rudger is," Ivan said evenly. "If he's working against me, or if this is some sort of power play put on by the two of you, then I'm going to come at you with everything I have."

"Is that a fact?" Phillipe asked. "Do you really think I've just been on a wild ride trying to find him?" Another rustle came over the line, and a woman's low cry pierced Ivan's ears.

"Ivan? I'm so sorry. I didn't know what—"

Ivan shut his eyes. "Millicent?" The stupid cow. She'd seen Rudger's corpse and had cleaned up the blood.

Phillipe came back on the line. "If you want her back, you'll meet me in Seattle."

"Kill her." Ivan ran scenarios in his mind. "Your brother was weak, and you're definitely the brains of the duo. Don't let emotion rule you right now."

"You killed my brother."

"Yes, but he was an idiot. I'm sorry he's dead, but you and I have a business to run." With the young demon watching him alertly, Ivan kept the conversation as vague as possible and tried to hide the flush of anxiety roaring through him.

Phillipe coughed. "I'm going to find you, and your death ain't gonna go easy."

The line went dead.

That stupid woman. He should've killed her the second she'd finished cleaning up the office. Now he had the demon nation, the Coven enforcers, and Phillipe Sadler after his ass. Not to mention the consortia members. He needed to mate Felicity Kyllwood and move his next plan into motion. "Your mother had better show up." If nothing else, just having her captive would give him leverage until he could take care of his enemies.

Logan snorted. "My mom is gonna be pissed, asshole. Believe me, you do not want her to show up."

Ivan frowned. "You know how weak she is."

Now Logan full on laughed. "Man, don't let her size fool you. You're pretty much a dead man sitting there talking to me."

Impressive. Such loyalty and blind faith from a real soldier. Ivan smiled. "Well, she's mad at me anyway."

"I'm sure."

"Considering I killed your father."

The atmosphere altered. The young demon changed into a soldier right before Ivan's eyes. "Excuse me?" Logan asked.

Ivan forced a smile. The promise of death in the kid's eyes didn't unnerve him even a bit. "You heard me." He expected an explosion and a string of threats. What he got, instead, was dark silence.

He swallowed. Maybe he would have to kill the kid before Felicity arrived.

Chapter 24

Daire's penthouse was still smoky, and the boarded-up window turned the place a little dark and gloomy. He ignored the state of his once pristine place and concentrated on his mate, nudging her toward the bedroom. The talk with Zane had exhausted her, and she'd been through enough of an emotional turmoil for now. So it was time to take care of her.

Zane sat in an only slightly damaged chair by the stone fireplace, reading property records, while Felicity had been drinking tea in the kitchen. When she'd returned, she'd looked pale and wan. "You need a warm shower and some sleep," Daire said.

She shook her head. "Ivan will call."

"No." Daire leaned down and smoothed hair from her face. "He's going to let you stew for a while, and he's going to make plans for the moment you walk into his trap. He's not hurting Logan, but he's preparing for a fight." Daire turned her around and pushed gently. "In order to fight, you need a hot shower and sleep." She'd been pale and shivering since they'd talked in the rain, and he was finished with that.

Zane glanced up from the table. "I agree, Mom. Shower and sleep."

Felicity rolled her eyes. "Don't gang up on me."

Daire pointed at her still wet socks. "Go. Warm. Up."

She twisted her lip and glanced down. "A shower wouldn't hurt." With a defiant toss of her still damp hair, she grabbed her cell phone off the sofa table and squished over the wooden floor to the bedroom.

Zane waited until the bathroom door had closed. "I don't think Bychkov will call tonight."

"I agree. It makes more sense to wait it out and make us tense."

Daire rubbed a hand over his hair. "He's also not interested in Logan and doesn't have a history of torturing people."

Zane nodded. "Are you trying to reassure me?"

"Aye." If it was Daire's brother being held, he'd want all the logic he could get. "Bychkov goes for the quick kill, as you know, and he won't kill Logan while your mother is safe here."

Zane nodded. "I know."

Daire exhaled slowly. "There's a guest bedroom off the kitchen. Both your brother and Garrett have stayed there, so I make no claims as to the cleanliness, although I do have a service that comes through once a week."

Zane leaned back in the chair near the fireplace. "You are not setting foot in that bedroom."

Daire grinned. He couldn't help it, although the last thing he needed right then was a fistfight. "Listen, kid. That horse is out of the barn."

Zane leaned forward. "I can put the horse back if I cut off your head."

True. "Your mother is a grown-up, and she can make her own decisions. If she wants me out of the bedroom and here on the sofa, I give you my word I'll be out here." Daire turned for the bedroom.

"I'm more worried she wants you in there," Zane grumbled.

Daire swallowed down a chuckle and shut his bedroom door, heading immediately for the bathroom, shucking clothing on the way. He was nude by the time he reached the bathroom.

Steam coated the mirror and the phone set on the counter. He prowled across the stone tile and stepped around the stone wall to find Felicity, pale in the soft light, under a hot stream.

She jumped when he walked in behind her. "Daire."

"It had better be," he rumbled, sliding a palm down her hair.

"Um, you shouldn't be in here," she said.

He grinned and squirted shampoo in his hands. "This is exactly where I should be." Indulging himself, he threaded the soap through her thick hair and then rubbed it into a lather. "You have the most beautiful hair I've ever seen." His fingers went deeper, and he massaged her scalp.

She leaned into his hands with a soft moan.

The sound licked along his skin to kiss his cock. He kneaded her nape, noting the knots and working on each one until she'd relaxed. She turned around.

He bent her back. "Close your eyes."

She complied, and he washed the suds from her hair. He wiped a couple of suds off her forehead. Her eyes glowed a dark onyx in the steam, a sexy contrast to her light hair. The warmth cocooned them. "We shouldn't."

He chuckled. "There's nothing else for us to do right now." A part of him wanted to relax her so she could sleep, while another part, one deeper and more primal, wanted to plant himself deep inside her and keep her safe. "I know you want to meet Bychkov by yourself, but that can't happen."

She flattened her palms over his pecs. "Getting him alone has always been my plan."

Crazy woman. Why did her insanity arouse him so? He reached around and palmed her ass, lifting her up against the stone. "The idea of you in danger makes me want to really hurt somebody."

She smiled and clapped her knees around his ribs. "Ditto."

Now wasn't that sweet? He lowered her and pressed against her sex.

She hummed and lifted her head, arching against him.

He slowly slid inside her, taking his time, enjoying the devastating heat surrounding his shaft. The warmth slid through him to take root in his chest. If he had a heart, she was in there.

Her cheeks flushed and her eyes darkened. "I love when you're inside me."

Such sweetness. He leaned down and took her lips, teasing her with soft licks at the corners of her mouth. "There's nowhere else in the world I'd rather be," he said, meaning every word. He'd lived long enough to contemplate the afterlife, and he was fairly certain heaven existed. But he knew without question that heaven on earth did, and right now, he was there.

Her smile was slow and so sexy his heart ached. "Just so you know, even though it has been crazy, I've really enjoyed the last week," she whispered, tilting her pelvis and taking more of him.

He pulled out and thrust inside. "As have I." He stilled as her words sank in. "That almost sounded like a good-bye."

"No." Her nails dragged down his chest. "It's a true statement just in case. We don't know what's going to happen tomorrow."

He did. He was going to take down Bychkov, get Logan home safely, and keep her away from danger. Everything had happened so quickly between them, and there had been excitement after dangerous missions after close calls. She needed time and peace to figure out what she wanted, and he was going to give her that. Then they could figure out the mating and slowly get to know each other.

He'd never been in love, but this was probably how it happened. Forget docile and sweet. He wanted wild and willing.

She bit his bottom lip.

Desire roared through him. He kissed her deep, seducing her mouth, tasting the desire in her kiss. His hips moved on their own, thrusting harder, taking him home.

Felicity returned the kiss, moaning under his onslaught. The cool stone behind her back was no match for the heated male along her front. He angled her up, just enough that he brushed across her clit.

Stars flashed behind her eyes. A moan built in her throat, and the muscles in her thighs trembled.

He held her weight with such ease, butterflies winged through her abdomen. His hot mouth peppered desperate kisses along her jawline and down her neck to nip the bite wounds near her shoulder. His bite.

Her body convulsed around him in a mini-explosion. More. There was so much more coming. The steam surrounded them, providing haven in a dangerous world. The man holding her so tightly, dedicated to keeping her safe, was more than she could've wished for while so alone the last few decades. Her last love had been calm and gentle, and she'd appreciated him.

Daire was anything but calm and gentle, and he brought out a side of her she hadn't even known existed. A crazy, free side that just wanted to ride his wildness.

He licked the bite again, and she shivered.

"You like that bite," he murmured as a satisfied statement.

She nodded and clasped her feet at the small of his back. "That feels amazing."

"Hmmm." His lips enclosed her collarbone, and his tongue lashed her.

She moaned.

He kissed the wound. "I wonder if that'll work with other bites."

At the mere thought, her body trembled.

"I'll have to bite your inner thigh and see."

She groaned and he chuckled.

Yeah, she knew they needed to slow down and figure out reality, but a part of her wanted to keep living hard and fast with the tough enforcer. Though dangerous, he had a sweetness to him that she doubted many people had ever seen.

For the first time in way too long, she felt special—and she owed that to Daire Dunne.

His fingers brushed across the brand on her hip, and she gasped. Coils unfolded inside her. She caressed down the hard planes of his chest and hummed while tracing each rib. Slowly, wanting to hold on forever, she moved around and flattened her palm over the Z he'd allowed to remain on his hip.

They were both strong enough to heal the burns, and yet, neither of them had done so. The thought brought tears to her eyes, the emotion coupling with the raw desire setting her on fire. Fire made up Daire, and he was sharing that warmth with her.

He stopped moving, embedded deep. "Felicity."

She blinked, her nails curling into his flesh. Time slowed down.

"Say my name," he whispered.

The order rippled through her, heating every nerve. "Daire," she rumbled.

His cock stretched even farther inside her, swelling. Her clit pounded, and her nipples hardened even more. Hunger claimed her, stealing her breath.

"Your voice destroys me every damn time."

She smiled. "Daire," she murmured, allowing her voice to go deep and throaty.

He shuddered. "You're a dangerous woman."

"That's what I've been trying to tell you." She leaned in and bit right above his heart. They should probably talk about the markings and their future, but at the moment, she just wanted to feel. Life was going to get even more dangerous, and she fully intended to sacrifice herself for Logan, so maybe the present was as close to forever as they'd get. She couldn't say that, so she said the only thing that was safe. "Daire Dunne, enforcer for the Council of the Coven Nine and the sexiest man I've ever met."

He groaned and pulled out to hammer back in. He brushed her clit and pressed hard.

Time awoke and sound roared in. So much, and all at once. Her legs shook.

He pistoned out and thrust back in, pounding into a rhythm so intense all she could do was hold on and feel. So close. So damn close. The sound of flesh slapping together filled the massive shower and echoed off the stone tiles. Her body tightened and he went deeper. So much deeper.

Each hard thrust battered her clit, and she held her breath, exhaling when he withdrew. Dizziness played with her.

Her breath began to pant out with his rhythm, speeding up just as he did. His intense gaze pinned her in place stronger than any hold. Need dug deep into the lines by his generous mouth. His nostrils flared like a predator's finding his mate, giving him a primal look right at home on his rugged face. Water dripped from his thick hair, sliding down his powerful shoulders to his abs. Fire danced down his arms, crackling with righteous hunger. The flames spread from his skin to hers, sizzling across her backside and wandering up to cover her breasts with sparks of heat.

She fell over the edge, sharply crying his name. Her eyes closed, and her head smacked the stone. An avalanche of pure pleasure consumed her, forcing her to ride the wicked edge until it finished with her.

So amazing. Daire Dunne was just amazing. He dropped his chin to her neck, as she'd known he would. The act of intimacy, of understanding what he'd do as he came, filled her with wonder. With joy.

He shook as he came and then slowly licked along her collarbone.

She shivered and clenched around him.

He groaned. "You're garna be the death of me."

She loved, fucking loved, that brogue. "Probably," she murmured sleepily against his shoulder.

He leaned back, and water dripped from his hair onto her arms. "It'd be a hell of a way to go."

She smiled, her eyelids dropping.

"Let's get into bed and go for round two." He carried her out of the shower and immediately surrounded her with a warm towel not nearly as heated as his ripped chest.

She bit into his shoulder again. "I could go another round."

His chuckle filled her with pleasure, and she wished more than anything to be able to hear it forever.

Chapter 25

They spent the next day poring over documents in the still smoky penthouse and waiting for the phone to ring. Felicity held it together all day, as did Zane, but tension hung in the air like a heavy mist.

Finally, darkness arrived and Daire began to prepare for the phone call. He poured another glass of water and handed it to Felicity. Allies had been reporting in for several hours, and so far, they didn't have a line on Logan.

Garrett leaned against the counter, his gray eyes taking on metallic vampire colors as yet another day wore on. "Titans of Fire is having a board meeting in an hour to discuss club business, and I'm thinking somebody knows something."

Daire exhaled slowly. Since Adam and Kellach weren't home yet, he was the only one with the rank to attend the meeting. Dealing with the human Fire members held little appeal to him at any point, and right now, with Logan in a killer's hands, he didn't want to waste time. But Fire distributed Apollo, and Bychkov mined the planekite that created the drug, so that connection was the closest thing Daire had to information on Logan. "This is so frustrating."

Felicity looked up from a stack of papers, dark circles marring the pale skin beneath her eyes. "Do you think the Fire members know where Logan is?"

"No." He said the word gently, wondering how he could reassure her. "But they may have information that leads to Bychkov." It was the only in they had, so ignoring it would be a bad idea.

Zane sat at the table next to his mother with deeds spread out in front of him. He rubbed the back of his neck. "Go ahead to the meeting and see what you can find out. We'll be fine here." His gaze remained shuttered.

What had Daire gotten involved with? Patience had never been one of his strengths, and he was losing what little he had. He didn't take orders from a demon, and he sure as shit didn't take orders from Felicity's kid. The door burst open behind him, and he instinctively turned, putting his body between her and the threat. Zane was already up and over the table to stand by his side before the newcomer skidded to a stop.

Black hair, green eyes, cut features.

"Sam!" Zane said, striding forward to clasp what had to be his younger brother in a hard hug. They were more like two wild broncs clashing horns than a couple of guys hugging.

Daire moved to the side as Felicity hustled by him to hug her boy. The vampire-demon was twice her size and held her gently.

The door hung drunkenly from one hinge, damaged even further. Daire sighed. At this point, he should probably just move.

Felicity drew back.

"Logan?" the vampire-demon asked.

She shook her head. "Zane called you?"

"Of course."

Felicity turned and drew him by the hand. "Sam, this is Daire. Daire, this is my middle son."

Daire frowned. With a mental shrug, he held out a hand to shake.

Sam shook his head. "We haven't met, but I've heard of you and your brothers."

Felicity coughed. "We, ah, mated."

Sam's eyebrows went up. He glanced at a hard-faced Zane, down to his mom, and then at Daire. In one incredibly smooth motion, he freed his hand and jabbed it toward Daire's chin.

Daire caught the fist, and the echo of skin pounding skin echoed around. "I've already taken one punch from a Kyllwood, and that's all it's going to be." He shoved back.

Sam didn't move.

Nice.

Zane chuckled. "We can kill him later, Sam. For now, let's find Logan."

The demon leader probably wasn't kidding. Daire sighed and glanced down at his mate. "I swear, you had better be worth it."

Her smile settled something deep inside him. "I figured out in
the shower yesterday, when we got all hot and heavy, that I totally
am worth it."

Yeah. He figured. Grasping her hand, he led her toward the hallway. "I'd like a moment before I go." His back stiffened, but he chose
to ignore the tension suddenly emanating from Zane and Sam. Once
outside in the hallway, he turned and grasped her hands. "Logan is
a smart kid, and he's tougher than most soldiers ten times his age.
I'll get whatever information I can from the Titans of Fire, and we'll
go from there."

Dark circles marred the pretty skin under her midnight-dark eyes.
But her chin was up, and her shoulders remained back. "I know.
Thank you for helping."

He couldn't help rubbing his knuckles along her cheekbone.
Her skin was unbelievably soft. "We'll get him back, Cee Cee. I
promise."

She blinked and her eyes filled.

His chest ached. Slowly, not wanting to spook her, he lowered his
head and brushed his lips across hers.

A throat cleared. "Ah, Mom? We have some files to go over."

Daire slowly turned his head to catch Sam's hard glare from the
demolished doorway. Jesus. "Go ahead. If you hear any news, call
me," Daire said, nudging Felicity toward her nosy kid.

She nodded and headed back into the safety of the penthouse.
Sam cut Daire another threatening look before turning on his heel.
Daire glanced up at the ceiling. What had he ever done to fate to de-
serve the Kyllwood three sons as family? At least he could be sure
Felicity would be well protected while he was gone and dealing with
Fire.

"Boy have you stepped in a pile of it," said a soft voice from the
penthouse down the hallway.

He turned and grinned at Simone. "No shit."

Her dark eyes sparkled. Dressed in faded jeans, black boots, and
red leather jacket, the woman looked like an Amazon queen. "Kellach and Alexandra just landed at the airport. She's heading into the
station to see if there have been any police gains on the Apollo issue,
and he's coming here to help find Logan. I've been going through
surveillance for cameras along the route we think the redhead took
Logan, but all I've found is one picture of them leaving the bar."

"Send it to my phone," Daire ordered.

"Already did."

He rubbed his eyes, caught between two duties. "I need Kellach on the files pertaining to you and whoever is trying to set you up. Enough people are working Logan's case."

Simone snorted. "One catastrophe at a time."

"No." Daire exhaled slowly. "It's bad, Simone. Whoever is after you has excellent resources. If I didn't know you as well as I do, I'd even be questioning some of the documents."

She leaned against her doorjamb. "But you know, with certainty, that I'm not involved?"

He scowled. "Of course I know."

She smiled. "Thank you."

Daire paused. "You said that Alexandra and Kellach are home. What about Jennie?" Alexandra and Tori's mom was a kick in the pants but somewhat difficult to keep track of.

"She stayed in Dublin and is having a ball with a bunch of the Dunne sisters." Simone shrugged. "Odd pairing, if you ask me. But who knows."

Simone and Tori were an odd pairing for friends, too, but they seemed to be getting along like they'd known each other for decades. Daire glanced at the time on his phone. "Garrett said he and Logan have been staying with you." He looked back up.

Simone flushed a light scarlet. "Those two idiots just moved in because I'm the only one with food. They're like cockroaches. I can't get them to leave."

Daire smiled. The woman was definitely protesting too much. Why she hid her gooey center was beyond him. "It's okay to like them."

"I don't." She snorted but her eyes sparkled. "Go to your meeting. I've got things covered here." She turned on a high-heeled boot and went back inside her apartment. Her door, unlike his, closed nicely.

He sighed and rubbed the back of his neck. Two steps took him to his cracked doorjamb. "Zane?"

The demon glanced up from the pile of papers on the table. "What?"

"Simone Brightston is next door, and she's a member of the Council of the Coven Nine. It's my job to keep her protected, and right now, she has enemies after her." Daire spoke evenly.

Zane glanced at the doorway. "We'll keep her covered while you're gone. You have my word."

He nodded. "Thanks." He would've had to have been blind not to miss Felicity's dazzling smile as he and her kid worked together. If only it were as easy as that. "I'll be in touch." Grabbing his coat decorated with the Titans enforcer patch from the closet, he strode down the hallway and stairs to the underground garage. Straddling his bike calmed him, but he'd have to hurry to make the meeting.

Garrett jogged into the garage just as Daire was about to light up his engine. "What?" Daire asked.

"Coming with you." Garrett reached his Harley and swung his leg over. "The prospects and other members hang out in the bar while the board meetings take place. I'll see if anybody knows where Logan is or if anybody knows about Apollo. I may ask to score some, if I get the right vibe."

Good plan. Daire turned the key and his pipes roared to life. He drove into the misty Seattle evening and allowed the movement and rumble to ease his senses and focus his mind. The kid stayed on his six, and they easily made it through Seattle traffic and onto open road. The scents of pine and rain soon filled his senses.

His mind remained on one tiny blond demon. How frightened she must be with her youngest son in the hands of a bastard like Bychkov. But she'd held it together, showing the strength he'd come to expect from her. While she seemed to think he and her sons had reached a détente, he knew better. Family complicated everything.

Soon the road condensed, and way too soon he was parking outside of the Titans of Fire Motorcycle Club headquarters. Music and the smell of spilled tequila poured out of the open doorway to the main bar.

He crossed inside, catching several furtive looks. When he'd created a fake motorcycle gang in Ireland in order to merge with Fire, many of the Fire members had objected to the partnership. His driving both Harleys and Ducatis had also been a bone of contention and led to more than one remark about pansy foreigners. So he'd promptly put three Fire members in the hospital and then assigned Kellach to be the main contact with the club.

The three members remained in-patients for quite some time, and one guy still needed physical therapy. So Kellach hadn't been bothered much when he'd started his duties.

Daire stepped inside, and the heat from many bodies slammed into him. The last time he'd made that step, he'd seen Felicity for the first time. It seemed like a lifetime ago. He crossed through the crowd toward the back of the bar, grabbed a beer, and proceeded into the long hallway of Fire bedrooms to the main conference room.

Garrett would probably wait a few minutes and then join the party. The Fire members didn't know Daire was working with either Garrett or Logan, who were posing as prospective members.

The heavy oak door required a hard shove, and Daire pushed, prowling into the quiet room. A thick oval table took precedence with several chairs around it. Pictures of club members and several old cuts lined the walls. Pyro, the Fire leader, sat at the head of the table, his hair greasy, his eyes bloodshot, his cheeks red. An empty chair sat next to him, and three other members filled out chairs.

Daire slowed and then shut the door. The empty chair had belonged to Duck, Pyro's nephew and former vice president of the club. Duck had been murdered just a week before, and from the look of Pyro, he wasn't taking it well. Daire relaxed his body and tuned in to the club's president, noting altered biorhythms, sluggish blood flow, and burning lungs. The guy had definitely been self-medicating with cocaine and alcohol.

"Is Kellach still in Ireland?" Pyro asked, his voice weary.

"Aye." Daire leaned back against the door. "I thought I'd attend the meeting."

Pyro shrugged a shoulder beneath a T-shirt stained with motor oil, ketchup, and something green. "Fine. Where are my guns?"

"Kellach is working on the holdup right now, and the new guns should arrive sometime within the next week." The guns Daire had moved to the States and stored near the airport had somehow been confiscated by the Seattle Police Department. Aye, he'd called in the tip, and since Alexandra had been in Ireland, no way could the betrayal be traced to him. "When's the next shipment of Apollo?" he asked.

Pyro flipped through a series of papers in front of him. "Tuesday." He scrubbed down his face, his eyebrows rising when whiskers scrunched. "Our dealers are almost out of stock, and since they've been educating buyers about not taking too much of Apollo, we've only had three new deaths reported."

The key to that sentence was the word *reported.* Daire lifted his chin. "Who's supplying us?"

Pyro glanced up, his head swaying a little. "Who's *our* gun supplier in Dublin?"

Daire forced a grin. "The supplier doesn't like anybody knowing his name."

"Neither does our contact for Apollo." Pyro scratched his elbow and stared off into the distance.

One of the other members, a newly paroled longtime member named Jamm, tapped his fingers on the table. "You okay, Pyro?" he asked, his voice raspy after years of smoking without filters.

Pyro nodded his head. "Fine." He glanced around as if surprised to find everyone at the table. "Uh, any other business?"

Jamm pushed away from the table. His dark beard reached his chest, while his hair had been cut short. Tattoos covered both of his arms to the wrists. "No. Just get some rest."

Nobody mentioned the empty chair, although somebody would have to become vice president at some point.

Daire cleared his throat and reached for his phone. "We're missing one of the prospects, and he left Short's Bar last night with this woman. Any ideas?" He held out the phone.

Jamm took it and studied the screen. "We're missing Logan?" His chest rose. "That kid is great with bikes. How long he been gone?"

"Almost twenty-four hours, and he's not answering calls or texts," Daire said.

Jamm twisted his lip. "With this chick, I don't blame him."

Pyro stood and grasped the table until he appeared steady. "Prospects are supposed to be reachable at all hours. Let me see."

Jamm handed over the phone.

Pyro's head jerked back. "That's one of the Grizzly skanks."

Daire reclaimed the phone and studied the picture. Tall redhead with presence and broad shoulders. Could be a bear shifter. "I'll call Bear."

"Hell no." Spittle flew from Pyro's mouth. "I've had enough of the Grizzlies. My nephew wanted to take them out, and I was too stubborn to listen. Enough is enough. Our men are hurting, and the only way to cure that is to draw blood."

Daire slid the phone into his pocket. "I'll talk to Bear first and see who the woman is. Our priority is finding our prospect."

Pyro shook his head, his pupils so wide the blue was barely discernible in his eyes. "No. This is for Duck."

"Amen," Jamm said, smacking his hands together.

The other board members stood. A guy named Knife grabbed a blade from his back pocket. "For Duck."

Shit. Daire couldn't stop all of them without using plasma, and letting them know he was a witch was an incredibly bad idea. So he faked a smile. "I guess it's war."

Chapter 26

Zane Kyllwood didn't particularly like witches, and he really hated sitting around and waiting in Daire's penthouse. As a soldier, he was trained to go in fast and hard. This hanging out, studying deeds and maps, made him want to rip off his own head. Sitting at the table was not working for him.

An enemy had his brother.

A cold lump settled in his gut, and he had to work to force down the rage. And fear. Logan was trained and smart as hell. Even so, he was a kid. The idea of his little brother being tortured or beheaded made Zane's head swim.

Kellach Dunne barked orders into his phone while pacing the long wall of windows, and Simone Brightston worked a computer on the counter, looking for surveillance footage. There had been a brief but entertaining scuffle between Kell and Simone when he'd ordered her to work in Daire's penthouse. The woman had nicely refused, but Kell hadn't taken no for an answer.

Based on the materials Zane had read, if Simone really wasn't involved in the mining and sale of planekite, somebody sure wanted her to look guilty. He would've ordered her into safety if she'd been his to protect, too.

Sam slid an energy drink in front of him, and he took it gratefully. There was nothing like having his brother at his back. "Anything?" Sam asked.

"No." Zane shoved another manila file across the table.

Their mom flipped through a series of maps, muttering to herself. Zane kept an eye on her, having no doubt she'd take off at some point to meet Bychkov without any backup. If there was a chance to save

Logan, she'd sacrifice herself. He knew that much about her, if nothing else.

Sure she was young, but she'd always been steady and forward moving.

Not bat-shit crazy. And fighting polar bears, robbing banks, and plotting revenge against somebody as powerful as Bychkov was bat-shit crazy. Not to mention mating one of the Coven Nine enforcers. They were dangerous and nuts. Now Zane would either have to watch her take a dangerous experimental drug a second time to negate the mating bond, or he had to cut off Daire Dunne's head.

Something told him neither path would be an easy one.

"I'm staying mated," his mom whispered, turning a map around and holding it up to the light.

The woman had always known how to somehow read his mind. "No, you're not."

An eyebrow lifted, and she glanced around the map of Europe. "Behave yourself, young man."

It took every ounce of control he owned not to reply with a "yes, ma'am." He bit back any other response, cutting Simone a look. The witch had abandoned the computer and was watching the scene with sparkling eyes. "You might want to get back to work."

"Watch yourself, demon." She sniffed and turned back to the computer. "I'll burn you to a crisp."

Witches. He was suddenly surrounded by witches. "They're all insane," he whispered to his mom.

Simone snorted, typing away quickly.

"I like 'em," his mom responded.

She would.

Sam, ever the peacemaker, leaned against the demolished front doorjamb and crossed his arms. "Mom, don't you think you rushed into this a little bit?"

She shrugged. "Life can be short."

Zane didn't know her at all. Who was this woman? "Which is why we plan carefully and proceed slowly."

"You've never done either, son." She returned to studying her maps.

Okay, he needed to rein in his temper and fast. He had a mate and baby girl in Idaho, and the second he found Logan, he was taking his entire family there for some quiet time. His mom and all three of his brothers would remain at demon headquarters for the near future, and they'd all live in fucking peace.

"I'm not going to retire in Idaho and knit stuff," his mom murmured.

"Are you reading my mind?" he barked out.

"Of course not." She looked up from the map and blinked her pupils smaller. "I just know how your mind works."

Yeah, which was why he hadn't gotten away with anything since he was two years old.

Kellach switched off a call, and his phone buzzed instantly again. "What?" He stilled, and his shoulders stiffened.

Zane leaned forward. Was the call about Logan?

"When?" Kell barked. Then he listed, his entire body going stiff. "Got it. Thanks." He slowly turned, and his gaze sought out his cousin.

"What?" Simone asked.

"The deeds, manifests, and corporation documents tying you to the mining, manufacturing, and distribution of Apollo have been leaked. The Coven Guard is on its way to fetch you and take you back to Dublin." Kellach's jaw hardened, and a muscle pounded down his neck.

Simone stood and clasped her hands together. "Then I should get packed."

"No," Kellach exploded. "You will not go with them. Not until we figure out what's going on and clear your name."

Her eyes darkened. "Kellach, you're an enforcer for the Nine. You can't hide me, and you can't commit treason. I have to go."

Zane watched the interplay. He kind of liked the spunky witch, and his best friend was pretty much in love with her. Probably. Nicholai Veis would kill Zane if he didn't interfere. "I can offer asylum."

"No," Simone said.

"Yes," Kellach shot back.

Zane reached for his phone and quickly texted Nick. "I'll have one of my top soldiers escort you to safety."

Simone threw back her hair, and a gorgeous blue flame danced down her arms. "Absolutely not. I am a member of the Coven Nine, and I will not run. It's time to face these charges."

"When will he be here?" Kellach asked, completely ignoring his cousin.

Zane glanced at his phone. "As soon as he lets me know where he is, I'll get him." Zane had an above average ability to teleport, and he'd transport his buddy, who unfortunately hadn't inherited the gene. But Nick was a hell of a fighter even without the skill. "Right now he's undercover on an operation that has nothing to do with planekite or witches, so as soon as he sees the text, he'll call in." But it could be hours.

"What kind of operation?" Simone asked.

Did she want to know out of curiosity, or was it something more? Zane rubbed his chin. "We're negotiating a peace with the shifters out of Alaska, and Nick has gone under to, ah, obtain information." Blackmail was fine in Zane's world.

"I'm going to Dublin," Simone said.

Kellach shook his head. "You're in danger, and as an enforcer, I can order you to safety."

She set her hands on her hips. "You can't order me to break Coven law and hide, Kellach. You know that."

Kell's phone dinged, and he lifted it to his ear after reading the face. "Get back here. We have a prob—" His head lifted. His shoulders dropped. "You're kidding me." He shook his head. "No. Simone is busy." Then he bit his lip. "Keep me informed."

Zane lifted his eyebrows. "Problem?"

"You could say that." Kellach studied the group at large. "Apparently the Titans of Fire are going to avenge a member's death by attacking the Grizzlies."

"When?" Simone asked.

"Right now." Kellach shook his head and quickly typed something into his phone. "I'll let Alexandra know, and hopefully the cops can stop the fight before it happens."

Simone grabbed Zane's drink and took a big swallow. "If Daire gets arrested, he'll need his lawyer, because with Felicity about to meet an enemy, no way will Daire allow the Seattle cops to keep him." She smiled. "I'm his lawyer. So I guess I can't go into hiding."

Frustration lined Kellach's face, and Zane could relate. "Why don't you warn Bear, so he can prepare to get Daire out of the line of fire in case there is a problem?" Zane asked. It'd be easier to avoid arrest than to get out of one.

Kellach nodded. "Good idea." He punched in more keys on his phone.

Zane sighed and stretched back in his chair. He was getting way too involved in Coven business.

His mom smiled. "They're our business, too."

Felicity turned the map around. No matter what happened, she had to figure out a way to destroy the Sjenerøse mine. She'd gone through all of the stolen deeds, and so far, there weren't any surprises. But planekite was so important, she wouldn't be shocked to find a mine or two well hidden.

The tension in the penthouse was palpable, and it wasn't coming from just Zane. Kellach continued to pace at a rapid speed, and Simone glared at him with her hands on her hips.

"Simone?" Felicity asked. "If you don't mind a couple of questions, I was wondering what would happen if the Coven guards escorted you to Dublin."

The stunning witch turned her focus on Felicity. "Charges will be read against me, there will be an investigation, and I'll probably go on trial."

Fascinating. The witches had been secretive for so long. "Who's the trial judge for your people?"

"The remaining members of the Coven Nine will sit as judges." Simone shoved curly black hair away from her face. The mass cascaded down her shoulders to the small of her back.

Felicity fingered her straight hair. She'd always wanted curls. "Um, what are the possible repercussions?"

"Removal from the Nine or death." Simone stood straighter and rolled her shoulders. "For these charges? Death."

No wonder Kellach Dunne wanted to force his cousin to safety.

Felicity's phone vibrated against her leg. She stood and headed for the bedroom and bathroom, feeling everyone's gaze on her as she moved. She hustled into the bathroom and locked the door. "Hello?" she whispered.

"Hello. Are you ready to bargain?" Ivan asked.

"Where's my son?" Anger threaded through her, and she fought to keep calm.

"Logan is fine and will remain so. I have no wish to harm your son." Ivan cleared his throat. "Last time we chatted, you were at the Seattle airport. Now, I can see you're at Dunne's penthouse."

She frowned. "Yes."

"Where?"

She glanced around. "The bathroom. Don't worry. They can't hear us."

"Good."

Felicity paused. "Well? What's the plan?"

A bomb ripped through the night, and the entire building rocked. The mirror fell off the wall, and she barely had time to jump toward the door before glass exploded. She fell, her knees impacting shattered glass. Pain rippled up her legs. She scrambled for the doorknob and yanked open the door.

Smoke assaulted her.

Her kids. She crawled out and pushed to her feet, trying to kick past a bunch of pillows that had been blown from the bed. A gaping hole in one wall sent rain billowing inside.

She coughed out smoke and tried to focus, but the smoke stung her eyes. Tears streamed down her face. She stumbled into the other room to find black smoke. Kellach and Sam were sprawled unconscious next to another yawning hole in the outside wall. Rain and wind pushed their way in. If either of the men tried to get up and tripped, they'd drop ten stories to the concrete street.

Simone lay in the kitchen, only her legs visible.

Zane crashed through the inner wall, fighting furiously with two men in gas masks.

Oh. Gas. Her mind spun, and her stomach heaved. Trying not to breathe, she slid over to Sam and grabbed his pants legs. Grunting with the effort, she dragged him away from the hole. Her shoulders protested, and her back ached, but she left him and grabbed Kellach under the arms. He weighed as much as Sam, and she was sweating by the time she got him to safety. A quick check of their necks confirmed they were out but alive.

She searched for a weapon in the demolished room. Nothing. With a shriek, she flew across the room and landed on the back of one of the guys fighting with Zane.

Her vision blurred, and her lungs burned.

Whatever was in the grenade slid into her central nervous system. She had to fight to remain conscious. Even as she watched, Zane's movements slowed.

The guy in the mask punched him hard in the face.

The man she'd jumped on reached back and yanked on her hair. Pain exploded in her head. She jabbed her elbow into her attacker's neck, right in the sweet spot. His neck cracked. He dropped to one knee, and she jumped off him, spinning a side kick into his temple. He toppled to the floor.

She swayed. Three more men in masks ran through the door.

One of them reached her just in time to grab her before she fell. Her last thought was that she hoped Zane didn't fall out the window while fighting.

Chapter 27

Daire signaled for Garrett to break off and fall behind the motorcycles roaring toward Bear's headquarters to wage war. The kid nodded and began to make his move. He couldn't afford to get taken down to the police station, and Daire couldn't afford for the king of the Realm, Garrett's uncle, to be pissed off right now. Hopefully Bear would diffuse the situation once they arrived.

If Bear stayed true to form, he wouldn't diffuse shit.

Trees sped by, and a fine Seattle mist covered their bikes as they rode hell-bent for trouble. The Fire members reached the Grizzly courtyard, and two rows of Grizzly members were waiting. Wearing their cuts and pissed-off expressions, they looked as dangerous as the mountains rising high above them. Apparently Kellach had decided to warn them, which may have been a good idea. Or maybe not.

How could humans not see something immortal within these guys? It was so obvious they were bear shifters.

Daire growled low and cut his engine. He needed to get back to his mate and not fuck around with a bunch of humans and bears. Why the hell had he agreed to this mission in Seattle in the first place? Of course, if he hadn't agreed, he never would've met Felicity.

The Fire members silenced their bikes. It looked like the numbers were about even, but the humans had no clue they might face bared teeth and three-inch claws.

Bear stepped forward, irritation sizzling in his deep eyes. "What the fuck?"

Pyro disembarked. "Where is our prospect?"

"No clue, man." Bear lowered his chin and actually looked like a bear. Tension vibrated from him with an animal ferocity, and several of the Fire members shifted their feet uneasily. They might not know Bear was a bear, but their instincts seemed to be kicking in. "Why the hell are you here?" he all but growled.

Pyro motioned Daire forward. "We have a picture of one of your skanks with our prospect leaving a bar the other night. Where is he?"

Daire handed the phone to Bear.

Bear studied it, and his eyebrows rose. A growl rumbled from his chest. "That's Tasha."

"One of your skanks?" Pyro asked, triumph in his voice.

"No." Bear returned the phone, his jaw tightening. "She's a nice girl and not a skank. This was the other night?"

"Aye," Daire said. There were many female members of Bear's club, but in order to stay under the radar and appear like other clubs, nobody knew it. Women were either old ladies, skanks, or visitors to the outside world. To the inside? There were some badass female warriors in Bear's group, but Tasha looked fairly young and probably wasn't a full club member. "Any word from her?"

Bear lifted his head and surveyed his men. "Has anybody heard from Tasha?"

Nobody stepped forward.

Well, shit. "We think the prospect disappeared with her the other night." Daire tried to communicate more.

"Leads?" Bear asked, fury flowing from him.

"Not yet. Working on it." Daire glanced at Pyro.

Bear stepped toward him. "Does the prospect's family know he's missing?"

"Aye." Daire bit back a snarl. "They're here, in fact."

Bear winced. "Sorry."

It was nice to have a buddy who understood. Dealing with demons wasn't easy in the best of circumstances. Daire stepped closer to Pyro. "Bear doesn't know anything, and we need to get out and find our prospect. Let's go."

Pyro waved him off, the stench of smoke and booze pouring off him. He swayed in his battered boots, but determination hardened his jaw. "I promised the boys a good fight, and I figure we're due. For Duck!" He rushed toward Bear and was instantly taken down by Lucas Clarke, Bear's top lieutenant.

The Fire members billowed forward, already throwing punches.

Lucas wasted no time in flipping Pyro over and smacking his

forehead into the concrete. A genuine smile, dark and grim, curved the shifter's lips when Pyro began to gurgle up blood.

"I told you not to attack," Daire muttered.

Two Fire members ran for Bear, only to be stopped by two angry Grizzly members.

Bear grabbed Daire's arm, pivoted, and tackled him through the open door. Daire landed hard with a fucking bear on his chest. His lungs protested, and his ass hurt from smashing onto a wrench. "Get off."

Bear kicked shut the door and stood, holding a hand to Daire.

Daire took the hand and jumped to his feet, rubbing his butt. "Put your damn tools away."

"You're welcome." Bear reached down and grabbed the wrench to toss it onto the counter. It clanked away and landed on the other side. "Damn it all to hell. Can't you control those Fire idiots?"

"Apparently not." Daire shoved rain off his face.

Bear sighed. "We have about five minutes until the cops show up."

Sirens echoed down the lane.

"Make that one minute." Bear hustled for a back door. "Follow me."

Daire ducked his head and followed Bear through an office to a garage holding a Bentley, a new Porsche, and a Spyder. "Nice," he muttered, careful not to touch anything.

"My mechanics are the best in the Northwest." Bear ran through a back door to where a couple of bikes were parked. "Take the Harley." He jumped onto a Victory Gunner.

A helicopter's rotors split the rain-filled night, and a beam of light poured down from a police helicopter.

"Shit." Bear started the bike and roared toward what looked like a trail.

Daire followed suit, his head down to avoid the rain.

The light swept to and from, and he tried to keep to the tree line. Garrett Kayrs had better have gotten clear before the cops showed up.

Red and blue swirled through the clouds, and the screech of vehicles stopping competed with the helicopter noise. Gunfire pinged through the air.

Shit. Who was shooting? Pyro had completely lost it. If Daire could get him alone, he might be able to finally get a line on both the distributor and manufacturer of Apollo. Or maybe it was time to just torture the club leader for information.

Daire followed Bear down a narrow path, ducking several times to avoid tree branches. Wind whipped into him, and the rain traced a chilly path down his neck and underneath his cut. He thought about using fire to warm up, but the helicopter might see the flames and investigate. Adrenaline flowed through his veins, and the need to get back home to Cee Cee compressed his lungs. Instinct bellowed for him to return and shield her.

The path wound around trees and bushes for several miles, finally ending up at a logging road halfway up a mountain.

An SUV blocked the road, and Detective Alexandra Monzelle leaned against the passenger side door, gun out and pointed at them. Rain matted her no-nonsense blond hair to her head, and her eyes glowed a dark blue through the darkness. She was small and lean . . . and knew how to shoot. She was also mated to Kellach, but that didn't guarantee any cooperation, unfortunately. She'd shot him a couple of times, Daire was fairly certain.

Bear rolled to a stop first, and Daire followed suit, both cutting their engines.

"Welcome back," Daire drawled, twisting his neck to look inside the vehicle. Empty. Good. She'd come alone and not with any other cops. "How was Ireland?"

"Lovely. Your aunt sends her love." Alexandra jerked her head. "Want to tell me what's going on?"

Bear rested his arms on his handlebars. "Want to tell me how you even know this road exists?"

She eyed him. "I memorized every escape road within miles when I was investigating you."

Bear grinned, flashing a dimple. "I think you're still crushing on me, Detective."

Daire rolled his eyes. "Bear, now isn't the time to set yourself up for a death match with Kellach."

"Ah, but she'd be worth it." Bear winked.

Alexandra tightened her hold on the gun. "I'd prefer not to shoot you, Bear."

"Sounds like foreplay to me," the bear retorted.

Man, he really wanted to get shot. Weren't most bears a honey pot away from insanity? Daire shook his head. The woman was as close to a sister-in-law as possible in his world, and while he had enough to deal with, he still felt concern. Though she'd mated Kellach, and her chromosomal pairs would increase to those of a mate and grant immortality, that took time. Right now, she was vulnerable. "Alexandra, you were shot way too recently. How are you?"

"Already healed," she said.

Good. Daire cleared his throat. "You should have a partner or backup."

She sniffed. "If I had backup, I'd be cuffing you and putting you in the back of the SUV. This way we can have a nice chat, and you can try to convince me not to cuff your asses." She smiled, her aim staying true. "Give it a shot."

"You can do whatever you want with my ass." Bear chuckled. "I think I love you."

Aye. Bear was nuts. Daire dug deep for patience yet once again. "Does Kellach know you're out here alone?"

She released the safety on the gun.

Daire bit back a sharp retort. Something caught his eye. He twisted his head. "Is that a diamond?"

She blushed. "Yes."

He smiled. "You're engaged."

"Yes. So please don't make me shoot you." She held out her left hand and turned it to reveal a diamond surrounded by emeralds.

Man, she was tough. He nodded. "Congratulations."

"Thank you," she huffed.

Bear winced. "I think you could do better."

Daire reached over and punched him in the arm. He could let his friend get away with only so much. "Stop hitting on my brother's woman."

"Your brother's *what*?" Alexandra hissed.

Shit. He'd forgotten the cop didn't like archaic language and was just fine with shooting members of his family. Or Bear. She'd even shot Bear at one time. Daire had forgotten that fact. "You know what I meant."

Bear grinned and shook his shaggy hair. "No, Daire. Tell the lady with the gun what you meant."

That was it. He was going to have to kill Bear. "Alexandra, I have to get back to the penthouse, and it's life or death."

"It's always life or death, and you're not going anywhere until you both explain what's going on," she said, not moving an inch.

Daire glared at the barrel. Though a bullet wouldn't kill him, it would hurt like hell and slow him down. He could leap over the handlebars and take the weapon, but that would just make Kellach mad. "Fine. Logan was with one of Bear's members before disappearing, and I made the colossal mistake of showing the picture of the pretty redhead to Pyro. He figured it was time to avenge his nephew and wage war."

"Kellach said that Logan had disappeared, and that's why I headed down to the station early. But there wasn't any information about missing prospects or anything interesting that happened around the bar where he disappeared." Alexandra frowned. "Why is Pyro attacking now? Bear didn't have anything to do with Duck's murder."

"I know, but Pyro is not thinking clearly." Daire eyed his cell phone. "I really have to go."

"Wait a minute. You said the woman with Logan had red hair." Alexandra asked slowly, "What does the woman look like?"

Bear stiffened. "Why do you ask?"

"We have a head with red hair at the morgue. I just checked in and was assigned the case immediately," she responded.

Daire brought up the picture and handed the phone over the front of his bike. "You've only been back a couple of hours."

"It's my job, and I'm good at it." She glanced down, made the picture brighter, and sighed. "We have a redhead in the morgue." She grimaced. "I'm sorry, Bear. We actually have her head but haven't recovered the body yet. It's definitely her."

Bear growled, losing every inch of his teasing persona and showing the predator he usually kept veiled. "Where was her head discovered?"

"It was found in a garbage can outside of a restaurant on the north side. All the way across the city from the bar where she and Logan disappeared." She shook her head. "I'm so sorry."

"Time of death?" Bear asked.

"We don't know yet." Alexandra handed back the phone and holstered her weapon.

Bear rubbed rain from his face. "Was her head ripped off or cut off?"

"Cut off with a blade. Surgical precision and immortal strength," Alexandra returned, all business. But sadness glimmered in her eyes, and once again, Daire could see what had taken his brother to his knees. The woman was tough and sweet, and Kell hadn't stood a chance.

Bear half turned toward Daire. "Tasha was one of mine, Daire. Not a warrior, not a soldier, but a nice kid who probably was just hooking up with Garrett for fun. She didn't deserve to die, and she doesn't have any other family to avenge her death. If you know who did this, I want in."

"I know who did this," Daire said. The phone buzzed, and Sam's face came up on the screen. "Sam?" he asked.

Sam coughed hard. "We, ah, were attacked." He erupted in a fit of more coughing. "Smoke and drugs," he gasped.

Daire gripped the phone. "Felicity?"

"She was taken."

Chapter 28

Felicity coughed herself awake and sat up in a cushioned bed. Her lungs ached and her head swam. Whatever they'd pumped into her veins had taken hold and lasted far too long. Her mouth tasted like she'd eaten coal, and no saliva wet her tongue.

She tried to focus, but her head lolled on her neck.

A glass of water near the bed caught her eye. She reached for it, her fingers fumbling and almost knocking it over.

God, she needed that water.

Lowering her chin, she reached out with both trembling hands and encircled the glass. Slowly, she raised it to her mouth and tipped it back to drink. The second the liquid touched her lips, she lost all control.

Water cascaded down her throat, over her mouth, and across her chin.

She didn't care.

The second it landed in her stomach, she groaned. Okay. Better. Much better.

She set down the glass and wiped her chin, allowing her eyes to focus in the dim light. Her head throbbed and her muscles felt lax. She glanced down. Silk bedspread, plush pillows. Fear sizzled through her until she'd patted her arms and looked at her yoga-pants-covered legs.

Okay. Good. She might be in a bed, but her clothing had remained on. Except for her socks. Her feet were bare.

Silence surrounded her, deep and pounding. No outside sounds at all penetrated the walls.

A dim light glowed from the bed table, and she kicked free, trying to stand. Her knees wobbled, and she had to hold on to the bed for several precious moments, trying to regain her strength. Finally, she could stand without falling.

A door took up the center of a far wall, so she shuffled across plush carpet to reach for the doorknob. The golden knob didn't even turn. Swallowing, she reached for the light switch on the wall and flicked it up.

The light slashed pain through her skull, and she winced, closing her eyes. She took in several deep breaths and exhaled, trying to calm her galloping heart. She opened her eyelids enough to let a little light inside. Then, taking her time, she slowly opened them all the way. A deep purple carpet covered the floor and matched the bedding. A feminine dresser and end tables were set in the room. Two doorways led to a walk-in closet and fully appointed bath, also in purple.

An original oil painting by Juno Dungs above the bed added more vibrancy to the already colorful room. The walls had been painted a muted beige.

She quickly scoured through the dressers and only found lingerie, yoga pants, and some jeans. More clothes, probably in her size, filled the closet.

Damn it. There had to be something she could use to pick the lock.

Staggering only a little, she made it to the bathroom. Typical feminine makeup, all unused, filled the drawers. No bobby pins or nail files. Damn it.

She searched for a weapon but only found a black eyeliner. So she slid it up her sleeve just in case. Maybe she could use it to poke an eye out. She meandered back into the bedroom and crossed to examine the door.

As she reached it, the knob turned and it opened inward.

Ivan Bychkov stepped inside. "Felicity. It is so good to see you."

She lost all reason. Yelling, she leaped across the foot separating them and slammed into him, jamming her elbow down on his collarbone. The cartilage cracked with a very satisfying crunch.

Using his uninjured side, he grabbed her arm, swinging her out and throwing. She spun through the air and landed on the bed, rolling off the other side. Pain lanced up her shoulder. She stood, grasping the bed covers for balance.

Ivan frowned and rubbed his collarbone. "Good lord, woman. You're wilder now than you were a century ago."

"Thank you," she said, showing her teeth.

"That changes and now." He stood about six-foot-six, long and lean, with stark white blond hair and purebred demon black eyes. To most women, he'd be handsome.

But she could see all of him, and real evil lived in him. "You know I'm going to kill you, right?" she spat.

His eyebrows were a light brown, and he drew them down. "I just don't understand the hostility."

She blinked. "Are you kidding?"

He sighed. "The drug we used will hamper you for a while, and according to my doctors, you need protein and sugar in your system. If you'd please come with me, we'll get you fed."

The guy was crazy. "Where's my son?"

"He's fine and is safely secured in the mine area of the mountain." Bychkov rocked back on his heels. "The dizziness you're experiencing can be quelled by a good meal."

Okay. So her vision was a little blurry. "What did you drug me with?"

"A cocktail created by a friend of mine by altering normal tranquilizers."

Damn witches and their potions. Of course, that's exactly how she had drugged Daire. She winced. Man, would Daire be pissed that she'd been kidnapped. She stepped around the bed. "Fine. I'll eat, and then I want to see my son." At the very least, ingesting protein would help her regain her strength to take on Ivan. "Where am I, any—" She gasped upon entering the hallway.

Sparkling rock surrounded her, while a long carpet stretched over more rock. "We're underground," she breathed.

"Yes."

That explained the quiet. "Where?" she asked, adrenaline heating down her back.

"On the island," he said, pivoting on his boot and leading the way.

Her lungs seized. "On Fryser Island?"

"The one and only." He clasped his hands at his back and strode past several closed doorways.

"We're at the Sjenerøse mine," she murmured, tripping and regaining her balance. "How did you get me here?"

He glanced over his shoulder. "Once you were knocked out, I teleported you here, of course."

Crap. She hadn't thought of that. Sure, a majority of demons could teleport, but she hadn't counted on being squired a world away from home. "I can't teleport."

"I know." He sighed, stopping in front of a silver-plated elevator and pushing a button.

She hovered near the wall and planted her hand over the sparkles. Many minerals glowed, but a shiny greenish pink one held promise. Obviously not silver or coal. "Is this planekite?" she asked.

"Yes." The elevator door swished open and he stood back, gesturing her inside.

The mineral felt cold and innocuous. It was hard to imagine that something so pretty could actually kill an enforcer with Daire's strength. Even walking down the hallway would weaken him and subdue his powers.

Which led to another problem. She turned and stepped into the elevator. "Isn't this mine only accessible by parachuting in?" Her stomach dropped.

"And teleporting," Ivan said, following her and pressing a button near the top. "Every man I have working here has the ability to teleport in and out, just in case of mine failure or attack."

Futility slammed into her stomach. Neither she nor Logan could teleport. Hopefully Logan would someday gain the ability; he was young yet. But she'd never have it, and now the only way out of the mining area for them was to climb down a series of frozen mountain slopes to the arctic tundra miles away. They'd face many predators, and she had no interest in going up against wild polar bears ever again.

Ivan cleared his throat. "By the way, we have all the surrounding area covered with land mines. Anybody trying to leave here by any way other than teleporting will be blown into tiny pieces even a witch couldn't put back together."

The Humpty Dumpty nursery rhyme trilled through her head. There had to be a place for a helicopter to land.

"We're covered by trees with no cleared space," Ivan continued as if slapping away each idea that occurred to her. "Any clearing big enough for a helicopter is fully planted with explosives." His voice remained matter of fact and almost cheerful.

Felicity kept her face stoic. Her only chance was to somehow get word to Zane as to where they were, so he could teleport in and get Logan out of there. But first she had to find Logan.

The elevator door opened, and bright light cut inside. She blinked several times and followed Ivan into an opulent dining room with full floor-to-ceiling windows looking out over a cliff. The world outside was blue and white. Blue sky, blue condensed ice, and white ground with white covering the trees. Sunshine sparkled off particles in the ice, glittering and cold.

"This is so weird," she muttered, stomping forward to take one of the two seats at the table decorated with fine red linens and sterling silver accents.

Ivan reached for a bottle of 1973 Richebourg and poured them each a glass. "A nice Pinot Noir for lunch," he said as the red wine filled their glasses. Then he sat across from her.

A waiter, impeccably dressed in a white uniform, entered from a side room and quickly deposited soup in front of them. The fragrant scent wafted up, and Felicity's stomach growled. There was only a soup spoon on the table, but the candlesticks appeared to be pure silver. While they were elegantly shaped with no sharp points, she could still use them. Blunt force trauma to the temple might take down Ivan.

He sipped his wine. "Eat up so we can get you healthy."

She frowned, the spoon halfway to her mouth. "Why do you care so much about my health?"

He swirled the wine in the glass and watched the play of light. "My doctors have informed me that we can't inject you with the mutated Virus-Twenty-Seven until all of the current drug is out of your system."

She dropped her spoon. "You have vials of the mutated virus?"

"Yes. The queen doesn't believe in proprietary information and made the concoction available to the world at large." He smiled. "It didn't take much of an effort to find a clinic and buy samples. Of course, the queen also sent very strong directions that the samples were for research purposes only."

Nausea swirled down Felicity's throat to thud in her stomach. "The mutation is still experimental."

"Right, but as I can see, the drug already worked on you, or you wouldn't have been able to mate Daire Dunne." Ivan smiled.

She shook her head. "No. I mean, yes, it worked. But the queen made a few tweaks before we experimented, and you probably don't have the newest samples. In addition, nobody has ever tried to negate a mating bond twice in the same body." God only knew what the mutated sample would do once inside Felicity.

"I'm willing to take the chance."

Felicity sat back in the velvet chair. "Why?" she breathed. "I really don't understand. Why is this so important to you?"

He blew on soup before shoving the spoon in his mouth. "Your brother and I had an agreement."

She cocked her head to the side. "Why else?"

His dark eyes darkened further. "You've been in my dreams for a century. Perfect golden hair and black eyes. A purebred female demon."

"I'm not some trophy."

"Sure you are." He smiled again. "Do you have any idea how rare you are?"

She leaned back. "Yes." The guy was a narcissistic asshole who'd rather see her dead than living away from him. "Have you tried seeking professional help for your narcissistic, sociopathic tendencies?" Steeling her shoulders, she dug into the soup to banish the dizziness.

He chuckled. "I like your spirit. You've caused me so much trouble, I now have my own people wanting to spill my blood. Mating you, the mother to Zane Kyllwood and a purebred demon, will put me back in control. Especially when I combine your fortune with mine and start investing again."

"I'm broke." She finished the bowl and sat back. As if by magic, the waiter appeared with her next course, a big steak. She winced.

"We both know you have plenty of money." Ivan handed over his soup bowl. "You still don't like meat?" He shrugged. "For now, I'd eat it anyway. Protein is the key to flushing your system of the current drug and preparing you for the next one."

Yes. The queen had had Felicity eat a high-protein diet for a month before trying out the mutated drug. But Felicity had taken time to find protein she liked and didn't have to eat meat. She had no objection to anybody else eating meat . . . she just didn't like the taste or texture. Even so, she immediately reached for the fork and steak knife left by the waiter. The knife would come in handy.

She cleared her throat and tried to use reason when all she wanted to do was shove the blade through Ivan's jugular. "Listen, Ivan. I hate you. With a white hot, raw need to see you decapitated." Her voice shook, and she forced air into her lungs. "I want you dead. That is not going to change ever. So if we stay in the same vicinity, I will kill you. Dead."

He sighed. "I know."

"So what the hell?"

He wiped his pale mouth and set his napkin back on his lap. "Since you're being so honest, so will I." His dark eyes burned with an odd light. "You'll take the drug and negate the mating bond with the lowlife witch. You and I will mate, or I'll kill Logan." Ivan sat back and eyed his steak. "Mating you will get me back on track professionally and personally? I want two kids. Purebred demons."

She shook her head, her chest aching. "You're crazy. No way will I have children with you."

He lifted a shoulder. "My doctors tell me all I need is to mate you and then harvest your eggs."

Her mouth dropped open. "What?"

"Yes. Using the technology created by humans, I can just harvest your genetic material and use a surrogate." His face lacked any sense of humor. "But we have to mate first, or the pregnancy won't take, as you probably already know."

He was over the moon crazy, but what if a crazy plan like that actually worked? She couldn't leave any of her kids alone, and no way could she have a kid with the bastard. "Under no circumstances am I giving you genetic material."

He smiled. "After we're mated, I don't see that you'll have a choice. You're stuck on this mountain, Felicity. And if you want Logan to live to see his next birthday, you'll mate with me."

She coughed out and tried to keep from puking. While the plan was absolutely insane, Ivan did have the resources to make it happen. "Then what?"

He smiled, his canines glinting. "Then I'm going to cut off your beautiful head."

Chapter 29

Daire took the stairs two at a time, rushing up the stairwell and bursting into the hallway. A still smoking hole gaped where the wall to his apartment had been. Somebody, probably Kellach, had created a shield in the air that would keep humans from seeing or smelling the smoke and fire. At least for a while. Quantum physics and magic at its finest. He gingerly stepped through, his heart thundering.

Rain and wind billowed inside from a hole in the outside wall. Sam and Kellach sat with their backs to the couch, bruises covering their faces and blood flowing from various injuries. Both were typing furiously on their phones and grunting something at each other. Simone sat over on a burned ottoman, an icepack against her face, her lip fat and bleeding.

Zane paced near the smoldering kitchen, barking orders into a cell phone.

Daire took a deep breath.

Simone saw him first. "We're trying to find her, but so far, no luck."

His knees wobbled and he growled.

Zane ended a call. "Six-man team, smoke grenade, and some kind of drug that knocked us on our asses. Well trained and prepared for both demons and witches." He rubbed a hand over a series of bruises on his forehead. "Mom fought hard, but the drug took her out."

Sam looked up, anger and concern in his green eyes. "We'll find her. Garrett is hitting the pavement up and down the block, trying to talk to anybody who might have seen them. Kell and I are working on traffic cams, store surveillance, and hopefully satellite pictures."

Kellach didn't even look up, his fingers were flying so quickly over his phone. "I have a German satellite that may have been in the correct position. The Realm boys are on it, and they'll relay all data to me."

Daire fought the urge to hit something. "She's smart and she's tough." He was reassuring himself more than anybody else. "Her main concern is Logan, so she'll play along until she finds him." That was crucial, because based on the information he'd gleaned about Bychkov, the guy would ultimately decide to kill her. He wanted to make her pay for making a fool out of him years ago. Mating a full-bred demon would help him with his followers for a while, but he'd have to kill her at some point, or she'd definitely kill him.

Daire coughed out smoke, his gut churning. His mate was in the hands of the enemy, and he had no clue where she was being held. He nodded at Simone. "Let's take this to your apartment."

She glanced around, her eyes unfocused. "Oh. Good idea." Her hand visibly trembled when she pushed off the chair, and Daire braced himself to catch her if necessary. But she made it over the legs of the two sitting soldiers and toward the door.

Kellach shoved to stand and reached down a hand to help Sam. A bone protruded from Sam's upper thigh.

Daire winced. "You need to fix that before you do anything else."

He nodded and didn't protest when Kellach ducked under his arm and helped him out the door and down the hall.

Bear crashed into the room, his eyes wide, rain dripping from his shaggy hair. "Holy crap." He looked around the demolished room. "What's our plan?"

"Next door," Daire said. "Simone's place wasn't hit, and we're going to plan there."

Bear nodded and loped through the gaping hole and down the hallway.

Zane stared at Daire.

"What?" Daire asked.

"I have an idea, and it's far-fetched, but we at least need to try." The demon crossed his arms.

"Fine, but heal that bleeding wound in your forehead." Daire tried not to look at the wound.

Zane wiped blood from his head and set his stance, his chest moving as he inhaled and slowly exhaled. The hole closed. "Better?"

"Somewhat." Daire eyed his ruined penthouse. "What's your plan?"

"You've mated. It's probably too early, but there may be a chance to communicate telepathically," Zane said.

Daire lifted his head. He'd totally forgotten that mated couples could usually reach each other through thoughts. Hope unfurled in his chest, and he shoved the emotion way down. "We've only been mated a couple of days," he warned Zane.

"I know, but demons have stronger telepathic gifts than other species, so it's not unheard of to learn the skill quickly." Zane stretched out his hand to reveal several broken fingers. With a growl, he narrowed his gaze and the breaks healed. "Plus, she's done it before with my father. At least give it a try."

Daire nodded. "Since Felicity can't attack minds, do you think she'll be able to read thoughts?"

"Yes. It's a totally different ability." Zane leaned back against the ripped and torn wall. "Well?"

Daire shut his eyes and centered himself. Then he sent out a call for Felicity.

Nothing.

He tried again.

Nothing.

"I feel like a dumbass," he muttered, opening his eyes.

Zane rubbed his chin. "I know, but it's our only shot right now. You have to believe you can do it, or it won't matter."

"Can you speak to your mate?" Daire asked.

"Yes. Easily."

Well, all right then. Daire inhaled the scent of smoke and blood. He then exhaled slowly, pushing out all the bad air. His mind wandered to the arctic and their night in the tent. Their first night together. He smiled and concentrated. *Felicity? If you can hear me, or sense me, ah, say something?*

A buzz tickled through his brain. He stilled. *Felicity?*

What?

The word stormed through his brain, sizzling along his synapses and shooting down his spine. He dropped to one knee, his heart convulsing. "Holy shit."

Zane winced. "She, ah, couldn't control the power with my dad, either."

Daire pushed to stand. "You're telling me that the woman who can't attack minds has the ability to destroy mine since we've mated?"

Zane's lip twisted. "Yeah. I mean, she probably won't."

"I'm the one person in the world she can mind attack?" Daire asked, his breath heating.

"Yeah. I guess you are." Zane studied him thoughtfully.

Well, shit. His heart warmed that he could actually get into Cee Cee's head, but the idea of her melting his brain accidentally didn't set well. "Why isn't she calling out?"

Zane shrugged, his eyes a little wild. "Maybe she remembered how dangerous she is."

Daire didn't care. He forced away thoughts of what could be happening to her and tried to focus. *Cee Cee? I'm fine, baby. Tell me where you are.*

The Sjenerøse Mine! shrieked through his head.

He staggered but kept his feet this time. Holy fuck. She was across the world. He focused on an intent Zane. "She's at the Sjenerøse mine on Fryser Island."

"The asshole teleported her," Zane muttered.

Daire nodded and tried to send another message. *We'll be right there.*

No! Entire place surrounded by land mines and covered in planekite!

His left eardrum exploded, and he clapped a hand over it. Her power was frightening. *Got it. You okay?*

Yes! You can't come get me—I think there's planekite everywhere.

I understand, but I'll deal with that when I get there. His head jerked twice, and blood dribbled from his ear. He blinked away blindness. *Find Logan?*

Not yet!

Pain exploded at the base of his neck and reverberated through his vertebra. Nausea exploded, and he turned to the side, his hand going to his stomach. It took several deep swallows, but he didn't puke. *Hold tight, baby. We're coming for you.*

Thankfully, she didn't answer.

He crammed the palm of his hand against his right eye to regain sight. "How many people can you teleport?"

Zane bit his lip. "I can probably take two in, but after we fight, if we find a fight, I may not be able to bring two out immediately. And weapons can't teleport."

Shit. He'd forgotten that fact. "I already know that Logan hasn't developed the skill yet. Can Sam teleport?"

"Yes."

So he had two demons who could teleport with him, and two to rescue who couldn't teleport. If the fight was fierce, then whoever Zane and Sam took in might not make it out. "Okay. Here's the plan. You, Sam, and I go in. You and Sam get Felicity and Logan to safety, and then when you're strong, come back for me. I'll take care of Bychkov and anybody else."

"That plan gets you killed," Zane said, crossing his arms.

Maybe. "The key is that we get your mom and brother to safety." Daire put it into words Zane couldn't dispute. "That's all that matters."

Felicity followed Ivan through a labyrinth of tunnels along thick carpet, then thinner carpet, then a series of bath mats, and then cold, hard stone. The jerk had confiscated her knife and eyeliner, damn it.

The hallways narrowed and the lights dimmed. Her mind spun. Daire had reached her, somehow. Man, she hoped she hadn't hurt him when she'd responded. She'd actually blinded her first mate for a week once years ago. Since she'd never had the ability to attack minds, she hadn't learned to control the skill.

Finally, they reached a secured room guarded by two men.

She stopped breathing. Was Logan inside?

Ivan unlocked the door and stalked into the chamber. She ran after him, frantically looking around. It was a war room.

A sprawling onyx table surrounded by heavy chairs took up the center of the room. Computer screens covered one full wall, and maps concealed the other side. A group of computers and stations were currently empty across the room. "This is where I work," Ivan said.

The door shut behind her and she jumped. "Where is my son?"

Ivan turned and smiled. "I think we'll wait to see Logan until after you are injected with the mutated virus. It'll be much easier to get along, I think."

Temper roared through her. "Is he alive?"

"Yes." No expression settled on Ivan's angled face. "I give you my word, he's alive, and he's here."

"Your word doesn't mean shit to me."

He sighed. "Language."

"Oh, fuck you." She wandered over to the maps, which clearly showed his mines. "You should probably use a different colored pin for the mines I've destroyed."

He swore. "That was very unkind of you, you know."

Her fingers itched with the need to draw his blood. But she couldn't harm him until she found Logan. Keeping casual, she studied the maps. "Who's your partner in these mines?"

Ivan laughed. "I'm afraid he's the silent type."

"I'm thinking he has a couple more planekite mines out there that you don't know about." She recognized all the known mines.

"Maybe, but he still needed my mines, so I guess he doesn't produce enough."

The door opened, and a blond demon in white coat walked inside. He had a medical bag under one arm and a syringe in his hand.

Felicity backed away.

"He's only going to take blood to see if the tranquilizer is still in your system," Ivan said, tossing a notepad back and forth. "I can hold you down until he gets blood, or you can offer your arm. I prefer to see you fight."

Heat coated down her throat. She might be able to take both men, but she still didn't know where Logan was, and there were at least two guards outside the room. She held out her arm. "Take too much, and I'll kill you next," she said to the doctor.

He nodded, dark blue eyes somber. "I won't take too much." His black hair had been slicked back, and his hands were cool as he searched for a vein.

She turned away from the needle as it slid into her skin. The bite didn't hurt overmuch, but her stomach still ached and her head began to pound. What if she didn't find Logan before they tried to inject her with the mutated virus? Her system had been through too much lately, and who knew what the injection would do to her? Tears threatened to fall, and she batted them back.

Her legs trembled. Not from fear, but from the urge to take down both men and go find her son. What she needed was a schematic of the facility.

The doctor retracted the needle and pressed a cotton ball to her vein. She took over and jerked away from him.

He nodded at Ivan. "I'll let you know if the tranq is out of her system." Without another word, he gracefully exited the room.

Felicity glared at Ivan. "I'm done cooperating if you don't let me see my son."

He threw the notebook onto the desk, and it clattered across to stop against a keyboard. "I don't require your cooperation, and you know it."

The earth rumbled and shook. Part of the map fell loose.

Felicity grabbed on to the table, her feet planting for balance. "Earthquake?"

"Yes. We've been getting quite a few of them since you destroyed the other mine on the island." He shook his head, using a chair to steady himself. "I'm hoping it settles down, but to be frank, some of the earth's movements have revealed new veins of both planekite and silver. Your little stunt not only has given me the opportunity to make a lot more money, but it has allowed for the rapid mining of the mineral that will kill those damn witches."

She frowned. "What do you have against witches?"

"Nothing until you went and mated one. My partner has a problem with the Coven Nine, but I don't really give a care."

She glanced around, not feeling much movement from mining activities, which meant that she wasn't in the mining part of the mountain. The offices and bedrooms were on one side of the mountain, and the mine on the other. The two had to be connected somewhere underground, and if she were creating a connection, it'd be close to the war room. The room only had one door, so she needed to look around meticulously when she exited.

A knock echoed hollowly, and the doctor poked his head in. "The tranq is out of her blood. I have the room ready to commence with the injection."

Felicity twirled around and bunched her legs to attack.

Ivan held steady, a green gun in his hand. The laser kind that turned into bullets upon impacting flesh.

She faltered.

"I'm absolutely fine shooting you and carrying you to the medical room," he said.

Her heart rammed against her rib cage.

He pointed toward the open doorway with the gun. "Go."

She swallowed and walked toward the doctor, her knees shaking. Stepping outside, she glanced around. The tunnel continued down the way to another large metal door.

Blood roared through her veins and filled her head.

She followed the doctor, pain before her, and a gun behind her. Where the hell was Logan?

Chapter 30

Daire shucked his belt and examined his boots as the familiar scent of Simone's penthouse filtered around. Spicy moonflowers. "No metal." Shit. They wouldn't be able to wear bulletproof vests because of the metal content, and no guns or knives would make the trip. "Teleporting is more dangerous than I thought." Considering they couldn't take weapons.

Sam finished removing his watch and cell phone to place on Simone's feminine walnut desk in her home office. "Accidents are rare. There's less than a ten percent chance that your molecules will be torn apart by cosmic forces." He smiled. "If you're demolished on a subatomic level, we won't ever find your particles, so if you'd like to leave a message for loved ones, now is a good time."

Zane snorted over by the satellite pictures glowing on the wall screen from the computer.

Daire cut them both a glare. His mate's kids were assholes, but he couldn't blame them too much.

"I want to go," Garrett grumbled for the tenth time from where he sprawled across a plush sofa.

"Too risky," Zane said. "We can get you in, but we might not be able to get you out. I carry Daire, and then Sam brings back Daire while I bring back Mom and Logan."

Daire nodded. "You give me your word that if you can only get one person out, you take your mother, and Sam takes Logan."

"No problem," Zane said easily.

Daire was suddenly sorry he'd sent Kellach to Titans of Fire headquarters with orders to get to the bottom of the Apollo connections no matter what. He was done taking it easy and going slow, although right now he could use some backup of the friendly variety.

A knock sounded on the outside door, and Simone glanced up from the computer screens. "Now who is here?"

Daire winced. He'd already had a discussion with Zane, and this might've been a bad idea.

Heavy footsteps echoed through the pristine penthouse, and a rumble of tension violated the atmosphere. Nicholai Veis crossed into the room.

"Bloody hell," Simone said, sitting back in her chair. "You called the damn demon?"

"The Coven guards are on the way to fetch you, and I'm a little busy right now," Daire shot back at his cousin. He'd had to scrap his plan to get her away from Nick in order to save her neck. "So aye, I called for backup."

She stood, dark eyes flashing. "I don't need backup."

Darkness settled on Nick's face, making him look every inch the dangerous demon he was. "That's too bad, *Zaychik moy.*" Sucking in air, his lowered his chin, and the air in the room slowly relaxed.

Daire's shoulders untensed, but he kept an eye on his cousin. Being called *My Bunny* wouldn't set well with her, but he was fairly certain she wasn't currently armed. Well, except with her natural ability of being able to create and throw fire.

Nick turned toward Zane. "As your first in command, I have to say, take me instead of the enforcer." His eyes held no expression as he nodded at Daire. "No offense."

Daire rubbed his chin. "None taken." As an enforcer, he understood duty. "But my mate, my fight."

Nick nodded. "Zane?"

Zane glanced at Daire. "I'm with the enforcer. Plus, he can communicate with my mom and so far hasn't burst a blood vessel in his brain." The demon leader turned back to the picture on the wall. "Yet."

The family love was going to suffocate Daire. He rolled his eyes. "Simone, I need somebody on you." Then he winced at the language. "As a bodyguard. Leave here, get somewhere secure, and as soon as I get Felicity to safety, we'll figure out our next step."

"No." She crossed her arms over a pretty red shirt.

Daire sighed and nodded at Nick. "Thanks for your help."

"Not a problem." He took two steps into the room. "Come with me willingly or not, Simone. Your choice."

She stood and planted her feet. "Daire, I can't believe you're on board with this."

He dug deep for patience he really didn't have. "I'm about to cross dimensions and end up a world away, cousin. In order to concentrate and then probably fight to the death, I need to know you're safe. So aye, I'm on board. Get to safety, and you can yell at me later."

She eyed him, no doubt fighting both loyalty, concern, and a glorious temper. "Fine." She tossed her hair and strode toward the demon. "You're garna regret this, Nicholai Veis." Her huff as she swept by him promised a wonderful fight was on the way.

Daire gave him a look containing both gratitude and warning. "I owe you."

He smiled. "Zane, I have my phone. Call if you need backup." Without waiting for an answer, he followed the furious witch.

Zane pointed to the satellite picture. "I'm thinking the planekite mine is on this side of the mountain, with offices and such here. See the entrance?" he tapped the screen. "So try Mom again, and ask her for a visual of where she might be."

Daire leaned against the desk for support and closed his eyes. *Felicity? Don't answer for a moment. We're getting ready to come in and get you, but all we have is satellite pictures to go on. Give me a picture, a mental image, of what you've seen so far.* Hopefully her pictures wouldn't burn his brain as badly as her words and emotions had.

Terror rippled into his head along with a hot blade of pain. He gasped and slapped a hand to his eye. *What's going on?*

Nothing. Sorry. I'll try pictures.

Boiling pins pricked his eyeballs. Slowly pictures began to form in his mind. A dining room. Bedroom. War room. Now a long hallway. Even though her sending pictures didn't hurt as much as her thoughts, an underlying fear hovered around the message. Whatever was happening had her frightened.

The walls sparkled an odd green glow. Planekite.

His eyelids snapped open, and he strode over to the screen to study the picture. "Based on the hallway, I'd say she's somewhere here." He pointed along an area. "But it's hard to tell, and she hasn't seen Logan yet." He dug deep and tried to calm his heart. "She's scared right now, so the sooner we go, the better."

"Scared or angry?" Zane asked, a muscle visibly ticking in his jaw.

Daire blew out air. "Scared. Definitely scared." The primal being at his core sprang awake, ready to wage war. "We need to go. Now."

"Okay. Go with your gut. Where do we land?" Zane asked as Sam rose to stand next to him.

Daire pointed to the entrance to what he believed was the business side of the mine. "As much as I'd like to go in center mass, I'd hate to land in the middle of a rock."

Zane nodded. "Keep in mind, one second we're not there, and the next second we are. If there are guards or anybody with a weapon, they'll shoot us before we regain our equilibrium."

Fucking fantastic.

The demon leader leaned in, gaze serious. "Take a deep breath, go as calm as you can, and don't fight the universe."

Daire nodded. He'd never really been one with the universe. "We don't have to hug, do we?"

Zane rolled his eyes. "No." With a hard lunge, he tackled Daire, and they both went down.

Through nothing. They fell through earth and reality, transporting between dimensions of time and space.

Darkness and an odd whistle echoed around Daire. His body flew away and then reassembled. For the briefest of seconds, true peace surrounded him.

Then he hit a freezing floor and rolled, coming up to face a slack-jawed guard. The guy lifted a weapon and fired.

Felicity entered the medical room and stopped short. Sterile white examination table, white counters, even white tile. Talk about a nightmarish room.

The doctor bustled around, flipping on different monitors. "We'll keep track of your heartbeat and oxygen levels after injecting the mutated virus," he mumbled, reading a chart and then scurrying over to the counter.

She shook her head. "Why? If I have a bad reaction, what exactly do you plan to do to counter the drug?"

He turned around and scratched his chin. "I don't have a plan. This mutation is so new, there isn't a lot of information about it."

His light-colored eyebrows rose. "To be honest, you're the first person I've met who has already taken the mutation to negate the mating bond. Perhaps if you tell me about the experience, I'll know what to do." Curiosity glowed bright in his eyes.

What an asshole. "I'm not a research experiment, and we both know there's nothing you can do if I have a bad reaction," she countered, chills clawing down her back.

Ivan prodded her in the kidneys with the gun. "Hop up."

She stormed away from him, noting the tray of surgical instruments on the counter. "Planning on operating?" she hissed, turning around and jumping onto the table. The smooth sheet bunched under her butt.

The doctor shook his head. "No." He grasped a small clasp and shoved it on her index finger, and one of the monitors began to beep. "Those are just in case. Your oxygen levels look good."

"What a relief," she snapped out.

Ivan shut the door and leaned back against it, gun hanging casually in his hand. "How long does the process take?"

The doctor glanced at Felicity. "Based on my contacts, it takes about two days to fully negate the mating bond."

Three days, actually, and then about a week of regaining energy and strength. The process was like a human experiencing a very bad flu bug. Felicity shoved hair away from her face. Was it really like the flu? If so, would this one take her down, or would she have created antibodies against the mutation? She swallowed and glanced at the syringe already filled on the tray. "This is such a terrible idea."

Ivan laughed. "Let's hope it works."

She'd known him forever. "Ivan, this might kill me. At least let me see my son once before we take the risk." She tried to force the hatred from her voice, and it came out quivery.

He shook his head, not concealing the hatred from his eyes at all. "Perhaps this will give you incentive to survive."

Fear and anger flushed through her. "You are such a prick."

The doctor cleared his throat and moved to attach a couple of nodules to her upper chest. Her heartbeat blipped on the screen, way too fast. Then he reached for the syringe and glanced at Ivan.

The demon nodded.

"Just take a deep breath and relax," the doctor said, grasping her arm with chilled hands.

Shots fired in the distance.

Felicity's head jerked up. Daire was there.

In one smooth motion, she grabbed the syringe, twisted her wrist, and plunged the syringe into the doctor's palm. He cried out and backed away, windmilling his arms. His ass hit the counter, and the tray of supplies tumbled to the floor. Sharp knives and hooks clattered across the hard tile.

"I'm mated," he cried out, yanking the syringe free.

"Not anymore," Felicity hissed, throwing the oxygen counter at his head.

Ivan darted forward, and she kicked, nailing him in the balls. He doubled over with a pained *oof*.

She grabbed onto the bed, swung around, and hit the doctor under the chin with a hard kick. His head snapped back, his eyes fluttered shut, and his body pummeled down onto the tray.

He'd only be out a few minutes.

Felicity slid to her feet just as Ivan stood up to his full height.

"I'm going to fucking kill you," he said, turning the gun on her.

Cold purpose flowed through her like bubbling rage. She stood and held out her hands. "You really need the gun for that?" Her lip twisted.

His chin lifted. "No." Slowly, he shoved the gun in the back of his waistband. "I rarely like to get my hands dirty, but I'm going to bathe in your blood."

She smiled. "I've been waiting for this way too long." Bunching her knees, she jumped into the air, clapped her thighs on his head, and twisted. Gravity did its job, and she dropped, taking his head with her and forcing his body to follow.

He bellowed and punched her in the hip.

Agony spread along her lower back.

Her hands slapped the floor, and pain ricocheted up her arms to her shoulders. She released his head, rolled, and came up swinging. A jab to the throat threw her back against the counter.

She wheezed in air and sent healing cells to the broken trachea, her eyes wide.

Ivan stood to his full height, blood streaming from a cut on his forehead.

She scrambled down and grasped a scalpel to hold up in front of her.

He chuckled, the sound low and evil, before drawing a jagged knife from his boot. "Mine is bigger."

"It's not the size—." She ducked into a slide, went past him, and cut his heel as she went. Blood spurted.

He bellowed, turning and yanking her up by the hair. Quick as a shifter, he flipped the knife in the air, grabbed the base, and jabbed the handle against her mouth.

Pain shrieked through her lips, and blood spurted. She jerked her head, freeing it. Her entire face felt like it was on fire. Gasping, she wiped her lips with the back of her hand and maneuvered to the side. He took one step toward her, swinging out and backhanding her left cheekbone. Stars exploded behind her eyes, and she careened into the wall.

Tears clogged her vision.

Another punch came out of nowhere, right to her stomach. She doubled over, and her knees went weak.

She kicked out, her heel impacting his nose. Cartilage crunched with a satisfying thud. He yelled and clapped a hand over his bleeding nose. She took advantage of the weakness, jumping up and spinning a kick into his ribs. At least two of them shattered.

He swung out, nailing her in the temple. Her stomach lurched, and she went down.

He grabbed her hair and dragged her over to the examination table, lifting her up and slamming her down. She bounced, and her vision turned black.

He planted a fierce grip around her throat and held her down, scrambling through drawers to the left.

She struggled and tried to stay conscious. For so long, she'd trained to fight him. It couldn't end like this.

"There." His voice filled with triumph, and he turned toward her. "I changed my mind." He squeezed with enough pressure to cut off all oxygen. "First I'm going to stick you full of this shit, and then, if you survive and negate the mating, I'm going to make you mine. You deserve to be fucked and often until you can't live any longer."

She struggled, trying to stay awake, trying to free her throat.

He held the syringe up high as if to jam it down into her chest.

She calmed. For years, she'd trained to fight somebody bigger and stronger. Her boys needed her. Daire needed her. The monster couldn't win. Drawing on strength she'd only hoped for, she lifted her legs, slammed them down on his shoulders, twisted and shoved. He dropped, his head hitting the examination table.

The hand at her throat loosened.

She slashed his wrist with the blade, and he yanked back. Following his movement, she levered up and jammed the scalpel in his eye.

He screamed in unholy pain, his hand dropping the knife and going to his eye.

The room quieted. She centered herself. Grabbing the knife, she propelled herself up on her knees and brought it down in his neck. Blood spurted up, covering her face and burning her skin.

She ignored the pain and shoved with all her weight.

The knife sliced through cartilage and muscle. His body convulsed like a fish stuck on the dock. She set her knees and used her entire body to yank the knife to the right and then the left.

His eyes closed.

She swallowed as more blood flew up to coat her shirt.

Breathing through her nose to keep from tasting blood, she sawed back and forth, using every ounce of strength she owned. Finally, his body dropped to the floor while his head remained on the table.

She released the knife and fell away from the head. Her body shook and her stomach lurched. Blood coated her from head to waist and dotted along her pants. The liquid burned like acid.

The gunfire suddenly stopped outside.

The door flew open and Daire stood there, bloody and battered. His eyes widened as he took her in. "Felicity," he breathed.

Chapter 31

Daire's mouth gaped open. The woman was covered with blood. His gut spasmed and he rushed for her, grabbing her biceps. "Cee Cee? Baby?" Slowly, being as careful as he could, he ran his palms down her arms. Then he patted her chest. "You're okay. You're going to be okay." She was still standing, although shock filled her eyes and she began to sway.

He shook her. "Stay awake." She had to be all right. "Please. I need you." He pushed both hands through her bloody hair. "I love you." He wanted to shout the words, but whispering them might save her. Somehow. If she allowed him to help her.

She smiled, her eyelids fluttering.

"No." He yanked off the shirt to find the wound. Forget taking it slow and courting her. She was his, damn it.

Her chest looked intact.

He patted down her legs and then turned her around, scouting every inch and finally shooting his hands into her hair. "You're all right," he said slowly.

She nodded and turned. A low sob escaped her, and she fell into his chest.

He patted her back, and only then did he see Ivan's head on the table. The body had fallen down on the other side next to a guy slowly regaining consciousness. "Honey?"

She leaned back, and tears streaked down her face. "Not my blood."

Three better words had never been invented. Daire stepped away and ripped his shirt off to shove over her head. He reached for a

paper towel and quickly wet it, wiping off her face. Demon blood
burned skin. "You killed him?"

She nodded, her face paling under a couple of quickly purpling
bruises. "I said I was going to."

Aye, she did. He grasped her hand and saw the empty syringe on
the floor. His world stopped. "Did they inject you?"

"No." Her fingers threaded through his. "We're still mated."

His body settled. "Good." Leading the way, he kept his body between her and danger. She'd taken out Ivan, and damn if that didn't
make Daire want to roar in pride, but that was her last fight to the
death. Ever. Unfortunately, with planekite living in the walls around
them, his strength was slowly ebbing. "Keep on my six."

"Go left. I think Logan is to the left," she said, her hand trembling
in his. "Wait a minute. You should stay here—there's planekite everywhere."

"I'm fine—don't worry. Zane and Sam are fighting their way
here, and we can't wait. The alarm went out the second we landed."
Dizziness still catapulted through his head, but he shook it off in
order to fight. Teleporting was not for him, that was for damn sure.
Or maybe it was the planekite messing with his equilibrium. He
loped into a jog, and the hallway narrowed. A soldier ran toward him
from a locked door, and he lifted a gun he'd taken off a demon
soldier, firing off two shots. The guy dropped.

Felicity shook her head and pointed at a metal doorway in the
rock. "I think the mine is that way."

He halted. "We don't know who's waiting on the other side." More
than anything, he wanted to grab Sam and have him take her to
safety, but Logan's time could be limited. "How about you wait here
for Sam?" Daire asked, releasing her.

"No." She slid to the side.

That's what he'd figured. "Fine, but get on this side of the door."
He slapped the gun into her hand. When he opened the metal, she'd
be protected on the other side.

She opened her mouth to argue.

"No." He nudged her gently out of the way. "I know you're a
badass who can fight, but I need you there so I can concentrate. My
weakness, not yours." Because he fucking loved her. One thing at
a time, and he had no problem confessing to a weakness if it kept
her alive.

She stayed put, settled her stance, and gripped the gun.

"Plus, gotta be honest. The planekite around us is messing with my system, and my aim is surely off." He slowly opened the door. Nothing. "Come on," he whispered, sliding inside a stone hallway similar to the one he'd just left, sans the carpet. Mining lights shone along the walls, and he stalked silently, heading down gradually.

Silence pounded eerily around him. The mining operations probably halted when the alarm had gone out. Chances were the miners weren't soldiers and had headed for safety. Even so, if Logan was being kept in the mine, there'd be more soldiers to fight. "What makes you think Logan is down here?" he asked.

"Gut feeling?" she answered. "Besides the bedroom I was locked into, it didn't seem like there were prison cells on that side of the mountain."

"Bedroom?" he muttered.

"Yes." She pushed him in the back. "Hurry up."

The corridor reached an exposed mining elevator. A numbness tingled through his extremities, and his temples pounded. "Can demons teleport from inside the earth?" he asked.

"Depends how deep they are." She leaned around him. "Looks like we go down."

He nodded and stepped onto the platform, which swung from his weight. "Do you have any idea how many levels make up this mine?"

"No." She took his hand and lifted her leg over the guardrail to stand next to him. "Sorry."

Huge problem. They could have a dozen levels to explore, and they sure as hell didn't have that much time. He had about ten more minutes left in him before he collapsed from overexposure to the stupid planekite. He pressed the lever, and they began to torturously descend. Soon a level came into view. A sprawling orange sign proclaimed the area held EXPLOSIVES. Nobody guarded the area, so perhaps any soldiers had headed for the breach. Hopefully Zane and Sam were doing all right.

Daire kept his finger on the lever, and they continued down into the cool earth. The next level stretched out dark and formidable before him with a narrow tunnel. He stopped the lift. "It's too narrow to mine here—not enough room for vehicles or equipment." He jumped over the rail and turned to lift Felicity to solid ground. "The mining operations will be down farther, so if Logan is being kept on this side of the mountain, this is probably the place." Before them extended a dark tunnel that veered sharply to the right. "Follow me."

"Do you want the gun since you're on point?" she asked.

"No." He glared at the dim yellow lights strung too far apart. Uneven stone lined the walls and floor. Unlike the hallway they'd just left, this one had been chiseled out without much care. Finally, they came upon a door secured with a metal rod. "Get ready." He waited until she'd pointed the gun at the room before tugging the rod free. He then jerked open the door.

Mining picks and small equipment in pristine order lined the walls of a room big enough to hold three trucks. He shut the door and swung around to run down the tunnel to the next door.

Five doors later, and all they'd found were supplies, a massive amount of alcohol, and equipment. The tunnel narrowed and shortened until his head almost scraped the ceiling. "I don't think Logan is down here," he said, noting the dust filling the air.

Felicity didn't answer.

Another door, same as the rest, was set into the wall ahead. "At some point, we should find weapons," he whispered. He waited until she'd gotten into position and then unsecured the door.

The second it opened, a hard body slammed into him, throwing him into the opposite wall. Shards of rock slashed down, nicking his cheek. He turned and threw instinctively, dropping to a knee and slamming his hand over the guy's jugular as they hit the ground.

"Logan." Felicity dropped to her knees, her hands frantically patting her kid's chest. "Are you okay?"

Oh. Daire released Logan and stood.

Logan sat up, frown lines cutting next to his mouth. "Mom? What the hell?" He reached out and wiped blood off her face. "Are you *hurt?*"

"No." She pushed up and held out a hand for him. "I'm fine. Are you okay?" Pleasure and relief sparkled in her stunning eyes.

Logan took her hand and used the wall to stand up. "What are you doing here?" He turned a hard glare toward Daire.

Felicity grabbed her son's hand. "Long story. Right now, we have to find Zane and Sam."

"Zane and Sam are here?" Logan shook his head, bewilderment slacking his jaw. "What is going on?"

Felicity reached up and patted his face. "Are you sure you're all right? No wounds?"

"No, I'm fine." He grabbed her other hand. "Really. Starving, but no wounds."

"We'll get you food," she said.

Daire staggered past them toward the tunnel. "We have to move and now."

"What's wrong with you?" Logan asked.

"Planekite," Daire said simply. "In about five, I'm passing out." So he had to get his mate to safety. Stretching into a jog, he knew the two would follow him. His boots rang on the cold stone as he passed the useless rooms and finally reached the lift. He jumped over first and reached for Felicity. She gave him her hands without hesitation, and her trust warmed him head to toe.

Logan gave him a hard glare once again, and it didn't cool his heat at all. Finally, they were once again moving on the lift, heading up this time. They reached the main level and stepped off.

Footsteps echoed. He jerked back, moving to shield Felicity.

Three soldiers ran around the corner. Vadim and two others. With a fierce roar, Logan leaped for all three of them, taking down one. Vadim smiled and lifted a gun to fire. Three darts instantly impacted Daire.

He growled and shot forward. His vision fuzzed. Shit. Apollo darts and not simple tranquilizer darts. He didn't have long to fight.

Green laser bullets whizzed by his head from Felicity's gun, and the third soldier dropped to the ground.

Daire impacted Vadim with the sound of muscle slamming muscle. If the darts held planekite, the poison would flow into his bloodstream any moment. Vadim jabbed him in the throat, and Daire countered with a knee to the groin.

Vadim's eyes widened, and he stepped back.

Sometimes a guy just couldn't play fair. Daire grabbed Vadim's head and slammed it down on his knee. Vadim countered with a double-edged blade, slicing up Daire's torso.

Daire hissed in pain, and his central nervous system misfired. His vision dimmed.

"Daire?" Felicity called from far away.

Her voice. The tone of fear in it, shot his eyelids open. He didn't have much time, but no way was he leaving her in fear. Rocking back, he shot a hard punch to Vadim's nose. The cartilage shattered, and the demon yelled in pain, striking up with the knife again.

Daire grabbed Vadim's wrist, twisted, and used the demon's momentum to plunge the knife into the demon's throat.

Vadim gurgled and reached for the knife handle. Blood flowed around the blade.

Daire shoved and let gravity take them both down, making sure he landed on the knife, which shoved all the way to the ground. A couple of really strong twists, and Vadim's head rolled away.

The air whooshed out of Daire's lungs, and he fell to the side, trying to sit.

Logan grabbed his armpits and shoved him up.

The cold stone scratched his back, while fire lit him up from inside. Daire glanced down at the two darts protruding from his chest. Electrical shocks rippled through him, and his stomach cramped. He closed his eyes and his back began to burn. "Get me off the rock," he mumbled.

Logan swore and tugged him away from the rock. "Sorry."

Felicity knelt next to him and cupped his face, her touch so cool he leaned into her palms. "Stay with me, Daire. Just dig deep and imagine your body fighting the planekite."

He nodded.

"I love you. Please don't leave me." Her voice sounded thick with tears.

He wanted to reassure her, but it took every ounce of power he had left in him to concentrate on not allowing his heart to melt in his chest. The pain was unbearable. But her voice, those sweet words, provided something for him to hold on to.

The veins and arteries in his body swelled to the point of bursting. His heart beat too quickly, and his lungs began to shut down in protest. Fighting the pull of unconsciousness, he opened his mouth and yelled.

Fire roared out of him to crackle against the wall.

Felicity leaned in closer, and he tried to push her way. "Get back," he ordered through gritted teeth. "Back. I'm going to explode." A raw burst of energy uncoiled deep inside him.

"Get back!" he yelled.

Chapter 32

Felicity gaped as the veins in Daire's neck turned a shocking, sizzling red. He threw back his head, tightening the muscles along his jaw and elongating his jugular.

Pain rode the air around them. She glanced at Logan, her lungs seizing. "Go get your brothers."

He shook his head. "I'm not leaving you."

"We're fine. Go now." She used her best mom voice. Logan faltered but then turned to do as she said.

She immediately pushed forward to straddle Daire's legs. Her hands shook, but she pressed them to his furnace-hot cheeks. Her heart hurt to the point her ribs vibrated. "Listen to me, Daire Dunne." She leaned in. "I finally found you, I love you, and I'm keeping you." Risking the burn, she pressed a hard kiss to his scalding lips.

He shook his head, sweat pouring down his rugged face. Red cut into the whites of his eyes, and with the green created a Tim Burton distortion of Christmas. "Get off me, Cee Cee."

"Never." She lowered her chin, keeping his gaze. "You mated a demon, witch. So suck it up, use whatever power you can get from me, and fight this planekite."

He blinked, and blood trickled from the corner of his right eye.

She pressed harder. This had to work. The man meant everything. "Listen to me. Planekite doesn't hurt demons. You mated a demon and should be able to tap into my powers, such as they are. Close your eyes and imagine a cooling balm inside your veins and around your organs." She would not lose him now. "I love you. Use that."

His gaze softened. "I love you," he whispered.

"Right back at you. Now concentrate." She closed her eyes and tried to visualize every ounce of power she should've had in life going to him. To saving him. The walls around them were weak, and he had to beat the drug inside his veins. That was the one that mattered.

He began to shake, low mutterings escaping from his mouth in an ancient language she couldn't interpret.

She kept in the moment, trying to help him. Instead of words, she tried to force a healing balm into his brain. Since she could hurt him just by communicating telepathically, why couldn't she help him with images? They'd mated, and she could help him.

His face heated to the point that her palms burned, but she still held on. Smoke billowed up from his jeans. Blood flowed, already burned, from his ears.

Yet she held on.

Finally, with one final shudder, he fell back.

"Daire?" Panic clogged her throat as she followed him down, peering at his face.

He blinked open his eyes. Green and white with black pupils. Beautiful green. "Cee Cee."

She smiled and fell flat on top of him, kissing him with everything inside her. The relief flowing through her nearly made her sway. He was all right.

He wrapped his bare arms around her, taking over the kiss, overwhelming her with sensation. One hand palmed her butt, rubbing her against him.

"Jesus," came a low exclamation. "Get a room."

She leaned back, and amusement bubbled up. Glancing over her shoulder, she took quick inventory of her three sons. "Everybody all right?"

Zane, a purple bruise across the right side of his face, winced. "Mom. Get up."

She rolled her eyes and crawled off Daire to stand. "You okay?" she asked.

He accepted her outstretched hand and stood, wavering only for a moment. "I'm fine. Thanks to you."

Logan snorted. "Could we get out of here, then?"

She cleared her throat. "Ah, would you all mind just staying here for a few moments? I have something to do." Without waiting for an answer, she turned and started for the lift.

A chorus of male protests echoed behind her, so she turned to face her family. "I said I'll be right back."

Sam wiped blood off his arm. "What is happening right now?"

Logan shook his head. "She's gone nuts."

Zane poked at a hole in his wrist. "Mom?"

She glanced at Daire, who was watching her intently. "Well?" she asked.

His lips twitched. "I'm just guessing here, but I think your mom has plans one level down. Right?"

She smiled and nodded. "I swear I'll be quick."

He chuckled, love definitely glinting in his eyes. "I'll come with you."

"What's the plan?" Zane exploded.

Felicity sighed. "I've always planned to blow up this place, and since we're here . . ." Her sons looked at her like she'd gone completely insane, their eyes wide, their mouths open.

Zane finally turned his wrath on Daire. "You're okay with this?"

Daire studied her.

Felicity held her breath. Either he got her, or he didn't.

Finally, his grin widened. "Aye."

Her heart swelled. She smiled so big her cheeks hurt.

Logan shoved away from the wall. "You're as crazy as she is."

"I hope so," Daire returned, sauntering over to her and holding out an elbow. "Shall we?"

Laughter rumbled up from deeper than her physical body as she slid her hand along his arm. "We shall." She glanced over her shoulder. "We'll be right back, boys. By the way, after we finish off the planekite mines and maybe rob a bank or two, I'm thinking about having more kids. Say a few girls?"

Her boys paled.

"Demon-witch hybrid girls?" Sam said slowly, shaking his head. "As our *sisters*? We'll never get to sleep again."

Daire patted her hand. "Sounds like a plan to me."

She nearly hopped as they reached the lift. "I never thought I'd say this, but it's so good to be alive."

"I agree." Her mate pressed the button, and within moments, they were at the right level.

They studied the explosives, which were fairly simple. Setting one to blow would blow them all, and there were enough piled high that the entire mountain would go.

Daire carefully engaged one with a timer and gave them five minutes.

Felicity's chest felt way too full. She paused at the control section of the level but did the right thing. Flipping several buttons, she grabbed the microphone and made sure all speakers in the mine and adjoining business part were fully on. "Hello. This is your one warning. Since all of you can teleport, if you haven't already done so, you're gonna want to in the next four minutes. This place is going to blow."

Daire clapped. "Nicely done."

"Thanks." She slid out from behind the console and ran to take his hand. They hustled up the lift and to where the boys were pacing frantically.

"Mom—" Zane started.

She walked right into his arms. "The mountain is going to blow in about three minutes."

He shook his head and grabbed Logan in a half hug. "Sam? Get Daire."

Then he whisked them from danger.

Daire left Felicity sleeping peacefully in a guest bedroom in Simone's penthouse after a long shower. A very long shower where he'd made sure all the blood was washed off her for good. He stalked out to the living area and paused to take in the Seattle skyline. Stunning and sparkling. Just like his mate.

The Kyllwood three lounged on sofas and chairs in the massive room after having eaten what looked like several pounds of cheeseburgers.

"Transporting takes protein," Sam said around a mouthful of French fries.

"I wouldn't know," Logan muttered, grabbing for a plate of what looked like mini-tacos.

At this point, Daire would need another job just to keep the kid fed. "You have plenty of time to learn how to teleport. Stop worrying about it."

Zane finished texting something on his phone and glanced up. "How's Mom?"

"Exhausted." Daire padded barefoot around the sofa, grabbed a lone cheeseburger, and dropped onto a chair. "I figure we all should talk."

"We've already been talking," Logan said, pulling a beer from a bucket and tossing it at him.

Daire caught it one-handed. He'd figured. He studied the three men. Black hair, green eyes, and their mama's stubborn chin. He could do worse for family. "What did you all decide?" Not that it mattered, because he was keeping Felicity for good. But getting along with her kids would probably be a good thing, and truth be told, he liked all three of them.

"Nobody is good enough for our mom," Sam said, eyeing the fries still on Logan's plate.

"Agreed," Daire said evenly.

Zane breathed out. "If she has to be with somebody instead of being a nun like I suggested, then we talked, and you'll do."

High praise indeed from one of the most powerful men on the planet. Daire took a drink of his beer. "Thanks."

"Truth be told, I'm glad somebody else can be looking out for her," Zane said, leaning forward. "I'm not sure, but I think she has completely lost her mind."

Logan snorted. "Nah. She just feels safe for the first time in her life, and now she's exploring a little bit."

Zane sobered. "I guess she feels safe because of you, Dunne."

That warmed him all over. "I won't let anything happen to her. You have my word." It was heartfelt and the least he could promise.

"I can't believe she killed Bychkov all by herself," Logan breathed.

Pride lifted Daire's chest. "She had a plan." The woman was amazing with a good plan. "She said she was going to take him down, and she did exactly that."

"Your mating will secure an alliance between the demon nation and the Coven Nine," Zane said.

"No." Daire tipped back his beer and allowed the local brew to cool his throat. "I mean, aye, it probably would, but my mating is not a political issue, and it'll remain private."

Zane grinned. "Nicely said."

Sam snorted and swiped a couple of Logan's fries. "You know she's a grandma, right?"

Daire lifted an eyebrow. "So?"

"Welcome to the family, Grandpa," Zane drawled.

Daire blinked. He wasn't old enough, not by a long shot, to be a grandpa. Hell, he wasn't even a dad yet. "Can't wait for your mom to give birth to a sibling for you three." His grin even felt a little dangerous. "You know, twins run in my family."

"Oh God," Zane breathed, falling back in his seat.

Daire nodded with just a hint of smugness. None of them, and that included him, were ready for witch-demon crossbred girls. God help the world. Take in their slightly crazy mother, add in a cranky witch for a father, and life would definitely get interesting. "Speaking of wild plans, what happened with the Sjenerøse mine?"

"Completely destroyed, set off a nine-point earthquake, and soon the entire island will be in the sea," Sam said.

Daire grinned. His mate was damn dangerous, now wasn't she? He couldn't even imagine being with somebody calm and docile. How boring. Thank goodness fate had other plans than what he thought he'd wanted. "I love her. Just so you know."

"Yeah. We caught that," Zane said. "Welcome to the family, Enforcer."

Chapter 33

Felicity snuggled down in the thick bedclothes not feeling an ounce of guilt for eavesdropping on the men in her life. Daire would be good for the boys. He was experienced, tough, and incredibly sweet. The boys would be good for him, too. There wasn't time to get cranky and stuck in one place when the boys were around, and Daire needed that, whether or not he realized it at the moment.

Her body ached, and her muscles pounded, but she'd never been happier. Who knew when she embarked on her crazy plan to drug an enforcer and glean information that she would've found love and happiness? Once again, she shook her head at the oddity of life, grateful beyond measure.

A tablet dinged from the bedtable, and she sat up, swiping a finger across the screen.

"Cee Cee Cee Cee," exclaimed a joyous toddler.

"My baby, Hope," she responded, just as much joy filtering through her as she took in Hope Kyllwood. At about fourteen months, the girl was adorable beyond words with huge blue eyes, curly brown hair, and very pink cheeks. A rim of green surrounded her blue eyes, and a prophecy marking climbed down her neck, but for now, she was just a kid happy to see family.

The girl clapped her pudgy hands together. "Cee Cee Cee."

Felicity laughed. "It's good to see you, too."

The baby gurgled, delight dancing across her face.

The screen widened, and Janie Kayrs, Hope's mom, came into view. "Hi, Felicity. I hope it's okay we called. Hope has been chanting your name for hours."

Felicity nodded at her daughter-in-law. "Always call. Any time and any place." Janie looked very much like her daughter, pretty with very intelligent eyes and was the perfect mate for Zane. "Zane will be home soon."

Janie grinned, flashing a dimple. "He says you're robbing banks these days."

"Um, yeah." That probably wasn't a good example to set for her granddaughter, was it?

"Awesome. If you ever need backup, please call on me. I'd love to rob a bank." Janie tugged on Hope's curls. "Mom wants to come, too."

Hope edged her way in front of the camera again. "Cee Cee Cee."

Daire slipped into the bedroom, and Felicity scooted over so he could sit on the bed. "You've met Janie, but this is Hope."

Daire leaned over and smiled into the camera.

Hope clapped her hands together. "Daire, Daire, Daire. Daire, Cee Cee, Daire, Cee Cee, Daire, Cee Cee Cee Cee."

Felicity laughed. "I see you've told her about Daire."

Janie's eyebrows drew down. "Um, no. I haven't said anything about Daire to her."

Felicity blew out air. Janie was psychic, so it wasn't a stretch to think Hope had inherited the gift. "For now, don't worry about it," she said softly. Hope's future was a worry for another day.

Janie nodded and hugged her daughter close. "All right. Say night, and we'll go call daddy."

"Night," Hope said, grinning. "Daddy, Daddy, Daddy . . ." The tablet shut off.

Felicity sighed and put it on the night table. "So, that's Hope. I'm young, really young, but I guess that you should know—"

"I know she's your granddaughter," Daire said, shoving down his jeans.

Felicity's cheeks burned. "Yeah."

"You're young Cee Cee, and we can have tons of kids."

"So I heard." Her heart actually warmed.

He slid underneath the covers. Warmth and the scent of fresh rain surrounded them. "Were you eavesdropping when I talked to your boys?"

She grinned and rolled into his side to play with the ripped muscles along his torso. So much strength, and it was all hers. *He* was all hers. "I have no problem eavesdropping or confessing to such. Looks like we just formed a solid family."

He brushed the hair away from her face, his touch gentle from a deadly hand. "I love you, Felicity. No matter what crazy scheme you come up with next."

She leaned up and kissed him on the chin, smiling as stubble tickled her chin. "I love you, too." For the moment, she allowed herself to bask in him. He was right in that she wasn't crippled or less than anybody else. Abilities were abilities, and she had her own. By viewing herself through his eyes, she'd finally gotten a clear picture. "We're going to have an adventurous life."

"I know."

She smiled.

"That smile. All mine." He brushed a kiss across her forehead.

Her smiled widened. "You, ah, don't see me as a bad person since I killed Ivan?"

"'Twas self-defense."

She sobered. That wasn't exactly true. "I planned to kill him, and I did. Even if he hadn't kidnapped me and tried to hurt me, I would've killed him."

Daire's lips twitched. "He killed your mate, and he would've harmed your sons. If you have an enemy, a real one, you take them out in order to protect your family." He brushed a gentle kiss across her lips. "I'd expect nothing less from the mother of the kids we'll have someday."

Her heart swelled so large she was afraid her ribs would break. "I love you."

"Love you more." He tickled down her rib cage.

She chuckled and shoved his hands away. How was it possible to be so happy, even while the world remained unsettled around them? Maybe having her kids in one place and all safe was something to celebrate, even if for only one night. "Any news on Simone?"

He traced her bottom lip, his eyes glittering. "Aye. She and Nick are on the coast, fighting it out. I believe they're safe for a while, and we have a little time to figure out who's after her." He breathed out. "I mean, if they don't kill each other first. That would take care of the entire problem."

She chuckled. If the tension vibrating through the room when Nick and Simone had been in one place was any indication, they were either fighting or making love at that very moment. "I've e-mailed all my research on the Coven Nine and planekite holdings throughout the world to you."

He grinned. "Thanks."

She believed him. If he said that Simone wasn't involved in those companies, then she trusted his judgment. "What about Titans of Fire?" she asked. "Was Kellach able to find out who's distributing Apollo?"

"Not yet, but basically because Pyro is still in jail." Daire sighed. "We'll figure out Fire next week. For now, let's just enjoy us."

How wonderful that they had an *us*. She'd never thought to find love again, and the reality of her good fortune made it difficult to concentrate on anything but the incredibly sexy body that was hers to touch. Forever. "All right, but I have to ask, is there going to be an issue with an enforcer mating a demon?"

He lifted a shoulder. "I don't care in the slightest, so no, there's no issue."

She grinned again. "I figured you'd think all of this happened way too quickly."

"Does anything happen in slow motion when you're around?" His warm palm caressed down her back to rest on her butt.

"Nope." She maneuvered herself on top of his strong body. Desire and love commingled inside her to create a comfortable craving she'd always associate with the enforcer. "So you're okay with every-thing?"

He placed a kiss on her nose. "You are everything."

Her heart jumped hard against her rib cage. Sometimes he was the sweetest person. "Are you sure we have time for a night off?"

He smiled. "I'm sure, and right now, I'm only thinking about you. We can return to reality tomorrow. For now, let's enjoy the fact that we're here, in a bed, and you're naked."

She chuckled, not missing the darkening of his eyes at her hoarse voice. "I've been thinking about robbing a bank I read about in Switzerland that hides money for criminals. It'd be a tough one, but I think I can come up with a plan. You in?"

He leaned down and kissed her, deep and strong. Finally, he lifted his head. "Oh, baby. I'm definitely in."

Read on for an excerpt from Rebecca Zanetti's novella

On the Hunt,

an introduction to her heart-pounding post-apocalyptic SCORPIUS SYNDROME series!

Extinction is the rule. Survival is the exception.—Carl Sagan

WEEK 1
Eight people dead
Likelihood of Scorpius Containment: *Definite*

Wind whistled a mournful tune around aluminum buildings and across the jagged concrete tarmac. Dr. Nora Medina shivered in the damp night air and ignored the water splashing over her flip-flops. The soldiers around her, armed to the nth degree, merely added to the pressure building in her chest.

Her nearly bare chest.

She fought to keep her balance while hustling up the metal steps to the third private plane of her day.

Enough.

She might be the only unarmed person on the quiet tarmac, and the only woman, but enough was fucking enough, because she was also the only person wearing a borrowed white blouse over a bright pink bikini top, barelythere wrap around her bikini clad butt, and sandals.

Temper roared through her, and she planted her feet at the top of the stairs, only to slide across the wet surface.

"Ma'am," said the nearest faceless soldier, reaching for her arm.

She jerked free and rounded on him. "I swear, if one more person calls me 'ma'am' or apologizes for the inconvenience of dragging me off a very nice beach in Maui several hours ago, I will take his gun and shoot him."

The man's expression didn't change. "Yes, ma'am."

She bit down a scream. "All right. Listen up. We are in Seattle, and I know we're in Seattle." She pressed her hands against chilled hips and tried to stand taller. "Do you know *how* I know?"

"No, ma'am." Well trained, definitely at ease, the soldier kept his gaze above her right shoulder.

"I *know*," she said slowly and through gritted teeth, "because I looked out the bloody window when we were landing. The next time you kidnap somebody, you might want to blacken out the windows."

"Yes, ma'am." He nodded his head, ever so slightly, toward the doorway to the plane.

"This is kidnapping, and I've had it. We're in Seattle, and yep, guess what? I live here. So I'm going to head home, take an incredibly hot shower, change my clothes, and then call—well, somebody. *Anybody* who will tell me what the hell is going on." Her rant would end perfectly if she could just get past him on the steps, but he easily blocked her way.

"All apologies, ma'am, but our orders are to escort you. Please embark." He kept his voice level and polite.

She swallowed. There were six of them, one of her, and no way would she win a physical altercation. "Not until you tell me where we're going."

"Nora?" A voice called from inside the plane. "Get your ass in here."

Every nerve she owned short-circuited. Her gut clenched as if a fist had plowed into her solar plexus. Slowly, spraying water, she pivoted toward the opening. It couldn't be. It *really* couldn't be.

The voice she knew so well. Male, low, slight Scottish brogue a decade in the States hadn't quite banished. Her heart thundered, and fire skidded across her abdomen to flare deep. How was this even possible? She steeled her shoulders and approached the opening of the plane as if a bomb waited inside. So many thoughts rioted through her brain, she couldn't grasp just one.

Warmth hit her first when she stepped inside, followed by another shock wave. "Deacan Devlin McDougall," she murmured.

He stretched to his feet from one of the luxurious leather chairs, standing in the aisle—the only place high enough to accommodate his six-foot-four frame.

All the thoughts zinging around her head stopped cold.

Nothing. Her brain fuzzed. The years had been good to him, experience adding an intriguing look of danger to his masculine beauty.

His green gaze, dark and piercing, scored her see-through shirt, light wrap, and bare legs. "I'm sorry I wasn't there for the extraction."

Her chin lifted. Heat seared through her lungs, lifting her chest, and she slowly tried to control her body. No way would she let him see how difficult he made it for her to breathe—even after all this time.

He wore faded jeans over long legs and a dark T-shirt across a broad chest—no uniform. But the gun strapped to his leg was military issue, now wasn't it? The weapon, so silent and deadly, appeared at home on his muscled thigh.

His dark brown hair, glinting with red highlights, now almost reached his shoulders. Very different from the buzz cut he'd had years before. His eyes, the green of a Scottish moor, held secrets, unplumbed depths, and promise. Chiseled face, hard jaw, and definite warrior features proudly proclaimed his ancestry, and even now, she could see the Highlander in him.

The door banged shut behind her, and she jumped.

He gestured toward the seat across from the one he'd occupied. The engines roared to life.

She faltered. "Where are we going?"

He reached into an overhead compartment and drew out a plush blanket. "D.C."

The plane lurched forward, and she stumbled. He grasped her arm, shooting an electrical jolt up her bicep.

His eyes darkened. "I'd wondered."

"Me too." As kids, they'd been combustible. So she hadn't imagined the spark from years ago. She blinked confusion from her vision and allowed him to settle her into the seat. The second he covered her legs with the warm blanket, she finally took a deep breath.

He sat down, gaze somber. "You haven't responded to my proposition."

Her head jerked back. "This isn't, I mean, you—" She gestured around the luxurious plane.

His lips twitched. "No. I did not execute a military extraction and secure three private jets to force you into making up your mind to meet me in person now that I'm settled in the States. Finally."

She plucked at a string on the blanket. They'd kept in touch through the years, and when he'd sent her an e-mail two months ago saying he wanted to meet up with her, she'd needed time to think about it. "I didn't think so."

Turn the page for a preview of the first novel
in the groundbreaking new series by Rebecca Zanetti!
Mercury Striking
will be available in paperback and e-book
in February 2016 from Zebra Books.

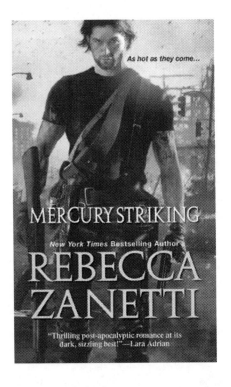

As hot as they come...

MERCURY STRIKING

New York Times Bestselling Author

REBECCA ZANETTI

"Thrilling post-apocalyptic romance at its
dark, sizzling best!"—Lara Adrian

"Nothing is easy or black or white in Zanetti's grim new reality,
but hope is key, and I *hope* she writes faster!"
—*New York Times* bestselling author Larissa Ione

With nothing but rumors to lead her, Lynn Harmony has trekked
across a nightmare landscape to find one man—a mysterious,
damaged legend who protects the weak and leads the strong.
He's more than muscle and firepower—and in post-plague L.A.,
he's her only hope. As the one woman who could cure the disease,
Lynn is the single most volatile—and vulnerable—creature in this
new and ruthless world. But face to face with Jax Mercury . . .

Danger has never looked quite so delicious . . .

Chapter 1

Life on Earth is at the ever-increasing risk of being wiped out by a disaster, such as sudden global nuclear war, a genetically engineered virus or other dangers we have not yet thought of.—Stephen Hawking

Despair hungered in the darkness, not lingering, not languishing . . . but waiting to bite. No longer the little brother of rage, despair had taken over the night, ever present, an actor instead of an afterthought.

Lynn picked her way along the deserted twelve-lane interstate, allowing the weak light from the moon to guide her. An unnatural silence hung heavy over the empty land. Rusted carcasses of cars lined the sides, otherwise, the once vibrant 405 was dead, yet she trod carefully.

Her months of hiding had taught her stealth. Prey needed stealth, as did the hunter.

She was both.

The tennis shoes she'd stolen from an abandoned thrift store protected her feet from the cracked asphalt. A click echoed in the darkness. About time. She'd made it closer to Los Angeles, well, what used to be Los Angeles, than she'd hoped.

A strobe light hit her full on, rendering sight useless. She closed her eyes. They'd either kill her or not. Either way, no need to go blind. "I want to see Mercury."

Silence. Then several more clicks. Guns of some type.

She forced strength into her voice. "You don't want to kill me without taking me to Mercury first." Jax Mercury, to be exact. If he still existed. If not, she was screwed anyway.

"Why would we do that?" A voice from the darkness, angry and near.

She opened her eyes, allowing light to narrow her pupils. "I'm Lynn Harmony."

Gasps, low and male, echoed around her. They'd closed in silently, just as well trained as she'd heard. As she'd hoped.

"Bullshit," a voice hissed from her left.

She tilted her head toward the voice, then slowly, so slowly they wouldn't be spooked, she unbuttoned her shirt. No catcalls, no suggestive responses followed. Shrugging her shoulders, she dropped the cotton to the ground, facing the light.

She hadn't worn a bra, but she doubted the echoing exhales of shock were from her size B's. More likely the shimmering blue outline of her heart caught their attention. Yeah, she was a freak. Typhoid Mary in the body of a woman who'd made a mistake. A big one. But she might be able to save the men surrounding her. "So. Jax Mercury. Now."

One man stepped closer. Gang tattoos lined his face, inked tears showing his kills. He might have been thirty, he might have been sixty. Regardless, he was dangerous. Eyeing her chest, he quickly crossed himself. "Holy Mary, Mother of God."

"Not even close." Wearily, she reached down and grabbed her shirt, shrugging it back on. She figured the "take me to your leader" line would get her shot. "Do you want to live or not?"

He met her gaze, hope and fear twisting his scarred upper lip. "Yes."

It was the most sincere sound she'd heard in months. "We're running out of time." Time had deserted them long ago, but she needed to get a move on. "Please." The sound shocked her, the civility of it, a word she'd forgotten how to use. The slightest of hopes warmed that blue organ in her chest, reminding her of who she used to be. Who she'd lost.

Another figure stepped forward, this one big and silent. Deadly power vibrated in the shift of muscle as light illuminated him from behind, keeping his features shrouded. "I didn't tell you to put your shirt back on." No emotion, no hint of humanity echoed in the deep rumble.

The lack of emotion twittered anxiety through her abdomen. Without missing a beat, she secured each button, keeping the movements slow and sure. "I take it you're Mercury." Regardless of name, there was no doubt the guy was in charge.

"If I am?" Soft, his voice promised death.

A promise she'd make him keep. Someday. The breeze picked up, tumbling weeds across the deserted 405. She fought a shiver. Any weakness shown might get her killed. "You know who I am."

"I know who you say you are." His overwhelming form blocked out the light, reminding her of her smaller size. "Take off your shirt."

Something about the way he said it gave her pause. Before, she hadn't cared. But with him so close she could smell *male*; an awareness of her femininity brought fresh fear. Nevertheless, she unbuttoned her shirt.

This time, her hands trembled.

Straightening her spine, she squared her shoulders and left the shirt on, the worn material gaping in the front.

He waited.

She lifted her chin, trying to meet his eyes, although she couldn't see them. The men around them remained silent, yet alertness carried on the breeze. How many guns were trained on her? She wanted to tell them it would only take one. Though she'd been through hell, she'd never really learned to fight.

The wind whipped into action, lifting her long hair away from her face. Her arms tightened against her rib cage. Goose bumps rose along her skin.

Swearing softly, the man stepped in, long tapered fingers drawing her shirt apart. He shifted to the side, allowing light to blast her front. Neon blue glowed along her flesh.

"Jesus." He pressed his palm against her breastbone—directly above her heart.

Shock tightened her muscles, her eyes widening, and that heart ripping into a gallop. Her nipples pebbled from the breeze. Warmth cascaded from his hand when he spread his fingers over the odd blue of her skin. When was the last time someone had touched her gently?

And gentle, he was.

The touch had her looking down at his damaged hand. Faded white scars slashed across his knuckles, above the veins, past his wrist. The bizarre glow from her heart filtered through his long fingers. Her entire chest was aqua from within, those veins closest to her heart, which glowed neon blue, shining strong enough to be seen through her ribs and sternum.

He exhaled loudly, removing his touch.

An odd sense of loss filtered down her spine. Then surprise came as he quickly buttoned her shirt to the top.

He clasped her by the elbow. "Cut the light." His voice didn't rise, but instantly, the light was extinguished. "I'm Mercury. What do you want?"

What a question. What she wanted, nobody could provide. Yet she struggled to find the right words. Night after night, traveling under darkness to reach him, she'd planned for this moment. But the words wouldn't come. She wanted to breathe. To rest. To hide. "Help. I need your help." The truth tumbled out too fast to stop.

He stiffened and then tightened his hold on her arm. "That, darlin', you're gonna have to earn."

Jax eyed the brunette sitting in the backseat of the battered Subaru. He'd stolen the vehicle from a home in Beverly Hills after all hell had broken loose. The gardener who'd owned it no longer needed it, considering he was twelve feet under.

The luxury SUV sitting so close to the Subaru had tempted him, but the older car would last longer and use less gas, which was almost depleted, anyway. Hell, everything they had was almost depleted. From medical supplies to fuel to books to, well, hope. How the hell did he refill everybody with hope when he could barely remember the sensation?

The night raid had been a search for more gasoline from abandoned vehicles, not a search party for survivors. He'd never thought to find Lynn Harmony.

The woman had closed her eyes, her head resting against the plush leather. Soft moonlight wandered through the tinted windows to caress the sharp angles of her face. With deep green eyes and pale skin, she was much prettier than he'd expected . . . much softer. Too soft.

Though, searching him out, well now. The woman had guts.

Manny kept looking at her through the rearview mirror, and for some reason, that irritated Jax. "Watch the road."

Manny cut a glance his way. At over fifty years old, beaten and weathered, he took orders easily. "There's no one out here tonight but us."

"We hope." Jax's gut had never lied to him. Somebody was coming. If the woman had brought danger to his little place in the world, she'd pay.

Her eyes flashed open, directly meeting his gaze. The pupils contracted while her chin lifted. Devoid of expression, she just stared.

He stared back.

A light pink wandered from her chest up her face to color her high cheekbones. Fascinated, he watched the blush deepen. When was the last time he'd seen a woman blush? He certainly hadn't expected it from the woman who'd taken out most of the human race.

Around them, off-road vehicles kept pace. Some dirt bikes, a few four-wheelers, even a fancy Razor confiscated from another mansion. Tension rode the air, and some of it came from Manny.

"Say it," Jax murmured, acutely, maybe too much so, aware of the woman in the backseat.

"This is a mistake," Manny said, his hands tightening on the steering wheel. "You know who she is. What she is."

"I doubt that." He turned to glance again at the woman, his sidearm sweeping against the door. She'd turned to stare out at the night again, her shoulders hunched, her shirt hiding that odd blue glow. "Are you going to hurt me or mine?" he asked.

Slowly, she turned to meet his gaze again. "I don't know." Frowning, she leaned forward just enough to make his muscles tense in response. "How many people are yours?"

He paused, his head lifting. "All of them."

She smiled. "I'd heard that about you." Turning back to the window, she fingered the glass as if wanting to touch what was out of reach.

"Heard what?" he asked.

"Your sense of responsibility. Leadership. Absolute willingness to kill." Her tone lacked inflection, as if she just stated facts. "You are, right? Willing to kill?"

He stilled, his eyes cutting to Manny and back to the woman. "You want me to kill somebody?"

"Yes."

He kept from outwardly reacting. Not much surprised him any longer, but he hadn't been expecting a contract killing request from

Lynn Harmony. "We've lost ninety-nine percent of the world's population, darlin'. Half of the survivors are useless, and the other half is just trying to survive. You'd better have a good reason for wanting someone dead."

"*Useless* isn't an accurate description," she said quietly.

"If they can't help me, if they're a hindrance, they're fucking useless." He'd turned off the switch deep down that discerned a gray area between the enemy and his people months ago, and there was no changing that. He'd become what was needed to survive and to live through desperate times. "You might want to remember that fact."

Her shoulders went back, and she rested her head, staring up at the ceiling. "I'd love to be useless."

He blinked and turned back around to the front. Her words had been soft, her tone sad, and her meaning heartbreaking. If he still had a heart. So the woman wanted to die, did she? No fucking way. The blood in her veins was more than a luxury, it might be a necessity. She didn't get to die. "Please tell me you're not the one I'm supposed to kill," he said, his heart beating faster.

Silence ticked around the dented SUV for a moment. "Not yet, no."

Great. All he needed was a depressed biological weapon in the form of a sexy brunette to mess with his already fucking fantastic daily schedule. "Lady, if you wanna eat a bullet, you should've done it before coming into my territory." Since she was there, he was making use of her, and if that meant suicide watch around the clock, he'd provide the guards to keep her breathing.

"I know." Fabric rustled, and she poked him in the neck. "When was your last injection?"

His head jerked as surprise flared his neurons to life. He grabbed her finger before turning and held tight. "Almost one month ago."

She tried to free herself and then frowned when she failed. "You're about due, then. How many vials of B do you have left?"

He tugged her closer until she was almost sitting in the front seat, his gaze near to hers. "Doesn't matter. Now I have you, don't I? If we find the cure, we won't need vitamin B." This close, under the dirt and fear, he could smell woman. Fresh and with a hint of—what was that—vanilla? No. Gardenias. Spicy and wild.

She shook her head and again tried to free herself. "You can have all the blood you want. It won't help."

"Stop the car," he said to Manny.

Manny nodded and pulled over. Jax released Lynn's finger, stepped out of the vehicle, and pressed into the backseat next to her.

Her eyes widened, and she huddled back against the other door.

He drew a hood from his back pocket. "Come here, darlin'."

"No." She scrambled away, her hands out.

With a sigh, he reached for a zip tie in his vest and way too easily secured her hands together. A second later, he pulled the hood over her head. He didn't like binding a woman, but he didn't have a choice. "In the past year, as the world has gone to hell, hasn't anybody taught you to fight?" he asked.

She kicked out, her bound hands striking for his bulletproof vest.

He lifted her onto his lap, wrapped an arm over hers and around her waist, manacling her legs with one of his. "Relax. I'm not going to hurt you, but you can't know where we're going."

"Right." She shoved back an elbow, her warm little body struggling hard.

Desire flushed through him, pounding instantly into his cock. God, she was a handful.

She paused. "Ah—"

"You're safe. Just stop wiggling." His voice was hoarse. Jesus. When was the last time he'd gotten laid? He actually couldn't remember. She was a tight little handful of energy and womanly curves, and his body reacted instantly. The more she gyrated against him, trying to fight, the more blood rushed south of his brain. He had to get her under control before he began panting like a teenager.

"No." Her voice rose, and she tried to flail around again. "You can't manhandle me like this."

If she had any clue how he'd like to handle her, she'd be screaming. He took several deep breaths and forced desire into the abyss, where it belonged. He wanted her hooded, not afraid. "If you were mine, you'd know how to fight." Where that thought came from, he'd never know.

She squirmed on his lap, fully contained. "Good thing I'm not yours, now isn't it?"

He exhaled and held her tighter until she gave up the fight and submitted against him. The light whimper of frustration echoing behind the hood sounded almost like a sigh of pleasure. When she softened, he hardened. Again.

Then he released his hold. "That's where you're wrong, Lynn Harmony. The second you crossed into my territory, the very moment you asked for my help, that's exactly what you became."

"What?" she asked, sounding breathless now.

"*Mine.*"

New York Times and *USA Today* bestselling author REBECCA ZANETTI has worked as an art curator, Senate aide, lawyer, college professor, and a hearing examiner—only to culminate it all in stories about alpha males and the women who claim them. She writes contemporary romances, dark paranormal romances, and romantic suspense novels.

Growing up amid the glorious backdrops and winter wonderlands of the Pacific Northwest has given Rebecca fantastic scenery and adventures to weave into her stories. She resides in the wild north with her husband, children, and extended family who inspire her every day—or at the very least give her plenty of characters to write about.

Please visit Rebecca at: www.rebeccazanetti.com/
www.facebook.com/RebeccaZanetti.Author.FanPage
twitter.com/RebeccaZanetti

TWISTED

DARK PROTECTORS

New York Times Bestselling Author

REBECCA ZANETTI

SHADOWED

DARK
PROTECTORS

New York Times Bestselling Author
REBECCA ZANETTI

TAMED

DARK PROTECTORS

New York Times Bestselling Author

REBECCA ZANETTI

MARKED

DARK PROTECTORS

New York Times Bestselling Author

REBECCA ZANETTI

New York Times Bestselling Author

REBECCA ZANETTI

WICKED
RIDE

DARK
PROTECTORS

THE WITCH ENFORCERS

Printed in the United States
by Baker & Taylor Publisher Services